Praise for Carol Edgarian

For THREE STAGES OF AMAZEMENT

"In this gorgeously written, haunting, and often hilarious novel, Edgarian conjures a particular moment in America's recent history and unleashes within it a collision of universal forces: love, desire, ambition, loyalty. I can't think of a book that more viscerally evokes the gritty challenge—and casual heroism—of motherhood and marriage."

—Jennifer Egan

"Furiously compelling . . . a fiery, deeply involving book."

—Janet Maslin, *The New York Times*

"A lovely, resonant novel . . . This story feels universal. Not to mention generous and graceful and true."

—O, The Oprah Magazine

"Thought-provoking, intelligent, wise, sad, and illuminating. If that makes it sound too lofty, it's not: it's humane and therefore sometimes funny, and it nails the complexities of adulthood with a steel hammer held gently in very capable hands."

—Ann Beattie

"Love, family, marriage, illness, and money—this is a life story and a love story for our era, beautifully observed, sharply etched by a master storyteller."

—Amy Bloom

"A brilliant and irresistible look at married life and happiness and the very human limitations of both. She's a wonderful writer."

—James Salter

"It's a great heart in a great author who loves the villains in a story while fully imbuing the heroes with human flaws and hungers. . . . Seldom have such true portraits of our era, or any era, appeared."

—Rick Bass

For RISE THE EUPHRATES

"A book whose generosity of spirit, intelligence, humanity, and finally ambition are what literature ought to be and rarely is today—daring, heartbreaking, and affirmative, giving order and sense to our random lives."

—*The Washington Post*

"The writing is so good it can raise the hairs on your neck."

—Elizabeth Berg

"A novel of extraordinary compassion, it's also a dead-on view of assimilation and the American experience."

—*The Phoenix Gazette*

"*Rise the Euphrates* begins with vivid, chilling scenes from the Armenian holocaust, follows one of its orphans to the New World, and becomes a commentary on the variety of the American experience. It is a wonderfully written family chronicle, full of observation and insight, that both moves and entertains. Its richly drawn characters and the haunted voice of its narrator will remain long in readers' memories."

—Robert Stone

"Carol Edgarian is a remarkable writer of intelligence and compassion. She has written an important story that is at once unique and universal. In *Rise the Euphrates,* history and personal story deftly intertwine to create a complex of emotions and questions about humanity, love, and family."

—Amy Tan

"Edgarian's sumptuous writing and uncommon wisdom about the human spirit and its maiming seep into a reader's heart, refusing to leave."

—*Miami Herald*

Also by Carol Edgarian

Rise the Euphrates

Three Stages of Amazement

The Writer's Life: Intimate Thoughts on Work, Love, Inspiration, and Fame from the Diaries of the World's Great Writers (coeditor)

VERA

A NOVEL

Carol Edgarian

SCRIBNER
New York London Toronto Sydney New Delhi

Scribner
An Imprint of Simon & Schuster, Inc.
1230 Avenue of the Americas
New York, NY 10020

This book is a work of fiction. References to real people, events, establishments, organizations, or locales are intended only to provide a sense of authenticity, and are used fictitiously. Other names, characters, places, and events, and all incidents of dialogue, are products of the author's imagination, and any resemblance to actual events or places or persons, living or dead, is entirely coincidental.

First Scribner hardcover edition March 2021

Manufactured in the United States of America

1 3 5 7 9 10 8 6 4 2

Library of Congress Cataloging-in-Publication Data has been applied for.

ISBN 978-1-5011-5752-3
ISBN 978-1-5011-5754-7 (ebook)

For Liv Far, Lucy Honor, Anne Riley

There is an old adage that the Investigating Officer can often remember to good purpose, namely, "*Cherchez la femme,*" "Look for the woman at the bottom of it."

—*Criminal Investigation: A Practical Handbook for Magistrates, Police Officers, and Lawyers* (1906)

When the bird and the book disagree, always believe the bird.

—James Audubon

First Things

I always thought of my city as a woman. But the house, it turned out, was a woman too. When the quake hit, she groaned. Her timbers strained to hold on to their pins, the pins snapping. And the rocks beneath the house? They had voices too. And if I ever wondered how long it would take for the world to end, I know: forty-five seconds.

An unearthly stillness preceded and followed the shaking. It's what we did and didn't do in the stillness that determined the rest of our days.

I lost two mothers that year. The first was Rose. I can't say where she was born or where her kin came from. The fact is, I don't know what mix of blood flows through me. I suspect there's some Persian, possibly Armenian. I understand there may be some Northern African and Spanish in the mix too, and a good pour of French. Spanish by way of Mexico. None of this Rose would confirm or deny. "We're mutts," she said, and left it at that.

One of the harlots claimed that Rose had been found as a waif in the slums of Mexico City. For a fee, she was brought north. I believe that; I believe most anything when it comes to Rose. She spoke five languages; her hair was blue black, her skin copper, her eyes green. In San Francisco, she became a much-favored prostitute, catering to the gold rush miners. Her next clients were the fellows who came after the miners, the suit-wearing bankers and merchants, who thought they could gentle a murderous, gambling, whoring town; they thought they could gentle Rose. Instead she became the grande dame of the Barbary Coast, the Rose of The Rose. She did not raise me. That duty fell to a Swedish widow employed to bring me up to be, I suppose, anything but a hooker. In that, Morie Johnson was successful. I am not a hooker. I am only a thief.

PART ONE

Birthday

Being a bastard and almost orphan, I never took for granted the trappings of home. My fifteenth birthday fell on a Monday that year, 1906. In nine days, the world I knew would be gone. The house, the neighborhood, our city, gone.

I am the only one left to tell it.

It was springtime. First thing before breakfast, my sister, Pie, and I made our lady loops—to Fort Mason and back. We were two girls exercising one unruly dog.

Pie walked slowly, having just the one speed, her hat and parasol canted at a fetching angle. She was eighteen and this was her moment. All of Morie's friends said so. "Your daughter Pie is grace in her bones," they said. And it was true: Pie carried that silk net high above her head, a queen holding aloft her fluttery crown.

Now, *grace* was a word Morie's friends never hung on me. I walked fast, talked fast, scowled. I carried the stick of my parasol hard on my shoulder, with all the delicacy of a miner carting a shovel. The morning sun blasted my cheeks, and anyone fool enough to come up behind me risked getting his eye poked. We were sisters by arrangement, not blood, and though Pie was superior in most ways, I was the boss and that's how we'd go.

As we turned from the house, our dog Rogue, a noble-hearted Rottweiler mix, ran into the alley after a bird. Rogue had been acting queerly all morning, flashing me the whites of his eyes, even when I called to him with a knob of cheese in my hand. It was as if he knew what was coming, as if he could feel the rumbling beneath his paws.

"Slow down!" Pie begged, knowing I wouldn't heel either. I had what Morie—Pie's mother, the widow who raised me—called *willful unhearing.* The welts on my legs from Morie's most recent whacking with the boar-bristle brush proved it. With every step my skirt hit where I hurt, and with every step I went faster. I would have flown like that bird if I could.

The day was unusually mild, fogless. You'd have to be a grim widow not to feel the lark in it. We lived on bustling Francisco Street, close to the canneries and piers, where the air was always cool and briny. Ours wasn't a fancy block, working-class. As we headed west, to our right sat the glorious bay—and beyond the bay, the Marin Headlands, green this time of year.

We were on Easter break, and free to walk the long way. Pie had arranged to meet up with her best friend, Eugenie Schmitz, at the corner of Van Ness Avenue. Pie was eager to tell Eugenie her big news. I was just glad to be out of the house.

"Make a wish," Pie called, pumping her arms to keep up, "for your birthday."

I glanced over my shoulder and rolled my eyes, pretending I didn't care. "Why," I said, "when it never comes true?"

My wish was urgent, the same every year. It made me cross to have to think it again. Instead I looked to my left, to where San Francisco rose on tiptoe. Seeing her in her morning whites always made me feel better. My city was young, bold, having burned to the ground five times and five times come back richer and more brazen. To know her was to hold in your heart the up-downness of things. Her curves and hollows, her extremes. Her windy peaks and mini-climates. Her beauty, her trembling. Her greed.

At Saint Dominic's, the nuns taught us that we were lucky to live in San Francisco, our city being an elusive place, easy to love, hard to keep—especially for those who don't deserve her. They taught us about the Spanish conquistadors, who sailed for years, fighting tides and hurricanes, scurvy and venereal disease in search of her; they starved themselves on hardtack, their ships battered, their tongues blistered from wind and a scarcity of water, yet still they managed to rape and pillage, and therefore, as God's punishment, they were standing on the wrong side of the boat when they passed the fogbound Golden Gate. All that trouble, all those years, and they missed the pearl—not once but twice. "Careful of handsome fools," warned the sisters.

"If I were a conquistador," I said to Pie, "I wouldn't miss what was right in front of my long Spanish nose."

"Not everyone is as vigilant as you," my sister observed.

The truth about Pie, and I loved her no less for this, was that she didn't question things, and I questioned too much. "Then pox on the Spaniards too," I said, just to hear her laugh. And because she was laughing, I considered it fair to ask, "Pie?"

"Yah?"

"I know you want to tell Eugenie, but tell me first: What happened last night with James?"

She stopped in her tracks and groaned. "You mean you heard."

I heard. After supper, when James O'Neill knocked on the back door and asked Pie to step outside, I put my ear to the glass. When I couldn't make out their whispers, I cracked the window. In the light of no moon, James O'Neill took Pie in his arms and promised this: in a year, if—he said *if* twice—if his store turned a profit, then he would ask her to marry him. The noodle went on to explain that as the sole support for his mother and sisters, he had to put them first; he'd gone into debt to open his notions shop, selling thread, tobacco, and buttons on Market Street; and, oh, he loved her. He loved Pie. He said it in that order, three things she already knew. As I knew, from the look on Pie's face when she came inside, that James O'Neill had given her a fraction of what she'd wished for; then, to add insult, he put love at the rump. How many folks take the meagerness offered and decide it's their due? How many girls accept a whacking with the boar-bristle brush and do nothing to stop it from ever happening again?

"I don't understand," I pressed. "He proposed to propose?"

"Don't put it that way," Pie begged. "Please, V. James may not be bold but he's good."

"Deadly earnest," I agreed. "But what does it mean?"

"It means I have to wait—" Pie faltered, tears in her eyes. "Some more . . ."

"Oh, Pie."

"And it means now we have no chance of paying off Morie's debt to the Haj."

We both sank at the thought.

Arthur Volosky was his real name, but Morie called him the Haj—Swedish for shark. The Haj ran the numbers racket in our part of town—among the cannery workers and fishermen and regular folks like Morie. The Haj took bets; he charged exorbitant sums on the money he loaned. Our Morie was a devout churchgoer, but when she drank she gambled. Doesn't everyone have at least two opposing natures warring inside them? I think so. One way or another, God or the Haj, Morie hedged her bets that she might one day live among the rich angels.

"You shouldn't have been snooping," Pie scolded. "James wouldn't like it. Not one bit." She lifted her chin, gathering herself. "Oh, drats. We're late. We'll miss Eugenie." Pie started to walk on. "Aren't you coming?" She squinted, shifting her focus to how she might fix me. "Sun's out. Put up your umbrella."

"Pie, Morie didn't hit me because of my umbrella."

"No." Pie hung her head. "Not only that."

Not only that.

Morie had tried to stop drinking, since the doctor warned

her of her heart. But when James O'Neill offered Pie half a cup of nothing, Morie filled her own cup with aquavit. And another and another.

I suppose I gave Morie a hundred reasons to hit me: my skirt was soiled, my tongue was loose. I reminded her of her lost pride. And this: my skin turned copper when I was too stubborn to shield it from the sun. If my skin was dark, while Morie and Pie were fair and pink, the world would know that I wasn't Morie's daughter and that our family was a sham.

A "dark affinity" lived inside me that Morie's boar-bristle brush couldn't beat out. So Morie's friends suggested, often to my face, as if there is only one black and one white ink with which to draw the world—one nasty, one good—and that is the dull thing society would make of a girl. Early on, the nuns at school granted Pie beauty and gave me the booby prize of wits. I was fine with wits.

"Same birthday wish?" Pie asked, taking hold of my hand.

"More or less."

Her face clouded when she heard that. "Why not something new, now that you're fifteen and a young lady."

"Oh, hell, Pie, I will never be a young lady."

I loved Pie; I loved her hard. But I would never believe that a man or a wish could save us. Having come from desire, I knew too much about desire. I knew San Francisco was a whore's daughter, same as me. If Pie and I were to rise, it would be up to me.

"Pie?"

"Yah?"

"How much is Morie in for to the Haj?"

She was about to tell me when a hired hack charged down the street and captured our attention. Our neighbor Mr. de Bretteville, who spent all day idling in front of his house while his wife gave massages to men inside, leaped from his chair.

"Bet it's her," Pie whispered, as the cab halted in the road in front of us.

Mr. de Bretteville's daughter, Alma, stepped from the hack in the same sparkle gown she'd worn when she left home on the previous night. When I took Rogue out for his evening walk, I saw her.

"Look at her," Pie hissed, in a rare show of envy. And I did. I looked at Alma de Bretteville, who was famous not just on our street but all over town.

There was a kind of woman bred in San Francisco then—bold, vulgar, and unapologetic—that was Alma. California was a young state, San Francisco was even newer, and Alma was the freshest thing going: twenty-five, buxom, ambitious, a fair Dane with soulful blue eyes. The men of the city were so taken with her, they'd used her face as the model for Victoria, goddess of victory, on the bronze statue that stood atop Union Square.

But that wasn't what got Alma known. It was the trial. Alma sued a miner who'd promised to marry her. His name was Charlie Anderson and she sued him in court for "personal defloweration." Alma demanded that Anderson pay her the whopping sum of fifty thousand dollars for what he'd taken, which could not be given back. "Pets, it's called screwing," she declared when she took her turn on the witness stand. All of which was covered in the morning and afternoon editions of the papers—and all I eagerly read.

Alma de Bretteville was six feet tall in her stockings, and if that was what shame looked like, I'd have it too.

"Hi, Pa," she said, sidestepping a pad of horse shit in her too-fancy shoes.

Here, any normal father—and what did I know of normal fathers?—might have had qualms to see his daughter return home from an all-night tryst. Not Mr. de Bretteville, who everyone knew was a fallen aristocrat.

"What news?" he asked, trembling with anticipation. He

reminded me of Rogue, wagging at the prospect of a fresh bone.

"Talk *inside*," Alma insisted as she dispatched her father to wait for her inside the house.

Only then did Alma show us her dazzling smile. It was the grin of someone who knew you'd been talking behind her back and would give a damn only if you stopped.

"Hello, ducks."

"Oh, hi," Pie said weakly, the sight of Alma making her doubly fearful that she'd end up an old maid who'd waited too long for James O'Neill.

Pie and Alma were the acknowledged beauties of our neighborhood. Though Alma was ahead of Pie by any measure of age, height, scandal.

I didn't speak to Alma, that was my thing. I hid in plain sight.

Alma fixed her gaze on Pie, that way pretty girls have of enjoying the sight of each other, as if standing in front of a mirror.

"Your hat," Alma said. "It's dashing. Care to sell it?"

Pie touched the wide brim with two hands, as if a malevolent wind were about to snatch it. The hat was navy silk with bold feathers and at the center a diamond pin. "My hat? No!"

"I'd pay something ridiculous," Alma assured her. "Even if it is used."

"You know perfectly well it's new." Pie gave Alma the stink eye. In fact, the hat was two years old. Even so, it was Pie's pride.

"How much?" I asked.

Alma's laugh was all bells and winks. "You're not too proud, are you?" She squinted at me. "I forget your name."

"Vera," I said.

"Oh, right, Vera." Alma sounded vague, as if she were trying to recall something she'd heard about me. Shrugging, she fondled her mesh evening bag—a bag no one on our street had any business owning, any more than Pie had any business owning that hat. Alma de Bretteville was bought and paid for, and so were we.

"Five dollars should put you right."

"We'll think on it," I said.

"Will not," Pie mouthed, so only I could see.

"Well, ducks, think on it while I visit my ma," Alma said. "I'll stay until one of us gets cross. That should give you all of six minutes." Laughing, she disappeared inside her parents' shabby house.

Pie waited for the door to shut, then wheeled in my direction. "What kind of girl buys a hat off a person's head?"

"Someone who's going places," I said.

Something was happening—something I couldn't yet see. The horn at the Ferry Building downtown was blasting and the seagulls overhead screeched in reply; on the corner boys in breeches were hawking the morning editions of the *Examiner* and the *Call*. Between here and there, the city was rising in its estimation, and we were rising too. I decided that one day Alma and I would be great friends.

"Think on it, Pie. Five dollars would buy you two hats."

Pie wouldn't hear of it. Her hat wasn't a hat but a dream.

Years later, when we were both quite ancient, I asked Pie what she remembered about the time of the quake. She didn't pause to consider. "All that we lost. Isn't it the same for you?" She peered at me from behind thick glasses.

I smiled, for of course I remembered the opposite: those I found. Alma being one.

"You sure were determined to keep her hands off your hat," I said.

"My hat?" Pie replied. "What hat?"

We walked on, faster now, so deep in our private worries that when Pie's best friend, Eugenie, called to us, we didn't hear her. It took Eugenie's whistle—diminutive Eugenie Schmitz had quite a set of pipes—to cut through.

Pie waved eagerly. "Smile, Vera. For cripes' sakes, smile."

Eugenie was with her father, the mayor. The papers called him Handsome Gene. They also called him a crook.

"I thought he was hiding out before he got indicted?"

"Shh," Pie whispered. "He'll hear you."

"Pie, I can't hear me."

Mayor Eugene Schmitz, German-born, with a thick head of hair, a handlebar moustache, and a beard, plowed toward us, all bells and smiles.

I supposed every era has a politician like him: good-looking and loose-natured, an ordinary person capable of extraordinary indulgences. He'd risen on questionable merits from playing the violin and conducting the two-bit Columbia Theatre to serving as San Francisco's mayor. The fact that Schmitz and the sheriff and every member of the city's Board of Supervisors were corrupt grafters wasn't news—the news was that anyone cared.

"V, not a word," warned Pie, "about James, and certainly nothing about the Haj."

I looked at my sister with wonder. "Why would I?"

"Why? Why do you say any of the things you do?" she replied. "Because you love to *stir.*"

I should have been insulted, but the fact is, it was true.

Half a block away, Eugenie, with her head bowed, clutched a small parcel to her ribs.

"What's that she's holding?" I asked.

"Your birthday present, silly."

"Quick, tell me it isn't a rosary."

Pie lowered her gaze. "I told her not to—"

"Why does she insist on converting pagans?"

Pie laughed. "That's what I said you'd say."

Even at a distance you could see that the Schmitzes' troubles rode heavy on their shoulders. They walked bent, as if facing a stiff wind. The mayor had his arm wrapped tight around Eugenie.

She had barely survived the most recent flu epidemic. She was thin and drawn, a handkerchief at the ready, half tucked in the sleeve of her coat. In contrast, her father radiated health; his thick, wavy hair required a Board of Supervisors all its own. He was accused of corruption on any number of fronts.

We'd known the family forever. Pie and Eugenie chose each other as best friends in the first grade—back when the mayor wasn't anything but a violinist. Somehow, even then, the Schmitzes lived in a better house than they should. But as we lived in a better house than we should, the friendship didn't seem so odd.

"Happy birthday, Vera!" boomed Schmitz as we collided with them at the side of the road.

Eugenie's eyes were red from weeping. She thrust her present at me. "I hope you like it."

I knew I wouldn't. Worse, I feared my real opinion would show on my face, as if my face were a page everyone should read.

Pie elbowed me. "Go on, open it."

It wasn't a rosary after all, but a pair of handkerchiefs Eugenie had embroidered with a thin, curly *V*. I was so relieved, I hugged her hard.

"Bravo," exclaimed the mayor, his smile fading as he scanned the road to see if anyone was watching. I'd heard reporters had staked out their house.

My gaze fell to the mayor's feet. There was a coin in the dirt beside his boot. The mayor and I reached for it at the same time, but I was quicker.

"Here," I said, offering him the coin. "It must have dropped from your pocket."

"Don't touch it!" cried Eugenie.

"Why not?" I insisted. "It isn't a bribe or anything."

"Oh, Vera." Pie shook her head.

But the mayor understood. I'd said the thing you must not say to a man accused of living on bribes.

"No, no," he protested, laughing. "Finders keepers."

For months the *Bulletin* and the *Chronicle* had been building a case against the mayor. His many transgressions included greasing city contracts, and the payola he received from the city's saloons, stockyards, and Frenchie restaurants. Schmitz held a partnership stake in the Standard Lodge, a truly wretched place, where a Mexican prostitute in the basement could be had for twenty-five cents, and a French whore on the top floor cost a dollar. He'd accepted bribes from the unions on one side and from the developers of the aboveground trolleys on the other. And that, for the moment, was his biggest problem. To be a crook in San Francisco was a thing so common it was almost a matter of pride, but to alienate your fellow crooks, that was a problem.

In our house, I ate the news for breakfast and dinner and had already formed a picture in my mind of the mayor rotting in jail, and poor, poor Eugenie.

Yet here he was laughing because a nickel wasn't real money, was it?

"Are you sure?" I offered it again, hoping in my optimist's heart he wouldn't take it.

He took it. Claiming it was for luck, he turned the coin over in his palm and slid it into his pocket.

I felt it was only fair to ask, "Have you got a good lawyer?"

"Vera," warned Pie, clucking and tsking. "You must stop talking *immediately.*"

Tears welled in Eugenie's eyes. "Papa says it'll all blow past. Won't it?" She looked to her father.

The mayor winced, knowing it wouldn't. "In fact, I have a team of lawyers. I'm not sure what good they do me, but they've been at the house all night. Eugenie and her mother are very upset, aren't you, darling?" Again, he asserted his arm around her tiny waist. "We thought we'd take a break, get some fresh air . . . find you girls. And here you are. Please, don't worry," he told his daughter. "Soon it will all be behind us."

At this Eugenie began to sob outright. Pie stepped forward and, being an old hand at comfort, took Eugenie's arm and led her away. As they walked on, we heard Eugenie cry, "He's going to jail and no one has the heart to tell him."

The mayor winced. "Walk with me?" he said. It wasn't a question. He took my hand, tucked it under his arm, and led me across the street, so that we were walking opposite them.

He got right down to it. "Vera, you're a bright girl. I can see you have good sense." He glanced across the road. "Those girls, they can't still be fretting about—"

"No, not about you," I assured him. I looked over, and seeing that Pie was the one talking, I explained, "They're talking about Pie's beau. When they're done with him, they'll move on to hats and dresses." I sighed. "Your daughter and my sister can talk about the wonders of a dress until even the dress gets bored."

The mayor smiled. "And you, Vera, you don't bother with dresses?"

"Not if I can help it."

His eyes raked over me. "How old are you today, dear?"

"Fifteen."

"Fifteen!" He flexed his arm, pulling me closer—so close I noticed that he'd waxed the left side of his moustache but forgotten to do the right.

As I studied him, Schmitz observed me. He clenched his jaw. "I would have guessed older."

Me too, I thought. I am as old as that bay and those hills—older, in some ways, than this man. I had made it my secret mission to find one adult—one single adult—who could show me how to behave. The mayor wasn't it.

"You aren't much like your sister, are you? Or your mother," he said.

There, the wretched question that had always plagued me. The question that folks in the neighborhood and the nuns at school and, God help me, Morie's church pals wondered whenever they saw me with Pie: How was it that Morie, the fair, blue-eyed Swede, had produced such a dark thing as me? And if they assumed my olive skin, brown hair, and dark eyes were the legacy of our dear father, they had only to glance at the portrait she kept by her bed: Lars Johnson was as blond and fair and dead as he could be.

"It's that terrifically sober face of yours," Schmitz declared, pointing to my nose. "I remember that look," he said, "from when you were quite small. Even then you saw through the malarkey."

I saw through *his* malarkey.

It was Eugenie's eleventh birthday party; I was just eight, the big girls having invited me to tag along. We were upstairs in Eugenie's room when Schmitz came home. He called to us from the bottom of the stairs, his eyes glassy with drink. All the girls ran down to greet him and he tapped each one on the head or shoulder, like a goose counting his goslings—all the girls but one.

"Vera!" cried Eugenie. "Come down and say hello to Papa!"

No matter how many times they called, smiling up at me like merry angels, I couldn't budge from the top of the stairs.

The girls soon moved on to the dining room for cake, but Schmitz stayed behind. Our eyes locked. All the joy leeched from his face, and I saw, in that child's way of seeing, a ghost. Then, in a flash, he was smiling again. He even winked at me. From then on I felt nervous when I was near him. For I had seen his real face.

"Vera, I'd like to trust you with a commission."

"You want Pie and me to look after Eugenie while you're in prison."

He threw back his head and laughed a single blast. "Ha! How

refreshing to hear what no one else will say." Glancing across, to where Eugenie was resting her chin on Pie's shoulder, he added, "What's the word on the street, eh? When do they plan on lowering the boom?"

"The papers predict next week."

Schmitz nodded. "My lawyers tell me next Wednesday noon." He wagged his head. "Looks like I need a miracle. Have you got one? Or maybe a prayer?" He smiled, the wily trickster.

"I'm not so good with prayers," I admitted.

"Neither am I. I try, but I'm not sure God hears me. Say, next Wednesday, you girls will still be on break, yes?"

I nodded.

"Would you find an excuse to spend the day with Eugenie? Make up anything you like, just keep her occupied. Can you do that?"

How could I deny him, even as I suffered having been branded at fifteen with a sober face.

We crossed the road and rejoined Eugenie and Pie, as Schmitz asked, "And what does your mother have planned for your birthday?"

I paused, the question of "mother" being more complicated than the mayor understood.

"I expect we'll have cake," Pie said, elbowing me again.

"Ah," he replied, for he wasn't listening anymore.

We had come full circle, returning to our block just as Alma de Bretteville was leaving her house. She had changed into a day dress, with an exaggerated bustle, her hair topped by a hat even finer than Pie's.

She called out, "Hello, Mister Mayor!"

"Alma!" he said, his voice shifting into another register.

If Alma was shocked or even interested to find the mayor in our humble part of town—indeed outside her door—she didn't show it. They said their how do's, but the look that passed between them was of a deeper knowing—a look of shared affinities reserved for rascally chums.

"What have you all been chatting about?" Alma asked, prepared to be amused.

"Vera's birthday," Eugenie said earnestly.

"I'm just the delivery man," the mayor explained. "I've delivered Eugenie to see her old friends. You know, we used to live not far from here."

"Oh, well, happy birthday," Alma said, showing me her best smile.

"Are you on your way?" The mayor offered his arm.

"I am." Alma hooked her gloved hand to his elbow. Eugenie mutely took the mayor's other arm. As they walked on, Alma looked back over her shoulder. "Keep the hat, pet. It looks right on you."

She said it without malice. She wasn't competing with Pie, after all; her sights were set on much grander things.

"I hate her," groused Pie as she tried walking faster to keep up with me. "What were you and the mayor laughing about?"

"His future."

"His future! Do you really think they'll put him in jail? I mean, has a mayor ever gone to jail?"

I paused. "Don't you wonder if he's guilty?"

"Is he?"

"Yes."

Even so, I wasn't quite ready to condemn Schmitz. Fathers were the rarest of creatures to me. I didn't understand the first thing about them. But I liked the fatherly wing he wrapped around Eugenie.

In front of our house, I whistled for Rogue. He appeared from a split in the neighbor's fence, running as if being chased, his ears flat to his head, tongue lolling. He dashed headfirst into my knees. I assured him he was the baddest boy in all of San Francisco, and he knew by my voice he was adored.

As we ran up our front stairs, I glanced over my shoulder. I was fifteen. Then, as now, I was impatient. Then, as now, I was in full possession of my adult mind. I had no power, no experience. My worldview was as flat as my girlish chest and as hollow as my longings. I was neither winning nor sweet. I was alone in every room I entered. But I could see things.

I could see where I was and where I needed to go. So, I made my birthday wish. I flung my heart high over the dairy farms of Cow Hollow, to Lafayette Square, which sat like a fat queen on the throne of Pacific Heights. There at the top of the hill was a great house of many rooms, where my real mother lived. I saw her just a few times a year: on Christmas Eve, and on a random night when the flesh trade downtown was running slow, and on this, my birthday.

I was always wishing to be with Rose.

At midnight, hours from now, she'd send for me. Her driver would arrive in a fancy Buick Model F with glossy red-brown paint and black leather curved seats. He'd approach in the dark, headlamps dimmed, just the chick-chick of the motor, then that too he'd cut, the car gliding noiselessly to a stop in front of our house. And with all our neighbors asleep, no one would be the wiser that the most successful madam of the Barbary Coast, the very Rose of The Rose, was coming to fetch me, no one would know she was mine.

Morie

Rogue headed for the kitchen and his bowl of scraps, but we were wanted in the dining room.

Morie had finished eating breakfast, her plate pushed back to make room for the shuffling of cards. As usual, she was dressed in widow black, her hair faded to the hue of cobwebs, twisted in a tight chignon. A thin, limp hedge of bangs lined her forehead.

"*Yah,* late," she said. "Did you wash hands after traipsing that beast?"

"Yes, ma'am." I was famished and the lie came easily.

Pie hid her hands in the folds of her skirt.

"So, Vera's hands are clean and Pie's are not? *Faa!* Sit. Eat."

There were plates with chops, burned at the edges, and eggs already cold.

Morie nodded at the present wrapped in cloth beside my plate. "And what is this, eh, birthday *flicka*?"

I already knew. She'd finagled the print folio of Audubon's *The Birds of America.* It was an odd gift; it was my heart's desire. I hated asking for it but I couldn't help myself. For months I'd campaigned shamelessly. Birds were beautiful to me. I liked to call out their different species on my walks with Rogue. I liked how the male was brightly colored while the female hid in plain sight.

I told Pie about the folio and she told Morie, and Morie sent word to Rose, who paid for my keeping and theirs. Of course, Morie inflated the price of the prints a dollar extra, but that was tax. The Morie tax.

"Two times I had to send a note. 'Birds?' Rose sends back. 'Why birds?'" Morie looked conspiratorially at Pie. "Do you understand this, *flicka*? I thought we had the bird."

She glanced at Ricky, my parrot, who was keeping watch from his bamboo cage. Ricky had been my birthday present when I was ten. He liked to ride on my shoulders, but on the long days when I was at school, Morie taught Ricky to squawk, "Pretty *svenska*, pretty *svenska*"—on and on and on. She taught him Swedish curses too.

"I'll thank Rose when I see her tonight," I said.

Pie and Morie exchanged a freighted look.

Morie wiggled in her chair, signaling we were moving on. "So, Pie-Pie." Morie shuffled, taking her time. "What did Eugenie say of your good news?"

Pie nodded at her plate. "I suppose she was happy for me."

Morie nodded in my direction. "Your sister, she has good prospects, no? 'Course, a girl's engagement takes money." I kept my eyes low, trained on Morie's garnet wedding ring, its gold inlay and seed pearls winking as she shuffled. Her flesh having thinned, she wore it on her thumb. "It takes lots of money to make a wedding."

Pie stared into me, eyes wide with warning. I stared back, trying to make out what I couldn't see.

"But you aren't officially engaged, not yet," I said. "Sorry, Pie, but it's true."

"Shut the mouth, bird," snapped Morie. Having dealt the cards into three piles, she clawed them back. "Tonight, we'll go with you to see her. We'll have the birthday, all nice, then we'll tell Rose Pie's big news. *Tings* must be said, and we will say them."

"But Rose doesn't want—"

"She wants! Always *she* wants," Morie boomed, the color rising in her cheeks. "Well, I want." She stabbed a bony finger to her chest. "This one, Pie, she wants."

All at once I saw it. She was going to ask Rose for money for Pie's trousseau and use it to pay off the Haj.

Morie grunted as she pushed back her chair. If she was threading a needle or lacing a boot, her hands stumbled and shook. But reaching for the bottle on the sideboard, she was sure. She gripped the neck of the aquavit with the authority of a cop seizing his nightstick and poured herself a glass—for her nerves. With the first drink, it was always love, a glad meetup with her sweetheart. With the second and even the third, she'd spin tales of the old country and we'd laugh along as Morie sang goofy songs from the homeland and cursed like a happy Swedish sailor. The fourth glass was when she turned lethal, turned to the boar-bristle brush.

Morie licked her lips and tossed her drink back.

"Skitstövel!" she spat. "What is *dis*!"

After she'd gone to bed—after, that is, the boar-bristle brush—I'd dumped the aquavit and filled the bottle with water.

As the glass shattered against the wall, Hank, Rose's do-man, having knocked on the back door to no avail, marched into the dining room with Rogue at his heels.

"Whoa there, sister!" boomed Hank, tall and lean as a redwood, his boots shined to a high gloss, the gold buttons on his black livery jacket so snug they quivered as he spoke.

Pie touched Morie's shoulder, quieting her.

"And how is the birthday girl?" Hank asked.

"I'm good, Hank." I was so relieved to see him. "And you?"

Hank answered with a decisive nod, then took a piece of jerky from his pocket and slipped it to Rogue. The dog thanked him with a moan-dance. Hank reciprocated by kneeling on the carpet and showering the dog with kisses.

"He's swish," Rose once said, to which Morie replied, "Swiss? I thought black Irish?"

But I caught on. I always did.

Hank said he had presents waiting in the car. When he went to fetch them, I followed him outside.

"You all right in there?" he asked. "Looks like someone was about to blow."

"Hank, Morie and Pie want to come with me tonight. Will Rose be mad?"

Hank lifted his cap and gave his scalp a good scratch. "Ack, you know the boss doesn't like the whole kit and caboodle coming to the house. Attracts attention, and she don't need that right now. The whole town's in a boil with this Schmitz business, and the boss, well, she and Schmitz, they all got a bit of bother on that score." Hank frowned, thinking he might have said too much. Being Rose's do-man, his job was to protect the madam and her secrets. So long as I was one of those secrets, I was in with Hank. "Still, I know she'll be glad to get an eyeful of you."

"Will she, Hank? Will she be glad?"

"Oh, in her way, 'course."

He opened the rear door of the car to show me the boxes hidden under a blanket.

"We got the full barrel for you ladies," he said with pride. There were new dresses and matching evening coats in boxes wrapped with ribbon.

"Dresses? What ever for?" I didn't bother to hide my disappointment.

"Oh, I expect you'll find out tonight," Hank replied. "Boss said to tell you to wear yours. I expect she'd like to see that it fits proper and all."

There was a crate of saffron and lemons and other goods bound for the kitchen on the hill, and bottles of whiskey, always whiskey, for Rose.

The Deal

And what of these two women who made me? Their deal was struck early on. No one expected a madam—certainly not one as canny as Rose—to get stuck in the family way, and being an expert at subterfuge, she hid her pregnancy well. When the time for my arrival neared, Rose boarded a ferry to Oakland, hired a coach, and headed east to the Gold Country, to Auburn. There amid the dusty saloons and forlorn banks that only a couple of decades earlier had bustled with the gold that built San Francisco, I was born.

Ahead of her trip, Rose hired a lawyer to place ads in the Sacramento and Auburn papers, and in this manner found a widow with three small children living at the end of a dirt road.

I was just a few days old, asleep in a basket inside the coach. The children were playing with sticks in the yard. Their clothes were rags and they had bruises on their legs and arms.

The widow rushed to meet Rose as she stepped from the coach.

"Where did they get those bumps?" Rose demanded.

"Why, how would I know? They're always mucking about, playing in the creek and bushes."

"Oh yeah?" Rose said. "Then why is her bruise in the shape of your thumb? And, look here, this welt is shaped like your hand."

The widow stared at the young thing with marks on her legs

and arms. When she turned back, Rose was already climbing into the coach.

Back in San Francisco, at Rose's brothel, the whores passed me around. One would keep watch in the early hours and another would feed me breakfast and another lunch and yet another would walk me up and down the halls while I dozed. Late at night, when the customers came around, I slept in Rose's office. An elderly harlot by the name of Sugar took care of me.

Some nights—many, I like to think—Rose took me home to her newly built house. Of course, I don't remember those nights, but the women have assured me this was so. I remember my mother's hands—quick, sure. And I remember her smell.

When I was nearly two, I opened my bird mouth and asked Rose why. Why this, why that.

Rose instructed her lawyer in Sacramento to find a person of refinement, with perhaps just one child. Elsa Johnson's husband had been a professor in Stockholm. He died in the flu pandemic of 1890, leaving her with a child and no means of support. This was a time in our collective history when folks simply fell off the shelf. The tenements seethed with sad stories, deaths from measles, influenza, meningitis, tuberculosis, whooping cough, or the slow creep of malnutrition, ringworm, polio, cancer. Of widows and babies starving. With few options, Elsa considered the one occupation available to a woman with a pretty face.

She wrote a letter and addressed it to a post box in Sacramento. Rose's lawyer responded with a different kind of proposal: Would she be willing to relocate to San Francisco and raise a second daughter? For her trouble, every convenience would be provided: a house, clothes, food, a weekly maid.

Soon there came the day when the women had to meet—if only to make the exchange. It was a Sunday. Elsa and her daughter attended church, where I expect they prayed for their souls ahead of meeting the madam and her bastard. The cottage in

Auburn was only slightly better than a shack. Rose pulled up in a fancy rig accompanied by two footmen.

She left me in the carriage with Sugar and went into the house, instructing one of the footmen to wait for her outside the door.

Rose turned her wide, bronzed face to the widow and nodded. Elsa was struck by Rose's crude beauty, a beauty so unlike hers in its too-muchness: the brows and eyes lined with kohl, the lips red with pigment, her city dress requiring some thirty-six yards of satin, lace, and flouncing.

What is she? Elsa wondered. Whatever mix went into making Rose, she had long since dropped her given names in the dirt. "I am everything," she said. She was Rose, irrefutable, fierce.

When I was very small I imagined she had gold flecks inside her, for they were sprinkled in her green, sardonic eyes. The freckles that covered her cheeks and her flat, straight nose were golden too. I always thought that those freckles were there to remind me that even Rose had once been a girl. She parted her black hair in the middle, her bun held in place by jeweled combs, their tips sharp as knives.

"So," Rose said, sitting wearily, "let's get to it, shall we?"

Elsa Johnson shivered despite the midday heat. "My daughter will need city clothes appropriate to her new station in society."

"Not so fast," warned Rose. "First, we deal with mine."

The widow nodded agreeably. She recognized a fellow survivor and the fact that she had little to bargain with. As the daughter of a Swedish Baptist minister, Elsa had been raised to believe in church four days a week, grape juice as Jesus's blood, and whenever her father drank, which was most nights, the rod applied liberally. She recognized that this madam slept in a big city bed, under covers of sable, while she perspired in the infernal Auburn heat.

"*Yah*, I expect the girl will need everything."

"Indeed," agreed Rose. "Everything."

Like seasoned traders, they talked of me, as the afternoon sun cast golden shadows on the faded carpet.

Elsa negotiated with the urgency of a woman with just two dollars in her purse, and the rent due, and her daughter, Piper, having a hole in her one pair of boots. That and a chorus of women from church assuring her she was bound for hell. The chorus couldn't decide which was more scandalous: serving tea to a madam or taking in the madam's bastard child. That and the fact of a trick heart, which she now mentioned.

"How bad is your heart?" Rose peered into Elsa's soul, arithmetizing on her internal abacus where the widow would prove weak or problematic. Anticipating, that was my Rose's genius.

"On the boat across, I took scarlet fever," Elsa admitted. "The doctor tells me I'm fine . . . a bit of hearing loss is all." She tipped her head and pointed to her right ear. "Then he died on me."

"Your husband? That was hardly his fault."

"Yet it's put me and my girl to shame."

"Shame you can survive," Rose declared. "Of that I'm certain."

She was seeing the broader picture now, of a Swedish professor falling for a bit of beauty. The desires of men being Rose's chief preoccupation. She considered that Lars Johnson might have been one of her customers: a man who wished for a little stroking of the box, be it the box on his shoulders or in his chest or in his trousers. Thinking of desires reminded Rose that she was far removed from the din of the whorehouse. This little cottage in hicksville made her eager to move on.

"And the child's father?" Elsa asked. "Will he be—"

"Not a factor," Rose declared.

"An actor?"

Rose let it pass. She banged her teacup to signal that time was short, her patience even shorter, and, anyway, tea was not what she drank. She had already made peace with the notion that I should never be hers. She had as much use for a baby as a lion has for fins.

"I should think you'd want to meet her." Rose called to the footman to bring me in from the coach.

Elsa sighed. There was no avoiding it. She stood as Sugar led me by the hand inside.

"Oh my," Elsa exclaimed, "she's . . . quite dark, isn't she?"

Rose squinted at the map of capillaries covering the widow's nose and cheeks—the distinct markings of a tippler. "I see all the shadings when I look at a face. I make it my business to do so," she said. "How 'bout you?"

"*Yah, yah,*" Elsa agreed. "Only, should folks ask why she is so different from me and my girl, I would have to *tink* on what to say."

"Oh, you'll *tink*," Rose assured her. "That, or me and the girl will move on."

It was Rose's observation that folks who begin the dance with a string of noes often prove the most malleable. Still, she didn't have all day and this pride-bound Swede would require a bit of the lash now and again.

"*Va' fan,*" the widow mumbled.

"What does that mean?"

Elsa wasn't about to say. Rose would learn soon enough that *fan* was devil. *Va' fan?* What the hell. *Hora* was what Elsa called Rose—in private.

"Our city neighbors," Elsa said. "They will just have to *tink* my Lars was—"

"Dark," Rose offered. "Mysterious."

Now that I was in the house, the pace of the negotiation quickened: hereafter I would call the widow what Pie called her—Morie, *mor,* Swedish for mother. Rose would build us a house in a flat section of the city; Morie didn't want to be climbing hills. It wouldn't be the best, not even the second-best, part of town, but maybe that was right too. Close to the piers.

"Good—far from the Jews," Morie said. Rose sighed at Morie's bigotry. The Jews lived in the finest houses in Pacific Heights. Where Rose also lived.

Rose arranged for her Chinese cook, his surname was Tan, to spend one day a week provisioning the larder and otherwise keeping tabs. Money for our food, necessities, school fees, and incidentals would arrive on the first of the month, regular as the Pacific railroad.

As Morie listened to all the bounty coming toward her, she held still, lest it pass her by. It was more than she dared hope for. She touched her heart, that organ that shut the day they put Lars in the ground—and felt it quicken. She touched her chest to be sure.

"The city," she said, blushing. "Lars always dreamed of going there. Won't he be proud."

"Chrissakes, let's not burden the dead with pride." Rose decided it was caraway, yes, caraway, the scent that pervaded the room. "I should have liked a bit of your akvavit," she said.

When she was frightened, Morie's pupils all but disappeared in a sky of bleached blue. "I don't expect you to be a churchgoer, but I won't have you ridicule. The doctor, he prescribes a tonic for my nerves."

"Does he now?"

Rose had planned to suggest a visit one evening each month. But hearing the widow connive—in Swedish singsong—she cut the visits to six times a year. Then, as Rose observed the low-slung cottage with the ceiling pocked where the rains seeped through, and the frayed rug, and the stale spritz cookies, she cut that number again. She would see me three times a year.

"And now I'd like to meet your daughter," she said.

Pie had been playing quietly in her room. Five years old, with blond ringlets and a sweet laugh, she ran into the room, took me from Sugar, and hugged me close. Morie had promised Pie she was getting a sister as a present.

"Vera is a funny name for a baby," Pie said.

"It means truth. Let's hope she grows into it," Rose replied. "Now, Piper, why don't you take Vera to your room and shut the door. I bet she'd like to play with your doll."

The part no one told me, what I must imagine, is what happened after I discovered they'd gone—Sugar, Rose gone.

Once Rose decided something, she never looked back. In San Francisco she had thirty girls to flick with her switch. The men who paid for those girls paid for me.

So, you see, I was a special bastard, a not-quite-orphan, a madam's mistake, a tippler's charge—provided for but never loved by either mother. And though that fact pained me in my early youth, I came to see my place as unique. I was never trapped by pretty frocks and expectations of home and hearth that plagued the other girls I knew; I was a secret, bound by a secret, and if all that binding kept me apart, it also allowed me a certain freedom. My mind was my sole company, and when the old world ended and the new world began, my mind would have to see us through.

But, oh, what a challenge I was for Morie. She played it corked and tight on that first visit with Rose. But with us, with Pie and me, Morie showed she had many sides. When sober, Morie could be funny, or salty as the pickled herring she forced us to eat. The stern side saw that I was scrubbed proper and that I knew where to put my fork and napkin. At dinner Morie talked of people and things. A girl was pretty or fair, a woman cultured or not-from-our-side-of-the-street, which is laughable, except in her mouth it was a serious charge; a man had means or he was nothing. She believed in keeping up with the news, and by news, I mean gossip. Thankfully, the San Francisco papers supplied an amplitude of celebrity and scandal. I taught myself to read early, and in the evenings I read the paper to Morie and learned the doings about town. Morie knew I would never be fair and pink, docile or sweet, like Pie. My hair was thick, coarse, nut brown; theirs was silky flax. I wasn't given to smile for company. I saw no reason to feign or flatter, as no one had ever flattered me. I would never be a lady but I could be useful. You hear a thing enough, and it is what you believe. I believed I had to be vigilant, be sharp. I believed that every day I had to work to earn our keep.

The Gold House

"Put on your new dress, mule," urged Pie, as she peered through a slit in the parlor drapes to check the road. "Hurry, before Hank gets here."

It was after midnight and Hank was late. Pie looked gorgeous in her new frock, while I'd thrown on my old blue with its too-short hem.

"What do I care? Rose doesn't give a fig what I'm wearing."

"Yes she does," Pie declared. "Why else would she send these?"

Rose had commissioned the best seamstress at I. Magnin to sew our new dresses, with silks from Paris, lace from Belgium, bone stays made from Pacific whales, and long French ribbons for our hair. The apricot silk with crème lace was meant for Pie and a fine navy satin for Morie, who'd spent the afternoon scandalized at the prospect of appearing in public in anything other than widow's black.

Even now, with Hank overdue, Morie was upstairs dropping her shoes and cursing, *"Skit! Skit!"*

Pie checked the road again. "I bet she's not back from the brothel. Do you ever wonder what goes on at The Rose?"

I shrugged. I wondered all the time, but I wasn't going to say.

Pie went on. "James heard some fellas talking. The girls, they stand naked, all in a row, like plucked chickens at the market. The men point and say, I'll have that one. Or that one. And the madam? She takes the money and says, 'You go with him.'" Pie wrinkled her nose.

"James is an idiot," I snapped. "The Rose is first-class."

"Oh really? How then? How does it work?"

In all my imaginings of The Rose, I'd considered the frivolity and the money, but till that moment I never thought of the women as anything other than cheerful participants, as actresses in a grand show.

Tan, Rose's butler and cook, was under strict orders never to speak of the goings-on at The Rose. But if I bribed him on the day every week that he begrudgingly worked at our house—if I promised, say, to unload the buggy for him or shine our three pairs of dusty boots—Tan would sometimes provide curt answers to my questions. "A paradise," he said, "a hell." What Tan lacked in articulation he conveyed in feeling, lowering his eyes and faintly shuddering whenever he talked of The Rose.

My mother had some twenty girls working the rooms upstairs, where there were suites with full five-course dining and canopied, gilded beds, and parlors for gentlemen's games; she had another dozen "hostesses" in the French restaurant-saloon on the ground floor. She had safes stuffed with gold bars.

In his way, Tan held Rose in high esteem—as a sometimes generous, sometimes ruthless boss. If interrupted during a meal, or while she was in the bath enjoying one of her thin cigars, she was liable to turn violent. She'd lash a girl with her tongue, Tan promised, or her whips.

"Of all the places downtown," I told my sister, "The Rose is the best."

Pie looked at me curiously. "Does that make you . . . proud?"

It did. In my mind, The Rose was strictly a high-end joint, where laughter flowed like the limitless quantities of champagne—you know, a warm, cozy sort of place, where all oddities were accepted and even celebrated, where no one was too bookish or stubborn or unsmiling. And, this was essential to me: The Rose was a place where no one was unwanted.

In my story, Rose called her workers *girls* but she treated them as professionals. She paid them handsomely, saw that they were schooled in the language of pleasing, with a fine appreciation for manners, music, and art, as their rich clients preferred. A doctor attended to them each week and money was sent to their families by courier, and there were even bonuses for the care of faraway children.

Faraway children. That was the part that stuck in my throat. No one had to tell me that Rose was expert at granting or withholding favors. I knew what a real mother's absence felt like, how it was never to have someone look upon your face with wonder or pleasure. My life was a mess of contradictions, of locked doors and secret assignations, same as at The Rose. Every time I visited my mother, I was sent away.

Overhead Morie's heels knocked on the floorboards.

"I'm starving," I said. "I wonder if she'll serve—"

"V, every day you claim you're starving," Pie said.

"And every day it's true."

We'd been waiting so long that when at last Rose's long, garish machine pulled up at the house—silent, like an eel sliding through ink—Morie was so flustered she ran out without her hat and shawl.

Rose had two places: the brothel downtown called The Rose, and her house. The Rose being off-limits to me, our visits took place at Rose's house, on the highest hill of Pacific Heights. It took a half hour for the motorcar to climb the distance of no more than a mile. Hank, grinding the gears, had to zig and zag to avoid the steepest slopes. Even so, the car huffed, gasped, crawled. When at last we arrived, the house looked shuttered.

"It's all right," I told Morie, who hadn't been allowed near Rose's place in years. "At night it always looks foreboding."

"Foreboding!" scoffed Morie, uneasy with things she didn't understand. "My, isn't that a fancy word."

Foreboding it was, at least at night. Rose's house was a grand Victorian dame, five stories tall—four up, one down—with a kitchen and laundry in back, a servant's room in the basement, and a garage with two stalls plus a stable. Rose had designed the place herself. In the daylight, one could see her eye at work: the house was a riot of ornamentation. There were chimneys and balconies, stained glass and decorative trim, and on every possible pitch and peak, gold leaf balls and posts. At midnight, with the windows covered by shades and velvet drapes, blocking all light within and without, the effect was of a dark hulk.

I was never permitted to enter through the front door.

Up the alley we came, like the farrier and the butcher and the ragman. Like the milkman pulling his dray cart. Up the wood stairs and into the kitchen, where Tan, Rose's butler and spy, was just finishing icing my cake.

"Oh, hello, Tan," Morie said in too jolly a tone. In the bright kitchen light, I could see she was perspiring. She dabbed her forehead with her lace sleeve and examined the tray of spirits Tan had set out on a cart next to a silver tea service.

"What kind of cake have you made for Vera's birthday?"

Tan shook his head contemptuously. "Lemon."

My heart sank. I liked all cake except Tan's lemon, which tasted both too sour and too sweet.

He'd made it for Rose. There was no love lost between Tan and me. Tan stocked our larder and cooked the only edible food served at Morie's table, but he did not appreciate that I was the reason for his extra work. Every Tuesday, he arrived in a buggy pulled by General, Rose's horse, and we had to pretend that Tan was just a tradesman come calling, though surely no one on Francisco Street believed that. The rig was too fancy and Tan was too polished, in his spotless black silks and starched white apron that fell below his knees, his impeccably braided queue hanging off his shoulder like a rat's tail. We ate his food mixed with his disgust, as he performed services that were beneath him. In short, he was a nasty piece of work, ol' Tan, and he impressed upon me early that while he worshipped Rose, he had no use for Morie or Pie, and viewed me as a particularly irksome opponent.

"What do you want?" he barked when he noticed me eyeing the cart to see what else he was serving.

"Send them in, would you!" Rose boomed from the parlor.

"Go, go," Tan hissed.

In we went. Rose had positioned herself on the velvet divan—my high-bosomed, terrifying mother, done up for the night in a lustrous green gown, fashioned by none other than the great Callot of Paris. Ropes of pearls covered Rose from neck to knees. They coiled in her lap.

"Ah," she said, "here you are: the whole uninvited kit and caboodle."

Rose's trick knee was propped on a silk cushion.

"*Yah*, and how is it today?" Morie asked.

"Killing me. Now, sit."

Rose never bothered with niceties, that was understood. She nodded in Morie's direction: an up-down jerk of the chin, sufficient to affirm their contract and to reduce Morie by a fraction, all in one economical gesture.

Pie got the next going-over: a fleeting glance, less business, more pleased. Rose was expert at assessing a girl from limbs to lips, and one raised brow told us that Pie was in good form, nothing new there.

The last and most piercing look Rose saved for me. "Your

hair's thick; men will appreciate that," she announced on my tenth birthday, her hand hovering so that I could feel her heat on my scalp. When I was twelve, she declared, "You're developing. Now let me see your teeth." I thought I'd die.

This birthday night, Rose looked me over and said nothing. And with that nothing, I decided to stand as far away from her as I dared, by the bookshelves in her wide parlor.

Next to Rose's divan, Morie settled into the settee, where a loose spring gonged in protest; for the rest of the visit, she would have to hold still so it didn't repeat. Pie took the low stool next to Morie.

Rose lit her pipe and puffed the fumes at the ceiling. "Tan!" she shouted.

Tan appeared at once, pushing the polished brass cart across the parlor's thick Persian carpet. These midnight soirees were a time for Tan to shine, since he'd worked at The Rose before being sent uptown to serve as Rose's majordomo, and ours. He halted his refreshment enterprise in the middle of the room. Here, I supposed, they might sing "Happy Birthday" to a girl. But no. Tan sliced the lemon cake and offered Rose the first slab. She ignored him. He set that piece aside and poured whiskey from the decanter into one of the china teacups with pansies blooming on its side, which Rose greedily accepted.

"I'll also have a nip," Morie ventured, eyeing the decanter. Rose shot Tan a severe look and he filled Morie's cup with tea.

"Tickets," Rose declared. "I've got tickets for you three to see Enrico Caruso at the opera house next week."

"Ca-ru-so!" Morie panted, taking her tea with a shaking hand.

It was to be the social event of the year in our newish city, where the popular tastes ran more to watching Miss Flora, the roller-derby queen, perform, or visiting amateur night at The Chutes. I'd read to Morie in the *Call* that the highest-priced tickets for Caruso were selling for one hundred and twelve dollars, an outrageous sum, given that a fur-lined lady's coat cost seven dollars and a Ford cost five hundred. The soprano singing the role of Carmen was Olive Fremstad, a Swede from Stockholm. Morie was dying to go.

"What Morie means to say," Pie suggested, "is that we're excited, really, this is beyond thrilling. Everyone in town is talking about Caruso." Pie's voice wobbled as she struggled to say something amusing to Rose, who was looking at her with a flat, bored mouth.

"I wonder," Pie continued, "do you think the mayor will attend, given his situation?"

"Ah, yes," said Rose, seizing the topic with vigor. "You've been chatting with Eugenie Schmitz."

"The girls saw them just this morning," bragged Morie. "Eugenie gave Vera a nice present of hankies and—"

"Did the mayor mention his troubles?" Rose seemed keen to know.

Pie allowed herself a little laugh. "Well, as usual, Vera cut through. She assured the mayor he was headed for jail."

"Ha! And how did Handsome Gene take that?" Rose shifted her gaze to me, but I kept on pretending to be engrossed by one of her leather-bound books.

"The mayor seemed . . . resigned," Pie admitted.

"I doubt very much he's anything like resigned," Rose declared. "Gene Schmitz will fight this case and anything else they try. We've done quite a lot of business together over the years, and I'm fond of him. You would do well, girls, not to judge a person who uses a few tricks or wiggles to climb. Why shouldn't he? That's called ambition and it's built this country. But Gene, ah, Gene, he's got his hand caught in the cookie jar one too many times. In that, he's worse than crooked; he's foolish."

"But somehow—" Pie said, thinking of Eugenie.

"Somehow has been tried, dear. Even in this town, there's

only so much one can do to fix a mess." Rose sighed wearily. "But you girls aren't here to talk politics." Rose motioned for Tan to refill her cup. "I was surprised, Morie, that you insisted on coming tonight. Something about *big news.*"

Over the rim of her second whiskey, Rose saw Morie and Pie exchange worried glances.

"Come on, ladies, out with it. Does it have to do with this fella of yours, Pie?" Rose urged. "Mister Buttons and Bobs."

"James," Pie corrected.

"You have your sights on marrying him, is that it?"

"That's it!" Morie erupted, embarrassing herself. "James proposed!"

"Well, he promised to . . . in a year," corrected Pie, who was honest by default.

Rose's gaze shifted from Pie to Morie, and back again. "What's this? Your young man proposed to propose?" She scoffed. "Is that your news?"

Pie shot a dire look in my direction. To think that Rose and I had said the same thing. "James is a serious person," Pie insisted, sitting higher on her stool.

Rose shrugged. "Ah, well. In a year, we'll know what the young man is made of, though by my lights he's shown you already."

"He's honest and reasoned," Pie said.

"And it's *reason* you want to marry? Well, reason you will have. And, oh, will it have you." Now Rose's voice, a honed instrument of pleasure, dropped into the low registers, where it was most lethal. "You won't hear me championing marriage. Marriage for a pretty girl is no better than a promise of servitude, yet all agree it's what she should want. No, sir. My girls are free. They come and go; they have money in their purses. They have skills—"

"They are prostitutes," blurted Pie, defender of love. She raised her snout in the air like a proud spaniel.

Rose smiled without showing her teeth. "May I remind you,

miss, it is these same prostitutes who put the food on your table and that pretty dress on your back."

Pie looked at her hands and nodded.

"Ah, well," said Rose. "Let's be jolly, eh? Elsa, how goes it with your playing the numbers? I forget, is it the church ladies you bet with? Are you winning these days?"

Morie, her face crimson, looked as if she were being forced to drink hot tar. "Yes, yes, I have won," she sputtered. "At times . . . I have been lucky." Morie searched Pie's face for a way forward and, finding none, inhaled sharply and sealed her mouth.

I wondered what Rose knew. Had she heard about Morie's debt to the Haj? It seemed likely Rose had eyes everywhere—same as Satan and God.

Rose observed the jeweled rings on her hand. "You know, Elsa," she said, "Caruso came from nothing: a mechanic's son. He is that rare creature, an artist with a capital *A*. Yet for all his gifts, he suffers from nerves."

"Oh, not him too."

"Truthfully, I don't know how he's going to perform. The man thinks San Francisco will be the death of him. And who's to say he isn't right? He's heard all the dark rumors and he believes every one. Did you know we are a city overrun by murderers and ladies of the night?" Rose chuckled. "On the train ride west, he had his valet step off to buy him a pistol. He spent the rest of the trip learning to shoot from the back of the caboose, *como un bandito*." Rose stuck out her pinkie as she sipped her drink.

Morie tried to regain a bit of ground. "Someone needs to show Don Caruso the *finer* parts of our city," she declared.

"My thought exactly," Rose agreed. "Last night, I sent two of my best girls to Caruso's suite at the Palace." Rose paused, deciding if it was indelicate to say more. She shrugged and went on. "My girls tell me he is keeping that gun *very* close. In. The. Bed."

Morie batted her chest with her palm, feigning delicacy.

"Oh, come, Morie, are we not all students of human nature?" Rose laughed. "You, calling me behind my back *hora* this, *hora* that?" Rose flashed her very white teeth, seducing Morie into having a joke on herself. "Pie, that dress looks very well on you," she went on, setting her whiskey aside and nodding to Tan, who once again handed her the plate of cake, along with a starched napkin.

"Thank you, ma'am," Pie said. "I love it."

"It loves you, dear." Rose nibbled her cake like a rabbit. "And what about you, Vera? I see you're intent on hiding from us in that ugly frock. You're not in love with your new dress?"

"I don't care about dresses."

"Oh, *flicka*!" Morie gasped. "Rose, ignore Miss Sarah Bernhardt!"

"Ignore at your peril," Rose said. "Child, what book are you pretending to read?"

I examined the cover. *"The Rubaiyat of Omar Khayyam."*

"Why that one? Did someone tell you to look at Khayyam?" Rose seemed truly interested. "Khayyam was Persian. Do you know where Persia is?"

"Yes. It's next to—"

"Right, I forgot, you're Miss Books. Speaking of, did you enjoy the Audubon?"

"Very much. Thank you."

Rose shrugged. "Birds. They peck, they shit, they fly. What is it you find so enthralling?"

"This girl," Morie piped in, "she wishes to fly out the window and be gone from all of us."

"Why do you talk about me as if I'm not here?" I snapped.

"Why do you insist on shouting from the shadows, eh?" Rose countered. "Come, bird. Come where I can see you."

If only I could have managed it. I saw the ghost of me do just that—step forward and smile. But no. Every time I was near Rose my knees got dippy, my cheeks blazed, my feet turned into cast-iron pipes stuck in old shoes.

"I'm fine here," I declared—stupid, proud.

"I'm not asking if you're *fine*, child." Rose's glance—one moment delighted, the next scalding—reminded me of another thing Tan had said: that Rose could make a man hand over his money, his hat, even his horse, with one look of displeasure. I was no man.

I took a small step, at least I tried. My heart was banging so loud I was sure she could hear it.

Rose pointed a long, lacquered nail at the carpet in front of her chair. Her gaze fixed on that.

"Girl," she said flatly, "I don't ask twice."

This was Tan's moment. As we'd been talking, he'd sidled to my side of the large room, where he'd busied himself adjusting some flowers on the table behind me. When Rose commanded, Tan turned and, punching his fist into the small of my back, propelled me across the carpet.

I looked back, to let him know just how much I despised him. He glared at me, pleased with himself.

Rose observed us, and I had no choice but to see myself in her cool gaze. I wasn't good-looking, so what. I had cowlicks—one in front and one in back—and any notion of turning me into some fashionable Gibson girl would prove ridiculous. I dreamed of being king, never queen.

"You think you're exceptional," she said, her voice soft, confusing. She was looking intently at me with those gold-flecked eyes.

"No," I admitted. "In fact, I think I am the least exceptional monkey in the zoo."

"Liar!" She laughed. "Come, here, closer."

I did as she asked.

"Good. Now, next time, hold yourself like this." She pointed her finger, with its long, sharp nail, at the ceiling. "Steady, especially when you're not. Steady, and no one will know you're uncertain. Do you understand?"

I nodded.

"Say so."

"I understand."

Satisfied, she downed her cup, then wiped her mouth with the back of her hand.

"Trust me, girl, they will always put their needs ahead of yours," she confided. "Our friend the mayor, he will beg, borrow, steal to avoid the cell that awaits him." She shook her head. "He will bring down both of my houses—this one and The Rose—if he has to."

"Can he?"

"Let's hope for all our sakes Gene plays it smart, eh?" She sighed, and I knew she didn't think that was likely. "Most people desire what they cannot have. There is no such thing as enough, not when a new, shiny thing beckons. I have made my fortune based on this one notion.

"Here, let's put it to the test," Rose said. She leaned forward, an elbow on each knee. "Take Morie here. Morie wonders if new dresses and expensive tickets to Caruso mean she'll have to do with less in this week's allowance. It's a reasonable question. She came tonight to get more money from me, for a proposal a year hence. Don't deny it, old gal." Rose chuckled. "We are old soldiers, you and I. I might ask, what's so urgent, but what difference does it make—Elsa, you always want more."

"I only was *tinking*," Morie sputtered, hands trembling.

"Tink away," Rose said. "A year is a hell of a long time in the lives of men and girls. Pie will muddle through, so long as her beau remembers his promise. But will he? A notions shop? Unless he's an idiot, I'd give him decent odds. Ladies always want new dresses." Rose nodded, agreeing with herself. "One day, Pie, you'll be Missus Buttons and Bobs. Not a grand outcome, but there you are."

Rose ignored the anguish on Pie's face, but it made me sick in my stomach. I watched myself siding one way, agreeing with Rose as the oracle, then swinging the other way, to how the world looked through Pie's and Morie's fearful eyes.

"Now, Tan," Rose went on, "we know, has notions of grandeur. Tan, tell us: What are your plans?"

"Roast beef tomorrow," Tan answered stiffly, and with that, he left the room.

Rose tasted her bottom lip, with its mix of whiskey and lemon cake. "That leaves only you, my girl."

"And you," I said.

"Yes, and me." She sighed.

She was only forty—so young, I think now. Vivacious, flirty, cunning. Still, forty years for a madam must be measured in dog years. Rose, my Rose, had been at the game a long time. She'd come to San Francisco when she was just thirteen. Oh, I'd see glimmers of the shiny girl she'd once been—more often when I was small, on those nights when I'd come to the gold house and she'd ask me to perform. I couldn't sing or dance, but I could spell *cockamamie* and *electricity* and she seemed to think there was a bit of magic in that. As I spelled, her lips moved. She didn't know her letters, but she knew in various languages the words required of a madam, and that had done her just fine.

Beneath the layers of powder and rouge and kohl that hooded her eyes, Rose of The Rose was tired. It was evident in the slight sag of the shoulders, the few strands of gray in her lacquered hair. I didn't understand, not then, that her ropes of pearls were in fact her armor. Rose talked of everyone's desire but her own. But I've come to believe she wanted what I've since learned everyone wants: to be brought to the other side by a surprise or a marvel or a song.

"Your pearls," I ventured. "Do you take them off at night?"

"What's this? My bijoux?" Her hands touched the strands of beads that covered her from her throat to her lap. "The dress didn't excite you, but these you want?"

How to say it wasn't the pearls but her?

"Pearls are awful expensive," Morie chimed in.

I knew they were expensive. I didn't care.

Rose understood. Leave it to a madam to comprehend the algebra of a young girl's desires. Rose raised her arms and grunted as she fished among the clasps at the back of her neck. I noticed that the great Callot of Paris had finished the armholes of my mother's bespoke sleeves with a darker shade of silk to hide her sweat.

The shortest strand, a choker, dropped with a pleasant sigh into her lap.

"Here now," she said, bunching the pearls in her fist. "Here's how this goes. My price for these pearls is for you, Vera, to tell me something I don't know. That will be hard to do. Still, I think maybe, just maybe, you can. I want to know your mind, girl."

My first thought, of course, was to tell on Morie. This was the moment I'd been waiting for, to tell of the aquavit and my suffering via the boar-bristle brush. To spill all regarding the Haj. What a good, diverting tale it would make.

Well, I didn't have it in me. All evening, I'd watched Morie being reduced to an embarrassment and it hurt my heart to see a weak thing made weaker. Even now, suspecting that I would give her up, Morie looked for mercy from the marble goddesses that perched on Rose's mantel.

"Tell Rose about school," Pie urged. "Tell her about the Spanish conquistadors."

"Not school." Rose chopped the air with her hand. "School we leave to the nuns. No, something else." Her eyes flashed with anticipation.

I'd been collecting facts and secrets for a moment such as this, to prove how smart and canny I was—how like her. Then she'd have to love me, wouldn't she? For I was indeed a student of human nature, as every orphan and hooker and unwanted kid must be.

But as I looked around that room, my mind went blank—except for another bit of madam wisdom Rose once told me: *Show the devil the devil and he'll say, How d' do.*

"Tan steals from you," I said. "Every week he adds an extra sum to the kitchen tally. He keeps that, plus extra he orders from the grocer and butcher, at our house. Every week, after he leaves us, he drops off a sack in Chinatown."

"How do you know this?" Rose asked.

"There's a box he keeps under the flour barrel in our larder," I said. "On Monday it's full, on Tuesday it's empty. Tuesdays are Tan's afternoon off."

"You go digging on a regular basis?"

"Tuesdays," I said, "are not my day off."

Morie gasped but Rose beamed with pride. "I knew the first part," she said. "What I didn't figure was you. Yes, you. I *am* surprised." She dropped the strand of pearls, warm as roasted chestnuts, into my hand.

What happened next, I will put here, though it shames me. I lifted those pearls to my nose like a too-eager dog. They smelled of her jasmine perfume; they smelled of Rose. It brought me back, far back—to, it must have been, when I was just a baby.

Then I caught Pie's look of distaste.

Just like that, the spell broke. "I'll say this for you ladies, you pack a good deal into an hour," said Rose. She tapped her pipe in the ashtray, a clear sign that she was moving on. At The Rose, the evening was just getting started.

Tan returned with our coats.

"Tan," Rose said. "I'd like a word with you, after."

Tan, thinking he was about to be praised, bowed and left the room.

We watched him go, and I thought: What have I done? Tan had been part of the scenery for as long as I could remember. He was never sick. He ran Rose's house and ours. Whenever Morie's ladies paid a call, he baked a cake, which she claimed as her own. He tended to Rose's horse, General, washing and brushing him, picking the muck out of his hooves, and shining the brass on the buggy. His English was serviceable except when speaking to someone he considered beneath him. He haggled and shamed shopkeepers into lowering their prices for a poor widow saddled with two gluttonous daughters; he fixed our lamps and gutters; he roasted and steamed and peeled and scoured; when so inspired, he could carve a face out of a radish; he polished our shoes. And for this he lived in a cramped cell in Rose's basement without a pot or cup of his own. He worked for scant wages. He stole. He was a liar and a cheat and none of that bothered me except that he took pains to prove his superiority over me, and to demonstrate his keen dislike. That was his crime. In a house of so little kindness, that to me was unforgivable.

With a heavy sigh, Rose watched Tan go.

"Right. The night of Caruso," she said, "Hank will collect you birds at six sharp. Be ready. Hank will arrive in the Ford," Rose added. "No need to stir talk."

"Oh, the Ford," Morie said, disappointed that it wouldn't be the fancy car after all.

Rose grunted as she stood on her sore knee. She walked to the small inlaid desk set in the parlor window, scratched something on a piece of paper, folded it, and sealed it in an envelope.

"Listen carefully," she said, coming to stand by me. And with a shock of recognition I saw that I'd grown taller than Rose.

"Well, look at you," she said. "Miss giraffe. You didn't get that height from me." She chuckled. "Very serious, eh?" She was looking into my eyes. "What do you have to be so serious about? Have you got big plans? I think you do. Good. But let's address a few things first, eh? Next week, at Caruso— Vera, are you listening to me?"

"Yes."

"Next week, all of San Francisco will turn out at the opera: the mayor, the Hearsts, the Spreckelses—and yes, Morie, the real Sarah Bernhardt. They'll be there, dressed to the bells, standing on their hind legs. Everyone who counts, and most who don't. I want you to be able to tell me who is who—who are the players and why. It's what you'll need to master if you want to make something of yourself. If you don't have beauty, child, work your smarts. They last longer. Do you understand?"

I nodded.

"The mayor," she went on, "he'll be there. He wouldn't miss a chance to welcome Caruso. Schmitz will be surrounded by the press. Everyone will want a picture of the mayor's grin on his last night of freedom. I don't imagine I'll speak with Gene—that's one photo neither of us can risk—but you'll want to say hello to Eugenie, yes? When you do, hand Schmitz this." She held out the envelope. "Go on, put it in your bag. Have you got a decent evening bag?"

"Good enough," Morie said.

Rose looked me over, hair to toe, one last time. "The nuns may teach you penmanship, Vera, but next Tuesday night will commence your real education. Now, what will commence?"

"My education."

"And how will you hand the note?"

"Subtly."

"You, with the words." She smirked. "That's right, subtly."

I was thinking of the difference between how she educated

a girl downtown and how she was bent on educating me. Let me live with you, I longed to whisper. But, of course, I said no such thing. Instead I asked the question whose answer I dreaded.

"At Caruso, will you sit with us?"

"Don't look for me," she said.

There is poor as in not enough to eat or drink—we would know that kind of deprivation soon enough. But there is another kind of poverty—of spirit.

I was silent on the way home, not at all certain I liked myself. My betrayal of Tan sat like a stone in my throat. That, and not being beautiful, which of course I knew, but to hear her say it?

Morie and Pie were likewise stunned. The visit had whittled us all.

Hank pulled up at the curb in front of our house and we hurried to the door. Morie headed for the parlor with Pie trailing behind her, but I escaped to my room.

I undressed quickly and climbed into bed. I felt wretched and lonely. I felt I'd lost—this may sound hokey and perhaps it is—I'd lost my honor. I feared I'd never get it back. With Rogue stretched out beside me, and Rose's pearls around my neck, I willed myself to sleep.

But sleep wouldn't come. Eventually, I climbed out of bed with the thought of going downstairs to get a glass of milk. As I stepped into the hall, Morie called to me.

"Vera?"

She was in bed with the lamp lit, my hag-of-the-night in her muslin gown, hair hanging loose to her waist. I was relieved to see she was sober. She smelled of the sandalwood soap she bought in a little shop on Fillmore Street. I'll say this, Morie was always clean. The scent brought forth our early life: how Morie wielded those hard sandalwood cakes as she scrubbed our young backsides and legs, how if she were jolly we'd laugh and pretend we were her little fishes; and those evenings, post-bath, when she bequeathed to Pie and me her tricks with cards.

"I can't sleep either," she admitted. "I am too much wondering—tonight, what stopped you from tattling on your old Morie? Eh?" She reached for my hand and tugged, not letting go till my bum perched on the edge of the mattress beside her.

I didn't rightly know. What was my fealty to this mercurial Swede, who every Christmas made us sing songs of Santa Lucia as we decorated the scarecrow-like Swedish tree with its *pepparkakor* ornaments made of gingerbread for Pie and me? I didn't know. But it pleased her to think I hadn't abandoned her after all, and if that wasn't love, well, it was something.

"You're not so bad, you know," she said, and to my surprise tears welled in her pale-blue eyes. "*Yah-yah*, we don't need to say, do we."

I shrugged, thinking: Every so often it wouldn't hurt.

"You're not so bad either," I said, and meant it. She had done the best she could.

"I am always telling them at the hall: Vera, she is the one with the smarts." Morie held my arm in a death grip. "Oh, but that *hora* of yours. How she turns us into little beggars in her big *hora* house." Morie sighed. "Ev-er-y day, I ask the good Lord: Shoot me with arrows, plague me with boils, send me like old man Job to the desert, but why did it have to be *her*?"

I took back my arm, thinking: And what would have become of you if not for Rose? Me and Rose.

But what I said, I meant so deeply my voice broke. "Morie, I am not a beggar."

"Not a beggar, eh?"

I glanced at the nightstand, at the daguerreotype of her with Lars. She had been so pretty—so pretty and young.

"How much do you owe the Haj?" I asked.

Not wanting to answer, she made a study of her hands, bending them into little church steeples, then folding them flat. She gazed at her portrait. "I wish you could have seen me. The time before last I was up-up-up. The people, they were wondering: How does she do it, winning week after week? They were all impressed, looking at me, you know, with the green eye."

"How much, Morie."

She shrugged. "Two, maybe three months."

"Three months! The full-boat three months? School fees and the rest—all she gives us?"

She hugged her ribs and rocked ever so. "Six—six months."

"Morie!" Rogue had followed me into her bedroom, and when he heard me shout, he growled.

"Shh, I know." Morie went on rocking as she set her eye on Rogue. "The Haj, he is a vicious man. I heard this woman, when she couldn't pay, he slit her doggie's throat and strung it up in her window like so, by the neck." Glancing at me, making sure I understood, Morie made another steeple of her hands. "Vera, you must *tink* very hard for us."

Going to The Rose

But if not a beggar, what was I? All night I tried, as Morie put it, to *tink*. By dawn, I had only one idea, and not a very promising one: I'd ask Rose for the money myself. It wouldn't be a gift. I'd tell her I was ready to work.

The next morning was Tuesday, Tan's day at our house. As soon as I heard him banging in the kitchen, I went down. I was already dressed, with a satchel packed with nightclothes, a dress, and a few other necessities, in my hand.

Tan had his own bundles neatly stacked by the kitchen door.

"I'm going with you to The Rose," I said, hoping my voice sounded more commanding than I felt.

Tan pretended not to hear me. He dipped a rag into a bowl of steamy water and wrung its neck. If Rose had beaten him or made him grovel, he didn't look punished. He looked exactly the same. Black fez, black silk tunic and pants. As usual he was in a foul mood, disgusted by our mediocre housekeeping, and therefore beating the life out of the kitchen table.

"What you think you know, *gurrl*," he said, smacking the wood table with a rag he'd folded into the heel of his hand. I hated the way he called me *gurrl*, low like a growl.

"What'd you take this time, Tan?" I asked. I pointed to his stash.

He lunged, shoving me against the wall, his face so close I could smell the fish on his teeth. He laughed in my mouth. "You know nothing, *gurrl*."

"I know what you do. I know you steal from Rose."

He followed with a string of Cantonese invective. Switching to English, he called me a pushy thing. He said I should learn how to be a *gurrl*, not a *snake.*

"Ha!" I cried. "You'll take this snake with you, won't you!" And wiggling from his grasp, I added, "I'll go where you go—"

"Nahh," he said. No *gurrl* would go where he went.

I said that was a stupid rule.

He said, "Stupid is you."

We were partners in this negotiation, each bound to play a part. The fact of our mutual and abiding loathing only heightened our performances. I made faces. I stuck out my tongue. Tan grunted. I grunted back, imitating him.

Then, before our pantomime turned truly ridiculous, I slapped the gold coin Rose had given me for Christmas on the kitchen table. Tan's brow raised ever so slightly and, knowing I'd impressed him, I was satisfied.

I hooked Rogue to his leash and went out the back door. It was a profound sorrow to give up that money, and I had no guarantee that Tan wouldn't just take the coin and claim he never saw it. But I understood enough of the world to know that for a girl to have any life outside the house, she had to risk. I had to pay for my future—Pie's, Morie's, and mine, that is—in gold.

I kept my eye on Tan all afternoon. At last he finished his chores, fed General a bucket of oats, and disappeared into the kitchen to fetch his bags. I seized my chance. Making sure neither Morie nor Pie saw me, I climbed into the buggy and hid on the floor, hugging my bony knees. My heart pounded with a heady mix of terror and joy.

Tan mounted the driver's bench in front. Through the buggy's small square window, I could see the back of his head, his black fez and narrow shoulders, his long braid brushed aside so he wouldn't sit on it.

If I wondered for even a second whether Tan knew he had a passenger trembling inside the carriage, he turned around and shook his fist at me through the window.

"All right, all right," I grumbled, and realizing there was no point in hiding, I climbed onto the narrow leather seat.

Tan showed General the whip and we set off at a trot.

I had never ridden alone in a hack—that was just how small my life had been. I'd never been downtown without a chaperone either. I decided I might as well enjoy this bit of freedom, for which I'd paid dearly.

The hack had been Rose's chief mode of transportation before she bought the motors; the walls were upholstered with her favorite red silk jacquard. Her perfume, thick and floral, pervaded the tight space, that and a rich mix of horse sweat and leather and grease from the large spoke wheels.

A ray of afternoon sun poured through one of the side windows and warmed my face. I took it as a sign of my bright future. I was giddy and I was on my way to The Rose.

I figured we'd go direct, down Columbus Avenue, but Tan had another route in mind. We wound our way toward the marina, then turned sharply onto Van Ness Avenue, the widest boulevard in town. Trees lined the curbs, with ornate and gabled mansions on either side, and six lanes of traffic—buggies and motors and horses cutting every which way—converging all at once. It was a beautiful dance with the pedestrians making way for the horses, the horses making way for the buggies and coaches, the coaches making way for the motorcars, which in turn blasted their horns, claiming their superiority. Everyone on the street expected everyone else to go around.

Tan wasn't having it. He whipped General into a quick trot and plowed ahead, forcing the other vehicles to veer sharply or halt. I gripped the bench with both hands as Tan made another sharp turn onto Sacramento Street.

We passed the church there. An old woman in rags, her shoulders rounded, her gait stiff, was slowly, painfully climbing the church steps. I wondered if she was sick, or perhaps in debt to the Haj too, or maybe she was just religious—all seemed equally likely. I wondered if she'd committed a crime and had come to repent.

Well, I, for one, didn't feel repentant. I was en route to my new life—on a mission to save Morie and Pie, to save myself. I never once considered the possibility that Rose would refuse me.

It was hard going for General to climb Nob Hill. The buggy lumbered with the horse's effort. I held my breath until at last we reached the peak where the road evened out—on top of what all of us natives referred to as Snob Hill. Picking up speed, General trotted past the palaces of Stanford, Huntington, Crocker, Hopkins, the mansions clustered like small countries bordered by iron gates. I thought: One day I'll live this high and owe no one.

But no sooner had we climbed than we started going down—down the treacherously steep grade that marked the approach into Chinatown. The buggy pitched forward and I was tossed to the floor.

General whinnied with terror. Horses routinely lost their footing on that hill. Going up was hard, but going down was bare-knuckles. One badly placed hoof, a too-heavy carriage, and the horse and buggy would crash. General was neither young nor nimble; he protested, snorting and arching his neck. Tan talked to him in Cantonese, his voice low and calm. The buggy rocked side to side with each of General's cautious steps.

My dress was dusty, and I'd skinned my knee. I climbed onto the seat and struggled to hang on. We entered Chinatown—five square blocks packed with twenty thousand Chinese.

I'd never been there either. And since I believed most of what I read in the papers, the recent outbreak of bubonic plague in Chinatown having been heavily trumpeted, as was the story of its underground zoo, I was predisposed to think of Chinatown as barren, haunted by tigers and vermin.

Well, I saw no tigers. Just throngs of Chinese packed in the brackish alleys and narrow streets. I saw no women. The few children, dressed like tiny emperors, were chasing each other through the doorways of the shops, while the men in the same black tunics that Tan wore puffed on their long pipes, their black bowlers and conical hats tipped back to take in the sun. I hadn't anticipated the bustle. Or the grimy alleys and blacked-out windows of the opium dens—in easy reach of the carriage. I hadn't imagined there would be so much life, from the overflowing bins of fruit and potatoes, to the stalls filled with trinkets and silk bags, to the butcher shop windows hung with fowl, their curled feet and droopy beaks, the live ducks strutting in straw cages, the crabs swimming in tanks of clouded water.

The girl was waiting on a corner, dressed like a bride. She looked up as we approached. The resemblance was unmistakable: a girl version of Tan. An elderly Chinese man stood beside her, his black garb hanging loose as if he'd recently been ill. The old man raised himself up, at attention, the moment he spotted Tan driving the coach.

Tan whoaed General to halt, reached under his bench, and handed the girl a sack. She passed it to the old man. Then Tan took hold of her thin wrist and hauled her onto the bench. That was it. The old man disappeared among the black hats. Tan rolled the whip across General's rump and on we went.

Why *her*? I wanted to know, feeling jealous and irked to have to share my ride to The Rose.

As if reading my mind, Tan flicked his whip, sending its popper, the hard leather knot at the end, flying through the air to land with a loud crack on the carriage roof. I shuddered as if struck. This way, Mr. Elegance silenced me.

We plowed through the knotted traffic at Portsmouth Square, straight on, each block of the Barbary Coast seedier than the last: the joss houses and saloons, the pawnshops, the dance halls with billboards overhead of girls doing the cancan.

It was three o'clock in the afternoon, downtime for the brothels and bars. Along the dirt-packed streets, things were quiet, with many of the joints shuttered, their doors and windows filthy with dust, their signs casting long shadows in the street.

Now we passed the truly sordid joints, the infamous Nymphia with a hundred and fifty cubicles on each of its three stories; on past the cribs and cow yards where customers weren't allowed to remove their shoes. Here were the joints where the music blasted from gramophones and customers routinely had their pockets picked; where thugs were hired to shanghai the unsuspecting, who awakened to find themselves chained in the belly of China-bound ships; where, in the worst of the worst, the wretched cribs, a prostitute might be forced to withstand scores of tricks in a single night.

How could this be the nexus of The Rose? I didn't want to believe it. I feared that it was a trick, that Tan was taking me to some new hell. I was about to bang on the window and protest when we passed a row of brick buildings, one with an unmarked, glossy black door. Above the door, hanging from iron fancywork shaped like a woman's outstretched arm, a sign painted with a single red rose.

Tan drove to the far end of the block, to the Hippodrome dance hall, where a pair of women were lazily leaning on the open Dutch door. Their dyed hair was crimped, their lips painted, their eyes ringed with kohl. Their blouses were cut where the bodice would have been, exposing their breasts. They were chatting lazily with the girls next door at the Bear. But when Tan steered General to the curb, they fell silent.

Tan climbed from his seat and tied the horse to a post. He moved deliberately, with a fierce solemnity, careful not to acknowledge their glances. Once, twice, he made a perfect knot of the leather lead and took the loose bit and wrapped it neatly. Next, Tan coiled his whip, just so, under his arm. He hefted a sack hidden under the seat, yoked it on his shoulder, then offered to help the girl down.

When she refused his hand, I thought, Ah, there's pride. That Chinese slip of a queen.

I moved toward the door, expecting Tan to come for me. He glared through the glass. *"Wait,"* he spat.

Was it ten minutes or thirty I stayed there? Well, it felt like a long time. At last I busted out of that perfume-soaked buggy and hurried like hell down the plank sidewalk, the women's stony gazes following me. When I reached the door of The Rose, I pushed into a world of darkness.

All these years of imagining, I had seen it lit bright. Candles, chandeliers, that kind of thing. In my mind, music played at The Rose all hours, with ladies in fine dresses spreading their professional merriment while the men, dressed as if headed to the theater or the opera, sat at white-clothed tables and smoked and drank.

The front room was low-lit and creepy. A first-floor tavern, stinking of beer and sweat and fetid flowers. As my eyes adjusted, I made out a vase of wilted roses, scattered wood tables and chairs, a dance floor, a long, waxy mahogany bar.

There was a certain coolness too. I mean temperature, sure, I mean time; I mean a deep, undeniable cool that you could push against, if you wanted to, but why would you?

There was a stage in back marked by a tired gold velvet curtain and matching gold swags. The chairs onstage were positioned at odd angles, the band's brass instruments, dented with knocks, haphazardly abandoned where the players had dropped them, as if it didn't matter one performance or the next; the real show at The Rose was always in motion.

In a week it would all be ashes.

Hank, Rose's man, was talking to a man behind the bar. The next thing I knew Hank was beside me, gripping my elbow too hard. "You all right, miss?"

"Fine, Hank," I said, "I'm fine." I never wanted anyone to think otherwise.

"Then stop all your shakin', Miss Vera," he said, moving me along. "You're with old Hank. Here we go, this way."

He didn't question my being there; he didn't question where we needed to go. My arrival had coincided with the brothel's off-hours, when most of the staff was asleep upstairs. Two women perched on bar stools were talking to the thick-necked bartender, who was hacking a bowl of limes. When they turned to look at us, Hank glared and shook his head. In unison they turned away.

At a table by a corner, a black woman was putting on a private show. Her skin was so uniformly, gorgeously dark, it looked blue in the light of The Rose. She was straddling the lap of a fat-bellied man, breasts to his tremendous paunch, feeding him shrimp from an icy silver bowl. She made a show of selecting each shrimp, plucking it from one bowl and dipping it into a second bowl of sauce. The man lifted his chin, honked like a seal, and she dropped the shrimp into his trap, giggling, then cleaned his mouth with her lips. I had never seen anything so disgusting, except perhaps when Rogue nibbled shit in the park; I couldn't look and I couldn't not look.

When she saw me, she cried out, "Oh my sweet Jesus," and crossed her hands over her heart. "What's the news, darlin'?"

Her name was Capability Jones and I didn't think I knew her from when I was small, except I knew her in my belly. I knew that broad smile.

"Damn it, Cap," barked Hank. "You don't see this." He pointed to the top of my head. "Hear me?"

Capability's grin folded in reverse, collapsing like a cardboard box. She cocked her head and looked appraisingly, unpleasingly, at the man on whose lap she sat, and said, "You full up, honey?"

Hank kept us moving, now crossing the room and heading for the far wall, our journey measured by his wide, booted strides. Next to a gold-framed painting of bare-breasted lady sailors, Hank pushed on a wall that was actually a door. The door led to a passage papered in pink damask, which led to yet another door and one after that, a maze. I had no idea where I was being led but I trusted that eventually we'd get to Rose.

I tried my best to keep quiet, to stanch the questions I longed to ask. And anyway, Hank was carrying on for the two of us. "Boss don't like surprises," he muttered, "you know it, still you've been barking up this path, I've seen it coming, and had you only asked, don't you know old Hank would have taken care? But her mood," he fussed, "oh, her mood. I cannot say."

"I'm sorry, Hank." In my heart, I almost meant it.

"Sorry is as good as yesterday," he replied. "Chip off the block is what you are. You and her don't know sorry." He didn't mean it unkindly. I even think he meant it as a form of praise.

The whole time we were walking briskly down narrow halls, passing row after row of doors. Some were open partway, and I caught glimpses of beds covered in shades of satin, no pillows or covers, just the sheet. In one room, a heavyset woman was lying on the bed wearing only a corset and bloomers. She was reading a newspaper, her enormous feet crossed at the ankles.

She called out to Hank, her voice a low bass. "Whatcha know, Hank?"

"Not now, Valentine," Hank grumbled.

I wanted to ask who Valentine was. I wanted to ask so many things. But Hank was shushing me as he hustled us upstairs.

We arrived at the top, and crossed what felt like a passage between two buildings, and beyond a row of nicer suites with private dining rooms and kitchens and fancy beds, then a final hallway, which ended at a door. Behind the door, muffled weeping.

Hank paused before knocking.

"Come," said Rose.

The Chinese girl was on her knees, begging. Earlier, I assumed she was a child, but I was mistaken. She was older, Pie's age at least, with a woman's high forehead, and breasts. She was weeping. Her tears dripped onto her white silk tunic, which, in the harsh light, shone threadbare. Tan stood behind her, grim and proud.

We'd caught them mid-negotiation, that much was clear, at the point where the girl had asked for something and had been denied. Rose leaned forward—as if speaking to a beloved child. With a lace hanky, she wiped the tears from the girl's cheeks.

When she saw me, Rose barked, "Hank, what the hell is this?"

Hank thought to explain, got half a word out, when I stepped forward. "I hid in the carriage. Hank, Tan, they didn't know I was there."

"Gawd," Rose said. "Suddenly, I am swimming in daughters."

That's right, she said "daughters." I didn't take kindly to being linked with the Chinese girl; she didn't take it kindly either. She glared at me.

"Tan, escort Lifang downstairs," Rose said. "Fix her something to eat."

Lifang began to argue, she had that in her, but she wouldn't, not then. She climbed solemnly to her feet, eyes downcast, the way you do when the fury you feel is so heavy, it weights the lids of your eyes. I knew that anger, I knew it well.

Hank saw them out and closed the door behind him.

I was alone with my mother. If I thought kneeling would help my cause, I would have knelt. But I figured I had to prove that I was stronger.

"That girl, she's also your daughter?"

Rose regarded me. "You have an odd habit of asking a question that is three steps ahead of where you belong. Has anyone told you that?"

"No one tells me anything."

"Ha, I bet." Her gaze softened ever so slightly. "So, you came down here on your own steam, did you? And has something transpired since last night—something terribly urgent?"

"I don't belong there; I never did. I've come to live with you. To work for wages. I . . . need the money."

"Good Christ," she said. She looked to her left and to her right, as if an audience were on hand to witness her frustration.

"I've known the family a long time," she explained. I thought she must be speaking about Morie and Pie, but no, it was Tan. She'd known Tan's family a long time.

"Tan came to work for me when he was just a bit older than you," Rose went on. "You didn't know that, did you? He's worked all these years to provide a better life for his daughter, Lifang. Now, it appears, she needs my protection. It isn't safe in Chinatown for a young, pretty girl. Tan wants her here, not as a working girl, no, never that, but in my care. Lifang, she is like—"

"Your chosen daughter?" Tears stung my eyes.

"Ahh, stop. You're angry at the wrong things."

"Am I? Tell me, what should I be angry about?"

She batted that away. "No one is coming to live with me," she scoffed. "A girl steps through that door and she is ruined." Rose glanced at me, letting that sink in. "Marching in here, you took a grave risk. Let's hope no one saw you. Or the jig is up, eh? Let's hope they think you're the butcher's girl, and in that dress—where did you get that awful sack? My God, why doesn't she put you in proper clothes, with all the money I give her? You must have grown two, three inches since that frock was hemmed. Shame on her."

"No one saw me," I declared.

"So you say." She tapped her palm with the tips of her long nails. "Tan has a serious problem. He has reason to believe that one of the tong gangsters running Chinatown has his eye on Lifang. They will kidnap her and force her to become one of their brides, or, should she prove difficult, they'll turn her into a slave in one of their crib dens. It's all the same to them—bride or whore—it's all the same. But she's special, that one. She doesn't think so, but I can see when a twig's so narrow it will break."

"I won't break." My face burned with too much feeling.

Rose showed me her fox smile, lips pressed. "Maybe not. But you've put me in a tight squeeze with Tan, haven't you? Making obvious his little bit of thieving. Let me tell you something: we're all thieves, Vera, one way or another."

"I'm not a thief."

She tipped her head, deciding. "Mmm. Maybe not. Or perhaps not yet. Let's see when you're pushed too far, then you'll know, eh? Meantime, there is to be no peace with you." She smiled wearily. "This place, you think it's fun and games. It's not. Trust me on that score."

"I can see for myself." I saw the piles of papers, the broken furniture, the tufted divan with its rows of missing buttons, her chair, sad and worn.

"Oh my, have we disappointed you?" she mocked.

I shrugged. I couldn't exactly tell her it was not The Rose of my Rose. That I'd imagined hallways lined with velvets and dewy flowers; I had pictured her inner sanctum with silk chaises and fine carpets—but that place didn't exist. The room resembled a cramped storeroom, with desks and cabinets overflowing with papers and maps and plot diagrams pinned to the wall, and bolts of fabric and frayed lampshades with no lamps, and boxes of candles stacked on top of crates of whiskey. A safe was fitted among the ledgers and newspapers and crates, and what she had hidden inside that shiny pachyderm, I needed.

"I'm good with numbers," I said, pressing my case. "At school I've won the arithmetic award four years in a row."

In the far corner, a man coughed. He'd been there all along, hidden by piles. He was seated behind a large desk, silently, steadily counting stacks of money.

"Martin, I remind you, you are not here," Rose said.

Martin dropped his head and continued on, his lips moving like bellows in and out as he tallied what I assumed must have been the previous night's haul. When he reached a certain number of bills, he tugged a band off his wrist, wrapped it around them, and set that stack aside. I figured four or five of those stacks would answer Morie's debt, and who would miss them?

Rose waved her fingers in front of my face, forcing me to turn away. "Why do you need money?" she asked. "What more could you want that I don't provide?"

The question threw me. There was so much I needed that she didn't provide, and none that I would admit. "I just do," I said.

Her eyes narrowed as she tried to see ahead of me. "And Pie?" she asked. "What about your sister? If you leave, I wouldn't be bound to pay for them, you know. Do you want to see Pie out on the street?"

"Pie is marrying James," I said quickly, and though it was true, true enough, it made my stomach ache to give up Pie like that.

"Marry James, so she says," Rose replied. "But you know as well as I, a lot can happen in a year." As Rose pondered my situation, she fingered her pearls, the beads on her ever-present abacus. "Tell you what: let's talk then. In a year, if you insist, we'll make a different arrangement. . . ." Her voice trailed off. "This, I can promise you, is not what I planned."

"What did you plan?" I asked, forgetting why I was there and remembering only that I wanted to be with her. For as much as she wasn't anyone's mother—not mine, not really—she was so familiar, familiar in my bones, the only one I'd ever met who felt like me.

"When you left me with Morie, what did you think I'd become?"

"Honestly?" She sighed. "I figured you'd be cared for, and away from this—" She waved her hand and her pearls chinked like a thousand tiny bells.

"Cared for like a beast, shod and fed," I muttered, then louder, "How do I know you'll stick to your part?"

"Listen to you. My word. Hank!" she shouted.

He must have been waiting with an ear to the door, for he came right in.

"Hank!" Rose bellowed. "This one here, she wants to know if I stand by my word."

"You *are* the word, mum. Everyone knows that."

"That's right, everyone knows." Rose shook her head. "All right, then."

"You need me," I said, making a last desperate stand. "You don't know it, but you do."

"Anyone I need, I can buy," she said. "But"—she held up a finger—"if I find otherwise, I'll call on you. How about that. Are we agreed?"

I did not agree, and worse, I'd failed: my pockets were empty. Even so, I was dismissed. The way we'd come, down the labyrinth of halls and doors, is the way we went, with Hank warning, "Now, Miss Vera, you made your deal with the boss and you don't want to be niggling. You want to show her you're made of solid stuff."

I dared myself not to cry. But the tears were at the gates, clogging my throat and stinging my eyes.

I figured now Hank would take me home in his car. My heart sank as he steered me toward the rig, where Tan was waiting, holding General's reins.

Hank opened the buggy door, and there was the girl, Lifang. She'd placed herself at the center of the narrow bench and had no intention of sharing.

"Move over," I croaked, my voice clotted.

"Now then, you two," warned Hank, "girls ain't cats, and girls behave. You got that?" Hank banged the door shut.

Lifang shifted a fraction, her fingers, the bare beds polished to a gloss, gripping the bench.

I sat heavily, shoving her the rest of the way with my hip. Tan put General into a choppy trot while Lifang and I stared out separate windows onto our mutual disappointment. We didn't dare look at each other. Still, being a tough girl is a lonely business; it took a fellow tough girl to comprehend how difficult it was to stand before the madam, flagrant with your wants, only to be sent packing.

"I hate cats," I whispered.

"I love them," she countered, wiping her tears with the sleeve of her dress.

Lifang took her father's hand as she stepped from the buggy at the corner in Chinatown where he'd fetched her. Without a backward glance, she disappeared into the crowd. In a few days, he would collect Lifang again, take her on the ferry to Oakland, then east to Sacramento, where she would be safe; Rose had it all arranged. Tan and Lifang were being sent away. Looked at in a certain light, it was a promotion.

"Stupid *gurrl,*" Tan hissed at me, his hand on the door. "She don't want you." And with that, he slammed it shut.

Block after slow block, Tan proved to me his rage by whipping the poor horse.

I felt every blow on General's back, and, alone in the buggy, I wept. I was ashamed—of myself for wanting, and of Rose, for being so much less than I'd hoped. I couldn't very well return home empty-handed, but home was where we were headed. With every sting of the whip, every lurching clop of General's hooves, we made our slow dread creep to Francisco Street.

Tan pulled up a block from the house. He didn't bother to offer me a hand as I climbed down. I suppose I wouldn't have accepted it anyway.

Tan kept his eyes on the road, his neck sunk into his shoulders. "Rose is no place for you," he said.

"You said she didn't want me."

"Nahh, same-same."

I thought of Lifang and her tears; she wouldn't say it was same-same either.

As I stood by, feeling my unjust fate, Tan made a show of setting his whip aside. He had only to roll the reins across General's back to set him in a trot. I watched them go. I couldn't imagine going home with my bag and heavy heart. So I lingered, as the late-afternoon fog poured in like the fingers of God—the city's famous wet wind relentless and insistent, asking me, Whoareyou, whoareyou, whoareyou?

Morie and Pie were waiting in the parlor. They stood as I came in. I must have looked wretched, for Morie wrung her hands and said, "I'm glad you're home."

"Tan isn't coming back," I replied, and let that sink in.

Morie covered her mouth with her palm. She had always bragged about her prowess in the kitchen, her Swedish meatballs adored by Lars, her lingonberry jam. Now she'd have to prove it—day after day. And the shopping and housekeeping too.

She and Pie exchanged glances. No doubt they'd passed the afternoon in a fit of worry, fearing and guessing where I'd gone. They'd spend the evening working over this new alarming turn.

"And . . . the other?" Morie asked, trying not say what was most on her mind, the Haj. "Did she—"

"She said no to everything." I turned for the stairs.

"I'll bring up supper," Pie called.

"Don't bother."

But later that evening, Pie knocked on my door. She had a cup of hot milk and a plate of toast and cheese. She smiled shyly. "Stop. I know you're starving."

"Please, Pie. Leave me alone."

She joined me on the bed. "You might as well tell me everything." Pie wrinkled her nose. "Was it awful?"

I paused, thinking of how to answer. I was a jumble of feelings, most of them wretched; I was stuck and the urge to stick the next guy, in this case Pie, was powerful. She looked so earnest—I was tempted to make up a sordid tale of the whorehouse, just to shock her. But the truth was much worse, and it would have broken me to have to tell it.

"What do you want, Pie?"

"How do you mean?"

"I mean, what do you really want? Is there anything you'd die for? Or is everything with you always sensible?"

She dipped her chin, the way she did when faced with unpleasantness. She knew me so well: my weaknesses, my worries. I thought I knew hers. I had never liked playing with other children, only Pie, while she had all kinds of friends, and a special understanding with Eugenie. Pie insisted that whenever she went visiting, I should be allowed to tag along, though I was never any fun for her friends and only stared at them, memorizing their faces and the black velvet chokers that bobbed on their thin throats, and the silly thoughts that spilled from their idle heads. Afterward, Pie would gently ask: V, couldn't you manage to smile just a little? I'd try and fail, and she would let it go. The one thing we never discussed was the deal that made us family; we never talked about the two women who'd decided our lives.

"Same as you," she said. "Same as you, I want my own life."

"Is that why you're marrying James? Do you even love him?"

Pie blushed. "Sometimes I forget you're a child."

"You might as well call me stupid."

"Oh, no, not stupid." Pie looked unusually focused, intense. "Do you think you're the only girl with dreams?" Her face was shiny with passion. "I just don't go about it . . . the same. I mean, where does it get you?" She paused, choosing her words carefully. "Rose knew you were clever. You had nothing more to prove, yet you ratted on Tan. And today, you had to push the point. I suppose you thought it was for us—I'm sure you did—but it was also to prove you could go where a sensible girl isn't allowed. You think the rules don't apply to you because of *her* but you're wrong. It was a fool's errand." She shook her head. "Don't you see? If Rose wanted you there, why—why all this?" Pie opened her arms wide.

"Go away. Go away," I cried. "You don't understand . . . you couldn't possibly—"

"Oh, I understand." Frowning, she smoothed a pleat in her skirt. "I think about you all the time," she declared. "I think you are the bravest and the loneliest girl I ever saw."

She looked me in the eye and nodded. She climbed to her feet and added, "I just don't see the point of pushing on a locked door. I pick my time. You might try that for a change."

She was halfway out the door when I said, "Pie? Next summer, after you announce your engagement, Rose said I could move in with her."

"Did she, now?"

"Pretty much, yes."

"So, she proposed to propose. Is that it?"

I nodded.

"Well, then, I guess we're both set."

But set was not what her face read, nor mine. Set was the furthest thing we felt.

Caruso

Later, folks recalled that on the night of Caruso, the horses in front of the opera were jumpy, impossible to control. Did they feel the quake coming in just a few hours? We humans had no sense at all.

Yet everyone had the same notion to arrive early. Inside the main hall, the ushers were still sweeping the trash from the aisles of the matinee, while three thousand San Franciscans decked in their finest were pushing through the narrow opera doors.

The night was unseasonably warm for April. Pie and Morie hadn't planned for it. By the looks of it, neither had the other women. They were so determined to give Caruso their best, they'd put on every pelt and sparkle they owned, including their fur coats.

"Now, mind you, ladies," warned Hank as he ushered us inside. "Keep close."

I planned to. I had Rose's note in a mesh bag dangling from my wrist.

I held on to Hank's elbow as we pushed through the doors, into a blinding haze of photographers' flashbulbs. The actress Sarah Bernhardt had just arrived, accompanied by an entourage of ten drunken sailors. The chief of police looked like a stuffed penguin; ditto William Randolph Hearst, accompanied by Mrs. Hearst, who more closely resembled a parade float. As my eyes adjusted, the faces I knew from the papers seemed both familiar and strange—less and more. The Magnins, elegant and restrained; Blanche Partington, the music critic for the San Francisco *Call.* The Rooses had brought along a party of ten, as if one outrageously priced ticket could be bettered only by a dozen. The Crockers and Floods, the Lippman Sachses, Senator Belshaw. Miss Helen Woolworth came alone, which I thought sad and strange.

"That's ZumZum Sykes and his sidekick Jay Masters," Hank explained of the two men standing in front of the concession stand. Hank went on to say that there was one concession on the main floor and another upstairs, the Club, reserved for folks in the private boxes. Upstairs and down the champagne flowed, but it was a better vintage upstairs.

Hank seemed to know everyone—at least, he knew the men. He nodded and, as we passed by, called them "captain" in sotto voce. "Evening, captain . . . Evening . . . Good evening, captain."

"How is it they know you?" I asked.

"Ah, miss, leave it that The Rose is popular with these sorts. Now, you ladies want to push on to your seats?"

"Quit hurrying us, Hank. We're here, aren't we? We want to lookie-loo." Morie squinted at the fancy folks, her mouth frozen in a little-girl smile.

For once I agreed with Morie. AB Spreckels, the renowned bachelor, and Alma de Bretteville—our Alma—were in the house, though not together. Spreckels was on one side of the hall, talking with a group of men in tails—their wives with their furs and headdresses forming a hedge beside them.

"Oh, look, girls," gasped Morie. "There's Claus Spreckels." She pointed with a gloved hand at AB's father. "The sugar king."

"That's right, ma'am," Hank said. "Papa Spreckels, he's the money behind the push to send the mayor to the graybar hotel."

"Graybar?" Pie asked. "What is that?"

"Jail. The stony lonesome. See, old man Spreckels is out to

get Handsome Gene, 'cause the mayor went against Spreckels on the trolleys deal," Hank explained. "You ladies might have got a whiff that his son AB Spreckels, standing over there, courts Ms. Alma de Bretteville on the sly."

Hank leaned in and added for my ears only, "Miss Alma and AB, they's weekly customers—strictly top-shelf, private digs upstairs."

Hank, the fount of the evening's gossip, included Pie and Morie as he further explained that AB could not be seen with Alma. Instead, he'd purchased tickets in the orchestra section for Alma and her relatives while he planned to sit upstairs in the Spreckels family box. It was the same deal Rose had divined for us.

Morie had strong opinions regarding Alma de Bretteville. "That girl is a cheap trick," she declared.

"Ahh, say what you like, mum," countered Hank. "She'll get Spreckels to marry her, if I know a thing or six. Alma's the horse to bet on."

At the center of commotion, Alma was easy to spot—six feet tall. As usual, she looked stunning, dressed in a blue satin gown with a low-cut bodice the likes of which was seen only in Paris, and even then, not in proper society. Top-shelf, Hank had said.

"Look at her," Morie hissed. "Carrying on like she's someone."

"She is someone," I declared.

"Over here, Alma. Over here!" cried the photographers from the *Call* and the *Chronicle*, the tabloids jockeying to get her picture.

Alma scanned the crowd, mocking everyone. Where did she get all that confidence? How did she know to turn a certain way, so that the flashes illuminated her just so?

"Hey, Alma, nice dress. Did your sugar daddy buy it?" queried a brazen reporter.

Hank didn't appreciate the question. He headed for Alma with my hand locked against his ribs. We cut the marble hall on the diagonal, piercing the crush, with Morie and Pie trailing behind, trying to keep up. No one questioned Hank's authority. He reached Alma and offered her his free arm, which she gladly took, patting Hank's biceps with a gloved hand.

Alma smiled at me. "Well, look who's dressed up, and very nicely."

"Alma de Bretteville, may I introduce Miss Vera Johnson," Hank said with obvious pride. "A special person."

"Why, hello, Special." Alma beamed, looking ahead and smiling for the cameras. "I'm dying to know what makes you Hank's special friend."

"One day I'll tell you," I said.

"Good. I warn you, though, I make it a habit never to wait long." She grinned as Hank took a step back, joined Alma's hand to mine, and disappeared.

I looked back nervously, but Alma tugged on my hand. "Here, pet," she said, plucking a gardenia from her hair and slipping it into mine. "There. Now smile."

She signaled to the photographers one last picture. The bulbs flashed in a dazzling freeze.

"What's your name, doll?" a reporter asked.

"Fellas, meet Vera Johnson," Alma said rapturously. "Now, consider yourselves warned, boys," she added, and with that benediction, Alma released me to the masses. She had other people to see.

The photographers moved on as well, a gadget-toting school of fish, now clustering by the mayor, who did not wish to have his picture taken on the eve of his indictment. The mayor, *my* mayor, I thought possessively, agreed to pose just once, with his wife, Julia, and, of course, Eugenie and her siblings, Evelyn and Richard.

A reporter called out, "Mrs. Schmitz? Do you plan on visiting the mayor in San Quentin?"

"Gentlemen, tonight we're here to enjoy the opera," the mayor replied, his voice strained. "We don't see the likes of Enrico Caruso every day, now do we?" He held up a hand, signaling that was all.

Morie and Pie rushed to greet Eugenie and her mother.

That gave me my chance with the mayor.

"Ah, Vera!" he boomed, addressing me with his public voice. "How are you?"

I tugged on his lapel so he would stop that nonsense and meet my gaze. "I have something for you." I opened my bag and showed him the envelope.

He pushed my hand away. "Good God, not here," he huffed, looking over my shoulder. I looked behind me as well. Abe Ruef, the lawyer and mastermind behind Schmitz's political graft operation, was approaching at a clip. A small, bespectacled, grim man, Ruef, having eyes only for Schmitz, missed the pack of photographers who were following behind him, angling for their shot. It was the photograph the papers wanted—Abe Ruef and the mayor, the infamous grafters.

"Vera, this way," Schmitz said, leading me by the elbow. "Now just keep talking. Is that a new dress? Lovely, lovely. This way." Schmitz kept on with a string of babble as he steered me toward a side door, through that door, down a short hall, then through another door, which led to a service area where they stored props and broken chairs and discarded sets and trash, a sort of alley that ran alongside the auditorium proper.

I was glad to be out of the crush but tired of being led, especially where I did not wish to go. I shook off the mayor, whose grip was bruising my arm.

"Sorry about that," he said. "Just a bit farther." He looked back to see if anyone had followed us. As we neared the far door, this one marked "Stage," he halted.

"Whoa, you startled me back there," Schmitz admitted. "You know there are scores of reporters watching my every twitch. What's so urgent?"

"This." I handed him the note.

He stepped back, as if stung. "What does it say? Am I supposed to read it—*now*?"

"It's from Rose," I said, lowering my voice in case anyone was listening.

"Rose?" he whispered. "Rose who?"

I looked at him evenly. "The madam? Rose of The Rose?"

"Rose of the—? How do you know—?"

I lowered my eyes and waited for the picture to take shape in his mind. He wasn't stupid, my mayor, not by a long shot, and if I was to learn anything from him, it was to observe the way his conniving mind flowed nimbly from one possibility to the next: a violinist becomes a conductor becomes a mayor becomes a wealthy grafter, then a hunted man, the up-downs like the notes on a musical score.

"So, you're . . . ahh." His face bloomed with recognition. "Hers?"

I nodded. It was odd—I'd waited my whole life for the truth to be known, but the way Schmitz was looking at me, with unsavory interest, I had the urge to shield my face.

"Julia and I, we always wondered—I mean, we thought early on, you didn't quite stack with Pie." Schmitz made an unfunny twist with his mouth as he worked it out. "We assumed . . . guessed, you must take after your father, who passed . . . what was his name?"

"Lars," I said.

"Ah, right, Lars." Schmitz nodded, agreeing with himself. "Jesus Christmas, Rose has a . . . daughter." He shook his head. "Rose's daughter," he repeated, as if the words wouldn't make sense until he'd said them a hundred times. Schmitz nodded at the envelope. "So, what news does your Rose have for me?"

"I don't know." I pressed the envelope into his hand. "Maybe it's your miracle."

"I doubt it," he grumbled, but being just the sort of person who would believe in a divine reprieve, he added brightly, "I thought you didn't believe in miracles."

"I said I didn't believe in prayers."

"Ah, right. Right you are."

He winced as he read. "Well, that's that," he said, crushing the note in his fist and tossing it into a bin of trash. "At least I can count on you to look after Eugenie."

"Of course," I said.

With no topic safe to mention, we fell silent. That was its own kind of intimacy; I didn't like it. In the vast reaches behind the stage door, a woman was singing. She was doing scales.

The mayor pointed his nose in the air like a hound. "Hear that? That's Carmen." He cocked his head to listen. "Flat on the E. Poor Olive, she's nervous."

I didn't care about the E. I was thinking that the mayor should have stayed a violinist. Then he wouldn't be such an obvious crook, and Eugenie wouldn't have to see her father hauled off to jail. I felt bad for Eugenie but I didn't feel too awful for Schmitz. I expected he deserved what he got. I was regretting that I'd revealed to him, of all people, my secret about Rose.

"Let me ask you, Vera, something I've given thought to, considering my, uh, circumstances. You're someone who thinks for yourself, right? Who hasn't had, well, clearly not, a conventional life." He searched my face, as if I were a door he needed to pass through to get to a better hideout. "Strictly in the abstract, do you believe the ends justify the means?"

I thought for a moment. "I guess that would depend on what ends and what means."

"Eh . . . family?" He showed me his empty palm and lifted it skyward.

Watching that empty hand, I had a sudden inkling of the play before me, that is, the mayor's secret orchestra. The whole lot of them, lawyers and bookies and saloonkeepers, were on the take or contributing to the take—this underground society of wheedlers and bargainers—all fed into and drank from the same filthy, civic trough filled with cash and favors and gold. In the crowd, Abe Ruef had looked to me like a rodent with glasses, scurrying for his next bit of cheese, and my own Rose too, oddly, decidedly nervous when I went to her place and offered myself—she was sharp and tired and dug deep. The game, I was beginning to comprehend, had to do with trying out words to hide deeds—words and more words till one fit, like a shoe or a hat, till the ends justified the means.

And what was worse, far worse? As I stood by Schmitz and considered him with a good deal of righteous scorn, it occurred to me that the same trough that fed him and Rose fed me too. If I wasn't careful, I'd grow up to be as dirty as the rest of them.

"Ah, what difference does it make?" the mayor lamented as he ground his jaw. He turned toward the stage door. "I'd best get on, pay my respects to Caruso. Vera, would you mind terribly . . . can you find your way back?"

Of course I could.

But I didn't go directly. My heart was torn. The buzz from the lobby grew louder. I inched the door a crack just to see. A congealing nervousness, a decided edge, had taken hold out there. What the mayor and Abe Ruef wouldn't carry, the room had absorbed. The uneasiness touched the shoulder of my new friend Alma, whose attention had been divided by her haughty, impoverished parents on one side, and a gang of young, laughing belles on the other. The feverish push-push, the jockeying for advantage, made me queasy. I saw ambition, beauty, fear, and envy. I saw the fervent desire for something more, something just out of reach, that would always be the mother's milk of my city, and this country too, the more-and-more-ness of the ladies with their painted lips and bejeweled hair, the men in their tall hats and starched collars. I didn't see Rose. I did not see Morie or Pie. The pack of reporters, having been denied a photo of Ruef and the mayor, had shifted their rabid gaze to Mrs. Evelyn Whitehall, whose husband had recently dumped her for a vaudeville actress.

I didn't want to go out there, not for anything. I shut the door and headed the opposite way, in the direction of the singing. There was no one to stop me. On the way, I retrieved the note the mayor had tossed in the trash.

"Excuse me, miss, are you . . . with the opera?" The bald man with the thin wire glasses and a beard that stuck out like a hearth brush spoke with a German accent.

"I'm looking for the mayor," I fibbed. "Have you seen him?"

He smiled, his grin elfish. "I'm afraid, miss, he's gone to his box. Come, come, let's see." The man led me as though we were engaged in a curious conspiracy. He gestured for me to poke my nose, as he did, through a split in the curtain.

"Look up," he whispered. "First balcony, center box. See?"

Schmitz was just taking his seat, between his wife and Eugenie; behind them sat Eugenie's siblings. And there was Abe Ruef seated with the City Supervisors. A united front. Naturally, Schmitz had taken a seat in front. He was leaning on the box's padded railing, studying the orchestra.

"I see him," I whispered. "Thank you."

Before the kind man could ask me to skedaddle, a stagehand approached, calling the man I'd been speaking to Herr Director. While they talked, I peeked through the curtain, to see if I could find Morie and Pie. The house was nearly full. Everyone was finding their seats and there was much dawdling in the aisles, with folks having to stand to make room for latecomers.

Four rows back from the orchestra, I spotted them, and the empty seat beside Pie. Morie was fanning herself with the program while she madly scanned the crowd. Pie looked stricken, searching the aisles for me.

Then a commotion in the balcony boxes. A collective gasp.

The stagehand took my place at the curtain to see what it was. "It's the duke, Herr Director. From Paris," he whispered. "He's taking his seat. Look who he's with, Madam Rose."

"Madam Rose?" Herr Director asked.

The stagehand whispered something and the director chuckled. "Old friends, my eye."

I peeked through the split in the curtain.

They were acting as a team: the duke bussing the cheeks of the ladies in the boxes on either side, while Rose, head high, flirted with the men. Her gown was all bosoms and silver, her elaborately piled hair embedded with a tiara.

"Miss, if I may, please, would you kindly stand over here." The stagehand, pulling me back several paces and to the side, addressed me with all deference, which Herr Director did not correct. Backstage a world had assembled—in the wings and on the stage proper, actors and singers had magically taken their places.

Herr Director signaled the maestro in the orchestra pit with a decisive nod.

"Now," he said to the stagehand. "Now."

The lights dimming, the first whine of strings, the curtain rising, I scanned the boxes one last time. Mayor Schmitz was looking right at me, his expression both bemused and surprised. We'd been here before: one upstairs, one down. And just like before, he winked.

• • •

Before the third scene in the first act, Enrico Caruso appeared beside Herr Hertz. The tenor was shorter than I'd pictured, barrel-chested, with a monobrow. He wore a silk robe across his shoulders, like a king. The director did not speak to him though they stood shoulder to shoulder; no one dared break the great tenor's concentration.

This was the moment Rose had prepared me for—Caruso was the one who mattered, after all.

I'd read up on him since the night at Rose's, and assumed, as one does of a famous person, that I knew him. He'd followed his father into the trades; he'd sung in church and on the street. He was known as an amiable sweetheart. One day the great Vergine, the Italian impresario, heard Caruso sing. The voice was singular, so large, so tender. In its irregularity lay its genius; with training it would make audiences weep. Some said the maestro pushed Caruso too early. When Caruso debuted at La Scala, the snobby northerners booed the lowly boy from Naples. Caruso carried the wound of his debut for the rest of his days. He was celebrated the world over, but his own people had marked him an impostor. The shock weakened his nerves. The slightest shift of routine awakened fissures inside him. Backstage, to calm himself, he drew pictures, doodles with his likeness drawn at the center.

As he prepared for a performance inside his dressing room, he studied the two photographs he carried with him at all times: the first of his wife and children, the second, a portrait of him as a young man, singing on a street corner by his house.

When Mount Vesuvius erupted a few weeks earlier, it seemed a harbinger of bad things, he told the reporters at the *Call*. Getting to San Francisco had been a trial—ten interminable days on a train. The farther west he'd ventured, farther from his wife and sons in Naples, he couldn't sleep and longed for the sound of his children's voices. At night he was racked by ugly, prescient dreams.

What he didn't tell the papers, what I'd learned from Hank as we waited that evening for Morie and Pie to come out of the house, was that Caruso believed that we San Franciscans were grossly immoral—worse than Sicilians.

He'd arrived to the fanfare of mobbing crowds. Caruso's suites at the Palace Hotel offered the calm of gold-plated faucets and smoke and fire alarms installed on every floor. Each suite came with a butler on call day and night. The prostitutes, supplied by Rose, lit sweet-smelling candles and applied lotions to Caruso's frayed nerves; they employed tantric methods guaranteed to promote relaxation. Caruso's valet waited in the adjacent suite, should the tenor call for help. One of the girls was from Naples. Caruso asked the *puttana* if it was true, what he'd heard about San Francisco. She was a well-trained girl, clean, her fingernails unpolished like a good *napoletana*, her moustache barely visible. She didn't deny the rumors, for she understood that the notion of danger was intoxicating to a man.

Now, at last, it was time for Caruso to sing. A couple of feet, no more, from where I stood, Caruso's dresser removed his robe, revealing Don José's costume: a fitted leather bolero jacket, matching britches with silver studs embedded in the seams, and lace-up boots.

I tried not to stare at his heavily made-up face, his cleft chin, shaped like tiny upside-down buttocks, his small, pudgy hands. But when I spotted the pistol he'd tucked into his belt, I exclaimed, "Ha!"

Caruso looked at me with alarm, his kohl-rimmed eyes shocked. "Eh?"

I couldn't help it, I laughed. Oh, how I wished Pie were next to me, so I could say, "Look! Look, the pistol!"

Caruso strode onstage, and the audience—including all three rows of balconies—stood and applauded. Caruso's right hand went to his gun, just in case. The crowd clapped wildly, without the slightest regard for decorum. The hoodlums and loose women of San Francisco stood on their hind legs and banged their paws.

My new friend—his name was Alfred Hertz, director of the Metropolitan Opera—turned to Miss Vivian, the costume mistress, and asked, "What's with the pistol?"

Miss Vivian turned to her second-in-command. "Where did Don Caruso get the gun?"

As Caruso reached for the high notes of the libretto, the unschooled audience—my people, that's who they were: my crooked mayor, my madam mother, my drunkard Swede, my everyday righteous, my people run amok (oh, I could have wept for how much I loved and hated them and was part of them)—began to murmur. The tenor paused. Were they booing? Just the opposite. They had been schooled not at the opera but at the roller derby. San Francisco's finest in their tails and tiaras were commenting on how well Caruso was doing.

At intermission, I thanked Hertz and ran, in my too-tight, fancy shoes. Pushing through the crush of satin and silk in the lobby, the men inviolable as posts, I fought against the tide headed for the washrooms to climb the stairs. The Club was already filling with patrons intent on enjoying their share of oysters and champagne for as long as intermission lasted; the men had their whiskey and cigars.

Rose was chatting with the duke. He was an ugly man, with a hooked nose and pockmarked cheeks. Yet the longer I stared at him, the more striking he became; his tragic face underscored a regal bearing. He laughed easily, with pleasure and discernment. I had the feeling he was a genuine sort. The rest of their group, all men, not exactly top-shelf but jolly, were taking their cues from Rose, who was laughing riotously, as if she were acting in a play. Several of the stuffy men in the Club beamed when they spotted her, but the women, the swans and matrons, avoided her. In turn, Rose gave the ladies what she called the Invisible, a trick she used to disappear someone she didn't like by focusing her gaze on the air above their head. Highly effective, the Invisible took great control to pull off. I was certain I'd never have the poker face to employ it. But Rose had the Invisible down. She'd invented it.

A gong sounded, and the lamps dimmed. It was time to return to our seats.

I couldn't resist. "Rose!" I called out, though I knew I shouldn't.

Never before had I been on the receiving end of the Invisible, and for a moment I kidded myself into believing she hadn't seen me. But my heart knew she did.

Shaken

I lay awake thinking of all I'd seen—the who and what—preparing my clever treatise on the night of Caruso, not for Rose, who I'd decided didn't deserve it, but for myself. There was Schmitz on the one hand, corrupt and eager, and there was Herr Hertz, who seemed like a rare, upstanding adult. Then there was Caruso, whose voice transported a city.

The story of Carmen perplexed me, though, how she returned Don José's favor with her lovestruck hope. But her fate had already been decided. The girl was poor and sick, and love or no love, she died.

Frankly, it made me mad. Why did Carmen have to be poor? Poor then sick then dead? Why couldn't she and Don José live on together? What was the point? Then again, the spectacle, the adult world with its ersatz diamond satisfaction, its music and musk, filled me with more questions than answers. The mayor, on his last night of freedom, sat on high in his box and looked down at the citizens who would convict him. Come morning, he would be arrested. And the cogs of the city, corrupt as ever, would grind on. It disturbed me so much I couldn't sleep.

We'd been in our respective beds for what must have been an hour when Morie called to Pie and asked if she'd like to chat. My sister gladly joined Morie in bed. I could hear their giggles and sighs as they savored the night—the magnificent dresses, the ugly duke, and Caruso, talented but, oh, the opera went on far too long.

On the ride home, I had tried to tell them about my backstage adventure, but they were too full of their own impressions to be taken with mine. Morie scolded me for giving them an awful fright. "What would happen," she asked, "if you disappeared?"

In my room, Rogue refused to settle. One o'clock, two o'clock, he paced from the bed to the window, and stood there, his feet planted, hair erect along his spine, his snout poking at the cool glass. He barked and barked at phantoms. When he paused to listen, another dog in the neighborhood started up and Rogue, honor-bound, had to answer.

"What's the matter, boy?" I kept asking. He tried to convey his troubles with an unblinking stare. When I failed to comprehend him, he whined.

I woke with Rogue standing over me, his paw pinning me to the sheets. In my confusion, I thought the growl—low and deep—was him.

It was the sound of the earth breaking. The quake climbed through thousands of layers of soil and bones and dinosaurs and fossils and bodies of ancestors, known and unknown, through the roots of a million trees.

Next it was the moan-cry of the house, the old-growth redwood weeping as it bent, or tried to.

Forty-five seconds is an eternity. Time it, if you don't believe me. The shaking went on and on and on. Furniture collided, sections of the ceiling split and fell—no one thing distinct from the next, a cacophony of collapse. In the moonlit shadows, my bureau danced foot to foot then fell on its face; the bookcase leaped, tripped on the rug, and crashed. The windows bent in their sleeves, straightened audaciously, then burst. The floor undulated in short, choppy waves. The bed, with Rogue and me riding its top, sailed as if it were a flying carpet. Rogue jumped off and I had the wits to follow as the headboard hit the windows, busting the last panes of glass.

Then, mercifully, a pause. I got as far as the door.

The next temblor started under the house. It thundered as it traveled upward, building, expanding, this one stronger than the first. The earth was a bucking bull that wouldn't quit until it had tossed us from its back.

I tried to hold on to the door casing, but a jolt sent me flying, facedown, into the hall. I shielded my head and hoped I wouldn't get beaned by the chunks of plaster falling all around me. That's when Rogue decided to run. He leaped over me and bounded for the stairs. I heard him cry as he tumbled down.

I kept thinking: This can't be *it.* Oh my God, *it is.*

Then, abruptly, the shaking stopped. Then one more shift—a hip check, deep and low. The house swayed, and kept on swaying, even after the earth stopped, the house rolling as if on wheels.

That's when the front chimney gave way: a thousand tumbling bricks.

"Pie? Pie!" I crawled toward her, bloodying my hands and knees on the rubble. Her room, what little I could see in the shadows, looked as if someone had tossed the furniture against the walls. In place of the front wall, where the windows had been, there was no wall at all, only the predawn sky.

"Pie! Pie, where are you?"

Then I remembered: she was with Morie.

Moments before the quake, Pie had awakened with a full bladder. She was squatting over the chamber pot when the chimney roared down, taking with it a side of the house. She watched the wave of brick, like a great black shadow, roll toward her, burying the bed where she'd just been. So many heavy bricks fell onto the iron bed, it gave way, crashing through the floor, the whole business falling—with Morie asleep, buried beneath the beams and bricks and plaster in the parlor below.

"Pie!"

She'd managed to hold on to a narrow strip of floor that clung to the wall. She was rocking, hugging her knees.

"Pie, look at me. Piper!"

Slowly she looked up, her eyes huge and unblinking, from the hole into which Morie had fallen.

"Pie, are you hurt?"

She'd taken a good knock on the head, that much I could see, now with the first light of dawn coming on. That, and she was soaked in her own piss, the chamber pot tipped on its side, her hair and nightgown coated with a suet of plaster and dust. My angel Pie.

I crawled toward her, inch by narrow inch. I tried not to think about falling, or the raw gaping hole, or the next shaker. I tried not to think about Morie.

"Here we go," I whispered. "Pie, don't look down. Here, this way."

She clung to me, to my back, her arms wrapped round my neck. Inch by inch I got us to the hall as the next shaker rumbled toward us.

And the aftershocks kept coming, followed by the slide and combustion of more bricks and glass, and, from out on the street, the cries of animals, horses mainly.

The house rolled and swayed. Any moment, I was sure, it would all come down.

"Here, Pie, quick, put these on." I handed her a pair of boots, but she only cowered, limp as a doll. I put them on her, cursing her idle feet. And I got my boots on too.

"Pie. Goddamn it, stand up," I cried hoarsely, the dust coating my throat.

She fell, as if her strings had been cut.

Once more, I carried her like a sack, and my ankles wobbled but I didn't let them do more than that. Step by uncertain step I got us down the stairs. Everything was in shadow and not where it should be. Vases and books mixed with plaster boulders and swords of glass. Lars's paintings had flung themselves from the walls. At the foot of the stairs, the bird's-eye maple mirror, which had always shown me taller and Pie prettier, crunched beneath our boots.

The walls of the parlor were stripped to their lath. At the center, the top of one iron bedpost and a pyramid of brick.

I knew she was dead, but the strands of gray hair poking out of the brick, hair like yarn at the end of a blanket, made it certain. If Morie had stepped from the shadows and yelled, I couldn't have been any more shocked. But she wasn't there. She was nowhere and everywhere under all those bricks.

Pie looked to me as if I had the power to change what we were seeing.

But, oh, I didn't.

The house shuddered as another temblor came on, and more parts of the house crashed. Next, we'd be buried too.

My only thought was to get us out. The front door was blocked by a fallen beam and more brick. With Pie on my back, we worked our way to the kitchen, where the busted gas pipe sputtered and hissed.

Morie's shawl was on the chair; I passed it to Pie, along with a dish towel for the cut on her forehead.

At the back door, Rogue was whimpering, holding up first one, then another shredded paw. I set Pie on a chair and opened the back door and let him go first.

"I can stand," Pie said, wobbling.

We locked arms and stepped outside into a grave silence, weightier than the roar. Our neighbors were just coming out of their houses. Like moths hatched from a chrysalis, we emerged into a shattered world.

"Hold on tight, Pie," I said, her tethering weight a comfort.

"You too," she whispered.

We crossed the road with Rogue at our heels, and I set Pie gently on the curb. She tucked her legs under her, as we looked back to see what remained of the house. Rogue lifted his snout and followed my gaze.

Most of the front and one side wall were gone; where the chimney gave way, there was a massive hole. The furniture, the tables and chairs and sewing machine and grandfather clock, were shattered or tossed. Yet the upstairs bathtub still stood on its four feet, and a towel hung from the bar. Morie's lace curtains—she'd insisted on Belgian lace, had campaigned a year for Rose to buy them—flapped in the morning breeze, their hems shredding on the broken windowpanes.

A dollhouse, with its back open to the street.

Our neighbor Mr. Heffernan approached in his nightshirt, his pearly, sockless calves peeking out of his wife's boots.

"Vera, Pie," he said. "And your mother?"

Seeing our faces, he looked back at our house, where only a single white bedpost stuck out from the tomb of brick.

"Oh, my dears," he said.

Mrs. Heffernan, her hair curled in strips of rags, then said, "Your mother, bless her, has gone to heaven, girls. While I fear we may be lost in hell."

Pie flinched and bit her fist.

Anything could happen and no one could ever be shocked again.

More folks were emerging from the wrecks of their houses. Not a single house on the block had been spared: columns split, chimneys caved, roofs folded like paper. The house next door to the Heffernans', having slipped from its foundation, faltered on bended knee, genuflecting. Mrs. Fielder, at the far end of the block, had been crushed by a beam. The falling joist had spared her husband, who was asleep beside her. Mr. Fielder carried his wife's body into the road as if she were a bride, and there he stood, looking back at his life.

And the aftershocks kept coming, with everything perched on the earth's top, every brick and board, glass and book, every man and beast, trembling—forced to recommit or bust.

The roar as another chimney came down.

"Flynn's," Mr. Heffernan said to his wife.

Followed by the neighbors on either side scrambling to dig out the widower Flynn, who, in his youth, had been a miner.

Rogue sat on his haunches next to me, and with Pie on my right, the two of them leaned against my legs. They were leaning so hard, I had to lock my knees to keep from falling.

"Who else?" Mr. Heffernan asked the group of survivors, our neighbors, all standing in their bedclothes.

"Any sign of the de Brettevilles?"

We turned to ask their house. The chair where Mr. de Bretteville loitered was tipped on its side, but the house stood.

"Saw them last night. They were all turned out for Caruso."

"Maybe they spent the night downtown with the swells?"

A collective shrug. Unspoken agreement that the de Brettevilles would be the ones to make a fancy escape.

Pie held the rag against her head and rocked with her eyes closed. "V," she whispered hoarsely, "ask the men . . . to help Morie—"

I shook my head. "Shh. Not now."

"But . . . we have to—"

"Sorry, girls," said Mr. Heffernan, catching Pie's meaning, "it's the living we need to tend to. There's no telling when the rest of these houses are coming down."

"But, V," Pie pleaded, and for good measure she tugged on my skirt. All at once, I felt light-headed, queasy. I dropped to the curb beside her and rested my head against my knees.

"V, we have to do something," Pie begged. "It's Morie. She's . . . don't you feel her—"

"'Course I do."

I felt the last shake and the one before that and the one before that too rumbling inside me, knocking loose the marrow of my bones. I heard the roar and slide of the chimney as it brought the house down over and over and over.

Rogue whimpered and licked his hurt feet. I shifted him over, so his rump was between my knees, and set to work picking the tiny shards from his paws. Having Rogue's heart boom against mine, I felt a bit less scared. No, I was in awe. The magnitude of the thing. It was there in the eyes of our neighbors too: the wonder in having witnessed it, of having survived. In those first hours, I never saw a soul, not even a child, cry for what had been taken. No one believes they should have died when they didn't.

At the corner a broken water main gushed like a Maybeck fountain.

"Ah, damn," said Heffernan. "No saving the city now."

His wife was combing the plaster out of their youngest girl's hair. "What is it?"

"The water mains, Bess. If they've all busted like that one, there won't be anything for the fellas to use to fight that fire." Heffernan pointed toward Nob Hill, where the first lacy tendrils of smoke were rising, marring a fine, clear sky.

Pie lifted her head. "Downtown's all right, isn't it?" She was thinking of James. As I was thinking of Rose.

"Look there." Mr. Morris, our neighbor on the other side, pointed to a second plume rising to the south.

"Market Street?" I asked.

Murmurs and nods. The stockyards, fisheries, the factories and warehouses. As we looked on, the clouds turned from puffy white to gray to black.

"Feel that wind," Mr. Heffernan said. "Blowing this way."

Around us, folks were tending to their cuts and broken bones; they were gathering up bits before the next shaker or the next one took down their houses. Topography would determine one's destiny in every part of town, but more so on Francisco Street, where our homes had been built on sand.

Our neighbors were hauling their valuables into the street. Sewing machines and pianos pulled clumsily down busted stairs—a cornucopia of bourgeois life being dragged into the broken, dusty street. In the mayhem of that first hour, mistakes in importance were made. Would a silver picture frame be more useful in the days ahead than a knife? Mrs. Smythe, across and down, brought out her wedding dress and a small framed oil painting of flowers. Her husband waited at the curb to receive the next load, which he dumped into a pile. Their four children stood beside him. None of what Mrs. Smythe carried would feed her family of six—not the fox stole thrown across her shoulder, not her hat. Mr. Smythe's pockets were stuffed with cigars.

"Stay," I commanded Rogue, but I meant it for Pie too.

A couple of minutes—that's all I gave myself to run back inside. It was just enough time to stuff Lars's old valise with a change of clothes for each of us, a nightgown and some underthings, the tortoiseshell combs James O'Neill had gifted Pie on her birthday. I seized Pie's good hat and my straw boater. I grabbed Pie's new silk coat too, and her old black. But I was happy to leave my Caruso dress forever in a heap. At the last moment, as I swung out the door, I took Ricky, whom I could not bear to leave. That's how I honored Morie; I took the goddamn bird in his too-heavy cage, Ricky squawking Swedish curses as I hauled him to the door. To be sure, I slid an orange, his favorite treat, into my pocket for him to peck on later, and a blanket on top of the cage, so the smoke and dust wouldn't kill him. And I piled it all in our two-bit coal cart and dragged that into the street.

Pie and Rogue were where I'd left them, though Pie was hiding, burying her face in her hands. It took me a beat to see why. Standing in the road opposite our house was the Haj. Unlike our neighbors, he was fully dressed in a black coat and bowler. His back arched as he leaned on his cane, favoring a foot that must have been hurt in the quake. The Haj looked like a wretched crow.

When he saw me approach with the cart, he said, "Where's your mother?"

When I refused to answer, when I pushed past him, he followed me.

"Get on with you, Volosky," Mr. Heffernan barked. "Can't you see their mother is dead?"

The Haj looked from our house to Pie, back to me.

"Mark this, Volosky!" Mr. Heffernan balled his fist and swung it in the air.

The Haj ignored him. Meeting my gaze, he nodded. A shiver ran down my spine, as I understood he was issuing me a promise. "Bad luck," he said. Then he tipped his hat with the knob of his cane and moved on.

It was nearly six thirty in the morning, an hour and a bit since the first shake.

"We have to go, Pie."

She had such fear in her eyes. "You mean, find James, right?"

I tried to think of an answer. The smoke from downtown was filling the sky. In the days ahead, the advantage would go to a person who kept her wits—despite her suffering over Morie, or her fear of the Haj—despite it all. A person who thought to grab for herself and her sister not their best dresses but sensible wool and thick-soled boots.

Mayor Schmitz had been granted his miracle, and what kind of twisted miracle was this?

"Sure. We'll find James," I promised, and I coaxed Pie to her feet and made sure she was solid enough to stand. But instead of heading toward downtown and the flames, I pulled her behind a fence and changed her out of her soiled clothes. I changed too, then I started walking us in the opposite direction from downtown.

Pie gasped, as the notion dawned on her—as she followed the familiar path of my gaze up and up to that house of twenty rooms on top of the hill.

"No, V, no—"

Behind the smoke, in the east, the sun was rising, same as ever. It would be another freakishly warm spring day.

PART TWO

Up the Hill

Pie would say: What choice did I give her but to follow my unyielding backside up that steep mountain of Pacific Heights?

She walked behind me in a trance, refusing my offer to pull her in the cart, for which I was glad. The way up was ridiculously steep. With the fissures in the road two, sometimes four feet wide, and the bricks and boards and all kinds of debris blocking our path, we made our way slowly, step by awful step. The dust was fearsome, and the smoke too.

By now the whole city was on the move. Folks just like us were fleeing their busted or burning houses. They dragged their few possessions stacked atop wheelbarrows and sofas with casters and carts of all shapes laden with trunks of china and candlesticks rattling atop barrels and framed portraits of dead ancestors and needlepoint chairs and sewing machines.

We nodded in solidarity, a quick lift of the eye, as we passed. Soldiers and police with whistles were already on foot throughout the city, soon to be joined by several ships of soldiers from the navy. In the meantime, all able men were being commissioned to help with the impossible task of burying the dead and clearing the streets.

As we passed a woman wearing three coats, we overheard her explaining to her son, who was likewise dressed in layers, why they couldn't return to their house, since all of downtown was ablaze.

"Excuse me," I said, "is it true? Downtown's on fire?"

"What isn't flattened," the woman said.

"Along Market Street?" Pie asked.

"And well past," the woman replied. "South of the Slot is burning, and on this side too. There must be, oh, dozens of fires," she went on, stroking her son's head. "It's as if hell is burning, and I don't mean to be cussing, but that's where we are—hell." She looked at us with bloodshot eyes.

We walked on, too troubled to speak. The smoke and dust had lodged in Pie's lungs. Her coughing forced us to stop. "I wish . . . I wish I had just a little water," she gasped.

"Here, Pie." I guided her to a stone wall fronting a house that was tipped on its side. I peeled the orange I had put in my pocket for Ricky, and she sucked on a slice, closing her eyes.

"James," she said.

"I know, Pie. But it can't be that every building is on fire."

"Can't it? You heard Mr. Heffernan. How . . . how are they going to put it out when they don't have water?"

"I don't know, Pie. I don't know. I keep thinking: What if Rose stayed last night at her place downtown? What if she's—"

"Dead?" Pie slipped another wedge of the orange in her mouth and, with her eyes shut, gave voice to my nightmare. "What if she refuses to take us in, or what if someone should see us taking shelter in a *madam's* house? How . . . how could I ever explain that to James?" Pie dabbed her bloody head between coughs. "No one of good society would allow—"

"Oh, stop your yattering," I said. Society, as far as I could tell, didn't exist anymore. "Are we really in any position to turn up our noses at a bed or a glass of water from Rose?"

Pie answered by refusing to go another step.

Across the road from where we stood a family was just leaving their broken house. Having shrugged off its foundation, the house was tipped to one side, like a dozing drunkard. The windows in the bays, even the thick panes in the double front door, were broken.

The wife was in labor, cradling her enormous belly in her hands and moaning. As we looked on, her husband settled her in an old wheelbarrow and with every movement she gasped. Her three young children stood on either side of the wheelbarrow, holding on to a fistful of their mother's skirt. A small dog was harnessed to a cart, the cart stacked with a few belongings. It was the eldest child's job—he couldn't have been more than six—to hold fast to the dog's collar.

"What a god-awful day to be born," I whispered.

The husband turned to the house and, as if addressing a mirror, donned his hat. He took his time putting on his gloves.

"Cyrus, mind you, lock the door," his wife called between contractions.

Her husband looked from her to his busted door and back again. Its matching panes of ornamental glass were shattered. All a person had to do was reach in and turn the knob.

"Cyrus!"

He did as she asked. He fished in his pocket, removed a key, and turned the lock. It was a gesture so futile and civilized, it struck me hard. As did the dog, a mutt, half the size of Rogue, who shouldn't have been pulling a cart but was pulling it anyway, and the older boy stuffed like a sausage man in too many layers of clothes.

The husband walked to where his family waited and, turning back, latched the iron gate. As he hoisted the wooden arms of the wheelbarrow, his wife cried out in agony.

We watched them make their way to the bottom of the hill. Then Pie climbed to her feet.

"Don't scoff," she said. "You aren't married; neither am I. And we don't have Morie to . . . help us." Her voice sounded distant and hollow. "I mean, when this is over, who are we?"

"Pie, look around you. My God, if Rose doesn't take us in, we'll be searching like everyone else for a pot and a patch of grass."

She nodded, but I knew she didn't believe me. In those first few hours, it was possible to think that just over that hill, everything was normal.

From under the tarp covering his cage, Ricky let off a string of Swedish curses. *"Vad fan, vad fan,* pretty *svenska!"*

"Who are we?" My voice sounded bruised and hollow too. "We're a stuck-up Swede, a madam's bastard, a mutt, and a foul-mouthed bird. How's that?"

"Don't be crass," my sister replied. "We'll tell James that we're Rose's *distant* relations. Will you agree to that?"

Rose's House

If there was ever a morning when two girls, a bird, and a dog could enter a grand house without a proper invitation, it was the early hours of April 18.

"I always wondered how it would look in the light of day," whispered Pie as we hesitated at the curb.

In daylight the house looked grand. Five stories and a riot of gables and fancywork, plaster reliefs and gingerbread molding, four chimneys, a balcony, and dozens of gold-drenched balls and knobs fixed to every peak and post. Next to its equally large yet more refined neighbors, Rose's Queen Anne looked decked out for a burlesque show.

"Front door or back?" Pie asked.

"Back," I declared, pulling the cart into the driveway, with Pie and Rogue following close behind. The driveway ended at a trio of garages: the first was General's stable, the second housed the buggy, and the third was for Rose's fancy motorcar.

Beyond the garages, a gate led to a small, manicured garden I didn't know was there. It had rows of boxwood and roses, herbs, and several magnolia trees. There was an outdoor fireplace with a thick-necked chimney; a chicken coop, partially hidden by ferns. A bloodstained wooden block was beside the coop, where, I supposed, Tan cut off the head and feet of the Sunday bird in front of its compatriots.

We didn't linger. A section of the back roof had collapsed

in the quake, with stray boards and a small pike of bricks having landed on the roof of General's stable. As we approached, the horse whinnied and kicked at the boards of his stall.

"I don't like the look of that," I said, pointing to the precarious stable roof. "We better take him out of there."

"Let's find Rose first," Pie suggested, and she headed for the back door.

A sign was tacked there: "Beggars scat. Tradesmen knock. You know which you are."

"That's Rose's hand," Pie said, looking to me yet again to decide what we should do.

"I'm not about to knock," I declared.

She wasn't there. I knew it immediately: the air, shaken and thick with plaster dust, hadn't pushed against a living soul that morning.

Even so, Pie and I spoke in whispers; we were careful not to touch anything. Rogue likewise sniffed at the floor but stayed close to my heels. It was cold in Tan's kitchen, with its twenty-foot-high ceiling and steady chill radiating from the enormous icebox with six separate compartments. Rogue sniffed at the drip pans under the icebox and cautiously drank his fill.

"We shouldn't be here," Pie said, her voice ghostly, as she touched the wound on her head. "Whoa," she whispered, swaying.

I understood that her knees were about to give. "Here." I swept the broken glass from the seat of a kitchen chair and tucked her in close to the same table where Tan rolled his flaky crusts, where he minced vegetables and sides of beef with an ancient Chinese cleaver. It was all too strange.

Dipping a glass into a bowl of water in the sink, I handed it to her. "Drink, Pie, come on."

I set Ricky in his cage on the floor beside her and lifted his blanket. "*Pretty svenska, pretty svenska,*" squawked the damn bird.

Pie reached for my hand. “Sorry . . . sorry I was sharp back there.”

“And I thought I was the tough bird.”

“You are.” She smiled thinly.

There were dish towels—dozens, in a drawer. I dipped one in the water. “Pie, put your head back against the chair. Good.” And I got to work washing the plaster and brick dust from the deep gash on her head.

“Ow!”

“This cut needs a doctor,” I said, scolding the wound.

Pie closed her startled eyes. “V?” She reached up and stopped my hand. “I keep seeing her . . . and the bricks.” Pie bit her lip. “It’s just . . . I’ve never, I’ve never been without her. Not one day.” Pie wiped her nose on her sleeve. “I know Morie hasn’t always been . . . I know it’s not the same for you.”

I could have said: I’ve been with Morie my whole life too. I could have said that this was my mother’s house in name only. And where was this mother anyway? Where had she ever been? I could have said that I took pride in being smart enough to get us up the hill, but that didn’t mean my insides weren’t jelly. It didn’t mean that I wasn’t terrified too. Maybe, just maybe, I’d lost two mothers in one wretched morning.

“No, it’s not the same for me,” I said, and I took one of Tan’s starched aprons from its hook and wrapped it round Pie’s head, making a turban.

Pie tucked the ends of the apron and felt the turban to see that it would stay. Then she tipped her head back against the chair and focused on the high ceiling.

I followed her gaze to marvel at the roses carved there, each rosette set in its own square box and all of it made of tin.

“James.” She sighed. “He won’t find us, will he?”

“He’ll find us,” I assured her. “Or we’ll find him.”

I got up then, just to keep moving—moving feeling less

scary—and made a business of kicking broken glass into the corners and checking the food stocks in the icebox. I couldn't imagine who ate all the food Rose laid in, but thank God she had: there were two beef roasts already cooked and two more raw. I stepped into the larder, where the shelves went as high as the ceiling. The floor was a mess of smashed tomatoes and eggs and nuts and rice and apples, and broken glass. Whatever was here was all we had.

"I don't think she felt it, do you?" Pie asked.

I poked my head out of the larder. "What was that?"

"Morie," said Pie, now using the rag to clean the cuts on her arms. "She was sound asleep."

I pictured the mountain of bricks. "That's right," I said. "She never woke."

"V, we'll go back for her, right? Give her a proper burial. Promise me."

"I promise."

Pie stared at the rag in her hand. She was going through her list of worries and loves, loves and worries. There was no end to it.

"Hey?" I said gently. "How about we put the kitchen to rights, then when Rose comes, she'll be glad we're here."

Pie nodded. "I can start on the larder," she said. "If I get wibbly, I'll drag in a chair."

I found more of Tan's aprons in a drawer and tied one around her. Her waist was so tiny, I had to double-wrap the string. She tied an apron around me.

"You've got a nice waist," she said. "Do you know that?"

"Do I?" I had no idea.

So much I didn't know.

For instance, how many months it would take for the most basic parts of city life to resume—water flowing from the tap, the cable cars humming, a school day with the dread nuns. There'd be no gas or electricity or telephone service for weeks; no water, except the meager cupfuls doled out in the relief lines. It had taken less than a minute for the citizenry of San Francisco to be reduced to the hunter-gatherers of old. Cooking over fires, sleeping in coats, relieving themselves over buckets or in trenches. Society, with its rules and strictures, would have to be rebuilt brick by brick.

Standing in Tan's kitchen, I understood that neither sweetness nor tears would take care of Pie and me. Dust in our mouths; ash in our teeth. We were squatters in Rose's house, that's what we were. And in that, we were lucky.

"Pie, will you be all right? I'm going to check upstairs."

I wanted to go alone—to where I'd never been invited and was not now.

I climbed tentatively, like an archaeologist, like a novice thief, mindful that at any moment a tiger! a harlot! or Rose herself—might leap out to snatch me.

The first door on the second floor led to an enormous pink bathroom—with a pink marble tub and gold faucets and a gold wand for rinsing your hair. Not one but two marble sinks with fixtures cast as shapely swans, a vanity with a fur-covered stool. Mirrors, also gold leaf, covered three of the four walls; they showed my mouth agape, my face streaked and dirty. All the mirrors had cracked, same as the marble floor—same as the San Andreas Fault.

Pie found me staring at the gizmo next to the toilet.

"It was too scary to be down there alone," she explained. "What's this? What's it for?"

The ceramic bowl looked similar to the flush toilet beside it, only it had no seat, and hot and cold spigots. Our virgin minds strained to imagine what it could be used for, here in the madam's bathroom.

"For washing her bloomers?" Pie suggested.

I pointed to the pair of sinks and shrugged. Then I tried

turning the knobs of the twin taps. The pipes inside the walls groaned and shuddered; a single blast of water—all that was left in the house—shot upward in a jet, then flowed down the drain.

"It's for swishing your privates," I declared.

"Why ever would you—" Pie bit her lip before saying anything more.

Pie wasn't well. The dust in her chest made it impossible for her to catch her breath. I made her lie down in the room next to Rose's, in a bed with a velvet headboard and matching coverlet, of a richness we'd never seen. Pie curled in a ball like a princess waif. And there I left her, promising I'd fetch her if there was even the smallest tremor.

Next I went to check Rose's room. Naturally, she wasn't there. Was I disappointed? Of course.

Her room was twice the size of the other bedrooms; it faced the rear of the house and the garden, with a view of Nob Hill. A fine plaster dust layered everything. Quake dust. One long wall was devoted to a series of mirrored closets and drawers; in the quake, they'd flung themselves open, spilling her gowns and silk garters, stockings and corsets. Opposite the bed, a Victrola had miraculously clung to its gilded stand.

If she were dead, I wasn't prepared to linger; if she were alive, I wouldn't have wanted her to find me there. I shut the door.

But I kept on searching the house, every room and closet. Feeling like an impostor but acting like a huntress, I climbed the stairs to the next floor of bedrooms, and above that to the attic, where her two maids slept, their rooms turned over in haste, clothes strewn about and the beds unmade; I imagined they'd run back to their families after the first round of quakes.

A third room faced the street. It was slightly larger, with a cot against one wall and, on the opposite wall, a sewing machine fitted in a dark-hulled cabinet. It had a rag rug, a rocking chair. Light poured in through an ox-eye window—some three feet wide—that was the central feature dominating the top of the house.

The window hinged at the center; when I unhooked the lock, it pivoted on an axis. I opened and closed the window several times, marveling at how it was made. The room faced due west, toward the ocean and the sunsets and, closer, Lafayette Square. I imagined on an evening the maids would sit here, reading or mending. Here, you could rock at your leisure and watch the doings in the square, or you could wish yourself all the way to the ocean or, beyond the ocean, clear to Japan.

While I fussed with the window, Rogue made himself at home. He jumped on the cot and settled, his head nestled between his paws.

"V!" Pie called up the stairs. "What are you doing up there? Quick, come down."

I hurried. "Hell, you scared me. What is it?"

She pulled me to a window in the bedroom where she'd been resting.

Tan was standing on the far side of the road, on the grassy banks of the square. All manner of chaos and hurt was passing by him—refugees pulling carts, soldiers blasting whistles urging folks to help or move along. Tan struck an oblivious pose, hand on hip, his gaze fixed on the house. The dust of Chinatown's collapse had turned his black silks gray. He looked like a vestige from the apocalypse.

"What's he waiting for?" asked Pie. "Why doesn't he come inside?"

"I expect he doesn't dare till Rose says it's okay. You know, she sort of fired him."

"And when he finds out she's not here?"

"He'll find out soon enough."

The neighbors knew Tan. He had worked in the house for many years. All the grand houses and apartments of Pacific Heights employed at least one Chinese servant, who had to make do living in what they called the Chinaman's room in the basement. A few of the neighbors spoke to Tan; he bowed in response.

"We have to let him in," Pie insisted.

"Hush, Pie. Hush, while I think."

"While you're thinking, should I tell him to come in?"

"You want him bossing you around? You want him calling you *gurrl*?"

Pie shrugged. He didn't call her *gurrl.*

"He stays out till I say so—"

In the street, Tan raised himself proudly as another acquaintance, this time a lady, passed by.

"V?"

"Pie, stop pestering me—"

"Do you hear that knocking? Is it the horse?"

I bowed my head and listened. We were several floors up, and with all the commotion in the street, the sound was muted. But it was distinct; General was pounding his hooves against the sides of his stall.

"Shouldn't we get Tan? V, we ought to tell him."

Remembering how Tan had whipped poor General, I didn't want him anywhere near me or the horse. "I'll do it. I'll tend to the horse."

"Are you sure? Do you know how?"

"How hard can it be?" I said. "You walk him, give him some feed. He's just a big dog."

Pie looked skeptical. We had always been too kept to keep a horse. Too kept to buy our own food or dresses. Rose and Morie had trained us to wait for life to come to our door. And it did come.

• • •

General was trembling, poor thing, his flanks slick with sweat. His stall smelled sick-sweet, the stink of fear mixed with manure and grain. His water bucket had flipped over, drenching his hay, and he'd pulped that business with his hooves, turning the hay to a mash that clung like lumpy porridge on his legs and in the web of his long, coarse tail. He looked at me sideways, with one beastly, fearful eye.

"Here, boy," I said, "let's get you outside."

He dipped his head to show he was agreeable. I took that as a good sign. I covered him with a blanket, fixed the leather lead to his halter. When I opened the door, he proved himself a gentleman, letting me go first.

But once outside, the confusion of smoke and noise assaulted his already fragile nerves. He pulled up, and I thought, what will I do if he rears?

Fifteen horse strides to the street, fifteen back. I was careful not to lead him into the road, where any able nag was being put into service clearing, hauling. Flakes of ash from the growing fires danced before our eyes.

I knew we were being observed by Rose's neighbors. I nodded at them; they nodded at me. And we went on in the strangeness.

I dared to pat General's mane. This way, I let him know that we were on this shaky planet together, and that the world still had its sun and sweet grass and, look here, Rose's flowers.

When General stumbled on a stray brick, I cried out, "Careful!" my voice croaky and hollow, my hand with the leather shaking, and all that fear, my fear, rippled along his flank.

If I was suffering Morie's death, I didn't know it, even as I kept blinking to banish the ash, banish the thought of her under all that brick. The silence when someone is no longer walking this world—I have known it since, but that was the first time. I did not question whether I loved Morie; she took up too large a room in my heart and mind. If I loved Rose more than I feared her, I didn't know that either. All I knew was the packed dirt of Rose's driveway and that I felt a powerful kinship with this nervous horse.

I told him he was a fine horse. And that for every lash Tan had banged into his worn hide, Tan would get worse. I told him the world was not itself and wouldn't be for a long time. Somehow, we'd figure a way. I talked to let him know I was in charge, for if you can convince a beast, you're halfway to convincing yourself. I told him that though he and I were odd, maybe even ugly, all you had to do was look around: the world was in worse shape than the pair of us. I was young; he was strong. I had brains and bones as yet unbusted; I had a booming, wanting heart. He had the goods to take us to find Rose and James.

I told him all of this without uttering a word.

On our final lap, as we approached the road, I caught sight of Tan. He was shaking his finger at me. I could just hear him growling, *Gurrl.* He pointed to General and at the stable and, oh, I got the picture: he was ordering me to return the horse to his stall.

I was in no mood to be bossed by Tan, who, after all, hadn't heard General's cries, his banging hooves calling for help. Nor had he seen the fallen bricks on the stable roof. If it collapsed, we'd be without a horse.

I decided to tie General to the hitch post outside the kitchen door. I offered him a bucket with a few inches of water—water being more precious in the coming days than diamonds and pearls. He took a drink with his vulgar, delicate horse lips, then moved two steps sideways to commence mowing Rose's petunias. I left him to it.

I was pausing in Rose's garden when a neighbor called out to me, "Hello, friend, hello!"

I pretended not to hear him. I deeply hoped he would go away.

"Hell-o!" he called again, marching through his garden, lifting his knees high to avoid the thorny rosebushes.

His hair was a web of white, his moustache the black of his youth. Thin wire glasses covered only part of his round, beseeching eyes. Scrawny legs, a paunch. He was wearing a fine suit and vest—much finer than the men on Francisco Street wore. In the confusion of the day, he'd neglected to put on a tie; his pant legs were stuffed into galoshes.

He introduced himself as Dr. David Sugarman and offered his hand. "And you are?"

I said my name—I said it plain.

"Ah, Vera Johnson, glad to meet you." He smiled as if he were truly glad, his accent foreign, vaguely European. "Are you a guest of Miss Rose's?"

I nodded.

"Pearl, my wife, we've been worried. We didn't see her after the first shaker. She's all right, I trust?"

"We're not . . . sure," I confessed. "We—my sister and I—haven't located her just yet."

He sighed at this news. "I see. And you are . . . a relation of hers?"

I couldn't help it, I smiled. Pie had gotten it just right. "Yes, on my mother's side." I felt the flush of a half lie burning my cheeks.

"I didn't know Miss Rose had family," he admitted as he surveyed the back of Rose's house. "'Course there's much we don't know—she's a . . . bit of a mystery. Keeps to herself." Sugarman frowned at the damaged roof. "But here we are, all topsy-turvy, eh, Vera Johnson? Now, as to Rose, she didn't spend the night downtown . . . oh, I hope not. The fire—"

"I think maybe so." I swallowed hard, fighting a rush of tears.

"Oh, my dear. You must keep hope. Were you and your sister in the house during the quake?"

"We just arrived. Our house, on Francisco Street, is in ruins. We came here—there was no other place to go."

"I see." What had been friendly curiosity seemed to shift on his face, as if two distinct plates had aligned. Sugarman pulled his watch from his vest. "Look at that. Not yet eight. Three hours of living in another dimension." He looked toward the chaos in the street, and at his redheaded sons, who were struggling to carry a heavy trunk down their steps into the dusty street.

"Ack, I told them not to bother with that," Sugarman exclaimed. "Vera, would you mind saying hello to my wife?" Sugarman peered at me, this curious, intense man. "I know Pearl would be glad to meet you."

I didn't see how I could refuse him, now that we were neighbors. We trooped back the way he'd come, through a split in the hedge that divided the two gardens, and up the side alley of his house. As we were walking, an aftershock, this one smallish, came on and we halted in our tracks.

Sugarman put his hand on my shoulder. As we waited to see if the tremor would build, he studied my face and I had the feeling he was seeing into my soul.

How quickly we'd adapted to a shaking world, as if it had always been this way: when it was coming on—like a stomach flu, the roiling that wouldn't stop until you were sick, sick and tired—you braced with your knees and grabbed on to something solid while glancing overhead to see what might fall. Then you cocked your head, listening, listening to the earth's core. Was this the next big one, or merely an afterthought? The walls and doors wondered same as you, and being like you made of jelly, loose at the center. You had seen for yourself that the street can dance and ripple like water; you'd heard two houses in a single morning weep. And it was only eight o'clock.

"Oh, dear girl," called Sugarman's wife as she held tight to a knob in their iron fence, her feet wide and braced. "I hope you weren't alone this morning, not in that big house?"

She talked as if she knew me, as if we were continuing a long conversation that had no beginning or end—proving she was just as sympathetic as her husband.

Before I could answer, Pearl Sugarman looked over my head to Rose's house. "Ah, good. Tan put the horse back in the stable where he belongs."

While I'd been in the garden, chatting with Sugarman, Tan had spread fresh hay in the stall and brushed General, transforming him into a well-tended horse. I didn't care. All that mattered was that I had left the horse where I believed he would be safe, where the likes of Tan and a quake couldn't hurt him.

I ran, and when I reached the stable, I pushed Tan aside and led General into the alley, and once again tethered him, this time in haste, to the post. I tied the leather lead with a double knot, to be sure. And all the while I cursed Tan. My witnesses were the bricks on the stable roof, and the fire, and the strangers passing in the street. I seethed in a language I didn't recognize—it wasn't English or Swedish; it was the roar of terror and grief, and it surprised me and I didn't seem able to stop.

Tan spat in the dirt at my feet. Then turning on his heel, he disappeared into the crush of refugees crowding the street.

• • •

"You're scaring me," Pie declared when I returned to the kitchen. She was holding a jar of tomatoes she'd found in the larder.

"I'm scaring you?" I bellowed. "I'm scaring *you*?"

I left her then, and was halfway up the stairs, when the next rumbling started. Oh, come on, I thought. Enough!

The earth answered by coming on. Every nail, bolt, and board of the grand house protested—a chorus of old people clearing their clotted throats. Louder and louder. Rogue braced himself at the bottom of the stairs, paws set wide, and barked.

When the witch's cap gave way, it whistled as it fell four stories, to land like a bomb. Followed by the sickening pule of a wounded beast. Then, most terrible, a rifle shot.

I ran, with Rogue at my heels.

A crowd had already gathered, refugees in the road pausing to witness the latest horror.

The witch's cap, the cone-shaped roof that crowned the turret, with its gilded balls and fancywork attached, had exploded in the driveway. Next to this heap: General, on his side, shot in the head. His leather lead was still hooked to the post; his black eye stared at the sky.

Rogue nosed General's hoof and looked at me.

A soldier, one of General Funston's troops, had his rifle still raised, aimed into Rose's alley. He wasn't much more than a boy.

"What have you done?" I cried.

The soldier looked at me as if I were a fool. "Can't you see? His leg, miss, it's broken." He pointed at General. "See that bone? Snapped in two. I was only doin' him a favor." He reloaded and slung the gun on his shoulder.

There was agreement in the street that the soldier had been quick and correct. I had to hear the story multiple times: how General reared as the roof came toward him. And given that he was tethered too tightly to the post (my fault, my wretched fault), he had nowhere to land but which-way on the fallen boards. He'd broken his foreleg. I could see the white bone.

Next door, the jolt had tossed Dr. Sugarman to the ground. But he gathered himself quickly and ran over, with Pearl following behind him.

"What a *shanda*," he bellowed, and without another word he wrapped me in his arms.

I had no idea what a *shanda* was, but if it meant I could hide in Dr. Sugarman's embrace, that was all right.

He passed me to his wife. Mrs. Sugarman pulled me to her starched, capacious bosom. There, my cheek found its first maternal nest.

"Poor, poor," she said. "What else can this day bring? And you, pulling on that old horse as if he were a dog."

I breathed in the lavender of her underthings and the scratchy wool of her dress; with every exhale Mrs. Sugarman's flesh pressed into mine. I buried my cheek and squeezed hard, allowing the tears to come, though they wouldn't. I was dry as dust. Mrs. Sugarman rubbed circles in my back and said it was all right. Which it wasn't.

Pearl Sugarman had borne seven ginger-haired sons, the last two, the twins Henry and George, having died in the winter of flu. She wiped my dirty face and called me brave. And I didn't mind it at all.

When grand Mrs. Haas, who lived in a nearby mansion, pulled up alongside and asked, "What happened here?" Mrs. Sugarman made sure her hand was cupped on my ear so I couldn't hear. Her voice sounded garbled like underwater sea-murmurings. But something indeed was said, of which I caught this much: Mrs. Sugarman said, "She's gone missing, but on this of all days, no one should judge."

And when at last she let me go? I ran to Rose's garden, where glass from a broken window littered the bushes, and a finial from the top of the house had taken a chip out of the marble birdbath. I squatted on my heels and hoped I'd disappear.

No one had to tell me that had I kept General in his stall, he would be alive.

A hummingbird appeared from a nearby magnolia. He dipped his beak in the bath, then hovered not a foot from my face. His black pellet eye fixed on me. I had the vague notion he might attack my nose.

"What do I do?" I asked him.

He darted away.

That was it. No tears. No General. No Morie. No Rose. I climbed to my feet and went inside. I kept climbing till I reached that room in the attic, with its rocking chair and Singer sewing machine. I looked out the ox-eye window that faced the street. Tan wasn't there.

That afternoon, on the longest day of our lives, I was attempting to right the heavy walnut chest in Rose's room, doing penance by refusing to eat or rest, when Pie reported that Tan had returned and this time he wasn't alone.

He'd brought the old man from Chinatown and—God help me—Lifang. They'd been at work in the alley and had covered General with a blanket, so only his back end and hooves peeked out. The two men were breaking apart the witch's cap with axes. Board by board, they were untangling the mess.

Lifang had been put into service too, carrying scraps of cornice and odd brick, making neat piles. She'd traded her white silks for the black shapeless tunic and pants her father and grandfather wore. Her clothes were too big: the cuffs on the mandarin jacket hung past her fingers. She looked like a doll. Her little black slippers covered in dust, her black braid swishing the tops of her thighs.

Pie pressed her nose to the glass. "What did you say her name is?"

"Lifang. It means beautiful one in Mandarin."

"She's every bit that. How old is she?"

"Your age, I'd guess."

Pie dipped her chin like a sober judge. "I wonder if she has suitors."

"Hell, Pie, really? She's mean as a viper."

My sister seemed unconvinced.

"Look, she can't sleep in the house. Do you understand?"

Pie shot me a troubled look. "Where would you put her?"

"I wouldn't *put her*. Trust me, Lifang is no servant. She thinks she's better than you and me combined."

Below, Tan, the old man, and Lifang were fashioning the boards and bricks into a wall that blocked the view from the street into the garden. Soon enough we'd discover why.

I felt sick to my stomach and had to sit on one of the beds.

"V? I'm sorry about General. I know you wanted to help him."

"Let's not talk about it."

Pie nodded and, turning to go, swept her hand across the bureau in what was, at least for now, her room. "Where did her maids disappear to?"

"What's that? Oh, judging by their rooms, they took off in a hurry. I bet after the first shake." I paused, then added, "Upstairs there's a decent room next to theirs."

Pie squinted, taking that in. "You can't be up there, V. Rose would want you down."

"I don't think she wants me at all," I grumbled. "When she comes back, she'll probably give us the boot. Of course, she might be dead."

Pie grabbed my shoulders and shook me. "Stop that. You don't think she's dead, any more than I do."

I bowed my head and tried to hear what the bones of the house were telling me.

"V? Answer me."

"No," I said. "She's not dead."

That first day, Tan kept busy. He coaxed several servants from the neighboring houses to help him carry Rose's old cast-iron stove, the one stored on the back porch, to the curb. He intended to set up an outdoor kitchen since it wasn't safe to use the gas inside. He did so on no one's authority but his own. I suppose, like me, he was trying to prove himself worthy.

Once he had the stove in place, he used the boards from the witch's cap and fashioned a shack with a roof and walls open to the house and to the street.

As Tan worked outside, I worked within. Having decided that the house was our safest bet—on no proof other than it had survived so far intact—I decided we'd stay, at least for a few nights. I cleared the kitchen of broken glass and crockery, and started on the mess in the parlor.

And all the while the smoke from the fires grew thicker, alongside the steady *thunk, thunk* of Tan's father's ax at work in the alley.

At some point in the afternoon, Pie brought me a cup of milk and some cheese and crackers. "Don't be mad," she said. "I gave them a plate too. It seemed only right."

"What's stopping him from coming inside and getting it himself?" I asked. "It's his kitchen."

"Maybe he's scared of you."

"Ha! Hardly."

"Tan's father," Pie said, changing the subject. "His name is LowNaa. It means old tooth."

"Why do they call him that?"

"Here," she said, tapping her incisor. "When he smiles, his teeth sort of stick out, like a vampire."

"Oh."

"He's actually quite sweet." Pie had another coughing spell; I waited till it passed.

"Did you tell Tan about Morie?"

"Yah, I told him."

"And what else, Pie? I suppose you and Tan had a nice ol' chat?"

"He wasn't exactly warm, but he nodded, in his way. I suppose he didn't mind me serving him. I think it was all right." Pie held her hand on her chest, trying not to cough again. "He asked after you. Well, he asked where you were. I said you were upstairs, trying to fix everything all at once."

"What did he say to that?"

Pie picked her words carefully, as if she were afraid I'd blow. "V, Tan doesn't have any more wisdom than we do. But he's trying to be of use."

"I know what he said. He said I was an idiot. He said General's dead thanks to me. Well, he's right. I'm sure in some awful way he's pleased."

Pie started coughing again. "The fire," she gasped, "I can't—catch my breath."

"You should lie down. Rest."

But the fall of the ax below pulled her back to the window. "Oh, crikey."

"What now?"

"It's General. He's too big to lift so they're . . . they're taking him piecemeal."

I shut my eyes. "Please, could you please stop?"

The Fire

I am as old as the pharaohs now. If you ask me what I had for breakfast, there's a blank page. Food is nothing to me. Nor this day: I'll see it come, I'll see it go. I am and I am not. But if you ask about those days, those days that broke and made me, I can say with certainty that on Wednesday, April 18, 1906, we ate roast beef and apricot jam. Pie found the jar in Rose's larder. I broke the wax with my thumb and we scooped the jam into our mouths with our quake-filthed fingers.

That first evening, folks up and down the block followed Tan's example and dragged chairs and tables from their houses, and we feasted in the street. LowNaa cooked the extra roasts from Rose's icebox in the firepit in the garden, and Tan carved the meat in thin slices and served it with bread and butter. He must have made a hundred sandwiches that first night. Folks in the park came down and offered what they had, apples and boiled eggs and the heels of hams, and cakes and beans. Women and children, Dutch and Irish, Jews and Chinese, working folks and Pacific Heights swells ate together in the road.

Strangers asked Tan if he would fry their meat. He cooked with the precision of a master chef. And Lifang, she had this little knife she kept hidden under her tunic—who knows, she may have had a collection of knives under there. She snipped the ends on a bushel of green beans, cutting them at an angle, the way the Chinese liked to do.

LowNaa was the greeter. Since he had no English, he bowed and smiled. He was somehow pure, with freckled high cheeks, and when he smiled at you, you felt blessed. How such a father could produce Tan, so dour and scheming, I couldn't make out. LowNaa seemed content to serve his son, and if they ever exchanged a laugh or a joke, I never saw it. He greeted everyone with the same joy, nodding and grinning exuberantly with his tea-stained teeth.

Mrs. Sugarman and the neighborhood women donned aprons and passed cider for the kids. Whatever goblet or chipped glass or china or tin cup was presented to him, Dr. Sugarman filled with wine.

We ate and drank. That's the thing of it. We had survived the day.

"What a shame we never gathered like this before," Pearl Sugarman said, being the jolly sort.

"We're here to tell the tale now, eh?" her husband replied.

A young woman hovered by Tan's kitchen, a baby swaddled in her arms. She'd plucked her eyebrows and redrawn them with kohl into two thin lines. She made a point of gifting some freshly washed greens and a couple of potatoes wrapped in a towel.

"Madam Rose, she here?" she asked.

I told her she wasn't around.

"She told me if ever I needed, she'd put us up."

"She isn't here," I said.

The woman pointed toward the flames engulfing downtown. "Well, she isn't there."

"We have blankets to spare," Dr. Sugarman said, and he offered the woman and her baby his seat at the end of the table, far from me.

When a photographer, his name was Arnold Genthe, appeared out of the smoke, a lanky sort of fellow dressed in a khaki riding outfit, Sugarman welcomed him too. Genthe explained that his cameras and studio had been damaged in the quake; he'd borrowed a Kodak Special from a friend and had spent the day walking the city, recording the devastation.

Sugarman offered him a plate and a cup of wine, and, as payment, he told us some of what he'd seen.

"The Hearst Building went up at noon, followed by the Mechanics' Pavilion," Genthe said. "Then the top of the Call Building caught fire and Portsmouth Square, both going fast, by early afternoon. Still they thought they could save much of downtown. They were wrong. They dynamited around the Mint. But once Delmonico's restaurant shot up in flames, well, there was no stopping the spread."

Mr. Levinson, who also lived on the square, piped up. He was in the insurance business and he'd spent the day sending telegrams to Washington until the telegraph office caught fire.

"We have our suspicions regarding Delmonico's," Levinson said. "The Alcazar Theatre that housed Delmonico's took on a lot of damage, but that fire was later. Very neat. Not a whiff of smoke, then full-bore blaze."

"Gas lines?" Sugarman queried.

Levinson wasn't convinced. "Looks to me to be arson. An insurance job. 'Course, nothing on that front will go forward anytime soon."

Genthe then said that Mayor Schmitz had given orders for the police to shoot looters on sight, no questions asked. "The fellows, they've been doing just that—downright recklessly," Genthe added, his voice coarse from the smoke. "I'd say the fire is covering many tracks."

Dr. Sugarman turned to me. "Vera, that soldier, he did your General a good turn. Don't doubt it for a second." Sugarman turned to Genthe. "Please, go on."

"Chinatown in cinders. The clock tower at the Ferry Building cracked. San Francisco Gas and Electric's silo chimney split in two." Genthe shrugged. He had seen too much, and could only recite the calamities, as if reading off a list. "The Palace Hotel, touted as unburnable, burned to its foundation. And, of course, you've heard what happened to the fire chief." Genthe looked at the surprise on all our faces. "Oh, well, that was a blow. When the building next door collapsed on the firehouse, the chief fell several stories down and was scalded by the furnace in the basement. The poor chap, just when the city needs him most. Burned over most of his body. They don't expect him to live."

"Dear God," Sugarman gasped. "And where is Sullivan now?"

"They've got temporary hospitals set up in the Presidio and by the Ferry Building. Thousands of wounded. Thousands dead." Genthe hugged his arms and stared at the ground.

We all fell silent then. Till Sugarman nodded and said, "Go on."

Genthe sighed. "Next I went to see about the Ham and Eggs fire. That's what the fire chaps are calling it. A woman in Hayes Valley, she didn't want her kids to go hungry, so she made a fire in what was left of her busted chimney."

"She didn't even think about the broken gas lines," Sugarman said, pounding his fist on the table.

Genthe nodded. "That's right. By the looks of it, the whole mash will burn, everything south of Market, as far as Hunters Point."

"Oy." Sugarman cupped his hands over his eyes.

"City Hall," Genthe added, and shrugged. "The priciest building west of the Mississippi? All a fake, a palace of sleaze." Genthe's lip curled with contempt. "The columns, why, they aren't even marble. More like . . . papier-mâché. I took a photograph of these little bits of newspaper tooting out of their tops. I took it, 'cause otherwise, who would believe it?"

Genthe handed his empty cup to Sugarman. "As for City Hall, picture the carcass of your Thanksgiving bird picked clean."

Again we were silent, imagining what we couldn't quite imagine.

"And the mayor? Where's he in all this?" Levinson asked.

"Oh, I've seen him about," Genthe said. "Driving from fire to fire. His neck got saved for now. Actually, he's doing a good bit. Last I saw him, maybe an hour ago, he was up with the fellows on Nob Hill fighting to keep the Fairmont from burning. Good luck with that."

"Excuse me," Pie said, coughing while straining to have her voice rise above the roar. "Have you heard news of James O'Neill? He has a shop—"

Genthe looked at Pie and slowly shook his head. "Sorry, miss, don't know him."

Squinting, he turned his gaze to Tan. "Your man there. Why isn't he with the rest of the Chinese? You know, they've put them in a camp in the Presidio. They won't let them leave."

Pie and I exchanged a look. So that's why Tan was so nervous. And why he'd come.

"I'd like to have a picture with him," Genthe said. "'Course with all of you." He stood and everyone stood with him. Genthe herded the group to stand beside Tan's kitchen.

"Miss, may I ask you to pose with your Chinaman?"

"He is not my Chinaman," I said.

"Vera," Pie whispered. "No need to press the point."

"His name is Tan," I said. "And he is not and never will be mine."

"Right. So, are you in the photo or out?" Genthe's impatience was matched only by his dissatisfaction that no one seemed to be listening to his directives. He arranged Tan, LowNaa, and Lifang in front of the canopy, then rearranged them.

"Please, everyone, stand closer! Come on!" barked Genthe as he waved his arms.

I stepped out of the picture then, and moved behind Genthe, to take in his view. In one deft adjustment, he'd wiped the

Sugarmans from the frame and centered the shot on Tan—Tan, Lifang, and LowNaa, the trio, standing in front of their stove. He'd included Pie, but on the edge. Behind her was Rose's house, and behind the house, a sky full of fire and smoke.

"Let's have a photograph that marks us toasting our city." Sugarman raised his glass and cleared his throat. "Hearts and hills," he said, his voice thick with feeling.

"Hearts and hills," we roared.

"Hold that!" Genthe commanded. Even Tan held his breath.

Then Sugarman set down his glass and said, "Shall we?"

We assembled in rows on the steep, grassy banks of Lafayette Square and observed the spectacle coming toward us; our city was on fire and we watched the flames dance from house to house, hill to hill.

Women in hats, their shirtfronts stained with ash, men in suits, as if just home from the office, when in fact their offices were crushed or burning. Children stood beside their parents, hands on little hips, looking eastward. Even the smallest children mimicked the adults and shaded their eyes. The heat was intense. Black smoke puffed skyward. As we looked on, the tongues of fire, having ravaged downtown, reached the top of Nob Hill. The orange of the sky appeared soft and throbbing, as if the earth had returned to what it always was: a star.

And if I saw the ghost of a smile pass across those faces, I understood: For isn't it a marvel to witness the end of the world?

"Can you believe it?" Pie whispered.

I could. And what was coming, I believed that too.

"I say," Dr. Sugarman called over the roar. "I say," he repeated, never finishing his thought. He removed his bowler and passed his hand along its ash-flecked rim, his white hair circling his head.

A banker by the name of Halperin stood beside him. Halperin's offices had been one of the first buildings to burn. Twenty-five years of work, gone.

As Halperin watched the fire, tears ran down his face onto the lapels of his coat.

"David, my friend," he said to Sugarman, "I had ten cases in the basement of a very fine Château Margaux."

"Ah, Margaux," Sugarman said dreamily. "Excellent."

"I bought them on the day of Tildie's birth," Halperin explained. "We planned to serve them at her wedding. Along with some very nice bottles of Heidsieck."

"Fine champagne, Heidsieck."

"This morning, my cellar—"

"Second smashing of the grapes?" Sugarman suggested. "I'm sorry."

"By some miracle," Halperin went on, "a few bottles of the Heidsieck made it through unscathed."

Dr. Sugarman wiped his eyes with the heel of his hand. "I call that a bit of luck."

Halperin nodded. "Say we pull the cork on them tonight. No telling what the morning will bring."

"Let's do it," Sugarman agreed.

Neither man moved. Not then, not for a long time. I suspect they would have stayed on the banks of the square all night. At last Mrs. Sugarman took her husband's hand and led him home.

Once again Pie and I entered the house without Rose. It felt strange and wrong to be there, but there we were. And now it was dark.

"Go on up, Pie."

"You mean to bed? What if the fire—"

"Sugarman said he'd come for us. I trust him, don't you? In

the meantime, I think we ought to sleep, or try. Go on, Pie. I'll be up shortly."

She refused to go without me. So, I made sure the rag on her head was changed and helped her with her skirt and blouse and tucked her into bed.

"Stay," she insisted, and scooted over to make room in the twin bed. We held tight to one another till I was sure Pie was asleep.

It was now past nine o'clock—sixteen hours since the first shake. I put on my boots and took Rogue outside to do his business.

Tan, the old man, and Lifang were out front guarding their kitchen. They were eating rice out of bowls with chopsticks. As I walked by, they stopped their chatter to observe me.

The street was thick with folks fleeing the flames. The bright-orange glow from the fire illuminated their exhausted faces.

I had wrapped a handkerchief around my nose and mouth, but there was no help for Rogue. He snorted and sneezed, then dropped his square head and plowed on. We had gone only a few paces in the road when Sugarman called to me.

"Vera!" he shouted, blasting into the roar. "Where are you going?"

"I'm just taking Rogue here for a walk."

"A walk!" he gasped. "A walk?" As if nothing could be stranger than a girl taking a walk. "And where did you think you'd take this walk?"

I shrugged. "Maybe that way." I pointed vaguely at the fire. "Where were you headed?"

"North Beach," he said grimly. Then, as if just hearing me, he shouted, "Downtown? You can't."

"North Beach?" I parroted back, for there was no reason on earth to go to North Beach either. Except if you were Dr. Sugarman, who, in quick fashion, explained that Mrs. Sugarman's sister and her Italian husband lived in North Beach. Mrs. Sugarman couldn't sleep for fear they were out on the street.

"But wouldn't they come to you?" I asked.

"So I keep telling her," he agreed. "They'll turn up on high ground, if the fire gets close. And of course, we'd welcome them. But my wife cannot be easily soothed. She is verklempt."

"Verklempt?"

"Choked up," he said.

I nodded. He was full of strange words, this Sugarman. He had a way of peering into one with such intensity—it wasn't exactly curiosity or frankness, more as if he were deciding which, of any number of personalities, lived inside you.

"Downtown is impossible, Vera Johnson," he said. "You heard Genthe. The fire has eaten everything from the Palace Hotel to the piers. Rose isn't there. She can't be."

Sugarman's fine, well-worn boots were covered with dust. I nodded at them.

"Vera, my friend—may I call you my friend?"

Again I nodded.

"How old are you, dear?"

"Sixteen."

"In how many birthdays will you be sixteen?"

"I'm fifteen."

"All right, then." Sugarman slapped his knee with a glove. "Now let's get a few things straight, shall we? First, look at me."

I did.

He smiled kindly. "I'll ask you to listen to what an old man has to say. Then you can decide. All right? You see, not everyone on this block is asleep when persons come to call at the odd hour of midnight." Sugarman inhaled sharply. "There, the worst-kept secret is out."

"You mean, *everyone* knows?"

"Surely not. Maybe only Sugarman here." He removed his

glasses, blew the ash from them, and put them back on his nose. "Most nights I read until one, two o'clock in the morning—I find it the perfect hour for thinking. No one to disturb you. Sometimes I even walk the square at that hour. I walk and say, Sugarman: you are a free man and this is a great country. Like so, I take a little walk and think my thoughts." He made a stirring motion with his finger. "Am I the only one awake at that late hour? I cannot say. What I do know, or know a bit, is that I have made it my life's work to try to understand the human animal. I am a doctor of psychiatry. Do you understand what that is?"

I shook my head.

"It is the study of the mind and where it connects here and here—to the soul and the heart."

Seeing the confusion on my face, he went on. "All I know for certain, Vera of fifteen, is that at midnight there are at least two houses on this block not yet asleep." He held up two fingers. "Sugarman's. And this house belonging to a woman with one name, Rose. In Sugarman's house, we have an old man who cannot sleep for hearing the voices of his dead boys. And the house next door? Here, the lamps are lit once, twice, three times a year for the arrival of a special guest. What a surprise that we should finally meet, eh? What other secrets live inside these houses? If someone told me a week ago that this world could be unmade in less than a minute, would I have believed them? Can anyone tell you or me that ghosts and special guests do not belong on our block except when they do?

"Now, Vera, let us say a few things quickly. First, I do not speak of these things to make you . . . ashamed. I see in your manner you are a person of pride. What I witness on my nighttime perambulations, I do not speak of with others. I witness, yes; I wonder, yes. Sugarman broods, he ponders, he mourns. But I don't gossip, ever, not even to my wife. You have my word on that. Mrs. Sugarman believes the world is a certain way; let's leave her to those pretty notions, eh? What happens in the house next door is that house's business.

"But—" Sugarman hastened to add. His voice shook with emotion. "Vera, my friend, it is a *shanda* bargain your people have made of you, and I, for one, despise it."

Yes, *made of* me, was what he said.

Sugarman sighed. He put his hand on my shoulder. "So, my dear girl, let us be friends and talk without pretense. We'll do what we can, all right?"

I nodded.

"So, not a word from her . . . people?"

"Not a word."

"None of her girls, except for that Italian bit with her baby, come by looking for a handout?"

"No, sir."

"Well, they may yet. For now I'm guessing there are three possibilities of what's become of Miss Rose." And once more Sugarman counted on his fingers. "First, well, we won't consider the worst, eh? Number two, she's among the wounded. Three, she took passage on the last ferry to Oakland. All right. Let us go through—"

"She isn't dead," I declared. I knew this, despite what Genthe had said, that every structure within ten, twenty blocks of The Rose had collapsed or burned. Rose would have gotten herself out. Hank would have carried her on his back if need be. What I couldn't grasp was, had she taken one of the last ferries to Oakland? Or was she badly injured? I confessed my worries to Sugarman.

He listened, nodding solemnly. "Yet we cannot have a young girl walking the streets looking for a rose, eh? And how far would you get? The Palace Hotel is in shambles, and the streets beyond the palace, the saloons and dance halls, gone."

Genthe had said as much. Spider Kelly's, the Hippodrome, the Poodle Dog, the Bear—the cheap joints and the high-end pleasure halls—all ashes.

"It's a *farkakt* world," Sugarman declared. He had a hundred phrases, Sugarman did, to say things were good or shit.

"If she left the city—"

"She's here." I didn't know till I said it. But saying it, I was certain. She was here.

Sugarman sighed but did not object.

"Well, then, it looks like the hospitals by the piers and in the Presidio are where we go looking. Thousands wounded. Finding her would be like finding the proverbial needle in a haystack. But you already know that. Tonight, get some rest and we'll knock our heads together in the morning."

We'd walked in a perfect circle round the square, back to the house. To where Lifang and her grandfather were asleep under the tarp. Tan was in back, cooking over the fireplace in the garden.

"Buried the horse in back, did they?" Sugarman asked.

I nodded.

"That was a grim piece of work. Good on Tan. And good on him that he thought to put up this kitchen. Tonight, we were grateful to have it. But what of tomorrow, and the day after and the one after that?" Sugarman sighed, the weariness deep in him. "All right, then, Vera Johnson, can I count on you to stay put for the night? It's not safe," he warned. "It won't be safe for a long time."

Sugarman saw me to Rose's front door and handed me his lantern. I didn't have the heart to tell him that I wasn't allowed to enter that way—no, with him watching, I had to turn the great brass knob and go in.

How odd to be alone in her foyer. To sit in her velvet chaise with my dusty boots hanging over the side. To sneak a heel of bread from Tan's larder, to open and close his treasured drawers.

I roamed from one dark room to the next, then went upstairs to check on Pie. She was fast asleep.

My shadow, cast by Sugarman's lantern, moved as I moved, elongated and bold. With no one to stop me, I went to Rose's room and set the lantern on the mantel. The quake had made a mess of things. The drawers and closets thrown open. I began sorting. Starting with the wall of closets, I addressed her gowns. The silks and satins, the chemises and Oriental dressing gowns embroidered with flowers or dragons or vines. I returned each to its proper padded hanger, the arms of which were stuffed with lavender. Next, the shoes. Short boots with matching buttons, of leather and crocodile and silk and satin. I restored them to their special nooks. Next, I knelt before a pile of scarves and folded them. Her underclothes of four-ply silk required special handling. She was abundant, my Rose. I didn't know her. The gizmos of whale bone and wire required to lift her breasts and flatten her gut necessitated deep, capacious drawers. What was the message in her intimate underthings? I wrapped them in yards of tissue paper, scented with lemon verbena and geranium, that she kept in a separate drawer.

It was in the back of that drawer of paper that I discovered the box tied with ribbon, undisturbed by quake or dust. A collection of baby things—little dresses with bodices of lace, a quilted blanket, a pair of silk booties. I knew at once they were mine. I couldn't believe she'd kept them. Maybe they'd been there so long she'd forgotten. Maybe not. What secrets did they have to tell me? I turned them over and held them up to the light, as if Rose's and my story were writ on them—or better yet, our future.

Tan

I wondered what shenanigans Tan would bring with him. I didn't have to wonder for long.

By the second day, the caravan of people fleeing the fires had become a mass migration of some two hundred thousand refugees—all seeking shelter and something to eat. Much of this movable city had to pass by Rose's house. Tan took advantage of his prime location. There would be plenty of customers who wouldn't settle for the gruel served in the slow-moving relief lines. These folks had to eat, and why shouldn't Tan feed them?

That first day and night, he offered all comers a free meal. It took no time for news to spread that a Chinese servant who was mean with a cleaver and great with spices was serving free grub in Pacific Heights. Soon folks were standing in line with their plates and chipped cups.

Then, on the second day, Tan changed the rules.

"V, hurry. Come look." Pie pestered me relentlessly. Her coughing fits made it unsafe for her to venture outside in the smoke. Instead, she watched a new world rising from behind Rose's upstairs windows.

"Hurry-hurry," she pleaded, until I dropped what I was doing.

"What now?"

Pie pointed at the curb. Tan was at work in his outdoor

kitchen. He now had an enormous cauldron of tea boiling on the iron stove. A gateleg table from Rose's parlor had been recommissioned; he'd covered it with a decent cloth, not too good but good enough to give a semblance of polish. Mindful of the day when he'd return to being Rose's snooty butler, Tan thought to protect the wood. From the mismatched parts of the witch's cap, he'd laid a series of boards and fashioned a counter—one end for his customers and the other for his cooking.

"Well, he wasted no time," I said. "Looks like he snuck inside the house last night. What's he serving them?"

"Roast beef. But that's not it. Keep looking," Pie urged.

I touched my nose to the glass. Lifang had stitched a canopy using several of Rose's flowered tablecloths; they flapped in the smoke-choked breeze. There were stray chairs and a couple of oil lamps they'd snatched from the bowels of Rose's beneficence. Come evening, I supposed, they'd illuminate the place.

"You mean the canopy?"

Pie shook her head. "Look again."

"You mean the bread?" Some half dozen loaves were neatly stacked.

"No, he bartered for those. I think he's trading Rose's spoons and plates for goods." Pie stomped her boot. "Oh, V, are you really so blind?"

"What? Tell me."

"Jupiter Christmas—the sign! Read the sign!" She pointed to the board nailed to a post, with a drawing of a teacup and plate, and underneath, written in a steady hand, "10 cents." "He's charging our neighbors!"

Sure enough, Tan had tied a sack around his waist to hold the coins he was collecting. I wasn't fooled for a minute to think he was raising funds for our mutual benefit, but I'd be lying if I didn't admit I was impressed.

Despite the smoke and hot winds, and the relentless musket blasts of the fire, popping and banging and roaring as it consumed yet more houses and stores—despite the heat as fierce as any furnace—Tan's line of customers snaked to the far end of the block. Mrs. Haas in her wide-brimmed hat and Mrs. Sugarman with the two youngest Sugarman boys were among the patrons.

"I don't know, Pie. Can they really be called *our* neighbors?"

"They'll think we put Tan up to— Oh, if James were to see this? If he thought we were taking advantage of folks in bad straits . . . he might never—" Pie's coughing kept her from finishing the sentence.

"Never what?"

"Marry me! As if living in a whore's house isn't bad enough."

"Well, I for one am very glad for this whore's house," I felt bound to say. "I don't think you ought to be quite so ungrateful, and if James is such a prig—"

"Don't call him that."

"I don't see Mrs. Haas thinking she's too good to eat Tan's roast beef." I stopped, for just then I remembered that we'd finished the last of the roasts in the icebox on the first night.

"Wait a minute," I said. "Did you say Tan's serving Rose's beef?"

"Yes-yes. It seems that icebox of hers has endless meat."

I looked out the window again. Lifang was handing Mrs. Sugarman's boys two identical plates heaped with stew. The little vixen made a point of bowing as she took their money.

"Pie? Are you absolutely sure Tan didn't barter for the beef too?" I tried to hide the urgency in my voice.

"No," she insisted. "LowNaa and Tan were in the back garden cooking the roasts all night. I hear they have a secret recipe, famous in Shanghai. It's meant to be delicious."

As if summoned, the old man brought a fresh platter of grilled meat from the backyard to the kitchen at the curb.

"Where are you going?" Pie asked.

"Lie down, Pie," I said. "Your cough sounds awful."

"Are you going to stop Tan?"

"I don't know what I'm going to do."

Across the road, in the park, soldiers were setting up rows of army-issued tents. The fire, torching the city behind us, was only a hill away.

I was more frightened of Tan than the fire. The fire I figured we could outthink.

"Tan!" I called to him from the top of Rose's front stairs. I had no idea what I was going to say.

When Pearl Sugarman and her boys saw me, she pointed to her plate and nodded.

I saw a hint of a smile on Tan's face as he came up the stairs carrying a cup of tea and a full plate. I waited till he got very close.

"Tell me," I spat, "tell me you aren't serving them *horse.*"

"Nah," he huffed, but in no way denying it. He set the tea and plate on the stairs beside me—where I could plainly see he'd saved for me a leg of chicken from last night's supper and a slice of potato pie and a sliver of corn bread—a meal decidedly not horse.

"Horse is dead. . . . But not so dead he can't do. Look at these hungry people. This is good for them. Good for us."

"Tan, have you no shame?" I asked, surprised to feel my anger quickly dissipate, replaced by more practical concerns. Having seen the world from Tan's point of view, I couldn't *unsee* it, and while I wasn't about to admit that I agreed, I flicked my hand to show him that I was just as eager to move on.

He looked me over. I had the feeling he'd made a decision too, and that despite all I resented about him and him about me, we were somehow aligned. Slowly, reluctantly, he untied the silk purse from around his waist. "You the boss now?" He shrugged and handed me his purse.

I pinched the sack by its neck, as if it were stuffed with worms. I set it beside me on the stairs.

"How much did you keep?" I asked.

Tan shrugged.

"Show me."

He glanced behind him, to see who was watching. Then he made a show of turning out his silk pockets. The few scant cents he'd saved for himself tumbled to the steps with a hollow ring. He picked them up, weighed them in his hand, and offered them to me.

I shook my head, and Tan returned the coins to his pocket.

"Lifang," I said. "Where is she supposed to sleep? And the old man?"

Tan tipped his head in the direction of Rose's basement—where his windowless, unheated cell awaited, a subterranean existence made up of dirt floors, a cot, a slop jar, and cast-off furniture.

I took the cup of tea in my hands, grateful for its warmth. I was trying to see the angles, to guess at what I could not see. I considered the blunt, steady sound of the ax that had fallen all night; I hadn't wanted to think what it could be. I had wanted them to bury General so I didn't have to feel guilty. I wanted Tan to take care without bothering me.

I looked Tan in the eye. "Even so, you have to stop. Do you hear me? Serve them—I don't know—beans and rice. There's plenty in the larder."

He shrugged as if to say, why, when there's so much horse?

We never finished that conversation. While we were talking, a series of blasts shook the air. General Funston and his army were creating firebreaks throughout the city. They were blowing to smithereens the mansions along Van Ness Avenue, in the hopes that they could stop the blaze from jumping the wide boulevard and gobbling Pacific Heights.

The steady boom was worse than the quake aftershocks—every five minutes Funston's troops set off another blast.

The army had taken the dynamite from the Chinese but never thought to ask which dynamite to use. It turned out there were hundreds of varieties. The Chinese had fireworks for funerals and weddings, and for knocking down buildings—as many kinds of dynamite as spices in Tan's jars. Funston's troops had seized granulated dynamite: gunpowder, the most highly combustible. For every block the soldiers leveled in an attempt to stop the fire, they created new blazes, the sparks hopping from roof to roof.

The owners of the mansions along Van Ness were given just forty-five minutes to clear out, before the horn sounded and their houses exploded with their art and valuables inside.

Van Ness was just two blocks east of Rose's house.

"Saaa," Tan hissed as yet another blast exploded behind us. Rose's house shivered. Tan glanced at the roof, to see what might fall on our heads—or perhaps just on my head.

I wasn't about to show that anything scared me. I picked up the plate and started eating. I was famished.

Tan nodded, eyebrows raised; in his way he was pleased.

"We have to find her," I mumbled, my mouth full. I sopped up the chicken gravy with the last bit of corn bread.

"We wait. One, two, three days." He shrugged. "Maybe she took the ferry. May-be hospital. May-be—"

"She isn't dead." I looked at him to see if he agreed. I wouldn't have admitted it, but Tan's opinion mattered to me.

He studied the street and sighed. "Nah," he said. "Rose, she's not dead." He thought a bit more and added, "Rain tomorrow."

"Tomorrow will be too late," I said. "If the fire jumps Van Ness tonight, we'll have to run for it."

Tan nodded, agreeing with me. I gathered myself, stood, and

made a show of brushing the crumbs from my skirt. "Right now I need help upstairs. Will you come?"

He followed me up to Rose's study. Indoors, Tan was second-in-command—not as my servant, never that—but for the simple reason that Rose would have expected it.

In the library, her heavy walnut desk with its leather top had tipped on its nose. We each took hold of a corner. Tan was strong, all nerve and steel, but I was tough too. We heaved the desk to its place against the wall. Then Tan tried to lift one of the deep drawers full of papers and ledgers all by himself; he cried out in agony, "Ayyy!" and dropped it. His silk tunic lifted as he jumped, and I caught a glimpse of the welts that covered his low back. Someone had beaten Tan.

"My God, what happened to you—?"

He caught my words, but more so the command in my voice. I heard it too. It was part of me now.

"What happened to you?" he snapped. "What happened to *you*?"

Here's what happened to Tan.

The day I visited The Rose, she handed him his severance and tickets for the ferry. After he dropped me, he collected his things at Rose's—twenty years of service could fit in a single sack. He returned to the room in Chinatown where Lifang lived with her grandfather. That same night, as Tan feared, the tong boys came to the door at the behest of their leader—Hop Sing Tong—and demanded that Lifang be given as a bride to one of the gang's leaders. It was a simple transaction and there was no possibility of refusing. They promised to reward Tan handsomely as the father of the bride. Tan assured them that they could have his daughter in a week, but first he needed time to prepare her with the proper clothes. He'd use their money to buy the dress and other necessary items for the wedding. No one in Chinatown would dare go against the tong. No one except Tan, who used the money to buy train tickets to Sacramento; they were due to leave on the ferry the morning of the quake.

Their building collapsed in the first shaker; it folded as most of Chinatown fell, like a paper lantern. Tan, Lifang, and LowNaa clung to one another and rode the building down as it buckled into the street. The residents on the floors below them died, but luck kept Tan, Lifang, and LowNaa alive. Still, Tan had to dig with his bare hands to unearth the old man.

They'd rushed to the ferry, passing too many dead, Chinese and white folk alike, and a hundred dead steers who'd busted loose from the stockyards and were shot as they stampeded down Market Street. At the Ferry Building it was madness, only whites were allowed to board, and even then, only the rich. They spotted Sarah Bernhardt getting on with her dogs; Caruso was accompanied by his valet and dozens of steamer trunks. Tan, Lifang, and LowNaa showed their tickets. When Tan insisted, when he claimed the right to board as the butler of Rose's house, one of the toughs beat him with a rod. With no options—with the Chinese herded like stock to a guarded camp in the Presidio—Tan came to us.

Strange Lands and People

Pie understood that as long as the fires raged, she couldn't expect to hear from James. But that didn't stop Pie's heart from wanting. Nothing stops a heart from wanting.

On the third day of the fire, Pie and I were preparing to leave the house—we'd gathered our pails to take to the relief lines—when it struck me that Ricky wasn't singing. I checked Rose's parlor, where we'd put him that first morning, there in the curved bay where he could feel the sun pouring through the tall windows, an eerie orange light cast by the fires. He wasn't there.

Ricky had figged the bamboo latch on his cage. It wasn't the first time he'd used his beak to free himself, and in our old house we'd threaded a wire round the little bamboo stick to secure the cage's door. In the post-quake mayhem, I'd forgotten to twist the wire. Pie and I searched the house but Ricky was gone—out the busted parlor window.

"Oh, V, I'm sorry. What a thing," Pie fretted.

How I must have looked, absorbing yet another loss. Pie insisted that I sit on the divan and gather myself.

I stared at the carpet, seeing nothing, while beside me Pie coughed into her fist. "I . . . didn't think about him today," I admitted. "I even forgot to feed him."

"It's all right, I took care of it. I fed him this morning—" Pie's eyes got huge, as she realized she'd forgotten to twist the wire. "Oh, V, I'm so—sorry!"

I covered my face with my hands.

She suggested we look for him in the ring of trees that topped the highest point of Lafayette Square, and though I doubted Ricky could last long in the smoke and wind, I brought along an orange, to lure him from wherever he'd gone.

Pie put her arm around me as we looked among the neighbors' roofs to see if Ricky was up there.

"I don't blame you," I said. "It was a mistake."

"Well, I blame me. You're doing everything," she said. "And all I can be is sorry."

We crossed the road and looked back at what was left of our city. Where there had been block after block of fancy houses and apartment buildings, there were only smoldering ruins leading up to Nob Hill. At the very top, the nearly finished Fairmont Hotel, an edifice of white, had smoke piping out of its windows.

Pie shaded her eyes with her hand. "Do you think . . . Will it ever be good again?"

I didn't know. It seemed unlikely in every respect.

Pie wiped her eyes with her sleeve and the white of the cotton showed black from the ash. Pie frowned at her sleeve and said, "James once told me that San Francisco was built with miner's luck, but the rocks that made the gold want revenge—that's why the city's burned so many times."

I thought that might be the most interesting thing ever ascribed to James O'Neill. I didn't agree with it; luck was what you made of it, no more, no less, and the city had plenty of good luck, and plenty of bad luck too. It wasn't in the rocks and it wasn't in the air.

"For a person our age, James is awfully certain," I said.

"In his way, I suppose he is," Pie agreed. "He doesn't like Eugenie's father, that's for sure. James says that Mayor Schmitz will get what he deserves." Pie coughed again, and again we stopped to wait for the spell to pass.

"Sometimes," Pie said, her voice low and hoarse, "I want to disagree. And I do, gently. James is awfully tough on brothels." Pie smiled slyly. "He says in San Francisco there will always be more hookers than police, 'cause that's who started the city—miners and hookers. Well, you know, I have to bite my tongue. If only James knew."

"When do you plan on telling him?"

"About us and Rose?" Pie tucked her lips and gave a defiant shake of her head. "Never. Morie always said: Rose is a secret we take to the grave."

It struck me as rude to say the obvious: that Morie did take that secret to the grave. "What about now, Pie? I mean, here we are."

She paused, the way she did when batting away dark thoughts to welcome a more convenient notion.

"Oh," she said, "after James and I marry, I wouldn't expect ever to see Rose again. There'll be no need. Not for me, at least."

"You mean, you'd move on and I'd be left."

"Well, you'd be . . . Well, I don't know exactly what you'd be, but we just thought—"

She watched me step back, the empty tin pails I was carrying—one for milk, one for water—banging together like hollow drums.

So, it had all been arranged, talked over, on how many nights of whispering after I disappeared to my room? How many nights had Morie and Pie planned their new lives—their lives without me? At my birthday, Rose said that folks can always be counted on to put their desires first, and wasn't that so true.

"Oh, V, dearest, I don't mean you and me. We'll always be us," Pie protested, her voice as tinny and empty as our pails. She sidled next to me, to prove we were and always would be sisters, knit boots to hip bones to shoulders to the rims of our hats together.

"Forget it, Pie," I said, and walked on.

"V, honestly—" she called.

"Honestly."

Her cough worsened as she tried to keep up. I didn't bother to slow my pace. At the far corner of the square, a man had rolled his Steinway piano out the double doors of his ruined house and onto the wood planks that made up the sidewalk. He had put up a sign to let folks know that he was selling the piano for fifty dollars. To show its worth, or perhaps to mourn its loss, he was playing Schumann.

"'About Strange Lands and People,'" Pie said as she came up next to me.

"I know the song, Pie," I declared sullenly.

In our little house on Francisco Street, Pie played it precisely, without feeling. Morie acted the part of a metronome, clapping her hands till Schumann resembled the march of the Vikings.

Played right, it was hauntingly sad.

"I seem to be ruining everything," Pie lamented. "Please, V, forgive me."

"Shh," I said. "I want to listen."

"Thing is," she went on, "I don't feel him anymore. James, I mean. I don't feel him." To press the point, Pie squeezed my hand. "Do you think it's a sign?"

I didn't answer. I was thinking that it was time I stopped being shocked by my cold Swedes.

"V?"

"Shh."

"Fifty dollars isn't very much for a piano, is it?"

We decided to find Lifang in the relief lines, then look for Ricky. But as we neared the far end of the square, from a distance, we could see that Lifang was in trouble.

She was supposed to be holding our place in the milk line, alongside hundreds of refugees. The queues for the water, soup, and bread stations were equally long, a loop that went around the square and doubled back. Rich and poor, servant and Pacific Heights matron, had to stand for hours in the stiff wind and floating ash, with nothing to do but gossip. That, and read the list of dead in the *Call* posted on boards throughout the square.

The white matrons of the neighborhood, and several of the newcomer refugees, many of whom could only dream of a foothold in Pacific Heights before the quake, had cut the line in front of Lifang.

First they'd elbowed her out of the way, then they insulted her with their dirty looks. Lifang cursed them in Cantonese, and when they turned their backs to her, she spat at their feet.

Just as we arrived, a woman jabbed Lifang with the sharp end of her parasol. Lifang had her own stick and she was pointing it at the woman like a sword.

"Stop! Stop this," Pie cried. The women ignored her.

I took Lifang's stick and moved her back, so she was behind me.

"We were just about to call the soldiers," bellowed the matron. "Your girl, she's entirely out of control. She ought to be whipped."

"Yah? Should I whip this good servant who was only holding a place for me and my sister," I shouted, "two girls who lost their mother in the quake, and our house burned, and how is it for you ladies with your fine parasols and attitude?"

Pie, her cheeks rosy with indignation, looked into the women's faces and said, simply, "Shame."

"Well, I never," the matron remarked, as if Pie had been the one to strike her.

"I hope you never," I added. "I hope for everyone here, you never." And nodding to Lifang, I sent her back to the house, while Pie and I assumed her place.

Now the matrons turned their backs to us, but their voices carried.

"Our square is done, Emily. From here out, it's low-bred squatters and foul Chinese," said the one to the other.

Her friend groaned in agreement. "Why, you know, they've taken to calling it Millionaire's Camp on account of the views. Millionaire's indeed! Eck, I fear we'll never be rid of them."

The pair sighed from the tops of their shirtwaists to the bottoms of their corsets.

"And the mayor!" the matron went on, glaring at the soldiers who were putting up another row of army tents. "He's no help at all. Why, I hear he's running about, this way and that, gaping at the fire. He might as well play his fiddle."

"What do you expect from a con man? Bought and paid for, to our great regret," her friend replied. "And I never did like his music either."

"Pie," I said, loud enough so they'd hear. "This afternoon, let's call on Mayor Schmitz. I'd like to speak to him about this bad business in our square."

"Good idea," Pie said. "He might be able to help us find James and—"

The women turned as one and spoke to Pie. "What did you say your name is, dear?"

"She didn't say," I snapped.

But Pie, ever gracious, introduced us, then added, "Would you ladies have heard any mention of a James O'Neill? He's my fiancé—" Pie coughed; she couldn't help it. The women shielded their faces.

"Poor girl. You don't imagine he's on the *Call*'s list, do you? They've just posted today's, it's over there."

"Oh, no," Pie exclaimed. "He's not on any list of dead."

"What part of town are his people from, dear?"

"Well, they have a small shop—"

"Oh, a shopkeeper, is he? And what kind of shop would that be?" The one named Emily gave Pie the up-down.

I'd had enough. I flashed Pie the orange, so she'd know I was going to search for Ricky.

"V, wait—" Pie begged, wagging her finger at me as she went on yattering with the ladies.

Ignoring her, I headed toward the grove of trees at the top of the square.

"V, for heaven's sakes. Stop!" Pie wheezed as she marched behind me. "Look, now you've made us lose our place in line."

I wheeled round to face her. "I won't stand by listening while those snobs nettle you. I'd like to pull out that lady's tongue—that would teach her. In fact, I'd like to pull out your tongue. Really, Pie, shame? Is that the best you can do? You won't catch me singing Lifang's praises, but at least she showed some spine."

We were at a standstill—literally—poised between two rows of tents. Nearby, a family of some six souls perched in the grass, eating out of a shared bowl and watching us. They had staked their claim by placing a rug and a basket in front of their tent. Beyond the tent, the mansions of Washington Street, and beyond the mansions, yes, those million-dollar views of the bay.

Pie eyed the strangers watching us. "I said I was sorry," she pressed.

"Are you? For which part?"

Pie shook her head. "That bit about the mayor, were you serious? I'd like to see Eugenie, and the mayor may have news about James—"

"James *and* Rose," I said. "Tomorrow we'll walk down—" I stopped. Someone was calling Pie's name.

As if possessed, Pie ran toward that voice, searching one row of tents and then another.

"Pie? Pie Johnson!" It was James's mother. She was with his sisters, each of them holding an empty pail or basket.

Pie tried to embrace them, banging her pails with theirs as

she wrapped her arms around them. "Oh my golly. I can't believe it's you!" she cried. "James, where is James?"

"I expect he's at our tent," his mother said. "Here, we'll show you. It's just over there. We were lucky to get one of the good perches, on the hill with a bit of a breeze."

She led us through the rows till we reached their tent. James O'Neill, his shirt filthy but his wool vest buttoned, was banging the dents out of a pot that had a hole in its bottom.

He looked stunned, diminished. Pie saw none of this. She dipped her head and barreled into him, fiercely hugging her James. Her questions spilled out in a rush. "Did you try to find me, oh, James, is the shop all right? I was so worried about you—all of you. But look, here you are. James, it's all so awful. Did you see my note? Morie. Oh, James, you don't know about Morie—" Here she ran out of steam and began to sob.

James's mother watched from a distance with her arms folded. Soon she was explaining that they had suffered too, not a loss of life, but the shop, their house, everything they owned—and a good deal they didn't own, having borrowed from the bank. They'd barely made it to Lafayette Square ahead of the flames.

"Oh, darling," James said. He shut his weary eyes and patted Pie's back.

"Where are you girls taking shelter?" his mother asked. "Did you manage to claim a tent?"

Pie lowered her gaze to the grass.

"We're staying with a relation," I offered, "in a house just across the way."

"Oh, how wonderful for *you,*" his mother remarked, her tone suggesting that they had no people.

James released Pie and held her by the shoulders. He half smiled as he studied her face. "I didn't know you had relations in town. That's . . . good news."

"Yes," Pie agreed. "Actually, it was a surprise to us too. People are so kind in these dreadful circumstances. Don't you agree? Kind," she said again. "And surprising."

His mother and sisters frowned—clearly, they hadn't seen such kindness—and by the look on James's face, neither had he. "Where is this house—just over there, you say?" He craned his neck to peer over the hill. "Can we see it from here?"

"Oh, not quite." Pie waved in the general direction.

"It must be grand if it's on the square," his mother ventured. I could see she was bent on knowing exactly.

"The gold one," I said.

"Gold, you say? Not the one with all the doodads," his mother replied. "Why, I know that house. It belongs to that woman, what's her name? The madam."

"Her name is Rose," I declared.

"But how . . . could you be related to her, dear?"

"Only distantly," Pie assured them, and she looked to James for help.

"How distantly?" his mother pressed.

"Why does it matter?" I said with a good deal of indignation. "Seeing as how our mother is dead and many folks have nothing but a . . . dented pot. I shouldn't think it matters what a person is or does, nor how distant she is to us as kin, so long as there's a roof over our heads. For which we are grateful."

James's mother nodded at Pie. "Your sister has quite a tongue."

Pie beseeched James with her eyes. He had yet to let go of that foolish pot.

"Here, let me walk you, Pie," he said, clearly wishing to get away from his mother and, no doubt, away from me.

"Well," his mother sniped as the pair of lovers walked away. "Our mortification never seems to end."

"No," I agreed, "it doesn't."

And with that, I excused myself and took my foul mood to look for Ricky. I called to him until I was hoarse. But he wasn't in the tall trees at the top and he wasn't in the scrub at the base of the hill. He wasn't anywhere.

I waited for Pie on the corner nearest the house. Large flakes of soot floated around me, blanketing the grass and my hair and shoulders. It was snowing the bones of the city.

At last she appeared and I could see at a distance that she'd been crying.

"What. What did he say?" I asked, dreading the answer.

"Oh, V, I am so stupid. I thought he was—"

"Kind. Maybe he was, Pie. No one is who they used to be. What did he say?"

"He said he has nothing—no money, no store—nothing to offer me. I said it didn't matter. He, he didn't agree. I said of course you and your sisters and mother must come and take shelter in Rose's house, with us. He said his mother would never allow it. He said *he* wouldn't allow it." Pie wrung her hands, pulling at them as she went on. "He said now that his mother has a clearer sense of me, she'll never agree to our arrangement. She's lost everything, he said—"

"Stupid cow."

"James said he couldn't . . . possibly add to her sorrow." Pie wept. "Then I said, What about my sorrow, James? What about my sorrow?"

"Yeah, and what did he say to that?"

She was shaking all over. "He said . . . oh, my pretty Pie."

I took her home to Rose's and put her in one of the fancy guest beds, where she cried herself to sleep. By morning the ash and smoke were so thick, they blocked the sun.

To See the Mayor

At that time, Mayor Schmitz had two houses: a mansion in Pacific Heights and the house they'd left Francisco Street for, a modest Victorian, halfway up the hill. Several months before the quake, with the indictments imminent, the Schmitzes decamped to their smaller house—to show that the mayor was still half humble, and not a criminal living in a castle.

From Rose's house, it was a straight pitch down. I had to hold tight to Pie's hand, lest we trip.

There were soldiers on horseback guarding the house, and police on foot, and still more posted at the mayor's front door. Half a dozen soldiers were smoking on the grass inside the short iron fence. The soldiers ignored the cops and the cops shunned the soldiers, who were strangers to our city. Yet soldiers and cops alike watched our backsides as we climbed the stairs to the mayor's door.

Pie dipped her chin so as not to meet their eager gazes.

"Pie!" Eugenie cried as we passed into the foyer. The two girls collapsed in a heap on the hall stairs and began at once to confess their hearts. There was too much to cover: the quake and fire; Morie's death, our house, and James—awful James. On Eugenie's side, there was the miraculous reprieve the mayor had been granted, for which Eugenie had devoted months of prayer. It was all too much.

When Eugenie asked, "Where did you disappear to?" Pie had

a well-timed coughing fit, and Eugenie rushed to get her a glass of water.

Julia Schmitz, the mayor's wife, pulled me aside—with the house full of strangers, there was no place to talk but in the packed front hall. She paid her respects regarding Morie, and I thanked her and hoped I wouldn't have to say more. My heart was the opposite of shut: it was a house of feeling with no walls or doors.

Julia Schmitz, being a practical woman and no fool, understood. She had her own troubles. When the quake hit, she and Schmitz had been lying in bed, talking about what she and the children should do if he were sent to jail that morning.

Knowing that I didn't care to linger on my losses or hers, Julia Schmitz turned our attention to the dozens of men crowding her parlor. Men in coats, their faces recognizable from the papers.

A stink pervaded the rooms and I couldn't decide where it was coming from—it was soot, wool, and something I couldn't name.

"How, Vera, am I to feed them?" Julia asked in her Irish lilt. "When I have just the one wee ham?"

I suggested she slice it very thin.

Julia smiled and touched my arm.

"Hurry, Molly," she said to her freckled maid. "These men are famished. Tell Nell to stretch the ham. Tell her to slice it very, very thin."

"Gentlemen," boomed Eugene Schmitz to those assembled in the parlor. Schmitz had his back to the mantel, his arms raised as if he were leading an orchestra. "Let's divide into groups. There, with Phelan, Relief. Here, with me, Fire. Over there, Triage and Wounded. Over there, well, over there, the Chinese." He waved in the general direction of a bespectacled man standing at the far end of the room. It was none other than the mayor's partner in crime, Abe Ruef. As the men organized into groups, Ruef remained alone.

But Schmitz, he was surrounded. He'd understood at once the

magnitude of the disaster: the gods had answered his prayers by leveling the city. Within the first hour, he'd gotten himself downtown, where he organized the city's leaders—the editors of the largest newspapers, the heads of business, law, and the railroads, and other assorted kings; he dubbed them the Committee of Fifty and made sure to include the very men who wanted his scalp, who'd funded the effort to prosecute him. Good men; complicated men. Men who would lay down their lives for the city they loved.

"Look at them," Julia Schmitz tsked. "They loathe my husband, yet who do they depend on to lead them?" She was proud, angry. "He'll show them, Vera, he'll show them the stuff he's made of. And we won't let them forget; they won't be drinking Eugene Schmitz's blood."

Of course, Schmitz had already shown them and me what he was made of, but the times being what they were, a violinist who knew how to lead a disparate band of players might prove to be exactly what the city needed.

"I don't think you have to offer them his blood," I suggested, "but maybe some mugs of beer?"

Julia knit her lips to keep from laughing. "Gene mentioned you were a different sort of girl. He's quite impressed with you."

Had he told her *exactly* how different a girl I was? No, I could see in that churchgoing, righteous face, he hadn't.

"Beer, Molly," Julia said as the maid passed by. "Let's put up some trays of beer."

"But what of the coppers outside?" Molly fussed. "Don't they get—"

"These men." Julia pointed to the packed room. "These men first."

The fifty assembled in the first hour after the quake. They met at the Hall of Justice, where Schmitz made sure to put his enemy, the former mayor James Phelan, in charge of the Relief Committee. As their numbers grew, the committee crossed Portsmouth

Square and assembled at the Plaza Hotel. When the fire reached there, they hustled uphill to the Fairmont Hotel's ballroom, atop Nob Hill. After years of construction and untold delays, the Fairmont was due to open that week. Built of granite, wood, terra-cotta, and steel, it was supposed to be unburnable. The Fairmont took fire late in the afternoon. Schmitz fought alongside the fire crews to save the hotel; he discovered the cistern full of water buried in front of the Hopkins mansion. The fire didn't care. It roared across Nob Hill, devouring the mansions of Flood, Hopkins, Crocker. The mayor had shown uncommon courage, the courage of a man with nothing to lose.

When the fire's heat drove them back, they moved to Franklin Hall, where they'd stay, calling it City Hall Temporary. When the mayor excused himself to go home for food and a change of clothes, dear God, they followed him there.

"Vera, would you mind?" Julia asked when Molly couldn't quite handle the heavy tray of beer. "And make sure the mayor takes something. Oh, and Vera"—she touched my arm with thin, cold fingers—"tell Gene to meet me in the hall. Insist, if you have to. He'll want to say a few words of condolence to you and Pie."

Handsome Gene looked awful. There were flakes of ash on his coat and in his hair. Would he prove the leader the disaster required? I suspected he would be the last to know—his shoulders rounded, his bloodshot eyes darting from man to man.

He'd imposed a curfew immediately, and shut down the bars and saloons. As the flames neared Chinatown, he ordered the luckless Chinese rounded up and confined to an encampment in the Presidio. A triage center was established there, by Fort Mason, and another on the wharfs. Still, the fires raged, and what to do with thousands of dead, and hundreds of thousands of refugees who lacked shelter, food, water?

It was fear, that's what it was. The stink in Schmitz's parlor. Soot, sweat, damp wool, and fear.

"Would you like some beer?" I asked as I moved through the room with my tray.

There wasn't a man present who didn't have a strong opinion of the mayor—indeed, who hadn't lined up for or against. The three who were determined to bring down Ruef and Schmitz were standing by the windows: Rudolph Spreckels, former mayor James Phelan, and M. H. DeYoung each put up a hundred thousand dollars toward the prosecution of Abe Ruef and Eugene Schmitz.

AB Spreckels, Rudolph's brother and Alma de Bretteville's lover, was also present—looking ancient, with a walrus moustache and hunched back. He leaned stiffly against the back of one of Julia Schmitz's crewel-upholstered wing chairs, favoring a bad leg. He was an invalid, in pain. I couldn't imagine him kissing Alma.

He took a mug from my tray and asked if the rumor was true: Was Mrs. Schmitz following with food?

"I believe so."

"Ah, excellent. Between you and me, that's why we're all here." When AB Spreckels chuckled, I saw the spark that captured Alma.

"I hear it's ham," I said.

"Ah, did you get that?" AB said to a man I didn't recognize. "Ham's on the way."

The man nodded and I made the mistake of looking too keen; they fell silent and waited for me to move on. With the next group, I learned to avert my gaze, and they forgot about me. Being a girl and not pretty made me twice invisible. But I didn't forget them or what they said. I loved listening as they schemed—these sooty captains of industry—their urgency being akin to mine. For fifteen years I'd been waiting for a catastrophe greater than my birth. The quake gave it to me.

When my tray was empty, I traded Molly for her tray of ham sandwiches, and moved on, to the one man who was standing alone. He was perhaps the most important of all, and the most shunned—uninvited to the committee and to this house. Abe Ruef, the single member of the Chinese subcommittee.

He was someone I should have admired. In his youth he was brilliant. Accepted to Berkeley at fourteen, admitted to the bar at twenty-one. He spoke eight languages, including Cantonese. In college he started the Municipal Reform League to root out corruption; he'd corresponded with Teddy Roosevelt. How, I wondered, did that idealistic boy become the most corrupt, despised man in the room? And why was he wearing a foppish bow tie?

I offered him a bite of food, which he refused.

"What's the word?" Ruef asked.

"I'm sorry?"

He gestured at his enemies: Spreckels and DeYoung. "What stupidity are they brewing?"

"I'm not sure."

"I saw you, hanging on every word. A spy who won't give it up, eh?"

"I am hardly a spy," I said.

He asked my name. When I told him, he said, "Ah, Vera. You know it means truth. So, are you a truth teller, Vera?"

I shrugged. "They're talking about the fire, Mr. Ruef. How to stop it."

"Fools," he spat. "The fire will stop when it decides to, and not a minute sooner. Mark me, this fire is the best thing that ever happened to our city. You want a fresh start? You want innovation? You want to make a fortune building a city from scratch? Think of all the steel and lumber and nails and lunches and working men that are required. Think of it! Start with a blank slate and build, build, build." He glared at the men, daring someone to contradict him. "These fellows, they'll wring their hands tonight, crying: Oh my, what a disaster. But tomorrow they'll be glad to start pocketing new fortunes." He seethed from behind his little round spectacles. "What do you say to that, Vera?"

A year earlier, Ruef had begun a speech with the line "Gentlemen and Grafters." Everyone had laughed; they weren't laughing now.

I shrugged, not wanting to say.

Ruef nodded. "Good, go on then, spy." He turned to Herbert Schmitz, the mayor's less handsome brother, whom Ruef had appointed president of the Board of Public Works. Ruef was eager to share his next brilliant, urgent idea: to relocate the Chinese to the wasteland of Hunters Point.

"Crikey, Abe, the fire's still raging," Herbert Schmitz said.

"And soon it will be out," Ruef observed. "Mother Nature has provided us with a broom, my friend. Chinatown is five blocks of prime real estate, newly vacant. Generations from now, your people and mine will be asking: What did Grandpa do when he had a go at a clean slate?"

"Your slate, Abe, is hardly clean." Herbert laughed.

"Neither is your brother's," Ruef replied. "In fact, neither is yours."

Herbert attempted to move on, as did I. Abe Ruef blocked my way. "Spy, what do you think of the Chinese?"

"They won't give up Chinatown without a fight, sir. I know a few Chinese. They're tough customers."

"Ah, then we've got to be tougher, eh?" He nodded, agreeing with himself.

Julia Schmitz was displeased. I'd neglected my mission to summon the mayor, and now she had no choice but to cut her own path through the huddle of men. Dropping chin to chest, her forehead serving as an ax, she didn't stop till she'd reached her husband, till she'd placed her hand with its very nice ruby ring on his lapel and whispered in his ear that Pie Johnson, who'd lost her mother, her house, and her fiancé required a word. Did Gene Schmitz want to keep such a poor thing coughing in their hallway?

"Darling," the mayor protested, "I can't." He smiled wearily at the men.

"Gene, Vera is right here," Julia pressed, pointing to me.

My presence seemed to change the equation. Schmitz nodded. "Of course," he said to his wife. "Lead the way."

If he were merely an actor, he was a very good actor, for the anguish on Schmitz's face seemed real. He marched to the stairs and in one swift gesture pulled Pie into his woolly grasp, her cheek turned to the side, her curls smashed. Then he searched for me. His hand came round my waist and brushed my breast. I froze. It happened so quickly; his thumb flicked the flesh, the heel of his hand on my ribs.

"Oh, girls, dear girls." He looked into Pie's watery eyes. "I am so very sorry."

"Mayor Schmitz? My mother, we need to bury her," Pie replied, her face flushed with tears. "There will be no rest for her soul until she's—"

Julia Schmitz took over. "Of course he'll see to it," she said. "Of course. We'll give your mum a proper burial. I promise you." She led Pie up the stairs toward the quiet refuge of Eugenie's room. At the top of the stairs, Julia turned back. Only then did she seem to realize that she had left the other motherless girl below, working beside the maid.

"Vera!" she called. "Please, dear, leave that tray and come."

The thing is, I didn't want to leave the tray. I didn't want to leave Schmitz till I had asked him about Rose.

He took the tray from my hands and passed it to one of the soldiers.

"Vera," he said, taking my hand and, God help me, pressing my palm to his heart. "I'm so sorry. We couldn't save your house." He winced. "So many of them we couldn't save, not without water. North Beach, yes, but not—" His voice lost steam.

"You mean, our house, it burned as well? With Morie—" I shut my eyes.

"You must stay here, with us," he insisted. "You and Pie. Julia won't hear of any qualms."

"Thank you, but we're fixed, at least for now, up the hill."

A vein above the mayor's right eye twitched. He pressed his finger against his temple to quell it.

"Fixed? Whereabouts?"

"On Gough Street." I thought that was enough of a clue to get him there. "Across from Lafayette Square."

"Lafayette, you say?" He'd been awake all night, and his bloodshot eyes saw only the grids of his devastated city—what had collapsed, what had burned, what was about to burn.

"Which house?" The moment he asked, he saw it. The mayor lowered his voice. "You're staying with Rose? No kidding. That's . . . bold."

"Only we don't know where she is. I was hoping you could help me—"

"Wait a moment," he said. "You and your sister are *alone* in Rose's house?" The mayor's face was a jumble of competing subversions. "That won't do. You can't—"

"Could you . . . I mean, would you help me find her?"

His eyes darted from the door to the stairs and back. "Are you saying, during the quake she may have been at The Rose?"

"I think it's possible. Otherwise, where—"

"Good God, let's hope not." He pointed his nose at the ceiling, seeing those crushed blocks in his mind. "Pacific Avenue, that whole area, took it hard. The quake and the fire both." He looked at the soldiers guarding his door, guarding him. "Look,

I'll find out what I can. You must know, it's chaos. Stay put, for now. I promise you, I'll inquire—"

"The fire," I said. "Do you think it'll reach Pacific Heights?"

He shook his head. "We don't know. We're doing everything we can, but for now, no house in the city is safe. It isn't one fire, it's fifty blazes—the worst civic disaster on record. In our city. Our city!" His eye twitched madly. He cocked his head to hear what was happening in the other room. "Ah, listen to that, they're starting to argue. I better go back in." Schmitz moved in the direction of the parlor.

Reluctantly, I started up the stairs.

"Vera?" he called. "Try the hospitals. We've set up a triage center by the Ferry Building and another in the Presidio. Look for the big red crosses. Eda Funston, the general's wife, she's in charge. Formidable woman. Ask for her."

"May I tell her you sent me?"

He looked amused at the thought of his having any clout at all. "Tell her the mayor said if she were running the city, we'd be in much better shape."

Pie was lying on Eugenie's bed, her head in her friend's lap. Above the bed, a wooden cross with a crucified Jesus looked down on them.

"Pie, please," Eugenie begged as I paced at the foot of the bed, thinking how much I preferred the company of men, "please tell Vera to stomp elsewhere. She's crushing Papa's violins."

I looked down at my boots. I was standing on top of Eugenie's floral rug. "His violins?"

"Yes, there. Under*neath*—" Eugenie flapped her hand in the general direction of the floor beyond the bed, where she couldn't see. "Oh, forget what I said. Papa told me never to mention—" Eugenie sat up abruptly and violently shook her head. "It's supposed to be a secret. Please, Vera, come up here with us."

"A secret . . . compartment. Right here, under the floor?" I kicked the rug aside and dropped to my knees.

"Stop that, Vera! Pie? Help me," begged Eugenie. "Papa will be furious—"

"V?" Pie called, her voice thick with tears. "Eugenie said to leave it."

"Why, it's just us," I assured them as I ran my hand across the floor. "We won't tell."

There, cut into the floorboards and well concealed, was a rectangle about a foot and a half wide and several feet long.

Eugenie sighed. "Oh, what does it matter. We don't really live here anymore. And if I can't trust you two, well—" She sighed. "Everyone is always after Papa, it's so unfair. And with so many robbers about town, he says you can't be too careful. He says when you have something of value, you must protect it. So, Papa had his men build a safe under the floor. For storing his most special violins. I said to him, 'Why my floor, Papa, not yours?' and he said, 'Why, silly, you're so light, the violins won't have to worry about being trampled.' He told me not to fuss or think about them *at all*, and that's exactly what I've done. Vera? Vera, did you hear me?" Eugenie let out a little whimper to match Pie's. "Anyway, you can see for yourself, it's locked. Papa said it must always stay locked."

But it wasn't locked. There was a thin metal bar hidden in the seam of the floor, and when I pulled on it, the wooden top came up in one solid piece. A metal box had been custom-made to fit the space underneath, between the joists on two sides and the ceiling below. Sure enough, there was a keyhole for a lock, but whoever used it last had forgotten to turn the key. The box within was padded on all sides with velvet. But instead of violins, there were canvas bags stacked side to side and several deep.

"Vera?"

The throat of each bag had been tied with twine. I worked one open just enough to see that it was filled with cash.

At last the note Rose had me pass to Schmitz at Caruso made sense. After reading it, he'd tossed it into a bin. I felt inclined to retrieve it.

Gene, be assured I've taken care of my end of things. Now make sure to stow your fiddles. Rose.

"You're right," I said, "it's locked."

And thinking of all that money—wondering how much was there and if it had been counted, and surmising that while the mayor grabbed big, he wasn't so much a man of details, not like Rose, not like me—I climbed onto the bed and joined the girls.

The End of the Fire

There were thieves everywhere. Thieves pillaging the ruins of the grand houses; thieves stealing from the refugees in the park. Tan, LowNaa, and Lifang guarded their curbside kingdom. As evening came on, they hauled their foodstuffs, pans, and firewood—everything short of the stove itself—into the house. Tan lifted the iron lid off each burner and brought them in too, lest folks take them to cook over their fires in the camps. Cups, tin, kindling, soiled cotton, all came inside.

After dark, boys and girls from the camps were sent out to scavenge. They plucked horse hooey from the road for their families to use as fuel, and whatever else of value they could find.

The evening was also the time when Tan and I did our reckoning. Tan's magic meat had been stricken from the menu, and we were down to serving rice and beans. Tan, whose genius lay in exotic sauces, threw together a Cantonese version of Boston baked beans. The recipe would prove our salvation—for now. People went mad for it.

I perched at the top of the stairs with my back against Rose's front door and waited for Tan. It was the first time I'd stopped all day and a bruised weariness sat heavy in my bones. So far, I'd reconciled the mess in Rose's room and in some of the rooms on the main floor. I'd taken stock of the larder—what we had and didn't have of food, water. I had put aside a little bit of money I'd found in some spilled drawers. But there was much still broken inside the house and out, and too much I didn't know.

As long as I worked, I kept my worry at a distance. But sitting on those steps brought it on. I thought of Morie—her death a heavy, sharp stone lodged under my ribs. I wondered if it was true that a soul hovered three days on earth before moving on. And if so, it had been three days, though it seemed a good deal longer. Part of me was still a child, with a child's sense of time mostly lived in the present. Or had been, before the quake. Now I was counting the hours by how many rooms needed fixing, and how much food and water we had on hand—with the only clock that mattered being the unyielding fire advancing toward us, house by obliterated house.

I was tired and thirsty. My hair, clothes, even my skin had thickened with smoke. My burning eyes continuously seeped tears. Hugging my knees as I waited for Tan, I looked across at Lafayette Square and wondered when the fire was going to reach us. And if the fire reached the house, and beyond, to the ocean, were we all going to die. I didn't want to die, that's for sure. And it occurred to me that for all her sorrows, Pie was lucky to have been kissed before the world ended, even if it was by that noodle James. I decided I wasn't about to die, yet I would likely never be kissed, and I wiped my tears with the heel of my hand.

Tan came up the steps with my supper. In those first days, we ate, if we were lucky, one meal a day. Tan served me, as he served himself, from a bowl, though instead of chopsticks he brought me a fork.

If Morie could have seen me, shoveling my food. Well, I ate like the beggar I always felt myself to be—all the while sneaking glances over the rim of my bowl at Tan's unreadable face and beyond him, at the tents on the hill and the smoke-filled sky above. There was no denying it, Tan's food tasted sublime, and for those few minutes I forgot my sorrows.

When I finished, he took the bowl from me and handed over his silk purse stuffed with pennies and dimes.

"What's not here?" I asked. Tan repeated the show of turning out the pockets of his silk pants. A few coins tumbled to the ground, his humble share.

On a whim, I asked to see his hat, the fez that never left the top of his head.

He crossed his arms and evinced his most sour face for my benefit.

I didn't react. I hadn't thought about the hat till the words leaped from my mouth, and having asked for it, I held still.

Tan removed the fez with great sorrow. As if I were shaming us both by asking him to do such a dishonorable thing. His black hair beneath the hat was greasy, parted down the middle. He handed the fez to me and turned his back.

Inside the crown, he'd sewn a pouch. I felt with my fingers the coins, warmed by his head and tightly packed. All day Tan had been wearing stolen money on his bean. When I tugged on the thin silk string knotted at the pouch's throat, coins splashed into the bowl of my skirt. So many pennies and dimes—at least a third of the take.

"Damn you," I said.

Tan pretended not to hear me, though he couldn't hide the shiver that passed through his raggedy bones.

For the first time since the quake, I was afraid. I had no idea what role I should play in this game with Tan. But it seemed that whomever I chose to be, I would be forever.

I gathered the part of my skirt with the coins in my fist and slowly, unsteadily climbed to my feet. I carried the whole lot—hat, money, fear—up with me to my attic room.

And there I stayed.

Later on, when Pie came up to bid me good night, she found me kneeling on the rug, the coins spread out in front of me.

"I saw you had your lamp burning," she said, hugging herself with her shawl. "It's freezing up here. You should come sleep with me."

"Hush, Pie," I snapped. "Can't you see I'm thinking—"

"Oh, what now?" she asked, her voice ghostly from coughing, and from the grief she was carrying upstairs and down.

It never occurred to me to ask for my sister's help. The wonder had gone out of Pie, and I knew if I had any worry left in me, I should worry about her.

"Off to bed with you, Pie," I said, dismissing her with a wave.

I was trying to think of how to punish Tan—*if* I had to punish him. I considered the welts on Tan's back, and thought of my own from the dread boar-bristle brush, and I knew that would never be my way. But I didn't know what was my way. I didn't want to be Tan's boss, and the world was burning and I was afraid.

I decided to count the money. Tan and I were alike in that we trusted money and believed in its power, believed it was something worth desiring, akin to love. Money, I thought I understood. As Tan understood it.

But that girl I'd been just a few days ago, with her childish wants and beliefs, had abandoned me. She was as scarce as what money used to buy: houses and hats and chickens and wine.

I trusted there were answers in those pennies and nickels, a world entire, if only I could find it. The take for one day in Tan's kitchen amounted to six dollars—what would be some several hundred dollars today. If we made that every day, we'd be sitting high, but I already suspected that the outdoor kitchen was a temporary fix. Already folks were looking to rebuild their shacks and houses, and everyone was short on cash. The money Tan made might be enough to replenish our store of beans and flour and sugar, if we could get it, and to repair the holes in the house—the windows, the witch's cap—but not enough to buy a horse or see us through the summer. It wouldn't be enough should Rose turn up injured. Or, worse and unfathomable, if we never found her.

But how could I live with a thief I couldn't trust? And what would I do if Tan were to go away?

I was only a girl, so tired. I undressed, hung my soot-filled clothes over the banister in the hall to air out, and put on my one nightgown. I curled in a ball on the cot and tried to quiet my mind. Rogue lay beside me, warming me. I stared into the dark room for hours. At last, the word I fixed on was *fairness.* I didn't know exactly what it meant, having seen precious little of it in the world, but it came to me that maybe it was the opposite of Rose's *Show the devil the devil and he'll say, How d' do.*

Just before dawn, I ran downstairs, rapped on the basement door, and waited till I heard Tan's slow creep, the swish of his silk slippers as he climbed the raw wood stairs.

He opened the door tentatively, and, oh, what a sad sight he was. Hair hanging to his waist unbraided and stringy, his sleeping garb ripped. He looked as if he were about to face the executioner.

I didn't give him a moment to think otherwise.

"Look," I said, speaking quickly before I lost my nerve. "I'm not anyone's police. That's the first thing. Second, I'm bound to make the repairs, buy supplies, and there's no telling for how many months we'll have to feed ourselves, including you three, without running water or heat. There's no telling if or when Rose will show up." I gasped, having forgotten to breathe. Pulling the blanket I'd thrown over my shoulders tighter, I pushed on, "So, here's the deal: for now, we run the kitchen, and anything else we can think of to make some cash, and off the top we need to set aside seventy-five cents for every dollar, for expenses and repairs. Anything left we split . . . fifty-fifty. I may choose to throw my share back into the kitty, but you do what you like with yours. No more thieving, Tan. Fifty-fifty, fair square."

I paused so he'd feel it. I paused to catch up with the idea myself. The truth was, I didn't know what I would propose till the words spilled from my mouth. I wasn't sure if what I had said was right. But having offered the deal, I would stick to it. Watching Tan's expression, his brows lifting skyward, I knew at least I'd hit the target: he was shocked.

Between us, we had a hundred reasons to distrust, even hate, each other. Yet with everything turned on its side, the hate between Tan and me made us more alike than not. The hate between us was a kind of respect too.

"Partners," he declared, puffing his bony chest with pride. He jutted his chin and dared me to take it back.

I offered my hand. When I noticed it was clammy, I wiped it on my blanket and offered it again.

How was it possible that Tan's hand was smaller than mine? The skin on his palm was as cracked and dry as the shell of a crab.

"Good," he said.

"Good," I echoed, then added, "A couple more things we need to get straight." The ideas came quickly now, as if a part of me had been preparing for this day, my mind and heart fully awake. "Tan, you can't call me *gurrl.* I won't have it. And it doesn't do you any good, not with these fancy neighbors. From now on, call me Vera. Let me hear you say it."

"Vee."

"No, damn you. Only Pie calls me V."

"Missy V," he offered.

I thought about it for a second and decided that was good enough. "All right, next—" I paused, expecting him to snarl, to say, What now, *gurrl*?

"We have to find her, Tan. We can't wait for the fire to die out. Just think if she's badly hurt. Tomorrow, you and I will head downtown and check the area around The Rose." I told him what the mayor had said, about the temporary hospital near there.

"Point is, we have to start somewhere," I said. "With so many wounded, it may take days to find her. And even then—" I paused, my voice cracking. "Lifang and LowNaa can take over the kitchen for a bit, yes?"

"Nah." He shook his head.

"What?" I spat. "You don't care about finding her?"

He stared at me oddly. I can only describe his expression in terms of what it wasn't: not the usual grimace, or anger, or disgust. Tan looked, well, he looked sad, his hands curled into empty cups at his sides. It was a gesture so unlike him, it stopped me.

He waited till I understood. He couldn't go with me. It wasn't safe for Tan to be anywhere outside the protection of Rose's house, and certainly not by the piers, where they'd consider him an escapee and lock him in the Chinese encampment.

The fact that he wasn't able to go with me shamed Tan. It shamed me too.

I found myself apologizing for the unfair state of things. "It's all right," I said. "We'll figure another way."

I meant it, though I suppose I sagged a bit at the prospect of having to go alone.

We said our good nights with a simple nod. As I walked away, I looked back to find him watching me.

"Tan? Do you think the fire will—"

"Sleep now, Missy V," he said. "Tan will watch."

Before dawn, the fire stopped. As Abe Ruef foretold, it stopped when it decided to—having destroyed twenty-eight thousand buildings and five hundred city blocks.

The fire stopped at Franklin Street, a block from Rose's house.

Then, as Tan predicted, it rained. The rain amplified the gloom and stink. With so much soot in the air, it rained *black.* Tar poured from the sky, soiling the white army tents inside the encampments and the linen roof of Tan's outdoor kitchen. It rained black on the hillsides of Marin and Oakland, and in Napa and Palo Alto. And it rained black through the busted windows of Rose's parlor, staining her fine carpet.

The mansions on Nob Hill had been reduced to steaming piles of rubble. Already looters were at work picking the piles clean. The city, hill and flat, block after block, looked plowed, as if the tall buildings had been rows of corn or wheat—plowed then torched, with only the stalks remaining. People sat smoking on the steps of their charred houses, as if waiting for the parade to go by.

During the night, a thousand young soldiers disembarked from the navy boats at the piers. They patrolled the streets in search of criminals, and anyone discovered looting was executed and left where they fell—at least for now. Farther south, Stanford University was in ruins, and in San Jose, a hundred inmates and staff at the state insane asylum were buried alive. With no building to house the survivors, the remaining staff tied the patients to trees.

Around Lafayette Square a new kind of normalcy was setting in. After the rains passed, boys played dice in the street outside Rose's house. With the tent encampment now fully established, councils had formed to handle lawlessness and complaints. Ladies with diamonds and Limoges china resigned themselves to living next to squatters who'd escaped the fires without a pot or a blanket. My city was ashes, yet along the periphery of the square, you could buy the services of barbers and laundries, waffle makers, cobblers for your broken boots, farriers for your horses, a tinker to knock the dents out of your quake-battered pots.

On that first fireless morning, a young couple was caught having sex in the bushes of Lafayette Square. They were taken to the temporary Hall of Justice by two of Funston's soldiers. A slew of babies would be born nine months hence—for the rest of their lives they'd be known as quake babies.

I woke late on that fourth morning. From the warm nest of my cot, I could hear those dice-playing boys, four stories down, laughing in the street.

I didn't want to move. I knew I had to find her and I had to be quick, but would I find her in time? And if I did, which Rose would I encounter? The truth is I didn't want to go. No, that's not right: I didn't want to go *alone.*

My attic room was unheated, the floor icy. I scurried to the hall to fetch my clothes. Outside my door, Tan had left a tray with a bowl of oatmeal and a pot of tea. Tan, my new partner.

Next to the tray, my skirt and coat, formerly caked with ash, had been brushed and folded. For a bit of armor or maybe luck—I decided it was both—Tan had gifted me Rose's straw boater. The hat was too big for my head, but tipped low in front, it hid my eyes. As I set out to find Rose, I had to trust that the part that showed me most vulnerable, no one could see.

PART THREE

Bobby

I was barely fifteen yet ancient. As old in some respects as I would ever be. I'd witnessed the temblor's roar, and the city burning. I'd lost one mother and maybe a second. At night, my dreams were of bright-eyed hookers and velvet-lined vaults of cash, and a longing I couldn't name. The world, having been unmade, was being made new again.

In that gold house, Pie, Tan, Lifang, why, even LowNaa had to make it new. I think of us, our lives, their savor and spark, and all the ways we never could resist the three blind kings of want, stupidity, and brashness. The heart leaps, the head conjures, the soul yearns. Desire being the one renewable fuel we have on earth, here is how we burned.

Which brings me to Bobby. He's the one I've got my eye on.

You can't always know in the moment who will leave a mark on your heart. This one or that one.

Bobby.

I met him on that first clear day, after the fires.

I'd intended to strike out directly for downtown, but Pie's coughing had kept her up all night and she was desperate for a bottle of Dill's tonic to help her sleep. I took fifty cents from the previous day's haul and hurried to the square.

I was cutting across the grass when I spotted him. I assumed he was just another street kid, a tough, or possibly the worst in my estimation: an orphan. The piers were full of these scrappy, rough-mannered, cocky boys, walking tall but with zilch under their caps; they roamed the piers at night, swinging their slightly bent arms, their chins jutting forward, like orangutans.

He was surrounded by a group of kids from the encampment, their grimy hands outstretched, beseeching him for sweets.

My first thought when I saw him? Oh no.

I didn't like anything about this boy, not the wide smile, the casual friendliness, the rock candy, no doubt stolen, he was handing out to the kids. He had a girl's long lashes and green eyes, framed by a tough boy's mop, his uncombed hair flopping over his ears. He was handing a piece of rock candy to a little girl and she was looking up at her mother to see if it was all right. I decided I'd never trust him or the candy.

I sailed by him and headed for the far end of the square, where an apothecary had set up a temporary shop. I bought the tonic, slid it into my bag, then headed for the house, taking a different route, toward the grove of trees up top—so as not to run into that boy.

"Did you lose something?" he called.

I turned around slowly, knowing what a sight I must have made: hat low, mouth grim, arms pumping as I marched—with *him* following close behind.

Mortified, I tried to think of a snappy reply. I even tried to do a quick Invisible; I stared above his head into the trees. And who should I find there, in the crown of branches, singing with his newfound cronies? That's right, Ricky.

"Him," I said, pointing. The birds, there were scores of them—blackbirds, sparrows, varied thrushes, starlings—feathered in browns and blacks. Then there was Ricky—fatter by half and a brilliant green.

To impress this boy whom I'd already decided I didn't like, I pulled from my pocket the orange I'd grabbed on the way out—the last of the fruit in Rose's kitchen. Unpeeling it quickly, I took a bite, nipped another piece in half, and placed it on my palm.

"He eats oranges?"

"Watch." I hoped to hell Ricky wouldn't disappoint me. Sure enough, the flap-flap of wings, as Mr. Flyaway landed on my arm, strutted a few paces down my wrist, and attached his claws around my finger. He pecked at the orange, cocking his head this way and that, at the boy and me.

"Well, now I've seen everything," he said.

"Everything?"

His hands were stuffed into his pockets and he was grinning at me.

"I saw you, the other day, in the relief line," he said. "Was that your sister? She's pretty."

"Too pretty for you."

He laughed. "What's your name anyway?"

"Anyway," I said, being a smart-ass. "I saw you just now, giving candy to those kids."

"Want some? I've got two bits left." He showed his palm.

"I don't need candy."

He smiled. "What do you need, Anyway?"

I was shocked by his boldness. "I have to go," I said, taking a step back.

He crouched a bit, to see what I looked like under my hat. "Where are you going?"

I wasn't about to tell him that I was headed downtown. On the other hand, I didn't want to be without an answer. Tan had reminded me that if I were to find Rose in one of the hospitals, we'd need a cart and a horse to bring her home. So, I said what was true and also something I was sure never in a hundred years of Sundays this boy would possess.

I pushed back my rim and showed him my eyes. "I need a horse. Have you got one of those in your pocket?"

"In fact, I do."

"Do not."

He shrugged. "Come on, I'll show you."

"Come where?"

He glanced at me with a seriousness I liked even less than his smile, as if he were worried about me—for me. "You living in the tents?"

"That's right," I lied. "You?"

"Down the road a ways," he said. "Name's Bobby Del Monte. And, hey, if you won't tell me your name, I'll be stuck calling you Anyway, and that would be stupid."

I nodded. "Where's your horse?"

We walked to the opposite edge of the park, with him leading and Ricky riding on my shoulder.

Now, as to Bobby Del Monte's horse. I don't know how many hands he was—nineteen, maybe more—but imagine a house of a horse. A Percheron, he must have weighed two thousand pounds. Black as soot with a blaze on his nose and a shaggy fore-lock that covered his eyes. He had massive hooves. In another life, in France, perhaps, he would have been called into battle or he might have hauled logs or worked on a farm, but as it was, he had a swayback and was riddled with scars that spoke of years of hard labor. As we approached, a second boy—he was as shaggy as the horse—was brushing his tail with a lady's comb. It was ridiculous, except it wasn't.

"That's your horse? Where'd you get him, the circus?"

"Not exactly."

"You stole him."

"No, miss, I saved Monster."

"Monster! That's what you call him?"

When Bobby Del Monte laughed, he gave his whole self to it, closing his pretty eyes. "What would you call him? He's Monster, all right."

I took another look at the other boy. Something was off about him. He kept grinding his jaw, saying nothing, sneaking sideways glances at me.

"Does Monster come with a wagon?"

"No wagon," he said. "I suppose I could get one for the right price."

I thought a minute. "How much for Monster and a wagon to collect someone, say . . . by the piers? He would be taking me along to pick up this other passenger."

"Monster is a one-passenger horse," Bobby said, but I could tell he was working on changing his mind. "Ten dollars."

"Ten dollars! Are you a robber, or just a bum?"

"Bum," he said, laughing. "My friend William here is the robber." He glanced at the boy, who was staring at the dirt.

I lowered my voice. "What's the matter with him?"

"Nothing," Bobby said sharply, as if he'd beat anyone who suggested otherwise. "You got the money or not?"

"I got the money," I said, "but I'm not stupid enough to give it to the likes of you."

Now he was just flat-out mocking me. "Then you'll be a-walkin', Anyway."

I left it there, certain I'd never see Bobby again. Certain and so very uncertain.

With Ricky riding on my shoulder, I returned to the gold house. Since the bird's disappearance, Tan had nailed a couple of boards across the bottom half of the broken parlor window but the top portion remained open.

Pie was waiting for me in the parlor. She'd wrapped herself in the fur blanket on Rose's divan. I handed her the tonic and announced that if Ricky wanted to leave again, we shouldn't try to stop him. To prove it, I put Ricky on top of his cage and left the door open.

"He'll disappear again," Pie warned, wheezing as she twisted the cork and swigged straight from the bottle.

"Good," I said. "Let him come and go."

Pie licked her lips, her cough already subsiding, the relief palpable. "V, did something happen? You look . . . odd."

"What do you mean?"

"Agitated . . . beyond your usual." Pie's voice thickened. Dill's cough medicine was a mix of chloroform and heroin; its effect was instantaneous.

"I'm off to look for Rose, if that's what you mean," I said.

"Careful," she murmured, eyes fluttering closed. "They're . . . shooting people."

The soldiers, she meant. It was all the women in the relief lines buzzed about: the roving packs of desperate men, the looters, murderers, and thieves. In Pie's mind, the quake and fire had cleared the city of good people, leaving only the criminals to rove the streets. Soldiers from the navy had orders to shoot anyone doing anything suspicious, but there were only so many soldiers.

"Would you come with me, and be my protection?" I challenged my sister, who was already asleep. "I didn't think so."

Rogue was waiting for me by the front door. I longed to take him with me. Pulling my rim low, I told him, "Stay, boy. Hope I don't get shot."

Searching for Rose

Rose's street was a hive of activity, but as soon as I crossed Van Ness Avenue, the world changed. How to describe what it looked like, smelled like—the acid burned my throat. Now that the fires were out, folks were eager to see what remained of our city. Women dressed in their finest—or what remained of their finest—with parasols and hats, their men in suits, sidestepped the fissures and piles of bricks and wood and charred bodies of animals lying in the road. I flowed with them—with the tide of tourists out for a Sunday stroll to witness the apocalypse.

On the corner of California Street and Hyde, a grocer, his apron coated with soot, was handing out stale rolls. "One per customer," the grocer barked. When he noticed that I was alone among the adults, he wagged his finger, added a slice of cheese to my roll, and handed it to me on wax paper.

Was I too proud to devour my bread in front of strangers? I was.

I waited till I reached the top of Nob Hill, where I sat on the rubble steps of the burned Huntington mansion, the former grand house of a railroad baron. With all of Nob Hill a ruin, folks were poking among the smoldering piles with their sticks and umbrellas, scavenging for a stray piece of silver or a burned trinket. Minding my business, I devoured that delicious cheese sandwich, which I can still taste.

Nearby, a pair of dogs were nosing a pile, fighting over a bit of charred cake beside a teacup. I let them get their eats, then shooed them. It was the cup I wanted. Forged in the fire, it looked to be made of iron. I put that cup in my bag and went on my way.

It was now almost noon and slow going. First one road was blocked, then another. Bricks and mortar and deep fissures at every step. My body trudged on, my old boots were soon wrecked, the bottoms of my feet blistered and raw.

I didn't make it to The Rose that first day. Or the next. Each time the soldiers turned me back from the streets leading to downtown, where the fire and looting were the worst. I saw soldiers marshaling groups of thieves tied to one another by a rope around their necks, women and children among them. Each thief wore a sign: "I Were Cawt Looting" or "I Stole"—written in a crude hand and flapping on their chests. They were being marched to the temporary Hall of Justice.

Pie was right, it wasn't safe. I had been so determined, I'd forgotten my fear. But the fear was real and more than once I had to pretend to be with other folks, so that I wasn't accosted or worse. At the burned site of Shreve's jewelers, a thief had just been shot. A policeman stood over the body. I thought: That's all right, I've seen it, and now I'm pushing on. I talked to myself a lot in those days.

The world had returned to its prehistoric state, before the Ohlone Indians and Spanish conquistadors, before the sandy hills and craggy reaches were carpeted by redwoods and grass—before Adam, before sin—from born to unborn. Witnessing it so, I wasn't as miserable as I might have been.

Everything I saw felt peculiar and holy, the only holiness I have ever known. And if I say I looked for Rose with a good deal of dread in my heart at what I might find, it was also true that as I journeyed through the wreckage I felt lighter, even joyous. Later I could name it: I was no longer alone in my loneliness.

The one thing I couldn't stand to be—a *hittebarn*, a foundling—no longer mattered. The burden I had been carrying from birth was widespread. Everyone had lost her, I mean our city. The highest of society and the lowest had the same soot on their faces and dust in their teeth.

When at last I reached downtown, heading toward the hospital by the Ferry Building, I realized I was just a couple of blocks from The Rose. I suppose I had to see it: the pile of burned beams, the skeletons of iron beds. The chalked X in the road and beside it the number 7 for bodies recovered. My throat clotted at the thought of Hank, with his buttons and cap. Good ol' Hank.

There was a ring of burned chips and glass lying in the dirt—what remained of the vase of flowers I'd seen by the front door. When I touched the chips with my boot, they dissolved to ash. If Rose was alive, she wasn't there.

I moved on quickly, heading for the water, and was passing a row of abandoned houses that had escaped the fire but been tipped from their foundations by the quake. As I walked by on the opposite side of the street, a man and a boy approached one of the houses and tried the knob on its busted front door. Curious, I stopped to see what they were doing. The man whispered something to the kid, then lifted him through the opening where glass should have been in the double doors.

"Quick now," he barked, and the boy was indeed quick. He returned with two large silver candelabras that he passed through the broken window, gripping them by their necks with his little fists. The man caught them with a bend of his knee and stowed them in a large burlap sack.

The boy raised his arms to be lifted out. "Up," he begged.

The man gave the top of the boy's head a cuffing. "Get back in there," he barked.

I thought I should call for help—someone, a policeman—

but the street was deserted. I thought of shouting, Get outta there! But I wasn't a fool.

I ran to the corner, turned, and kept on going to the far end of the block, where I spotted a couple of soldiers. It seemed in those days there were soldiers everywhere. These particular fellas were waiting on a trio of navy sailors, just off their ship and still toting their duffels. They all converged and there among them was Alma de Bretteville, laughing.

"Hey-ho, look who's here," she called, ever friendly, as if we'd planned to run into each other.

I must have looked frightened. "Burglars," I sputtered, pointing in the direction of the house.

"Boys," Alma said, "quick, go see."

The soldiers ran down the center of the street with Alma and me following close behind. We reached the corner in time to see the boy pass a heavy silver urn through the busted door to the man.

"Hey there," shouted one of the soldiers. "Hey there, you!"

The man turned slowly and offered the soldier a greasy smirk.

"What's your name, fella?"

"Bailey," the man said. "Me and my boy are just securing a few bits from our house. There be thieves all round, don't you know."

"Yeah? Where's your key, Bailey?"

The man fiddled in his pockets. "Ah, must have dropped it. Willy," he called, "Willy-boy. Son, where have you gone with my keys?"

"Hey, Bailey, without turning round, tell us the number of your house," said one of the soldiers. Letting the strap of his rifle slide down his arm, he took the gun in his hands and aimed.

The number was painted in gold above the door: 172.

Bailey grinned, showing a gap where a couple of teeth were missing. "Ah, the number." He scratched his head. "Let me think. Since the quake, I'm shook up, fellas."

As he said this, the boy returned, this time with a fistful of silver forks and knives; in his exuberance, he passed the whole kit up and through, assuming his father was there to catch them. They clattered to the floor of the porch.

The soldier lifted his rifle and aimed. "Tell you what, Bailey, you got two seconds to tell me the number on your house."

That's when Bailey took it in his head to run. He was shot in the street.

Alma seized my hand. "Come, duck, this way." She tugged me and didn't let go till we reached the rocks that bordered the bay.

"Here." Alma handed me a handkerchief; I noticed the monogram A.B.S. sewn on one of the corners. "Go on," she said, "wipe."

Like a child I blew my nose and dried my tears. I had no idea I'd been crying. Alma, giving me privacy, studied the view of the water.

"The boy," I said, "I bet he's still crouching behind that door. What's going to happen to him?"

"Don't worry about the boy," Alma said, and she led me to a flat rock and made me sit beside her. "Those fellas, they'll see he's all right."

"But how?"

Alma got very still—a practice, now that I think on it, she must have developed during hours of posing as an artist's model at the Art Institute. It was a commanding stillness.

"I don't know," she said. "I guess I don't see much point in worrying about what you can't fix." Alma reached into the bag between her feet, popped open the top, and handed me a beer. Then she took another for herself.

"That's it," she said. "Drink."

And I did drink. I drank the whole bottle, then proceeded to burp.

"Look at you, sailor." She laughed. "Good, huh?" She held

the bottle up to the light. "I bought these to bribe those boys in case my charms weren't enough." She shrugged. "Here," she said, "let's split another."

I drank that beer too. It was cool, the temperature of San Francisco, and delicious. It gave me the hiccups.

"Boo!" Alma exclaimed, and when that didn't cure me, she added, "Don't think about them anymore. Think on something else."

"You do that a lot?" I said, hiccupping. "Think about something else?"

She gave me a long serious look. "How do you plan on getting on?"

I shrugged. "You know, everyone on Francisco Street wondered about you. You and your family disappeared."

Alma found that amusing. She went on to tell me how she and her family spent the night in a suite at the Palace, paid for by AB Spreckels. When the Palace took fire the morning of the quake, they made a dash for it, ending up in Golden Gate Park, along with thousands of refugees.

"I figure, while I'm there, I might as well be useful," she said. "I set up a school for the kids. Mostly, I'm teaching them to draw. What we need are desks. And who better to help a girl move some furniture around than a few strong navy boys?" She shrugged. "It's okay, there are more where those came from. And as for that burglar, he deserved it. He absolutely did." She smiled as she took back her handkerchief and slipped it into her sleeve. "Hey, you. Listen. Listen to ol' Alma. Times are tough and they're going to get a whole lot worse, by my reckoning. Girls like us can only afford to be soft in one or two places. All right, pet?"

"Are you always so sure?"

Alma thought about it for exactly a second. "Yes, yes, I am." We both laughed, for we were both just putting it on most of the time, and that was a secret we shared.

"Have you seen Spreckels since the quake?"

"AB?" She hesitated. "We had a row after the opera. I let him know I'm getting impatient." She took a long pull of her beer. "I think I overplayed my hand."

"How long have you two—"

Alma shook her head, so I didn't press it. She reached into her bag for a pack of Murads, lit one, and offered it to me.

"Thanks," I said. I cursed, I drank beer, I smoked—sure I did. I watched Alma to see how it was done.

She took a long drag and held the smoke much longer than I thought humanly possible. She exhaled like a dragon, from the spouts of her mouth and nose.

"Three years," she said. "He won't marry me. He thinks I'm lowbrow."

"Of course he'll marry you. Anyone with eyeballs would marry you."

Alma thought that was very funny. "Let me tell you something, pet. This town can burn to the ground, but the very last weed standing will be some rich matron's sense of the proper social order. And the proper social order will never abide you and me. *Dah-ling*, you don't marry the nudie artists' model, not if you're a Spreckels."

"Then he's an idiot," I said emphatically.

"That's lovely, but no. AB is the best man I've ever met." And she showed me her face, her real face, besotted. "He is as far from a fool as I'm likely to know. Of course," she added, "he's also filthy rich." And we laughed at that too.

"So long as we're making our confessions," Alma said, "how is it you know Rose, pet? I've been curious since I saw you on the arm of ol' Hank."

"I can't tell you," I said, not because I didn't trust her, but because I didn't trust myself enough to consider trusting someone else.

"Oh, I'm sure you can," Alma replied, and took a long drag of her cigarette while she worked out the next scene in the play that was my life. When she finished the cigarette, she tossed it behind her, a gesture both careless and practiced. She was the kind of girl who tossed things over her shoulder yet knew exactly where they landed. I had a lot to learn from her.

"Your mother," she said, thinking aloud, "the dried-up *svenska*, my father used to call her. I'm sorry, it's rude to speak ill of the dead."

"It's okay," I assured her. "Morie called your father the worthless Dane."

We smiled at each other.

Alma puckered her lips. "You look nothing like her. And you aren't like them, spirit-wise either. Pie is a sweet thing," she said. "Standard pretty. You have nothing in common with her."

"I guess I'm the black sheep."

"I don't think so. No." She tapped me on the knee. "Listen, if we're to be friends—let's agree, friends, shall we? I need one friend and I think you'll be it. I can promise you I have no allegiances other than to myself, and I don't fib, unless absolutely necessary, and I don't gossip," she declared. "In fact, I despise gossips. What about you? You're awfully young to have no shoulder to cry on. I mean, other than that dog. By the way, where is he? I don't think I've ever seen you without him."

"He's at the house." I paused. "Rose's house."

"Ah, there, see." She nodded, proud of me. "Are you going to tell me that story, or should I guess? I'm pretty good at guessing . . . and, by the by, you have her nose and hair. Has no one mentioned that? Very straight on, distinctive. If someone were to draw you, they would figure out in a second that you were hers."

"I can assure you, no one's ever drawn me," I said.

"Ah, not yet." With that, Alma finished her beer. "I might, one day. You're not pretty and you have no idea how to dress, but with help you could be . . . hmm . . . striking. That's almost better than pretty, you'll see. Say, are you going to smoke that thing or stare at it? Here." She plucked the cig from me and added it to her pack. Then she stood and arranged her blouse so it hung right, and said, "Okay, another day we'll tell our secrets. Right now I need to find me some sailors. What do you need?"

I pointed to the rows of tents just past the Ferry Building—there must have been two dozen tents with red crosses on their roofs. "I think Rose may be in there. Unless—"

Alma looked toward the hospital and I knew she was deciding if she wanted to help me. "What will you do if you find her?" she asked. "Have you thought of that?"

"Bring her home," I said.

"Home," Alma echoed. "To that hideous place on Lafayette Square?"

"You know the house?"

Alma laughed. "Oh my, you are fresh, aren't you? Vera, this town has a couple of dozen players that make the whole business go—same as everywhere, I expect. Your Rose is one of them. They play like they're your great chum, so long as it serves them. All I'm saying is be careful."

"I'm careful," I said. But I wasn't convincing, even to my own ear.

Alma collected her bag from the grass, the beer bottles inside rattling. "Should you find your Rose, how will you get her up the hill? There are no ambulances to spare, and until the roads get cleared, a car is pretty much worthless. You'll need to hire a horse and wagon," Alma said, figuring as she spoke. "That'll take real cash, not beer. Do you have any money?"

"Some."

"And do you know anybody with a horse?"

"I might." Suddenly, I was confessing what I knew of Bobby.

"Well, look at that." Alma beamed, triumphant.

"What?" I snapped.

Alma squinted, seeing what I didn't want anyone seeing—me. "You know what"—she laughed—"I think I'd better keep an eye on you. I think I better."

We parted then, with me having made my first real friend.

Eda Funston, General Funston's wife, had several thousand wounded on her hands. There were hundreds waiting to be evaluated, and scores of the critical in the triage tents, and hundreds of patients laid on stretchers and cots in the several dozen tents that followed.

"I'm looking for someone," I said.

"Everyone is looking for someone," remarked doe-eyed Eda Funston. Dressed all in white, a pencil balanced behind each ear, she was issuing orders without ever raising her voice. I trusted her immediately. "Who is your someone?" she asked.

When I told her who I was looking for and where she would have been found, Eda Funston's brow arched—not from any feigned delicacy regarding Rose's occupation, oh no, but because that part of town had suffered the quake and fire worst.

"Do you know for certain she's here?"

I had to admit I didn't.

"Well, then, I'm afraid you're going to have to hunt."

She walked me to the first tent filled with patients lying in rows of cots. As Eda Funston moved, a dozen nurses and regular folk trailed behind her, waiting for a word; she ignored them.

"Now, listen," she said, speaking slowly, as if to a not-very-bright child. "Do not disturb these patients by asking questions. Do not bother any of the doctors or nurses. Do not do anything untoward, or you will be asked to leave. These are our wounded and they are my priority. Do we understand?"

"Yes, we do." I smiled, thinking of what the mayor had said, that if Eda Funston had been in charge of the soldiers instead of her husband, the city would not have burned.

"While you're looking," she said, "make yourself useful by passing a bucket of water. Offer a third of a dipper per patient, no more, and—need I say it—don't bother with those who aren't awake." She looked into me, taking a final measure of my character, and smiled. "Good luck," she said, and handed me the bucket.

I went from bed to bed, tent to tent. Most of the patients were unconscious, and I was thankful I didn't have to bother with them. Those who were awake watched me with eyes pricked with pain—burns, mostly, and broken bones. I can see those eyes now. Their limbs and torsos wrapped in gauze—and what wasn't wrapped I wish had been.

It took all afternoon and into the evening. I nearly missed her. She was being moved, and when at last I found her, she was in the tent with the most gravely wounded—with the patients they expected to die.

She was mummified, her face and head wrapped in soiled gauze, her body a swath of stained muslin. Her pearls and diamond rings, gone.

How did I know her? By her nails, chipped though they were. Those painted spears that even in her present state terrified me.

A nurse passing through asked, "She yours?"

I nodded.

The nurse looked at Rose, a body among a sea of hurt. "Between the burns and broken bones," she said, "it's a mercy she's unconscious. The docs do the best they can, but it's a mercy."

"Why haven't her dressings been changed?" I pointed to her blood-soaked bandages. "Look there, and there!" I went on, accusing the poor nurse.

"My word, miss, are you blind? Look around. And more coming every hour. We do the best we can."

That much was obvious. Yet it didn't lessen my belief that Rose should be getting special treatment.

"I'll be by tomorrow to collect her," I said.

"Collect her!" the nurse scoffed. "You're outta your mind. This patient can't be moved. Unless you plan on taking her to the morgue."

A House of a Horse

When I asked in Lafayette Square had anyone seen Bobby Del Monte, one of the scruffy girls who hung around with the roughneck boys told me what had happened. A soldier had tried to enlist Monster to help with clearing the roads. Bobby wouldn't hear of it. He bested the soldier in a fistfight, and now he and Monster were in hiding.

"Where?" I asked.

The girl's mouth twisted as she looked me over. "Come on," and she took off down the hill.

Which is how I came to be running after that slip of a child, her legs scissoring, her blond hair loose and unkempt, flapping behind her like a wing.

Over her shoulder, she shouted, "Girlie, can't you go faster?"

She was no young lady; I was no young lady either. I couldn't stop grinning as I ran faster and faster.

We zinged along what was later called Cathedral Hill, a barren place where the houses gave way to fences and fields. In the middle of a large field loomed the dreaded Ladies' Protection and Relief Society, a Gothic stone box of a building, six stories tall. Commonly called the Children's Home, it was known to be a wretched place filled with unwashed, unwanted children in rags and castoffs, the boys and girls quartered on separate floors, and all the work of the farm done by these orphans, some as young as two or three. They tended the cows and chickens and horses;

scoured the laundry of a hundred souls; cooked the grim, gray porridge.

The Children's Home had been a favorite subject of Morie's threats—if I did another thing to cross her, I would be sent packing to the house of the *hittebarn*, the foundlings. Morie delighted in describing the home's disgusting porridge. The children got whipped, she said, if they didn't lick their bowls clean.

But this girl couldn't wait to get to the home. As we rounded the fence, following the brick walk that led to the stone ruin, she skipped even faster. The tiled roof had collapsed onto itself like an inverted triangle; the tall, arched windows were missing their panes. The front door had been knocked from its hinges. It leaned into the space where it previously hung, with only a narrow gap, barely wide enough for a skinny girl to slip through.

We entered a great room with a vaulted ceiling and a Spanish tiled floor. The windows on all sides were broken, with a steady breeze passing through. Yet the sun was shining, and fat, yellow rays poured through the arches and spread their warmth across the floor. The younger kids were playing hopscotch in the sunbeams.

When I was small, my greatest fear was that I would one day end up an orphan, an urchin of the street, a ragamuffin, a ward of the Children's Home. I imagined myself assigned to a narrow cot, ten to a row, ten rows to a room, one of a hundred kids eating porridge, that was the hollow inside me. When I started reading the novels in Lars Johnson's library, I shunned the orphan tomes. I couldn't bear to walk the road with Oliver Twist or Tom Sawyer, those books my own children would one day fiercely love. I could never stomach the Cinderellas or the Little Matchstick Girls. They cut me, those little lost souls.

But here were the real orphans—babies and toddlers and kids perhaps as old as twelve—playing tag or scrubbing laundry in buckets or sharing the open tiled floor with chickens and a pig and even a cow. In a far corner, Monster was chomping hay from a basket.

The kids had been shouting rambunctiously when we came in, but once they perceived a stranger was among them, they dropped to the floor and played dead. Twenty, thirty kids lying on the floor, their heads crooked in contortions of deadness.

I laughed. I thought it must be a game, and that I should be *it*. Ha-ha-ha, I laughed. But no, these children weren't playing. The boy lying nearest my boot, why, his heart was thumping madly, his eyes squeezed shut, as if he weren't dead but in dire pain.

Only the babies, three souls in a crib, their faces fixed with the quietude of orphans who don't expect folks to answer their needs, dared to look at me. They sucked their fists and steadied their unblinking eyes on my face.

I stared at that boy—I stared hard—till he opened one eye.

"You can't come in, miss," he whispered. "Bobby says no one must come in."

"Where is Bobby?"

The boy slapped his eyes with his palms, shutting out the world and me.

I jiggled his boot. "Bobby," I said. "I need to talk to him."

"He's out, miss," said a girl, one of the older orphans. She had two golden braids wound atop her head. Climbing to her feet, she brushed herself off and called, "Okay! Everyone up." And stepping over a girl who was stretching as if just awakened, she added, "Bobby's out getting supplies."

"Why didn't he take Monster?" I asked, intent on proving I wasn't a stranger.

"Faster on foot," she said. "Bobby's in and out before they know what's missing."

She was no more a woman than I was, yet she was dressed like a crone, with ripped stockings and worn heels. She was holding a feather, dancing it along her cheek, and I thought, I bet she's Bobby's girlfriend.

"I could take a message," she said, as if she were a secretary in a fancy office. Around her, the children, rising to their feet, watched us with a feral intensity.

"Tell him Anyway came by," I said, and smiled. "He'll know. Tell him: he can find me in the gold house on Gough Street, across from the square."

Bobby Del Monte had those orphans to care for and I was determined not to be another girl asking for his favors. When he showed up at Rose's door, he was grinning, as if glad to see me.

I made tough, hands on my hips. His smile faded.

"Okay," he said. "I'm here. You got the ten dollars?"

"Ten dollars," I scoffed. "We back to that?"

"'Course you'd have to show me you've got it. Monster isn't big on credit."

"I'll show you when you complete the delivery."

He laughed. "Go on." He peered behind me, at the naked marble goddesses posing on either side of the foyer. "Whose place is this?"

"Have you ever heard of The Rose?"

He shrugged—the first person in my new life who hadn't heard of her.

"She's an important lady and her people would be most grateful if you brought her home safely," I said.

"You her people?"

"Sure." I felt the color rise in my cheeks.

One thing about Bobby: he was never impressed by anything or anyone he couldn't see or touch. "The piers, eh?" he said.

"That's right."

Bobby nodded, seeing it in his mind. "That's a way, there and back. Coming this way, there's a hard hill for Monster to climb. That's a killer hill."

"That's a hill worth the price of . . ." I paused. I knew we couldn't afford to part with ten dollars. Reluctantly, I showed him my pearls, where they sat on my collarbone, just under my blouse. "These pearls are worth better than twenty-five dollars," I said.

"And you're going to hand them over, Anyway?"

"Uh-huh," I lied.

Bobby shook his head. "I'd like to see that," he said. "Tomorrow, then."

He borrowed a wagon from the Ladies' Protection and attached Monster to the rig. Then, with Tan's help, they took a ladder from Rose's garage, padded it with quilts, and loaded that in the wagon to use as a stretcher.

I insisted on going with him, though the ride nearly undid me. The hills of the city were impossibly steep, and with the roads split in places, we had to zigzag for blocks.

Bobby had thought to bring along his pal William to help lift Rose into the wagon. William rode in back, and every so often Bobby looked over his shoulder and asked, "How ya doin' back there, buddy? All good?" I expect William nodded, though he never said a word.

I kept my eyes on the road. When Bobby noticed that I clung to the little iron rail of the bench each time the wagon lurched over a bump, my knee and hip knocking against his hip and knee, he said, "Here, put an arm around." He was struggling to work Monster's reins, or I expect he would have grabbed me to keep me safe. When I balked, he replied, "You wanna fall and break your head, be my guest."

"I'm not falling," I said, and I put my arm around.

I had never so much as touched a boy. His ribs under my hand, his warmth, were a marvel to me. I had to struggle to keep my mind on where we were going. And I swore that if Bobby Del Monte so much as looked at me funny, I'd sock him.

At last the street leveled when we neared the water. We drove along the piers till we arrived at the hospital. With scores of wounded lying in the grass and in the road, no one paid the slightest notice as Bobby pulled up by the last tent of some twenty tents, and he and William slid the ladder under a flap in the bottom of the tent.

As we came in, a doctor, having just finished his rounds, was walking away, giving instructions to a nurse. I was glad to see that Rose had been wrapped in fresh bandages, and with no other nurses about, I snitched several rolls of cotton from a pile while those two scruffy boys made a quick business of lifting Rose, sheets and all.

Watching them jostle her into the wagon—well, I was convinced they'd drop her. I said as much.

"You sure know how to beat the drum, doncha," Bobby said.

"I'll do worse, if you—" But he gave me such a stony look, I stopped myself from saying more.

And good that I shut my mouth, for they got her up the killer hills and into the house, on up the stairs to her bedroom. Bobby took over then, settling her gently on the bed, and ever so carefully covering her broken body with the good sheets of the house. I suspected he wasn't a skunk after all. His pants may have been patched, but they were clean; his nails short and scrubbed.

"Talk to you a second, miss?" he said when we were back downstairs. "I don't mean to nose into your business."

"Then don't," I suggested quietly, knowing that Tan, Lifang, and Pie were listening on the other side of the kitchen door.

"She needs a nurse," Bobby said.

"I'm a nurse."

"'Cause at the hospital, I heard the doc say—"

I sighed dramatically. "For godsakes, can you talk any faster?"

"I could, if a person were pleasanter."

"I'm pleasant. I'm pleasant!"

"Goddamn," Bobby said. "Well, take this for nothing: That eye of hers? The one all bandaged? It needs to come out. There's an infection brewing, see, where the bones are broke underneath. I heard the doc say it. He said they don't expect she'll make it, so they let the eye stay put."

I didn't want to hear it. "Is that all?" I said, nudging him toward the door.

"You don't exactly strike me as the tendering type," he added, "nothing on it, miss, just saying—"

"You don't know me."

"Nope, I don't."

"Nope, you don't." I held the front door open so that he and his friend could move along.

Bobby studied the coved ceiling in the foyer, and the chandelier that held a thousand crystal stars. I guessed he was figuring how it was with me and Rose.

"If I had a relation with this kind of fancy rig, I'd call her Ma and get on with it."

"Thanks, but I didn't ask for your opinion," I said.

He looked at me as if I were a tune he couldn't quite recall. "Vera, huh? That's your name? I don't think so. I think I'll have to call you . . . Versus. It's a good word, isn't it, William? *Versus.* Means opposite."

"Ver-sus-sus," William parroted, missing the joke but comprehending the slight at my expense.

Inside the parlor, Ricky was also listening and the damn bird chirped, "Versus, versus!"

Now Bobby was laughing. "Well, Versus, time to settle accounts." He held his cap scrunched in his fist, and I could see that the lining was all torn.

This next part, I had prepared for: I handed him a sock stuffed with pennies and dimes that I had stowed ahead of time behind one of the statues by the door. "It's almost all there," I said. When he paused, I quickly added, "Tell you what. I'll throw in a bottle. Here. You drink whiskey, don't you, sailor?"

Bobby wagged his head, as if he'd heard something terrible about me and had refused to believe it, but now must. "Oh, now, would you look at that," he said. "We made a deal and I know Monster, William, and me, we honored our end. Those pearls, they gotta be worth twenty-five dollars, you said."

"What's a boy like you going to do with girlie pearls?" I replied, my voice thick with scorn. "Or are they for your girlfriend?"

Bobby Del Monte studied his scrunched, ratty cap and held still. There's a kind of person who slows the clock. Who holds too still. Bobby. He hovered at Rose's door, deciding what to do about me.

"Oh, fine," I said, and stomped my foot like a petulant child. Grunting and huffing, I reached for the clasp at the back of my neck.

"Don't," he said, and he took my empty hand and returned it to my side.

"Crikey," I blurted. "Guess you want a kiss."

"No." He laughed. "No, ma'am."

"What, then?"

He considered the question. This boy, he moved so slowly. "Just this morning, I was saying to William here, manners are what makes the world go. Good manners," he said. "Now, you've said thank you, not really putting your heart in it. That's a fact. Second fact: those pearls. You'd rather trade a dozen socks full o' dimes than see me walk outta here with that necklace, I get that. Now, my side? I did notice on the way in, you've got a couple of stalls out back. Monster, he needs a place where soldiers won't be nosing. They want to use that horse up. I won't let them. So, here's the deal and it's a fair one: I'd stay out of your way. I'm up at dawn, helping with the orphans and earning some scratch elsewhere doing odd jobs. I don't come home till after dark. I feed myself. We could call it even, two months' rent, for returning Miss Rose to the nurse of her dreams. Two months and the bottle," he said, picking it up from where I'd set it on the floor. "That, and a first-class thank-you. I'll take that too."

"You mean, you'd live in the stall alongside the horse?"

"I've stayed in worse," he said. "In the stall next to him will be fine."

I was surprised, delighted, but wasn't about to show it. "I'll need a few days to talk it over with my people."

"Your people?" he asked, looking over my shoulder. "Where are they?"

"Come back in a few days and I'll give you my answer."

"I'll be back at the end of the week," Bobby said. "But first, don't you have something to say to me?"

I smiled. "Thank you."

"You're welcome, Anyway."

The minute the door closed, Pie burst from the kitchen to tell me it was a god-awful idea to allow a boy—an orphan from nowhere—to stay with us.

But Tan nodded to let me know he was fine with the idea. He'd put his eye on that big horse.

Rose in the House

I'd scrubbed and settled her room. Beaten the rugs and pillows, washed the windows with vinegar. Where the panes were missing, I patched the gaps with paper. Her pink bathroom shone with my fervor; her drawers of silk corsets and stockings were tidy with sachets of lavender. There was no extra water or clean linens or cut flowers, yet Rose had all of these things—I made certain of it. The bed changed, clean cotton dressings for her burns. I handled it all. Pie and Tan stayed back—on my strict orders. Much as she longed to, Lifang didn't dare set foot on the second floor.

All was ready. All except me.

First off, I bathed her. I filled a basin with my day's water ration and sponged the dried blood from her scalp, her face swollen and purple, the nose pressed to one side, the landscape of cuts and bruises. I changed the dressings on her burns. I was careful, careful as I could be. When she groaned, low, cattle-like, I froze, fearing I'd harmed her worse. I saw all her parts, and all those parts I bathed, as if she were my baby. I cleaned her down there, where she was dark, almost purple. I thought: I'm purple there too. All the mystery that made me, made me dark like her.

I wound the Victrola and played it hour upon hour, happy tunes, for a celebrant who never woke.

Tan arranged for a Dr. Howell to set her arm and leg in plaster-of-paris casts. The doctor had been a regular at The Rose.

He came the next day, and each morning that followed, to work off what must have been a considerable debt.

The blow to her eye was serious but she had other injuries. Here and here, Howell showed me, where timbers from the roof had crushed her leg and arm and face. There was swelling on the brain and the swelling needed to lessen before he could remove the eye, which, without the gauze, bulged from the swollen socket.

Dr. Howell gave her less than a twenty-five percent chance.

"Please," I whispered, never finishing the sentence. Please don't die.

Those first days I did whatever was needed. But I didn't sleep in the same room with her. I had my cot in the attic, and for a few hours each night, I fell into a bottomless hole. As if I were the one dying.

I woke with Rogue behind me, asleep against my knees, and a view of the Singer sewing machine. Black, with a walnut case. Its narrow bench seat held boxes of buttons and another box of loose needles, pins, and bobbins. Its wrought-iron foot pedal was shaped like a fleur-de-lis. Its underbelly was a world of black covered wires and gears. Every cord and gear and bobbin played an essential role. I thought: That machine is me.

When Rose awakened, if she did, I decided I'd write my name underneath the Singer, where no one would ever see. I'd write: Vera.

I was just a girl. A scrawny, sharp-tongued girl. When I wasn't fretting over the money we didn't have and couldn't get, or fighting a silent war of wills with Lifang, who hated working in the outdoor kitchen and wanted credit for saving the madam should she awaken, I held my claim and hovered close to Rose.

But a house, even a fine one, can become a crude cave if neglected. Rattle any shelter, be it a hut or a castle, shake it to its core, then strip its innards of water, heat, electricity; smash the windows and bury the horse, and you'll see: the winds begin to howl.

One afternoon, a couple of days after I brought Rose home, I went down to eat whatever Tan had put aside for me, and he presented me with the day's list of problems. We talked them through, deciding what we could afford to fix or buy, and what of the many urgencies would have to wait. Then Tan lowered his voice and said, "Lifang, let her help you." His gaze lifted to the ceiling, to Rose.

I thought: What a devoted parent Tan was, he'd do anything for his girl. It touched a place in me that was raw and desperate to have such love.

I shook my head. "Tan, make sure Lifang understands. No."

As Tan and I talked in the kitchen, Pie drifted in, listless in her grief, her coughs and wheezing painful to my ear.

"Oh, you're back," she said. "Is Rose better?"

"No, she isn't *better*," I snapped. In losing both Morie and James, Pie had lost the thread of not just her story but any story, including mine.

In the relief lines, the women accorded Pie a kind of respect granted to the most serious of the grieving.

"Why do they look at me that way?" Pie asked. "Everyone has lost someone or something."

"You wear your grief on your face," I said, noting the barb in my voice.

"But I have no face," she insisted. "I have nobody and no face." It was true. Pie's pretty face had been replaced by a pale mask.

I was awed and irritated by Pie's grief. When I heard her in the night weeping for Morie, something in me condemned her. Saw her as feeble. The way she moved in those early days, listless as a sloth, as if she had all the time in the world to be sad—well, it irked me; her sniffles and coughs made me feel as if someone were plucking the hairs from the back of my head. How could I indulge her feelings, when I didn't allow them in myself?

I said, "Everyone in town is suffering the same as you, Pie—only on the inside."

At the end of that first week with Rose in the house, Pie knocked on the bedroom door.

"There's that boy downstairs," she said. "He says he's come for your answer."

"Stop pestering me, Pie," I snapped. "And eat."

In those days, women of means were nearly always stout—in the bosom and bottom. The fashions amplified the body's padding. On that score, it was lucky Rose was solid. Curvy, not fat, though she did love to eat and drink. On any given morning before the quake, Tan prepared her a breakfast of fried eggs, hominy, rolls, bacon, and pancakes with jam, and a fruit compote of grapefruit or oranges or berries. Hot chocolate. At night, if she was dining at home, Rose consumed a multicourse meal of fish or oysters, steak or chops, with potatoes mashed or plain.

She was unconscious for nearly two weeks, with nothing going into her but a saline-and-brandy drip attached to a rubber tube that the doctor inserted in her bum, and a catheter for urine, which he taught me to change.

Each morning Dr. Howell arrived to poke and prod her, and to bark orders at me, before hastily departing, with dire predictions and a growl. In all, there were tens of thousands wounded in the city, and if he didn't owe Rose big—for services I could only imagine—he wouldn't have troubled himself with a daily house call.

Later, I realized he was ill, his face narrow and sharp as a wolf's, his eyes ringed with exhaustion. The enormity of the collapse he carried with him; he was beyond appeal. I didn't try.

In his bag he had bottles and syringes and metal instruments and cotton bandages and snakes of rubber tubing. Every time he lifted his bag, he grunted, with a pain that harbored in his hip and ran along his right arm. He scolded me, and rubbed there, wincing. Watching him grimace, I imagined all the bodies he witnessed in a day—all the death and near-death, the pus and rot.

The doctor and I irritated each other—that was our bond.

When I refused to leave while he examined Rose, he rolled his eyes. When I made him tell me what he saw—what news of the infection in her eye, was it any better?—he grunted.

"Patience, miss," he barked.

He suspected I was one of her girls, and he spoke with his eyes addressing my chest or, worse, my crotch.

He said, "Your madam, she's not likely to wake, and what then for you girls?"

"She is not my madam, and I am not one of her girls," I replied.

Rose murmured when he removed the bandage over her eye. Her mouth opened and shut. I asked him what it meant.

He grimaced as he inspected her eye, then shifted that savage look onto me. "I'd like to know: What is this arrangement you all have?"

"What does our arrangement have to do with her eye?"

"Say I'm curious. Say she dies. Who's in charge here?"

"That's not why you're asking," I snarled. "You want a bit of gossip, a little lace and thrill."

He laughed. "Not likely," he said, and sighed. "We all have our secrets, miss. Meantime, this eye needs to come out. I don't have a nurse to spare." He paused. "So, are you brave, or just impertinent?"

"Impertinent and brave," I said.

"Ha! That'll have to do. We'll operate tomorrow." He gave Rose more morphine, this time dribbling a spoonful in her mouth and, seeing that she could swallow, he left me with the bottle. "Every four hours," he said. "And if she'll take it, give her some broth too. Not much, mind you. Couple of spoonfuls."

On his way out, I offered him a glass of whiskey. Rose stocked the finest whiskey. As I poured his drink, I was thinking that even in an apocalypse, for the privileged few, whiskey and pretty parlors and top-drawer service never cease.

"Tell me, miss," he asked, "are you religious? Seems all the folks in this godforsaken town are suddenly, fervently religious."

"I don't put stock in anything I haven't seen," I declared.

"And even then?" He was laughing with me now. He poured himself another glass and held it up to the lit lamp. "I've been an Episcopalian my whole life, but I feel these days we are very much on our own."

There was such a haunted look about him. I hoped I wouldn't have to hear his confession.

"Odd, this house," he mused. "It's a far cry from her other place." When he saw that line of talk made me uncomfortable, he hesitated. "Ah, you'll forgive me if I'm crude. You don't need to worry so much. The tough nuts like your lady upstairs tend to rebound. They built this city, you know: the miners and the Roses."

He drained his glass and set it on the mantel. "I have seen things these last weeks that would make Dickens weep. I fear our city has lost its soul." He shrugged. "Perhaps it never had one."

He sighed and something rattled in his throat. He was too tired to cough. "I wouldn't bet on much these days, but I think I'd bet on you, miss. Tomorrow, then," he said, and he put on his hat and coat and reached for the door. "Boil water. As much as you can spare. We'll need clean sheets and towels."

That evening in the square, we traded pots and china plates for extra water, which we set to boil in the morning, awaiting the doctor's arrival.

He didn't come, not that day or the next. Or the next.

Pie offered to walk downtown and check for him at the hospital, but no one had seen Dr. Howell in days, and there wasn't another doctor who could be spared.

I accused Pie of not pushing hard enough.

"I did push. I was rude like you," she said.

Rose burned with fever. Her arms became mottled. Still, her heart beat. While my heart boomed with every twitch. I feared that now that I was with her—now that she was mine—she was going to die.

In the kitchen, they caucused—Pie, Tan, LowNaa, even Lifang. They decided that we had to return Rose to the hospital. They were haggling over who should be the one to convince me.

I wouldn't hear of it. Instead I grabbed my coat.

Dr. Sugarman was at supper; he answered the door with crumbs in his beard. When I told him what I needed, he went to a closet and rummaged for his leather doctor bag. It was dusty from lack of use.

On the way back to Rose's house, I asked him if a psychiatrist ever did this sort of thing. "No, my dear," he said, "not since school." In medical school in Vienna, he had been a colleague of Freud's, his practice being the psyche, the soul, he explained; he hadn't tended to the bodies of patients in many years.

Sugarman was winded climbing Rose's stairs. He washed his hands in the basin beside the bed. As he tugged at the bandage covering her eye, his hands shook. He stepped back and bowed his head.

"Dr. Sugarman?"

He didn't answer me.

Finally, he said, "Vera, I think some whiskey."

He drank a glass and said, "You too, dear."

We covered the bedclothes with sheets, then sterilized the instruments in Sugarman's bag with whiskey. Again Sugarman bowed his head and mumbled in Hungarian and Yiddish a mix of hexes and blessings and sighs. He gave Rose a shot of morphine. With no further ceremony, he used a clamp to hold the lid in place, though it took him several tries. There was nothing to clamp onto, the bones in the socket were shattered.

He stepped back, rejiggered, tried again, admonishing himself and God.

"Vera, here," he said. "Hold like so."

There was a stink to the infection, and it made me sick in my stomach, but what could I do? I did. Sugarman held the lower lid with his finger. Grunting, he seized the scalpel, lifted the eye from the muscles surrounding it, and cut the ball at its root. The eye dropped, missed the bowl, and rolled onto the sheet, settling in the crook of Rose's arm. Sugarman pinched the ball with his fingers and put it in the bowl and set that on the bedside table.

I couldn't look but I looked anyway. The eye resembled a hard-boiled egg with a raw red knot attached to one end. At the other end, a fixed stare.

Sugarman peered through his wire spectacles, bending close to inspect Rose's face. Next, he scraped the pus in the socket with a tiny spoon. His fingers shook on approach; his fingers had white hairs on the knuckles. He bathed the cavity with yet more whiskey.

When I saw the thread and needle, I asked, "Really? That's how you do it?"

"That's how you do it," he said.

He stitched the seam and wrapped her head with a roll of cotton that Howell had left behind.

Where Sugarman stitched, the seam would eventually look like a crudely knit purse, but even so, I was grateful to him. When he finished, once again he bowed his head. I waited with him.

He glanced at me, and I asked, "Are you praying for her?"

"No, my friend," he said, "not her. You." He put his hand on my shoulder and squeezed.

The Ramble

Sugarman came by the next morning to check on Rose.

"How can I help you, dear?" he asked.

I didn't understand the question. He'd done more than anyone. I told him so, and said that I was grateful. I added, "Dr. Sugarman, I'm fine."

He said, "Vera, you are not fine." And he gave a great Sugarman sigh. "As to Rose, I should think we'll know anytime."

She faded in and out—two more days. I stayed with her, rubbing witch hazel into her hands and feet. She woke briefly, rolled her battered face in my direction, and said, "Hurry." Before I could answer, she drifted away.

Pie shook me as I dozed in the chair. "V, Bobby's waiting."

"How do you know his name?"

"They've been by, Bobby and Monster, every day. Sometimes twice a day," she said. "You have to give him an answer."

"Tell him I don't care."

"I can't tell him that." Pie twisted her hands nervously. She couldn't hide the hint of a smile.

"What, he's your friend now?"

"I think we ought to let him stay," she said with emphasis. "Tan agrees."

"Does he, now?"

"Yes."

"You've changed your mind."

"Yes," she admitted, "now that I've seen him a bit."

"All right," I said.

"That's it: All right?" Pie sighed with relief. "Good. I'll tell him." Pie paused before adding, "V? When was the last time you put a comb to your hair? You look a fright." She didn't mean it unkindly. "I could sit awhile," she went on. "I'd wake you the minute—"

"Go on, Pie. Tell your boyfriend he can sleep with the horse."

That night—always nighttime for the madam—when she woke, I managed to dribble half a cup of soup into her. When it was obvious that she was in pain, I gave her some spoonfuls of morphine.

"What happened," she asked.

I told her about the quake and the fire. Then I told her about Morie and the house on Francisco Street, and Tan with his curbside kitchen, and the city, all but disappeared. Speaking it, it seemed impossible that so much had transpired on the first day of the quake, and all the days since.

Her one good eye remained closed; the other, of course, was bandaged. She was so still, I was certain she'd fallen asleep.

"What happened," she said.

I thought: Ah, she wants to hear what happened to *her*. So, I told her of The Rose and how I'd found her in the tent of the dying.

"Vera," she said, "is that you?"

Those next few days, I stayed with her. The morphine, it turned out, loosened Rose's tongue. And if I gave her a little extra, so that she'd answer some of my questions, well, so be it. My hunger was vast.

For hours, she rambled, saying things she would never say—things no virgin should hear. Things like: the duke *came down*, they all came down—a woman's privates she called turkey wattles; penises were sticks or things.

Despite her delirium, Rose remained duty-bound, a working girl checking her lists. She sighed and fussed over the pending orders of crab and beef and shrimp—who would receive them? And the weekly deliveries of liquor; the silk stockings and robes, potions and creams, the mountain of laundered sheets and towels. There were the sheepskin condoms to order, the diaphragms made of vulcanized rubber; the house-made douche they called salad dressing, a mixture of lemon, lavender, and white vinegar.

Rose talked of her clients, their names, their predilections, their wives. But always she circled back to the duke and money, her two great loves.

It was my job to follow her through the bramble, and if every so often she winced, I gave her another spoonful of the morphine, chased by a dribble of tea.

From what I could stitch together, Rose and the duke had started sleeping together as a professional arrangement in their youth. When they were no longer young, they became lovers, confidants, investors, friends. Rose had seen the duke through four wives and seven children, five of whom survived. It seemed the duke had a baby in every port. Early on, she'd taught him to apply powder to his face to hide the pocks, and she'd seen to the deflowering of the young duke, the older duke's son. That the duke loved both men and women didn't seem to bother Rose; up, down, in/out, sex was sex that Rose provided.

The duke had a particular yen for sailors and rough boys who worked in the stockyards. Across the years, it seemed, Rose had made a handsome profit catering to her friend's appetites.

But what of my mother's heart? I wondered. What of her heart?

That night of Caruso, she and the duke left the opera and rode through the streets, the city as shiny and great as it had ever been. When they arrived at The Rose, the duke made a strange and rare request: he wondered if he might see some of the back rooms where the girls lived in their off-hours. Experiences, that was the key, my madam mother always said: you give the client what they cannot get elsewhere, and you have them in your pocket. Well, what the duke was asking for, Rose didn't want to give, any more than a magician wants to show the shitty cage where the rabbit-in-the-hat sleeps. She never allowed clients to see where they kept the makeup and menstrual rags; the toothbrushes and hair crimps.

But the duke was special and it had been a grand night.

She showed him the pink-tiled bath, its rows of tubs and toilets, its cubbies—one per worker, where they stored their towels, potions, and pumice stones. Overhead, the laundry lines were festooned with the whores' just-washed stockings and bloomers.

The duke ran his hands along the women's drying underthings, their filmy flags of nirvana.

"Rosie, Rosie," he said, titillated, as she knew he would be.

Two flights up, they made their way to her private rooms. There the duke asked his old friend if, on this most celebratory night, she'd permit him. For old times, eh, Rosie?

Pshaw. She confessed that she hadn't allowed a man in years. Even so, it was a special night.

Afterward they dined on what was known, in the parlance of The Rose, as the Full-Barrel: courses of beef, fish, poussin, and potato caviar, champagne and strawberry roulade.

It was nearly three o'clock in the morning when the duke suggested that they continue on to his suite at the Palace. But Rose's pride prevented her from entering a hotel on a man's arm—on this night, a fateful error, to be sure. Likewise, she made it a point never to spend the night at The Rose. A restorative nap now and then, all right, but only while seated in the red chair, or on the divan where they'd been frolicking—then fully clothed, heels peeking over the edge, hands folded across her tummy.

She sent the duke on his way. The champagne and rich food and pleasure had made her delightfully sleepy. She thought she'd take just a short nap. Hank was nearby, and with The Rose wired with a series of buzzers and bells, all she had to do was press a button and he would bring the motor around to ferry her home. The last thing she remembered was closing her eyes.

At some point, I fell asleep in the chair beside her. When I woke, she was looking at me with her one good eye. "I heard you, with the doc," she said. She touched the bandage that covered her eye. "Did he do this to me?"

"No, that was Dr. Sugarman."

"Sugarman? The Hungarian philosopher next door? Good Christ."

"He's a doctor, a psychiatrist. Trained in Vienna. He damn well saved your life."

"Crikey, bet he butchered me. Fetch a mirror, will you?"

"Uh-uh."

"No? What's this no?"

The wound beneath the bandage looked hideous; I'd seen it that morning when Sugarman came by to check. Bruised and seeping and ugly. Lifang's Chinese dumplings were more finely sewn than Rose's eye.

"I insist. Go on, fetch me."

"Fetch it yourself," I said dryly.

"Who do you suppose you are, lady of the manor?" she sniped.

"That's right. Catheter changer and lady of the manor." I stood to show I could just as soon leave.

Rose sighed. "And you're living here now?"

"Upstairs."

"Ah, the front room?"

"No, up top. The sewing room."

"With the maids? Dear God."

"The maids are gone," I said. And once again I told her of the quake and the fire, though she resisted believing me. I told her again about Morie.

"Ah, too bad, the ol' girl," Rose said. "How is Pie taking it?"

I paused. "Not very well, I'm afraid. James, you remember James?"

She hesitated and I had the sense she was ranging across the fields of her past, my life with the Swedes being a small patch in the corner.

"James," I repeated.

She grunted. "Buttons and bobs."

"That's right." I could tell by the way her good eye twitched that she was in some pain. I gave her more morphine, and when the folds of her face relaxed, I told her what had happened with James.

"Coward," she mumbled. "We . . . we had a bad feeling about him, didn't we?"

I thought my heart would burst, hearing her say *we.*

"Good riddance," she added.

"Yes, but Pie, she isn't all right—" I paused, for I didn't know what else to say.

"Losing two loves in one blow is hard," Rose filled in. "Have you taken care of her?"

"No," I admitted. "I've been full up with you."

Nodding, she looked at her hands. "Where are my pearls? My pretty rings? How . . . did you know it was me?"

"I knew you." I pointed to her nails.

She grabbed hold of my hand as if she didn't want to let go. "Here," she said, her body relaxing as the drug took her for a ride. Her hand twitched in mine and I held on tight. I wasn't scared, and I wasn't in awe of her anymore, though I didn't yet know what I was.

She woke with a start. "Hank?" she called. "Hank?"

I told her that we guessed Hank was the one to dig her out of the wreckage before the fire started. Then, we supposed, he went back in to save the other girls. They couldn't identify his body; they never would. Hank's name would never appear on the *Call*'s list.

The official estimate was several hundred dead, but everyone in the square agreed there were thousands more, burned beyond identification or never found at all.

Rose's one good eye tick-tocked. I sensed she was siding with the notion that things weren't half as bad as I was putting on.

I let her think so. I had lived the catastrophe, was living it now, but Rose, she was only a tourist. I didn't care to explain too much, not to a disbeliever, not if it made those days small. I have felt that way all these years. There's a privilege of having witnessed the wrath of the gods.

"Tan's here," I said. "He's all right." I left off the part about Tan and me becoming partners.

"You . . . still worried about him stealing?"

"I'm worried about everything," I admitted, "but not so much that. He's a thief, all right," I said with a smile.

She studied me with her good eye. "You're older," she declared.

I nodded. I was older at the very least.

Rose leaned back into the pillows and I sensed she was getting tired. Or maybe she just didn't want to hear any more. As I stood to leave, she moaned.

I gave her another spoonful of morphine.

"Where are—" she murmured, her voice high-pitched and breathy inside the drug dream, her voice almost girlish. "Where are my . . . babies? Valentine? Mercy?" She was counting her darlings like beads on her missing strands of pearls, and if I hoped that at last I'd be one of them, my hopes were quickly dashed. "Where," she asked, "where is . . . my . . . Lifang?"

• • •

Rogue, sweet Rogue, greeted me as if I'd just returned from a long trip. All those days, he'd been waiting, guarding Rose's door. I fell to my knees, wrapped my arms around his thick neck, and buried my nose in his fur. He smelled of the fire.

"What are we going to do, eh, boy?" I whispered.

Did I expect that she would thank me? That she would hug me close, her long-lost daughter? Swallow as I might, I couldn't dislodge the stone of heartache in my throat.

Rogue nudged me with his nose.

We went downstairs. In my absence, a quiet rhythm had settled over the house. In the parlor, Ricky sang from his new favorite perch on the mantel. Pie and LowNaa were playing cards at the table by the broken bay windows. A cool afternoon breeze flowed into the room unimpeded. Pie had wrapped herself in one of Rose's furs, while LowNaa had a crocheted blanket draped across his shoulders. The flap-flap of the cards, mixed with Ricky's incessant chirps, made a kind of music. I looked on without them noticing me.

They were playing Beggar My Neighbor, one of Morie's favorite games. When Pie lost the next hand, she cursed LowNaa in Swedish, calling him in a lilting, tender voice a *din jävla skit,* or devilish shit boot.

LowNaa grinned as he replied in Cantonese. Back and forth they spoke, in tongues neither understood.

"*Va' fan?*" I called to my sister. What the hell.

"There you are!" she cried. "How long have you been standing there? Is she awake?"

I could only nod, the exhaustion hitting me all at once.

"V?"

"Mmm."

"Rose . . . is she talking?" Pie turned, giving me her full attention, while LowNaa dealt the next hand.

"Yeah," I said, "she's talking."

"Is she . . . herself? I mean, does she know what's happened? Did you tell her about Morie?"

I sighed. "I told her everything, but I doubt she'll remember."

Pie nodded. "You should get some sleep." She squinted at me and I understood without her having to tell me again that I looked ragged.

I went to the kitchen to get some tea. Lifang was there, eavesdropping, of course; when she saw me, she turned, squatted on her heels, and attacked one of the many dirty pots scattered on the floor.

"Who's that on the roof?" I asked. For days there had been persistent tapping.

"Bobby," Lifang said. Bobby was fixing the hole left by the witch's cap, and when he finished each day he was hungry—very, very hungry, she explained accusingly. Which meant more pots for her father to cook with and for Lifang to clean.

Lifang went on scrubbing a soup pot, its sides so deep, she had to use her whole arm to reach its bottom. She'd scour it using a rag and only a few scant drops of water. She'd work till it sparkled, her every movement a mixture of rage and pride—a tiny, complete revolution.

The one thing Lifang couldn't control was her desire for something better than pots. As she scrubbed, her gaze kept turning to the ceiling—to Rose.

Lifang had stayed back those first weeks, letting me be the one to change Rose's soiled bandages and catheter. Lifang let me trick myself into thinking Rose was mine.

But Rose was never mine and Lifang had only been waiting. How badly she wanted to ask about Rose, but wouldn't; she wouldn't allow me the satisfaction of knowing more than she did. Now that Rose was conscious, she would have no qualms about using Rose's convalescence as a way to escape the tedium of her father's kitchen.

As proof, on the table, she'd put up a tray with a fresh lace cloth napkin and a bud vase of flowers and a steeping bowl of broth. Floating at the top of the soup were little shavings of ginger and green onion.

"That for her?" I asked. "Too bad. She's asleep."

Lifang glanced at the ceiling and shrugged. But I understood. Desire was our common language. She would wait for as long as it took, until she had tithed herself to the madam.

A shiver ran through me as I imagined her upstairs, snuggling with Rose, or polishing her nails—all the girlie things I couldn't bring myself to do. Lifang would tell Rose what she thought she ought to know—the version of things that showed her in the best light, of course. She'd tell Rose how hard she'd been working, while Pie and I lazed. She'd claim that she, Tan, and LowNaa were the only ones keeping the wolf from the door.

Oh, my father is so tired, she'd say. I am so tired too, scrubbing and cleaning, day and night. Of course, I am not as lovely as I used to be.

Don't be silly, my darling, Rose would assure her. You are as lovely as ever.

I saw it in my mind's eye and in my mind it had already happened.

I paused with my hand on the back door. How curious I felt, how strange. Competing with Lifang for the madam's attention wasn't as compelling to me as it was on the afternoon we met, when the two of us foolishly pressed our claims with Rose. Could it really have been only a month earlier?

I had waited for Rose, longed for her, tended to her. Now, it seemed, I might be ready to let her go. That surprised me too.

"Lifang, your grandfather. Does he understand what Pie is saying?"

Lifang answered with a stern shake of the head.

"That's a relief," I said. "And what does he say to her?"

"My grandfather, he is sick of being alive," Lifang declared, tossing her rag on the floor as she climbed to her feet. "He says your sister cheats at cards. He says, 'The skinny Swede talks dirty with a hungry, cheater's mouth.'"

Lifang crossed her arms and glared, letting me know she considered herself my equal—perhaps better than my equal.

Now it was my turn to shrug. I didn't care a fig who was up or down. I had never thought of Lifang as less. In all the ways that mattered to me, she was richer. Her father and grandfather looked out for her, sacrificed for her, adored her. Yet she was greedy and wanted more. Did I blame her for wanting to take Rose for herself? I did.

"What are you staring at, bug-bug?" she griped. Mocking me, she grabbed two fistfuls of her silky hair and held them above her head, imitating the knotted mess of my bun.

I swung past her, seized that delicious bowl of soup in two hands, and gulped it down. I wiped my mouth with the perfect napkin, and set the bowl on the floor next to the piles of pots. "Here," I said. "One more for you."

It was a gorgeous day, clear and blue. Monster stretched his enormous head over the top of General's Dutch door, taking in the sun. Bobby Del Monte was five stories up, banging on the roof. With Rogue leading the way, I hurried across the street, and as I went, I pulled the pins from my hair and combed it with my fingers, letting it fall every which way, down my back.

I hoped Bobby or the neighbors hadn't seen me. I decided I didn't care.

Rogue tore up the hill past the rows of tents. There were some five hundred people now living in Lafayette Square. I ran after Rogue and didn't stop till we reached the uppermost hill of the park, where the trees clustered in a ring. I sat with my back against a large boulder and had a good, cleansing weep. Then I fell asleep.

When I opened my eyes, Bobby was standing a few paces from me, holding an orange in his hand.

"I figured I might need this," he said, grinning. He'd peeled the orange and fanned it in slices in his palm, the way I did when I lured Ricky from the trees.

"Where did you get that?" I asked. Fruit was impossible to find in the city.

"The madam's car," he replied, stepping closer. "There was a bag of them, hidden under the seat. I snitched a few."

"Those must have been for Rose to take downtown." I smiled, thinking of Hank and our evening ride to Caruso, a world ago.

"There's also a shotgun under the seat," Bobby said as he sat near me in the dirt and smiled sweetly. "Should I have brought that? You look like you might need to shoot someone."

I shrugged and popped a piece of orange in my mouth, not knowing what else to do. The boy unnerved me.

"Go on," he said, "have the whole thing."

"Guess this makes me a bird," I mumbled between bites.

"I think maybe you are. What kind, I can't figure yet. What kind are those?" He pointed to the high branches.

"There? That's a kinglet. On the branch next door, those are white-crowned sparrows. A couple of chickadees in that tree over there. See that crow? He stays at the top. No one wants to get too close to him." I kept pointing out more birds, but Bobby had his eyes fixed on me.

"I still don't see any of your kind," he said. Then, before I could stop him, he brushed back the hair that was blowing in my face and put it behind me. "See. Their feathers aren't as long as yours."

I didn't know what to say. I was so flustered. I didn't know if he was mocking or flirting with me.

"Why . . . why are you here, Bobby Del Monte?"

"To see you home, Anyway."

He let me be. That's all. We didn't say much; didn't need to. He let me be. Eventually, we made our way across the hill to the north side and took in the view of the bay. There were plenty of boats going by, and seagulls cawing, and the Marin Hills in the distance just beginning to turn golden with the onset of summer. As we gazed at the water, our backs to the encampment, the world looked almost the way it used to.

We stayed all afternoon on the top of Lafayette Square, till the wind picked up and shivered through the rows of canvas tents like a thousand flapping wings.

The Women

I sometimes wondered what it would have been like to be raised a normal girl, with no mention of brothels or folks who preferred it Frenchie, no talk of payola and crooked politicians. But that was not my story.

The women began arriving that next week, just as Rose knew they would. It was as if a call had gone out, announcing that the madam was now receiving at her gold house. They arrived hungry, broke, with just their first names—their professional names. They came with their hair curled and waxed, and their nails clean. Once inside, they filled the house with their sweet cloying perfume and the distinct insouciance of the high-end whore.

Capability was the first. She carried all her possessions in a small suitcase: an umbrella, four pairs of shoes, and a metal rod she heated on the stove to curl her hair.

"Oh, baby girl," she cried, clapping with the tips of her fingers like a happy child. Cap—that's what her familiars called her—smelled of the cinnamon and vanilla she dabbed each morning behind her ears.

"How are ya doin'?" she cooed. "I remember you so, when you were just a sweet, wee little thing. And when I saw you again, stopping by the other day, well—" When Cap smiled, the space on the left side of her mouth showed, where a drunk once hit her and knocked out two teeth. "Honey, whereabout is Ma'am Rose?"

Valentine arrived next. She offered her hand, her meaty palm twice the size of mine. "I'm Valentine," she said, in her slightly formal, silk-smooth bass. "Madam Rose," she added, "never talked much about you. Oh, she talked about a lotta girls, sure-sure, but not you. I think prob-o-bly she was saving you for herself, eh, sugar? Tell me, is she receiving?"

Mercy tried to sneak by me with a kitten in her basket. Out front, Tan paused over his boiling pots to see what I would do.

"No cats," I said. "House rules. No men, no cats."

Mercy wrinkled her nose and wobbled a bit in her high shoes on the narrow front steps. "Exactly how firm is this no-cat law? I mean, how much wiggle we got, honey—for a little bitty kitten?"

"No wiggle," I said.

She peered into the basket with besotted devotion, same way I looked at Rogue.

An hour later, Mercy returned from the square with two bottles of wine in her basket. "Found him a good home," she said.

That first day, Cap, Valentine, and Mercy took over the two rooms next door to me on the top floor.

I liked them instantly. And if I didn't think to ask Rose if it was all right if they stayed, I also didn't ask Pie. That's how much had changed.

Tan, of course, had an opinion, but the women were careful to lavish him with praise, as if he were their funny, taciturn uncle. They told him how much they'd missed his Sunday dinners at The Rose.

I went upstairs to tend to Rose, and when I came down Sophia had arrived. She was the oldest, trained in the burlesque shows in Paris. She didn't bother with the front door but came around back, meeting Bobby first.

So it was Bobby who announced we had another boarder.

"Listen to me," he said—always like that, his voice like velvet. He was the only person who could tell me to listen and I would. "There's plenty of room in the stable. I could make room."

"You mean you want to be with her," I said.

He chuckled. "Watch it now, Versus."

I thought about it for exactly a second. "She can sleep in the attic with the rest of us."

And that was that. Capability, Mercy, Valentine, and Sophia settled in the rooms next to mine; they hung their corsets and bloomers from the attic beams. At night, there were games and readings and songs in the parlor.

The women had come to Rose but were in no hurry to *see* her.

"That young man. Bobby. Is he your fella?" Mercy asked.

"God no," I said.

They paid nothing, slept till noon, and awoke famished. Once they took up residence in the gold house, they didn't bother to dress and instead lounged all day in their silk dressing gowns.

One afternoon in the kitchen, they were peeling potatoes—always piles of potatoes that Tan bartered for on the black market. Mercy had her feet propped on a chair and was begging Valentine to fetch her a bowl.

"Get it yourself, baby."

"Aw, can't you see my bunions are hurting?"

"Aw, can't you see I'm beau-ti-ful?"

They all laughed.

I couldn't stop staring at them. I couldn't stop staring at Valentine. She wore white gloves except when she was cooking, her hair waxed and pinned tall in shiny curls; she wore a pair of red satin slippers that a customer had made especially for her, she said, with a wedge sewn inside to save her arches.

When I asked Capability what it was about Valentine, Capability shrugged. "Darlin', I guess you could say she was just born with the wrong hat on."

"The wrong hat?"

"Oh, you know."

But I didn't know. Valentine called everyone honey, and from the first day she called me Honey V.

Seeing me stare, Capability snapped her fingers in front of my eyes. "Now, baby, why don't you come sit between my knees, and let's fix your hair for that nice boy."

"There is no boy," I insisted.

"Oh, right, I forgot." Capability laughed sweetly.

"I'm serious," I said.

"Serious, darlin', is this rat's nest on your head." Cap pulled a comb from where she kept it hidden in the nape of her hair and got to work on me.

There was so much laughter that even when it was at my expense, I couldn't see the harm. Their laughter washed over me. The women talked and sighed and exclaimed. They forgave themselves and all of humankind for its folly. The one thing they could not forgive was violence or abuse, of which they'd each had their share. Mostly, those early days, they marveled to find themselves on hiatus, for the first time in their lives. They hadn't just escaped the fires; the catastrophe had landed them in a gold palace.

Each had a story of how she'd made it through. Capability had been visiting a private customer at his home on Russian Hill. They'd hunkered down in the man's basement and waited out the fires, until Cap couldn't stand holding still anymore.

Mercy had been visiting an aunt in Santa Rosa; the quake leveled the town. It took weeks for her to make her way back.

Valentine was walking down Market Street when the quake struck. She witnessed a dazed Caruso standing in the road outside the Palace Hotel; he was dressed in his bathrobe, his valet hustling to carry down Caruso's many trunks.

"Let me tell you," Valentine said, "Caruso was terrified. *Ell of a place! Ell of a place!* he kept on saying. I told him, 'And you, Caruso, are an *ell of a singer*!'"

"You did not!" Mercy batted Valentine's shoulder.

"Honey, were you there? Were you?"

As luck would have it, the night of the quake, Sophia had the evening off. She was in North Beach visiting her sister, who'd married an Italian. Sophia helped them save their house. For the three days that the fire threatened North Beach, they soaked burlap sacks in the homemade Chianti they kept in the cellar and spread the wine-soaked sacks across the roof, just like their neighbors. They managed to save that part of town.

But after the fire was out? Sophia's sister let her know she wasn't welcome anymore. Her sister had young children and she didn't want them damaged.

"Damaged! What, did she think you'd give her children the pox?" Valentine asked.

"Something like." Sophia pouted.

They all agreed they were lucky to have been away from The Rose. The fire swept that part of town first. But there were others—Frankie, Bess, Sally, I can't recall all the names—who hadn't escaped. Neither, of course, did Hank.

"Damn shame," Mercy said.

"Quelle horreur," added Sophia, who always used French when making a point.

They were quiet then, shelling peas and peeling potatoes while Cap finished combing the snarls from my hair.

"Oh-oh, did I mention? I saw Jubee," Mercy said. "She's got herself a little thing of a baby."

"Aw, what's his name?" Capability asked.

Mercy's whole face lit up. "Tellem."

"Tellem? What kind of name is that?"

"Tellem when you see him, he's a father!" Mercy sang.

Oh, they laughed, even if the joke was as old as a worn penny. They slapped the table, slapped each other's knees; Cap nudged my shoulder to let me know I was now one of the gang.

Then Cap set aside her comb and worked her fingers through my hair, massaging my head and neck and shoulders. "That's it," she said. "Close your peepers and make dreamy."

I did just that, there on the floor of the kitchen, with Cap's knees holding me snug and her strong, knowing hands working the knots out of me.

"At last, at last," Valentine said. "Capability, you could pour love into that child from Sunday to Christmas and it wouldn't be done."

"Shush your mouth and let her be," Cap replied. She dabbed her finger to the inside of her wrist, where she kept a patch of Lucky Brown Pressing Oil, and set to work making sense of my newly combed hair. Coiling the strands around her finger, she fixed each section in a modest-hooker do, while I kept my eyes closed and the talk swirled around me. Idle talk, it seemed, that touched everywhere but the one place where it was required to go—upstairs.

At last Valentine said quietly, "We can't put it off into forever. We gotta go up, pay our respects."

When they talked of Rose, they pointed at the ceiling.

"Honey V?" Valentine mused. "Has she, you know, inquired after us?"

They turned as one, with the faces of scared, naughty children. "Not directly," I said.

"Well, then, maybe we don't need to be in such a lather," Mercy suggested. Nods and murmurs and the room fell quiet.

I decided to ask them about the duke.

"The duke! Oh my," Cap hooted. "Baby, we don't talk about the duke."

"Ferme la bouche," Sophia burst, slapping the table with her hand. "*Ferme* that door."

"Why?" I pressed. "Was he trouble? Did he come often?"

"Not often *e-nough,*" Valentine declared. "Honey, let me put it this way: when the duke showed his ugly face, Madam was all bells and giggles. We loved us some duke." Valentine looked round the table and chuckled. "'Course, we all *did* love us some duke, didn't we, now."

They laughed and slapped knees again.

"Say, what's that chittering? Listen." Capability cupped her hand over her ear. "Hear that?"

They cocked their heads and listened to the strange noises coming from the room above.

"Lifang," I grumbled. "That's her laughing. She's always with Rose now."

"So, she's taken with Tan's little girl?" Cap asked. "That little slip of a thing?"

It took all afternoon for them to get ready to see Rose. They had to paint their faces and prettify their hair and nails. Then they had to try on their best dresses, which they decided didn't look right in the mirror. Then they had to eat, so they wouldn't feel faint. Then they had to finish themselves with a dousing of toilet water.

When at last Capability knocked on Rose's bedroom door, it was nearly suppertime.

"Come," shouted Rose.

Lifang was sitting cross-legged on the bed next to Rose, her lap full of scarves; she was using little scissors to cut them into head wraps and matching eye patches.

The women filed in, like schoolgirls at inspection, to stand in a row at the foot of the bed. I lingered by the door to see what would happen.

They were actresses, all of them, but they couldn't hide their *horreur* at the change in their madam. Rose had been convalescing in the house for two, maybe three weeks. Lifang had done her best to cover Rose's wounded head with a turban fashioned from a silk shawl. She'd removed Rose's stitches too, with those sharp little scissors, and applied a foul-smelling medicated oil to Rose's wounds—my God, the stink in that room. With the lamp lit, Rose's skin shimmered with a greasy glow.

Even so, there was only so much Lifang could do. Where the eye and cheekbone had been crushed there was a pocket. Rose's lips, tweaked and stiffened, hardly moved when she talked. Then, of course, there was the fact of the missing eye. Below the sheets, Rose's fractured leg required her to be constantly, painfully turned.

"*Ça va bien,* Rose?" Sophia ventured. As the senior girl, she was allowed to use Rose's name, so long as she did it in French and not very often.

"That patch looks nice," Valentine said.

"*Très chouette,*" Sophia replied.

Rose looked them over. "I wondered when you all would decide to show your faces. And here you are."

"Here we be," Capability echoed. "You gettin' on okay?"

"Ah, girls, as bad as this looks, it's worse below. I can't walk," Rose said. "I'm all crooked down there."

"Shame, shame," they murmured. "Ma'am, what can we do?"

"Nothing, babies," Rose said. "Nothing to do. Lifang's taking good care of me."

That stung. Cap met my gaze and nodded knowingly. The rest of them fixed their eyes on Lifang's rapid scissors and the little bowl of nuts she had beside her, which she sucked on, one at a time.

"I heard it was Hank who saved you, ma'am," Cap said. "But Vera was the one to get you home. What a fine girl she's turned out, ma'am. She does you proud."

"Hmm," Rose said. "Where is she?"

I stepped away from the door, so her good eye could find me.

"How you getting on?" she asked. "Taking it easy?"

"Easy!" Cap exclaimed. "Why, Vera's running the joint, ma'am, runnin', tradin', cleanin', fixin', solving every-which-way worry—"

"Mother Rose, you want your soup now," Lifang said in a too-sweet, baby voice. She set aside her scissors and helped Rose to some broth.

"Ah, girls," Rose said after a bit of fuss with a napkin and some spill on the silk coverlet. "I don't remember anything about the quake, or the fire, or how I got to this bed. I don't remember."

"Well, I do," Valentine said. "Let's see. You came back straight on after Caruso. You and the Duke, all blush. He asked you to give him a tour—remember that, ma'am? He was pushing, that's what, for the private show. I heard him pestering you and you said, 'Val, what am I going to do with this man?' And I said, 'Ma'am Rose, there's only one thing a gal can do with a duke.' And we all laughed. 'Member? 'Course, it would take more than the duke to set you back on your heels."

"Thank you, Valentine," Rose declared. "I think that's enough of a walk down history lane."

Now it was Mercy's turn to speak her mind. She started out slowly, sweetly, "Ma'am Rose? I know you're ill and all, but have you . . . we were wondering . . . you thinking you might rebuild?"

Rose sighed. "You girls are welcome to stay on till you get your footing and I get mine. But when I say nix, it's nix. All right?"

Nervously, they picked at their cuticles.

"All right?"

Each nodded. And with that, they were dismissed.

"Vera," Rose said, "why don't you stay."

Cap was the last one out; she brushed my hand and closed the door.

"I see Capability has been doing your hair," Rose said. Lifang tittered into her cupped hand. Rose touched Lifang's knee to silence her. "That's all right," she said. "Just tell her next time, *less.*" Rose cleared her throat. "How are you getting on?"

"Fine. I'm fine."

"That's a lotta mouths to feed. Including that boy you got out back." As she spoke, Rose glanced at Lifang; just as I expected, she'd been filling her in on all the doings in the house.

Rose examined the state of her fingernails. "So, what are you thinking? These are my best girls. You've got the goods under one roof, maybe you think you could start a little business of your own."

"Me? God no!" I cried. "They . . . they had no place to go. There's nothing but burned houses between here and The Rose. Tell her." I waved at Lifang. "Tell her how bad it is."

Biting her lips, Lifang picked up her scissors and ripped a seam.

Rose shook her head. "If it's a charity you're running, let me tell you something: where those birds flock, men follow. One way or another, those girls are going to be doing the one thing they know how to do. So, I'll ask you again, what's your plan?"

"I have no plan," I admitted.

"That's what I was afraid of," she said. "Where there's no plan, time has a way of making its own arrangements." She leaned against her pillow and her turban tipped to one side. "All right, then. Go on. Send up Tan, will you?"

"Why do you need Tan?"

"Why? I don't believe I need a why," she declared. "I need him to fetch something for me downtown."

"What do you need fetched?"

Rose considered what, of her endless list of secrets, she was willing to share with me. "The safe at The Rose," she said. "It was meant to be fireproof. We'd better dig it up and see what's left, before someone else finds it."

"I'll take care of it," I said, and my heart skipped at the thought that the cash inside the safe might save us. I had a half basket of potatoes and eleven mouths to feed; the last of the chickens had gone under Tan's cleaver two nights earlier. But in her room, there was toast and tea and flowers—and Lifang.

"You'll handle it?" she asked, her mind trying to run ahead of me. "Ah, the boy out back. You'll send the boy and his horse."

"Yes."

The one eye tick-tocked. "Tan will need to go too."

Lifang looked up. "But, Rosie, it's not safe for Father," she whispered. "A Chinese cannot go downtown."

"It's safe enough," Rose replied. "Folks on the street know Tan. He may need to vouch for me, should there be questions."

Lifang thought to protest but decided against it. Instead, she tore the hem on one of Rose's fine silk dresses.

"Anything else?" I asked.

"Lifang," Rose said, "go on, now. Go help with supper and have some yourself."

Lifang sighed. It was in fact the opposite of a sigh—not a lessening of tension, but a gathering, a combustible storm of all the things Lifang could not do. She dropped her scissors in the drawer beside the bed and slapped the drawer closed. After she left, the room was so full of her silent protests, for a moment we didn't move.

"Come here, you," Rose said at last, and patted the bed beside her. I stayed where I was, perched on the edge.

"You know, I'm only blind in one eye," she said.

"What does that mean?"

"It means I see you."

"And I see you." Trying to make my voice sound reasonable, I added, "Why do you like her more?"

"Not more," she corrected, pointing her finger. "Easier. I can't explain better than that. It's easier."

I nodded, not because I wanted to agree, but because I couldn't deny it. Easier would never be me and Rose.

"She soothes you," I said, trying it on.

"Why, yes. That's it," she agreed. "Lifang has a way of soothing my mind."

"Don't you ever miss . . . having, you know, family?"

"Never," she declared.

"But," I started saying.

"What? What but?"

"You kept a box of my baby things. When I was putting your room to rights, I found it."

She rubbed her hand across the quilted silk coverlet. "Those dresses . . . I had them made special. With good lace in them. For you," she added, and she turned her hand over to show me her empty palm.

I said, "I want a family. Sometime." And I was seized with a longing so deep and wide, it took my breath.

"Then you shall have it." Her hand closed into a fist. "I hope you do."

"But not with you."

She shook her head. "I have no talent for it. That kind of feeling I don't ever recall. I felt responsible for you, but that's all. I suppose I'm more like a man that way." Rose chewed her lip, trying it on. "Hmm. The madam is a hard nut, eh, Vera?"

"I don't think so," I said. "I think the madam is used to hiding out."

"Ha!" She snorted. "Well, with this face, I suppose I should. You know, when I was a little girl in Mexico City, living on the street, the old slum dogs you'd see, the true mutts, why, they'd have one eye or an ear lopped off. No bother, no fuss. They'd be wheeling down the road on three legs. I've been thinking a lot about those old dogs."

"You never told me about when you were little."

"Ah, maybe one day," she hedged. "Maybe one day you'll give me another dose of your magic tonic, and I'll spill more of my secrets, eh? What the hell did I tell you? Well, I hope you make right use of it." She smiled, just a flash was all, a lopsided grin that made her look goofy.

But the goofy smile dried to nothing—I saw it hover for a beat, then run. She said, "Things are changing, Vera. I hope you're ready." She tapped the coverlet with a sharp finger. "On that score, let me save you a bit of heartache."

"Heartache?"

"That's right. First rule: you can't be both the boss and their friend. That strikes you as lonely, I know. But you get over it."

Gold

I expect she thought she was preparing me, much as a farmer tells a day laborer which rows to hoe and how much, at day's end, she would be expected to reap.

Eleven mouths to feed, eleven mouths. I went to bed thinking of the money we didn't have, and woke thinking of it. Everything was expensive. With the city being built again from scratch, prices from fish to lumber to apples to morphine were triple what they had been.

In the evenings, Tan and I settled accounts. I finished whatever task in the house needed doing—washing, cleaning, counting, sorting, worrying—and took a seat at the counter of his outdoor kitchen. He stopped scrubbing his stove and set a place for me.

One night, he poured a cup of tea and cut a slice of the corn bread he'd made that morning. The pan was nearly full.

"How many customers today, Tan?"

He held up three fingers.

"All day?"

All day.

While I'd been at Rose's bedside, Tan had suffered diminishing sales. Across the next weeks, folks in the camps settled into a grim acceptance of destitution, the long haul upon us. In the houses that were still standing, the gas lines were slowly being repaired. Tan hadn't wanted to add to my worries, but the demand for his stew, his fried rice and bean bowls, had ended.

"She wants you to dig out the safe from the rubble at The Rose and bring it here," I said.

Tan paused, and I knew he was figuring how to cart such a heavy thing. That is, if they could find it under a building's worth of burned wood and brick.

"Bobby can borrow the wagon from the Ladies' Protection," I said. "And we have Monster. But you'll need more men."

Tan nodded. He'd get more men. To pay them, we agreed to spend four dollars from the kitty—four dollars in dimes and pennies. Tan looked eager; he thought as I did that the money in the safe would save us.

I bid him good night. As I was coming into the house through the kitchen door, Bobby called to me. He was in the garden having a smoke.

"Hey, Anyway," he called, "you all right?" The concern in his voice was so real—intimate—it shocked me. I didn't know I wasn't all right till Bobby Del Monte asked me.

Knowing he was close ruined any hope of sleeping. My heart skipped ahead of me—fast and unthinking—to Bobby, as the one good thing.

That next night, after everyone in the house had gone to sleep, I was lying in my cot, thinking of Bobby, when Rogue picked up his head and growled.

My first thought was, Oh no, another quake. But Rogue was wagging his tail and happy-whimpering, his snout pointed toward the door.

"Pie?"

"Shh."

"Bobby? What are you doing?"

He dropped to his knees beside the cot and, reaching over me, patted Rogue, talking to him in that gentle voice he used with Monster. "There, boy. Shh. That's right. Settle."

Minding Bobby, Rogue stopped beating the cot with his tail.

I waited to see what would happen next.

"Hey," he whispered. "I could hear your brain ticking all the way down the stairs, through the kitchen door, across the alley, inside the stable. I thought I'd better visit and tell you, for Rogue's sake here, shh. The dog needs his sleep."

"Bobby, how'd you get up here without—?"

"Stairs," he whispered, kissing me, first on my cheek, then across my forehead and down the other cheek to my lips. "Stairs, Anyway."

"Bobby?"

"Shh—"

He had bathed and his hair was damp. He brought with him the coolness of the night air too.

"Bobby, if Pie hears us—"

"She'd be *appalled*!" We stifled our laughter by pressing our lips into each other's necks.

I reached for the lamp, but he took my hand and held it to his heart. "Nicer," he said. "Look, the moon." It was coming through the ox-eye window, from across the park, and across the sea; it was a moon from Japan and beyond, and it lit the curves of the window casing and put a shine on the Singer and a shine on us.

I snorted to tell him I agreed.

"You know sometimes you sound like a horse," he whispered.

I thought, I *am* a horse. I'm a horse and I have nothing on but this thin muslin nightgown.

He said, "You are the farthest thing from a horse. See," he whispered. "I've kissed a few horses and that was no horse kiss. But I may have to kiss you again to know exactly what it was."

"I'm a girl," I whispered.

"That you are," he agreed. "My girl."

In the dark, I nodded.

"Say, would you mind if I stretched out on the rug, just for a bit?"

"Bobby, come up here next to me."

"Do you think Rogue would mind?"

"He won't be pleased, but he won't mind." I snapped my fingers to prove it. Rogue groaned like an old man, which made us both laugh. I snapped my fingers again, and Rogue slunk to the floor.

Bobby pulled off his boots and lay on top of the covers next to me, on his side, with his arm around me. "Go to sleep, Anyway," he whispered, and kissed me again. "Rogue and me are gonna keep watch on you."

It took Tan and Bobby a week to dig through the rubble. And when they did find the safe, buried deep, it was still hot from the fire. Tan hired several workers to help lift it into the wagon and, once they got it home, to carry it from the wagon into the house. They used oven mitts, and even then, their hands burned. They hauled it through the front door and gave up. The thing was just too heavy.

Sargent & Greenleaf, the name blazed in gold on the safe's door, lived where it couldn't be avoided, in the foyer, its scars from the fire having blackened its painted cast-iron sides and top. Its bellyful of heat radiated throughout the main floor like a mighty furnace.

We'd heard stories of business folks downtown retrieving their safes, then opening them while they were still hot from the fire, much to their sorrow. The heat trapped inside exploded the moment the cooler air rushed in, burning whatever was flammable: papers, cash.

"When will it be okay to open it?" Bobby asked.

"When she says so," I replied. "Rose is the only one who knows the combination."

"What's she got in there, gold bars? It sure is a heavy joe."

Bobby was hoping, same as Tan and me, that this heavy joe would be our salvation.

Tan and Bobby had formed a buddydom hauling that thing, and Bobby was now invited to join us at Tan's outdoor kitchen. We understood that the days of Tan's enterprise were coming to an end, and so we lingered in the cool San Francisco night and savored a bit, after the day's work. For Bobby, that was hauling and repairing; for Tan, it was bartering for our food and running his kitchen; for me it was managing the house and its too many people. If the toilets were stopped; if the milk from the relief line turned sour; if the women ran out of thread or stockings or blankets; if someone stole-borrowed without asking someone else's curling rod; if a merchant on Fillmore Street would only barter with a white person who didn't resemble a prostitute, they brought the problem to me.

The thing is, I liked to work. That was among the many lessons of those fevered days. I liked to work and I liked feeling necessary.

I was just beginning to know that the only folks I could ever care about would be fellow scrappers.

June into July, the summer fog made the house tight with an unremitting dampness. With great reluctance, a defeat Tan suffered deeply, he and LowNaa packed up their curbside kitchen. We had seven dollars and twenty-two cents to last the summer.

And still Rose refused to talk about the safe. In an act of defiance, Tan draped Sargent & Greenleaf with a wrinkled cloth and we moved on.

At night, the women sang in the parlor. "Wait Till the Sun Shines, Nellie" and "So Long, Mary" were frequent numbers, but their all-time favorite was "Give My Regards to Broadway." They had excellent voices, and with Mercy keeping pace on the piano, their harmonic warbles passed siren-like from Rose's parlor into Lafayette Square.

When the women were downstairs singing, Pie hid in her room. I followed her one evening to see what she was doing in there. When I grabbed the book from her hands, she confessed she was reading the Bible.

"Why on earth are you bothering with that?" I asked.

Pie held up her palm to stop me from saying more.

"Do you really think God is watching?" I pestered.

Pie tipped her head, the bright hum of music rising through the floorboards from below. There was the insistence of the piano, and Valentine's bass underscoring all.

"That man," Pie whispered, "is he a man?"

"Valentine?" I shrugged. "Well, you know—"

"No, I don't know!" Her eyes were a brilliant, spiked blue. It seemed to me there were tiny icicles inside that blue.

"What's there to tell?" I said. "Valentine started as a man, now she's a woman. But Capability says Valentine prefers to date men."

"Herregud." Pie shuddered. *"Herr-e-gud!"*

"Pie, stop with the oh my God–ing. You sound like Morie," I said. "Talk to me. Just talk to me plainly."

She took a deep breath. "Yes or no, are you planning to start a brothel here, in the house?"

I had expected her to implore or beg, to tell me all the ways we were ruining ourselves by being associated with whores. I had expected the latest report of tongues wagging in the square about our boarders. And I was prepared to mock Pie, to say, Yes, and even so, Pie, would you like the ladies to starch and press your dress, in addition to having them wash it in Pearline?

But Pie said nothing of what I thought she'd say. She folded her hands across that thick book and asked about my business plans.

I shrugged. "And are you thinking of becoming a nun? You're not even Catholic."

"What about you?" she countered. "Are you the next Rose?"

Such a face she was making. No longer the old pleasing, if overly practical, sister, this new Pie was part schoolmarm, part zealot, and eager—as if she'd awakened from a long sleep.

"You didn't answer my question," she said, lifting that sharp Swedish chin. "And yes, I can become a Catholic. Anything is possible when you're living with harlots. Answer me, Vera."

"I don't know," I said. "They'd like to help out in some way with the bills, and that is their way. But I don't know. In case you haven't noticed, we're dead broke."

"I know."

"Do you? I wonder, Pie, do you remember that Morie turned to Rose when *she* was dead broke? Do you remember what she was prepared to do—"

"Don't say it!" Pie snapped. "Morie would never have—"

"She would have, if that's what it took to survive," I declared. "She would have done the same as those women downstairs—for you."

Pie shook her head, refusing that part of our story. Instead, she smirked as a new revelation came on her. "You don't want to," she crowed. "I know you, V. I know that look. You don't like the idea of a brothel any more than I do. You just don't want to admit it."

"That's not true."

"You're daring yourself not to be bothered, but you think prostitution is a sordid affair, same as me."

I crossed my arms. "I'd rather be a hooker than a nun—though both strike me as a lousy deal, whether you're the hooker or the nun."

"That's 'cause you have no relationship to God," Pie replied.

"Since when do you?"

Pie shrugged. She couldn't explain that since the quake—since losing Morie and James in one awful go—the Church made sense to her, its rules and expectations. Its clarity. In a fallen world, the Church stood. That, and she was spending too much time with Eugenie.

"You wouldn't understand," she said, talking in a calm, cold voice; it was the voice of a stranger. "How could you?" she went on. "You've never believed in anyone but yourself. In that, you're lucky."

"Lucky!"

"Yah, yah," she assured me. "I want to be lucky too. Is that so terrible? I've tried everything I can think of. I asked Eugenie if I could live with them. She wanted to say yes, but with the mayor's troubles—"

"So, you're forced to live here," I said. "Miserably."

She shrugged. "Eugenie helps out at the refuge with the nuns from school. I suppose I could work there too. Do you think Bobby would take me in the buggy? Alamo Square is too far to walk."

I thought: We sure could use help around here, and Bobby has plenty else to do. But I bit my tongue and said simply, "I'll ask him."

The next morning, I brought coffee and a plate of hash to Bobby. He was setting up Monster for the day, brushing him in the driveway. When he was finished, he'd walk Monster to Lafayette Square, where they'd hire out as a team, hauling for a day's wages.

Bobby saw me and laughed. He licked his thumb and wiped a smudge from my cheek. "There," he said. "And you don't need to bribe me to ask a favor. What is it?"

"The favor," I said. "It isn't for me."

"Oh no? That's disappointing." Bobby went on working the snarls in Monster's long, shaggy forelock. He was using General's old brushes. Since that one night, he'd visited me in the attic a couple more times. But he hadn't visited in a while and I feared I'd done something wrong.

"Bobby."

"Yeah?"

"Before you and Monster head out today, could you take Pie in the buggy to Alamo Square? There's a convent they've turned into a refuge for the quake orphans."

"Don't call them that," he said sharply. He was so gentle, Bobby, but he was also odd, like his horse. Any wrong noise, he jumped. "They're children," he insisted. "Call them children."

"All right," I agreed. "Would you take Pie to see the children? I think it would be good for her."

"Let me ask you a question," he said. "When was the last time you saw the ocean? I mean, we're surrounded by water."

I shrugged. "Before the quake, I guess."

He nodded. "Tell you what. I'll take Pie *and you*, if you say you'll come with me one afternoon to Ocean Beach. It would be good for you."

I nodded before I had time to think why I shouldn't.

"Look at that, Monster." He beamed. "She's smiling. We done okay."

I patted Monster to let Bobby know that it was more than okay. Bobby had his shirt tucked into his trousers, and his belt was an old brown strap he used to cinch his pants. He was too skinny by half and his ears turned pink when he was feeling good or angry, and he wasn't angry right now. His cheeks were scruffy where he needed a shave and I wanted to kiss him.

Instead I said, "Bobby, when are you going to tell me how you got ol' Monster?"

He paused. "I'll tell you when you tell me what's the story with that lady upstairs. Rose."

"What do you know?"

He sighed. "Too much and nothin'."

"I promise I'll tell you, but can you ask something easier first?"

"Here." He took my hand, rubbed it across the scruff on his cheek, then gave a quick kiss to my palm. He asked, "Is that easier?"

"No." I laughed.

"Ah, guess we'll have to keep hoping for a yes, eh, Monster?"

Bobby went on brushing the horse's legs and flanks. "I found him on Howard Street, just after the quake hit," he said. "Those blocks took it real bad. Monster was calling out, horse-wise—you know, panicky. I figured he was hurt. The house where he belonged had come down, I mean, it was nothin' but a pile of boards. I suppose everyone in it, well, there was no one around. Monster was in the back, tied up. They must have used him hard, 'cause there was just a dirt patch and nothin', I mean nothin', for him to graze on. There was a wagon, crushed to nothing. You said I stole him—"

"I'm sorry I said that."

"Well, I sort of did."

"You saved him, is what." My voice sounded all croaky.

Bobby read my face. "See that, Monster," he said. "I think maybe she's taking a shine to you." And when he saw me blush, he laughed. "Good gawd. Go on, tell Pie she's got a ride, and let's get to it. Monster's waiting."

That's what I did: I got to it. I hurried Pie with her dressing, and by the time we came out, Bobby had Monster hitched to Rose's buggy.

Pie and I rode in the carriage, with her chatting the whole way. When we reached Alamo Square, Bobby jumped down, opened the door like a gentleman, and helped us out.

"Thank you." Pie smiled sweetly. "Thank you very much, Bobby."

"Thank you," I whispered, and took his hand and didn't let go till he agreed to come with us inside.

It was a madhouse, and I mean to use that word; the bottom floor of the convent had been converted into a ward to house the insane. There were hundreds of patients, some chattering like finches, others reclining dully in the beds and chairs. Some stared limply out windows that had been welded shut.

A nun, her wimple damp with sweat, passed us, carrying heavy buckets of milk. Bobby took them from her without asking.

She asked him to leave them with the sister by the stairs and added, "If you're looking for Sister Raymond, go on up, top floor."

There was a formal set of stairs and a back way. Pie pushed us to go up the wide staircase. The second floor of the mansion had been given over to the Jesuits, whose building had burned in the quake. In the front rooms, people were kneeling, receiving blessings by a priest. He touched their heads and murmured a prayer softly and moved on to the next, while in a far corner, a curtain had been strung on a rope, behind which confessions were being heard.

A priest asked us, "Are you here to make your confession?"

"Oh, no," I blurted. "We have nothing to— No," I said firmly.

Behind me, Bobby chuckled.

"Stop that," I said, but the way he was looking at me, full of mischief, we were surely guilty, perhaps Bobby and me most of all.

The next two floors were devoted to the sick. There beds had been put in rows, many beds, with only a few nuns to care for the lot. The top floor was devoted to the nuns and orphans.

Pie was keen to find Eugenie. "This way," she said, and led

us to the back and up a narrow set of stairs, to the attic, the final floor, where the sisters had to make do, post-quake, by arranging their thin pallets in neat rows, head to foot, with only a few inches between them.

When Pie spotted Eugenie, surrounded by a flock of children, she squealed with delight and skipped across the pallets to greet her friend.

"There she goes," I said to no one, but Bobby heard me and said, "It'll be good for her to get outside herself." He said it without any edge, just plain, as if Pie were an animal, like the rest of us, and needed someone to show her which way to go.

Sister Raymond was just gathering herself. She adjusted her wimple as she marched toward us, robustly stomping on the pallets in her heavy black boots. At school, she taught us grammar and history, though once Sister Raymond confessed that if she hadn't been called to God, she would have liked to be a farmer. Here she was in charge of cooking for five hundred souls, two meals a day.

Sister Raymond lit at the sight of Bobby. "Vera, have you brought us an extra pair of hands?"

"Sorry, Sister," Bobby said, and he explained that we were expected shortly at the Ladies' Protection—to help with those children.

"Well, good on you, lad," the sister said. "And Vera? You're helping there too?" The sister didn't bother to hide her amazement that I would have molted into a Good Samaritan.

"Yes, Sister, I've been attending to the sick and downtrodden," I said, owing it wasn't a lie. "We all have to do our part."

"Well, I'm glad to hear you're using your smarts for good," she agreed. "I always hoped you would."

With that we left Pie and Eugenie in a state of what I can only describe as ecstatic servitude. They were joyously sorting donated clothes—rags, really—making a game out of it to occupy the children: a pile here for socks and another for shirts and another for trousers.

Bobby took my hand and led me down the servants' stairs of the once-grand house. We raced past the floors of wounded, to a large back room on the second floor that was occupied by the priests. Bobby caught a flash of something and said, "Whoa, horse." He stopped so suddenly, I nearly flew past him. But Bobby pulled me back, and up several steps, and from there I could see what caught his eye.

The room looked like a dragon's lair. Bobby pumped my hand, if only to direct me to the next marvel and the next, the piles of gold bars there, jewels over there, paintings and silverware bundled in haste.

"If you're here to drop your valuables," a priest said—it took us a moment to realize he was talking to us. He was seated at a small desk not a foot from where we stood. "Sign a card," he directed, and he placed one on the edge of the desk with a pencil beside it. Then he gathered some papers and walked into the next room.

Leaving us alone with all that loot. There were silver candelabras and pitchers, and cases and clocks, and money wrapped in newspapers or tied with string, and jewelry in velvet bags; there were oil paintings in heavy gilt frames stacked along the walls or leaning haphazardly against the legs of chairs. There were swords of various sizes, bejeweled and plain. Yes, a dragon's lair, or how I'd imagine the stash might look inside an Egyptian tomb. All within easy reach.

Bobby couldn't stop squeezing my hand.

"What the hell?" he whispered.

I thought of that first day of the quake and how folks had hauled the valuables from their broken houses and stacked them in piles at the curb. And I remembered Mrs. Sugarman's tears when someone made off with her silver. With the banks burned, folks who'd lost their houses had naturally turned to the clergy to safeguard their money and valuables.

"Come on, Bobby," I whispered. "Bobby?" I tugged on his hand.

"Wait," he said. I understood the orphan in him wanting to feast a little longer on the sight of all those riches. I did too.

"Bobby, please," I urged, pulling him along.

When at last we reached the buggy, he spoke harshly to me, his face and ears crimson with insult. "Admit it. You didn't trust me back there, did you?"

"What do you mean?"

"You thought I was gonna steal."

"Don't be silly," I said. But the truth was much harder to admit. "Bobby, I didn't trust me."

The next morning, first thing, I went to see Rose. She was propped on pillows, snoring. Lifang was asleep beside her, looking like a child of no more than eight or ten.

I was about to leave when Rose grumbled, "What's on your mind?" She'd lost none of her bearings. She was ever the vigilant madam in whatever room she was in.

"Money," I said. "Money is on my mind."

Rose grunted as she struggled to lift herself higher on the pillows. "What about the girls? No gentlemen callers? I thought you were working on that. They are looking to you, you know."

"They're looking to *you*," I declared. "We all are. And I'm asking, what about the safe? It's plenty cool by now."

"The safe is none of your concern."

"You mean you're not going to open it?"

"I mean, what's in there is not for general use."

"Rosie?" Lifang yawned and, raising herself to sitting, wiped the crust from her eyes with her dainty fists. "Rosie," she repeated, in that awful little-girl voice she used around Rose. "Madam Johanna started a house not far from here. Three French girls they call the Lively Fleas. And Madam Bertha? She has a house very-very near, on Sacramento Street. The girls wear little dresses. They sing gin songs."

"Gin songs?" Rose asked.

"Yes-yes, gin songs," Lifang insisted. "Very-very popular."

She was pushing me to start a whorehouse, even though that fat safe was begging to be opened downstairs. She was pushing, though she had once declared she didn't want that life for me. Well, that conviction, along with so much else, was gone. I wasn't having it. The thought of it made me sick in my bones.

"If you want to start up again, go ahead," I declared. "But I'm not doing it."

They pretended not to hear me. "You'd need a theme," Rose mused, her good eye fixed on the ceiling. "Home Away from Home?" She searched the walls, the ceiling, the curtains for inspiration. "Pacific Heights," she said at last. "Ha! That's it. You'll call it Pacific Heights."

Tan was waiting for me at the bottom of the stairs.

"She's not opening the safe," I announced glumly. "We have to think of another way."

Tan had his hands folded in front of him, his head bowed.

"Did you hear me, Tan, I said—"

He nodded sharply, in that curt way of his. "Lifang," he whispered. "She's with her?"

When I said that of course she was, he sighed with relief. "They are two snug cats," I added, then stopped myself from saying more. I realized Tan and I were having two different conversations, and that he was in a state.

"What is it, Tan? Why are you wondering where Lifang—"

He shook his head to silence me from saying more.

"Whiskey," he said, changing the subject. He pointed to the basement.

I thought for a minute. "Okay, let's see what you've got."

He'd been pestering me for days to go with him to see Rose's stash.

Tan lit a lamp and led the way, his silk slippers scratching on the unfinished wood stairs. The darkness of the basement was sudden, as was the wave of mildew and damp that assailed my nose.

Tan, LowNaa, and Lifang had done the best they could to make a home below ground, with cast-off sofas and tables perched on a foundation of sand. Planks had been laid end to end to form a narrow hallway between the walls and the brick foundation.

I don't know what I'd imagined, but it shocked me that one floor below Rose's palace of marble goddesses and twenty-foot ceilings and polished parquet, Tan had been relegated to living on sand.

We passed a closed door.

"What's in here?"

Tan shook his head.

"Please, show me."

It was Tan's room. He'd laid more planks to form a rough floor, which he'd covered with a rag rug. A narrow cot was tucked against one wall, and beside it an old dresser with a missing leg propped up by a book. On the wall opposite the cot, a threadbare sofa was being used as a second bed. I supposed that this must be where LowNaa slept. A lantern, a slop jar—everything neatly in its place. Tan stood behind me, proud of what he'd made out of nothing. I knew he'd consider it an insult if I showed that it hurt my heart to see him living like that. Instead I told him how remarkable it all was.

Lifang had a slightly better deal. Her room had a small window that looked onto the base of a rosebush, with its candelabra of green-leafed canes. A wire had been strung across the room, on which Lifang had hung two American dresses—the ones she was saving for her bright future.

Further on, the planks of the hallway ended abruptly at two doors. The first held odd bits of furniture and tools, and a repair bench with a vise. The second room stank of earth and booze. Rose had lost a fair amount of wine in the quake; the sand in the room was stained red. But some of the crates made it through unscathed. As luck would have it, some of the good stuff. Rose had kept her best hooch at the house so no one would walk off with it at The Rose. There was the odd case of Château Lafite Rothschild Bordeaux, Grand Cru Royal, and some Gruaud-Larose, Martell cognacs, and, of course, whiskey—loads of it.

Tan hefted a crate from the pile.

"How much?" I asked, money and barter being Tan's and my favored language.

"One month." He shrugged. "Maybe more."

"All for a case of whiskey?"

Tan flashed the briefest of smiles. "Rose, she buys the best."

I didn't hesitate. "Go ahead, make the trade," I said.

That first case bought us another month—a month of roles shifting inside the gold house. I left Rose completely to the care of Lifang. Tan, having already established a name for himself as someone who traded silk garters, perfume, and cigars for eggs and beef and beans, now became known for trafficking in whiskey. He found the customers and I struck the bargains. I kept the books and we moved a steady business of trade along that kept us in food and covered the repairs on the house.

Pie went every day to the refuge and worked with the nuns. Bobby did chores for the orphans at the Ladies' Protection, and at the house he fixed what needed fixing. He made extra money hiring out for day work with Monster. In the evenings, we visited.

If the women weren't going out to the roller derby or The Chutes or to see the occasional client, if they didn't feel like singing, they gathered in the parlor, and Bobby and I joined them, to listen to Miss Sophia read from a novel.

Sophia had been engaged once to a French poet.

"What happened, Soph?" I asked.

"Ah, baby, he quit me."

"Quit, Soph? You mean he left you?"

"No, baby. He died quit."

He may have died, but Sophia's poet gave her a love of reading that stuck. She insisted that new clients bring her a poem at the start of things. Capability told stories of how, in the days of The Rose, Sophia's clients stood in bow ties and suits at the foot of her bed and recited poems of love as she, a paid listener, lounged before them in her silk underthings.

Mercy claimed that Sophia often serviced her customers with a book in her hand. She read constantly—in bed, and every evening as we gathered in the parlor. Sophia would wiggle her hips in anticipation of the next chapter of whatever novel or play she decided to read aloud, the springs in the parlor settee gonging as she robustly acted all the parts.

That summer, Sophia taught me of the Greeks and D'Annunzio and Cavafy and Balzac; she introduced me to Chekhov, Tolstoy, Pushkin. These are the great men, she noted, the men who understand women.

September arrived, ushering in San Francisco's real summer, with dry, warm days and balmy nights. While Tan and I traded more crates in the basement for food and supplies, Sophia began to read aloud *Anna Karenina.*

Whenever he could, Bobby sat with me on the sofa. Given the circle we were in, we decided it was fine to hold hands. He had a way of holding my hand, his thumb working my palm, that sent shivers through me. I had never been happy before. And like every happy person, I was certain I had discovered happiness. Here, with the only gang I would ever belong to.

Now, the women approached life in a literal way. For instance, they believed what was happening to the characters on the page was unfolding in real time, much as their lives were unfolding. They had long ago decided to live in the present and therefore they had no compunction about interrupting Sophia as she read.

"Hurry up, Karenin," warned Valentine, "'fore Vronsky gives her a bang she won't forget."

"You know, you're ruining it. My reading," Sophia complained.

"Go on, girl. I'm fully engaged," Valentine insisted, and she pulled on the waist of her skirt to give herself some air down there.

"Engage yourself *si-lent-ly*," Mercy insisted. "And without all that flapping."

"If this is a book about sex, why are there no pros in it?" Cap wanted to know.

At which point I shocked them by asking, "What is it like? . . . I mean, do you mind, do you hate, you know, working?"

Sophia sat up. "What was that, belle? Someone tell me, what did the child say?"

"Honey V's wondering if we hate turning tricks," Valentine boomed. "Or was it more like, do we miss it?"

They looked to each other, deciding how much to say.

Cap spoke for the group. "Darlin', it's like this: nobody here is some little bitty poor froufrou. We're the best, you know? At least, I am." Smiling at her own joke, Capability flicked her nails. "Now, there was a time, well, there was a time, I wasn't this."

"That would be a *long* time ago," Mercy piped in, chuckling.

"Hush. I'm talking to the child," Cap said. "Darlin', don't

you worry about a thing. We may not have chosen it, but no one here is getting dragged from their mama's tit. Here is where we belong. And you've taken good care. Mighty good care. We're just keepin' easy, waiting for Rose to give us the word. You know, when you're part of a house, you can't be dancing solo. You probably don't know that. We're just sitting time—va-ca-tion-ing." She paused, studying me through her long lashes. "Oh my, now I've misplaced your question."

"That's all right," I said, feeling my face getting warm. Now that I'd made a thing of it, I wanted them to quit bothering.

"I don't think, by the look on you, we did right here," Valentine declared. "What is it, darlin', you want to know?"

"What is it?" Bobby whispered. "Can you tell me?"

I couldn't say, the words felt too dangerous. Company. Happiness. Love. I was afraid that having discovered that these exotic places exist—and they did feel to me like places, where one might visit and linger, and even rest, and like a house or a city—they could just as easily vanish. Here one day, then crushed.

The Difference between Want and Desire

The aftershocks may have lessened, but the rumbling carried on. The quake was my great teacher. Those early days with all of us together in the gold house taught me that on every street corner, in every shop, stable, and basement, is an entire world—of kings and paupers, rulers and ruled, and folks just getting by. I was starting to comprehend that knowing a fact is far less useful than knowing where to put it—where it belongs, in the greater chain of things. I wasn't sure if Rose was right—that leading is lonely, but a necessary loneliness. I was newly acquainted with the notion that want is a far lesser thing than desire.

Want is a ripe peach or a new dress; desire is the pang that keeps you awake at night, as if you're being chased.

I waited every night for Bobby to find me in the attic. On the nights he visited, I knew I loved him. On the nights he failed to show, I decided in my torment that I hated love.

One night I decided I was not the sort of girl to be kept waiting, and I went looking for him in the garage. He had rolled the buggy into the driveway and made a room for himself in the stall next to Monster's stable. His bed was a horsehair cushion from a discarded sofa; his pillows were lumpy sacks stuffed with batting and straw. He had a crate for a table and another crate to hold his basin. His boots and a few odd bits of clothing were folded and tucked. The garage smelled of oil and metal and of Monster, next door.

Bobby said nothing; I said nothing. He opened his blanket and I crawled in.

There must be a hundred, a thousand sorts of kisses, touches—we discovered them all. The air in that shack held us, the air buzzing with what else we were not yet doing. The not-doing was impossible. At last Bobby climbed to his feet and said, "You have to go now."

"Why?" I whispered. "Don't you like me?"

"No. Anyway, I don't *like* you."

"I . . . don't understand." I didn't want to understand. Had it been up to me, we'd be making love. We'd be doing anything and everything.

Bobby pulled me to my feet, blanket and all, and breathed into me, his lashes tickling my neck. "When will you be sixteen?"

"April."

"Okay, then April."

"Bobby, that's months from now."

"Yeah, damn it, I know."

I wanted to argue; it made me suspicious, scratching an old hurt place inside: to be cared for by being sent away.

"Well, damn you, Bobby," I said.

He seized me by the wrists. "Don't. Don't say what you'll regret."

"The only thing I'll regret is if you send me away."

He pulled me to him, kissed me, and whispered, "Go."

I returned to the sewing room, where I did not sleep.

In the morning, Tan was waiting for me in the kitchen. He looked beside himself, muted, in that way of his, when he was most angry or distraught. He wouldn't meet my eye.

"What is it?" I asked sharply. I expected that Tan saw me sneaking into the garage and that I was in for some withering disapproval.

"Lifang," he said, "is she with Rose?" I told him that's what I would expect, if she wasn't with him. Then I reminded him that I didn't usually bother with Rose till midmorning, after she had eaten her breakfast. All this, Tan already knew.

He studied the floor and, holding still, waited for me to read his mind. Tan's ways were maddening, but there was a poetry to them too. He didn't just feel, he combusted.

"I'll go up and check," I said, and I hurried upstairs, thinking of how much I missed Bobby and of the breakfast I wanted to eat—thinking that the house had too many hearts, and all of them wanting, and that was the greatest shaker of all.

Lifang was in Rose's bathroom, rinsing some underthings. "What? What?" she demanded.

I supposed I had the shine from being with Bobby—of wanting him—on me, for Lifang studied me in one of the many mirrors, and said simply, "Ha!"

"Ha, yourself. Your father's looking for you," I said. "He's worried. Does he have reason to be?"

She shook her head fiercely and went back to rinsing her bloomers along with Rose's.

I went down to tell Tan that I'd seen Lifang. Relieved, he turned to the business of breakfast, cracking the few eggs we had left in the larder.

But you see, I wasn't the only girl looking for love as the weather turned colder. Lifang had been sneaking out at night. For a good long while, she had managed to keep Tan at bay by varying the pattern of where she slept—one or two nights with Rose, then a night in the basement.

But Tan figured it out. She must have known he would. After all, he was the original conspirer. But, like me, Lifang was beyond caring.

I expect Tan's greatest fear was that she had been seduced by one of the tong boys. But it was worse than that: Lifang was sneaking into the square at night to be with a soldier she'd met while waiting in the relief lines. Worse still, he was white, a navy recruit from Seattle, where he kept his wife.

Tan discovered them making love in one of the tents. He beat the soldier with a belt that had a brass buckle at one end. Then he marched Lifang home.

Cap, Valentine, and I huddled in the kitchen as we listened to the shrieks coming from the basement. Tan was using the belt the way he'd whipped General—without mercy. It was awful. And it went on.

We never heard Lifang cry. No, it was Tan's keening that shook the house. With every stroke he roared. She was the love of his life, and he had failed to protect her. She was living with him, but she was gone.

When at last Lifang appeared at the top of the stairs, she was unsteady on her feet. Yet her body looked unscathed. What a tough, tough girl, I thought.

Later, when Tan showed his face, I understood. He had whipped himself and made her watch. And when she refused to bend or cry, he pulled out his hair, patch by wretched patch. His skull was a map of wounds.

Tan prohibited Lifang from visiting Rose's suite, or any room upstairs. He confined Lifang to the kitchen, reducing her once again to the scrubber of dirty pots. Capability took over tending Rose.

That night, when I couldn't sleep, I went to the kitchen to make a cup of tea and found Lifang. She'd been waiting for me. She nodded and dared me to *unsee* her misery—her tears that flowed, now that her father wasn't watching. How I wish we could have shown each other even a small bit of kindness—for if anyone in that house could fathom the wide, bottomless bowl of a girl's desire, it was Lifang and me. She glared at me, and I understood her rage to be a promise: one day she'd prove, finally and forever, that she was the freer, better girl. She'd win and I had to wait to see how. It would come when I least expected. It would come when I was most vulnerable, like her.

The Mayor

Six months after the shake, the city was a cacophony of saws and hammers, with drays hauling fresh-milled lumber to thousands of new building sites. The tents of Lafayette Square now had flower and vegetable beds to mark the various plots. In the Presidio the refugee camps gave over to rows of earthquake cottages. The rent for these one-room shanties was two dollars a month toward a purchase price of fifty dollars. For that you got four redwood walls, fir floors, a cast-iron stove, and a cedar-shingled roof. The cottages were painted dark green to blend with the surroundings. The latrines and kitchens were separate, as were the playgrounds and schools spread across twenty-six camps throughout the city.

With the building of the shanties, the newspapers reported widespread optimism: our new city was rising—bigger, bolder, cleansed. The papers failed to cover the extreme shortages of beef and milk and bread and lumber. And the thousands of victims still missing. The epidemics of cholera and influenza and scabies sweeping the camps.

I suppose the citizens of San Francisco, having lived the disaster, wanted good news. That, or they wanted revenge.

When Schmitz came to visit Rose, he arrived as I once did: at midnight, his car rolling into the driveway with the motor cut.

The women were upstairs, preparing for the reopening of the roller-derby rink. Miss Flora, the derby queen, had promised to put on a spectacle.

Schmitz always insisted on coming through the front door. I met him there. The mayor tried to embrace me; I offered my hand instead.

As ever, he was impatient, eager to talk about himself. Had I read the papers? Of course I had. Now that the initial crisis had passed, there were calls to reconvene the grand jury in the hopes of sending Abe Ruef and Eugene Schmitz to prison at last.

"Vera," he said, "I count on you to give it to me straight. What do you hear?"

"About you? Nothing good," I said.

He laughed. "Well, I wouldn't expect you, of all people, to put a bow on it." He cast about for something more pleasant, his eye landing on Rose's marble Venus. "I see the goddesses came through the quake." He smiled dimly, his eyes darting as he tried to think of something bright to say. "Good we stopped the fire, eh? Good we did a few things right."

It seemed that I should feel sorry for him; he had a genius for pulling on that string. I told him that Rose would be glad to see him and I pointed the way.

He hesitated. The devout Catholic, the huckster who made a living off of prostitutes, was embarrassed to be seen visiting the madam in her bedroom. He cleared his throat. "Up? This way?"

I walked him up, curious to see how it'd go, grafter to madam.

Capability had dressed Rose in a pink silk turban and matching bed jacket. She wore a flowered velvet patch, the effect of which made her look like a tropical pirate.

"Gene," Rose said, taking his hands, "the gods must love you fierce, to have burned our town just to save your German tush."

Schmitz snorted appreciatively. He was a good actor, I'll give him that. He saw the travesty of Rose's face and didn't flinch.

"Rose, I'm glad to see you so well."

"Well? I've busted everything but my spirit, Gene, and that sure could use a drink. Vera, would you mind?"

I fetched the whiskey—Tan was prepared to bring it, but I took the tray. As I came in, Schmitz was saying, "But if Abe is *coerced* into testifying against me—"

Rose held up her hand. "Hold that thought," she said.

I made a quick business of pouring their drinks while the mayor remarked, "You're lucky, Rose, to have such a daughter. I trust Vera has told you we're old friends."

"Yes," Rose agreed, "she's very resourceful, this one. She's been a help to me."

"I'm glad," he said. "Now, Mrs. Johnson, that was a tragedy. Julia and I were so fond of her. Vera, how is Pie getting on?"

"She's fine," Rose answered. "Better every day." Rose had hardly seen Pie, but that didn't keep her from having an opinion. "Though she's had a hard run, Gene. Death and heartbreak."

Schmitz nodded. "I'm afraid there won't be any school to distract you girls for another few months. But I did just hear that Alma de Bretteville has started a school for the younger children in Golden Gate Park."

"Alma de Bretteville started a school?" Rose said. "She's a scrapper, that one. Good on her. Vera, you know Alma. You should help her with her school. It would get you out a bit."

"I'm busy here," I said.

"It would get you out a bit," Rose repeated with emphasis.

"If you're amenable, Vera, I'm sure Alma could use the extra hands," Schmitz added. "Eugenie has been very active helping out at the refuge. In fact, she is so engaged, I fear we may lose her to the nuns." He sighed.

"Don't let her, Gene," Rose warned. "God does not need you to sacrifice a daughter."

Schmitz wasn't sure; perhaps the sacrifice of a daughter was exactly what God required.

"Vera," Rose said. "The mayor and I have some things to discuss."

I excused myself. As I was pulling her door closed behind me, Schmitz didn't hesitate to start in. "Rosie, what a fix we're in. I have soldiers with guns aimed at our citizens, citizens with no shelter, roads and schools nonexistent, and, to our greater worry, Spreckels and DeYoung are damn eager. They're pushing to reconvene the grand jury. I fear—"

The conversation was too rich—I couldn't help myself. I snuck into her bathroom, where the door leading to her room was always ajar. Lifang kept a stool in there, by the tub, for when she helped Rose with her bath. I sat on that little padded throne, my legs tucked under me, and held my breath.

"Gene, it is foretold this would happen," Rose said. "You can't expect the world to be grateful forever that you showed up for the disaster."

"Beg your pardon, I did more than show up. I organized them—friends and enemies alike—I had the balls to put them together. We worked for the common good—"

"Ah, very nice. Save that speech for court. The simple truth is: now that the crisis has passed and the city is rebuilding in earnest, your enemies have a greater appreciation for your scalp."

"They aren't just *my* enemies," Schmitz warned, his voice rising. His sense of injury, incredulity more than guilt, passed through the walls as a huffy impatience. Schmitz marched grimly around Rose's bed. I could just imagine her tracking him with her one eye while deciding her next move.

"Chrissakes, Gene, you're making me dizzy. Stop galumphing and sit the hell down."

He went on pacing. "And what will you do, Rose? Carry on, as before? All this talk of ridding the city of every hooker and saloon, that won't stand for long."

"Look at me, Gene. I'm not exactly fit to preside. The Rose is no more the flower she once might have been." She paused and her voice dropped to a whisper. "What's that rustling I hear? Is someone—?"

The mayor opened the door to the hall. "No one," he said.

"Vera, she has keen ears, that one. They all do," Rose grumbled. "Gene, check the closets. Go on—"

"Vera has a keen mind too," he remarked as he dutifully opened and closed the mirrored doors. "Reminds me of someone. You sure kept that apple hidden, Rosie. Any more daughters you've got tucked in these closets?"

"Plenty of your secrets I keep in there, Mr. Mayor. Careful what door you open. There are bound to be tigers."

Schmitz laughed. "Should I be scared?"

"Yes, Gene," she said with all seriousness, "you ought to be damn scared. But not of me."

"What are your plans for her? Will she take over the family business, then? The next madam?" asked Schmitz as he opened the door to the bathroom and found me curled on that little stool. I was fully clothed, but I felt naked.

"She doesn't have the skills," Rose declared. "The girl doesn't have a flirty bone in her body."

I winced at that, and Schmitz winced along with me. He shook his head to show me he disagreed—to show that we were, as ever, in cahoots.

"Nothing in here, Rosie," he called, "but these twin crappers. What's the second one for?"

"Oh, come now." She laughed. "Have you never seen a bidet? It's *très* French. For washing your stick and stones."

"No kidding," Schmitz said.

"I'm famous for clean, aren't I?" Rose remarked. "Hey, come back here. I think I've got the answer to both our problems."

He paused. Was he musing on what to do with me, what to do *about* me? He tipped his head, silently posing the question.

I looked the bastard in the eye and winked.

"Say, Mayor," Rose bellowed. "Have you considered that this would be a fine moment for you and Julia to take that long-awaited trip to Europe?"

"Europe?" Schmitz queried. "Were we thinking about Europe?"

"Yes, Gene. It's simple: if they can't find you, they can't try you. From now on, your middle name is stall, stall, stall. This would be an excellent time for you to disappear."

The mayor did as Rose instructed: he and Julia left for Europe in late autumn and didn't return for a month. During that time, Rose got busy. She had Tan and me organize the second-floor library to serve as her new office, and there she met with her lawyers and Martin, her accountant. She took her meetings in the late afternoon. If she felt robust, she saw the men in the study, and if she was feeling poorly, she met with them while reclining in bed. She used the bed as her throne, and directed the men to perch on lady-sized upholstered chairs—that, or she had us take the chairs away so they were forced to stand. I marveled at how the men got small and polite, seeing Rose laid out so.

When her meetings ran late, Rose summoned me, never Tan or Lifang, to serve the whiskey.

One afternoon, after the lawyers had left for the day, Rose called me to her bedside. Lifang had ingratiated herself sufficiently with her father that he once again allowed her upstairs. She was fluffing Rose's pillows, getting her ready for her pre-dinner nap.

"Here," Rose said, and she opened an envelope that Martin had left behind. She handed me a hundred dollars in bills.

"Now, stop selling my hooch," she sniped.

Lifang, that minx tattletale, cupped her hand over her mouth and chuckled.

Like the mayor, I took Rose's advice and visited Alma. The Geary Street trolley was one of the first to be fixed, and I rode it all the way to Golden Gate Park, where the tent encampments had given way to scores of newly built earthquake shacks. Alma had turned the park's former playground building into her school, with donated books and blackboards and even little desks. I passed the day helping her teach penmanship and arithmetic to children ranging in age from five to ten.

Afterward, Alma took a couple of beers from her secret stash, and though they were warm as piss, we enjoyed them on a grassy bank overlooking the Tea Garden.

"Ah," she said, "I am almost happy."

"Why aren't you completely happy?" I asked.

Alma rolled her eyes. "AB, of course. The man has one tragic flaw: he will be pushed only so far." She sighed contentedly. "Let's not talk about him. Tell Auntie Alma your troubles," she said. "I'll give you ten minutes."

"I have nothing that can be squeezed into ten minutes." I laughed.

"Oh, look, nine minutes."

She was funny, Alma.

I decided to tell her about my life with Rose. I needed to tell someone, and Alma was at that moment my only girlfriend. I told her everything up to and including the visits from the lawyers and Schmitz.

Upon hearing my story, Alma sat up, her brow furrowed. "The other night," she said, "AB was talking with some fellas and

I overheard a good bit. Everyone knows they're tightening the noose on Ruef and Schmitz. But it seems they're intent on casting a wider net. Rose's name was mentioned."

"How do you mean?"

"Well, I only gave them half an ear, because, my God, those men can talk round a thing, but they're calling it a grand sweep—as many big and little fishes as they can catch." Alma squinted at the bottle. "There was talk about proving the extent of the money trail. Bribes and more bribes."

"And that would include Rose?"

"Mmm." Alma nodded. "Has she said anything?"

"Uh-uh. She never shows her hand if she can help it."

"Well, keep an eye out," Alma warned, and having taken care of business, she looped her thin arm around me. "Now, tell me: What of that boyfriend?" Alma smiled. "Bobby Monster."

I laughed. "His name is Bobby Del Monte, and I thought you said I was out of time."

"Oh, we have loads of time for that," Alma assured me. "Tell me all about him."

As soon as Alma said the bit about Rose being in trouble, I knew it was true. The piece I'd been reluctant to see. It wasn't bribes from the folks intent on trolleys that would prove to be Abe Ruef and Gene Schmitz's undoing, and it wasn't the Standard Lodge, that seediest of brothels; no, it was the ho-hum everyday payola from the Frenchies that put them in the sights of the prosecution. The steady flow of cash that came from the tills of the Poodle Dog and the Pup, and a list of others—the restaurants and hotels from which the mayor and the Board of Supervisors had received regular kickbacks. The money was a melody that played under everything. Who had it, who gave it, and all along Rose acted as Schmitz's adviser, his greaser, and for that, she'd received a handsome cut.

If they were looking to lock up folks for taking bribes, Rose's name was high on that list. If it could be proved. Same as the mayor, Rose was looking for a way out.

After the holidays, as the charred hills of the city were being pounded with heavy rain, Schmitz once again visited the gold house.

I was upstairs with Rose. Schmitz must have rung the bell and been let in by one of the women, but I never heard the gong. He burst into the bedroom as we were finishing a conversation about the week's schedule. I was her secretary now, sending notes to her associates and arranging their visits to the house. I'd gone to fetch her a glass of water from the bathroom. Schmitz, dripping wet in his coat and hat, didn't bother with hello. "Rose, I've just been with the lawyers. Older and Spreckels have called on the president to appoint a U.S. attorney to handle the prosecution. Did you hear me? Teddy Goddamn Roosevelt is after me, Abe, and you."

I hovered in the doorway, in full view of Schmitz.

"The Poodle," Rose scolded. "I told you not to go there, Gene. We didn't need cash from every second-rate saloon and joint."

"Abe was the one with his hand out," Schmitz protested, his voice thin with self-pity. "They wanted protection. We couldn't let them—"

"You could have let them," Rose corrected. "Goddamn it, you could have let them," she barked. "Then you have to draw attention by being the first to get permits to rebuild? You, the mayor?" She went on, lashing Schmitz with her tongue. "And what do you rebuild, what classy operation do you choose as your flag, to show everyone you've turned over a new leaf? Why, the Standard, that dirty crib-joint with the girls taking abuse at twenty-five cents a go? You know, I've never cared for that kind of operation. The girls are sick, the customers are low-grade filth. But you, you have no ability to see the larger picture—"

"It wasn't me," Schmitz protested. "It was Abe."

"No, it was you, Gene. You think like a two-bit player. Worse, you're greedy," she bellowed. "You know, on the farm we had one rule: when the rooster starts acting like he's got a spare cock, cut that one off too."

"Ha!" he grumbled. "I never pegged you as a farmer's daughter."

"We're all farmers' daughters, once upon a time," she said, her voice husky with rage and pain and something unmistakable to my ear—fear. My Rose was afraid. "Now I have to worry about more loose ends? Christ, Gene. Tell me you've taken care of things."

"Yes! Yes," he vowed, but he didn't sound convincing. "There's just one, uh, bundle I can't get to—"

"*Can't* is for fools in prison," she spat.

"What can I do? They've impounded our old house," he whined. "I buy Julia a mansion but all she can talk about is cops putting their dirty boots on her old furniture. She's beside herself. Of course, knowing nothing about—" And here Schmitz looked at me, and I saw him decide that I was one of them after all, and that his problems were more urgent than any fear he might have of me. "Ah," he went on, "with the jail in ruins, they're talking about holding Abe ahead of his trial in our house—can you believe it?—with guards all over the place. Abe, of all people."

Rose turned her cycloptic gaze in my direction. "Oh, hello, big ears. You still there?" She nodded to Schmitz to keep on. "Ironic, your pal Abe under lock and key in your house."

If Schmitz saw the irony, he didn't appreciate it. "Abe is no pal of mine. My lawyers tell me his people are trying to finagle a deal—"

"Oh, he'll turn on you," Rose assured him. "The only question is, when they come digging for stuff to use against you—and dig they will—what will they find?"

• • •

I knew what they'd find. For Schmitz and Rose it was always about cash—cash in the safe, cash in velvet-lined boxes—the more bundles the better. Well, good for the police, I thought. They might as well pick Rose's safe and lock her up too.

I thought this out of spite, and oh, so many things. How the two of them had put me in the middle of their filthy antics—how I had put myself there.

"They're cold," I whispered when Bobby kissed me good night. "I didn't want to believe it, but now I know."

"Who is? Start at the beginning, and tell it to me," he urged.

I couldn't. I couldn't see the beginning and I surely couldn't see the end. Whatever I felt about Rose, and it was changing all the time, I knew I had to keep quiet.

I couldn't tell Bobby that as I showed Schmitz out, he asked, "Vera, what you just heard. How do you figure it?"

Once more he showed me his real face—that mix of scoundrel and choirboy that frightened me so when I was a little girl. Maybe there was a time when the choirboy could have won the day. Maybe if Schmitz had been gifted with a more expansive nature, and humility, maybe so. But Schmitz had only one real interest and that was himself.

"Are you asking, Mayor, if the ends justify the means?"

Schmitz grimaced, to hear his old question put back at him. The question whose real answer he never wanted to hear.

"They don't care about anyone," I whispered as I shivered in Bobby's arms. The tremble never leaving me, not in all those months.

"You're talking in riddles," Bobby said, and he kissed and kissed me, hoping to kiss the cold out of me.

Monkey Bread

Those winter afternoons when the weather was fair, Rose bathed in the sun. The sun, she insisted, healed her in ways no medicine could. She had Tan and Cap drag the velvet chaise from her bedroom onto the balcony, with its proper view of the garden and the blackened hills beyond. There, dressed only in knickers and a silk robe, which she opened to expose her breasts and belly and thighs—with the sewn eye pocket naked too—Rose gave herself to the sun. I think it must have felt delicious to have some heat on her bones, and though it was the fashion of the time for women of means to go around looking pale as cadavers, Rose preferred herself golden.

"Join me," she said one afternoon. She directed me to a second, smaller chaise Tan had positioned next to hers. "Go on," she urged, "no one's looking. Let the sun heal you, Vera. Let it turn you and me the same nice color."

I went as far as unbuttoning my blouse, so that the lace and ribbing of my combination was exposed.

"Look at you," Rose said dreamily, "going wild."

Was she making fun of me, or was she pleased? She lay back like a Mayan queen, with her eye shut and her chin raised to the gods.

I should add she was deep in the whiskey, the glass gripped in her hand. Rose wasn't Morie when she drank, but even so, I was cautious. Drink never did a single good thing for either of my mothers.

Yet I was free to observe her. To see that her hands were my hands, her bare feet the same as mine. We pointed our identical beaks toward the sky. If we talked, I expected we'd fight, so I stayed quiet. Still, I had the notion this wasn't to be a casual mother-daughter afternoon.

Tan had left us with a plate of monkey bread to share. Rose broke off a bit and chewed with her mouth open. "Have a bite," she urged.

I wasn't hungry but I ate anyway; it seemed rude not to. I ate one piece and, finding it delicious, ate another; she ate three pieces, all the while walking through the rooms of her mind.

"I make a point never to judge," she said at last.

With that, I knew I was in trouble.

"I've seen everything—everything," she said, taking another bite of the gooey monkey bread and washing it down with whiskey. She had my full attention.

She went on, "I've concluded that even a saint is capable of murder, and inside every murderer there lives a sweet, lost child. In other words, everyone has the whole organ inside them. Understood? And since I don't judge, I don't particularly care. All right?"

I sighed volubly to let her know I wasn't really interested in hearing another chapter from the madam's handbook.

"Now, no harm, no foul," she said, barreling on. "That boy out back: What's the story?" She sighed. "I hear all kinds of things. This house might as well be made of paper."

When she smiled, or tried to, only one side of her mouth lifted. "I expect you're trading favors. Do you know how to keep safe? Have my girls taught you at least that much?"

When she saw that I was too flustered to speak, she chuckled. "It's all right. I just don't want to see you in a fix—"

"Like you were?"

"Oh, fa."

"Here's something," I said, and flourished the copy of *The Rubaiyat of Omar Khayyam* I'd brought with me.

"My, my, where'd you unearth that thing?"

"Don't you remember? On my birthday, I found it on your shelf."

"A jillion years ago," she said. "Give it here."

"Not so fast," I said. "First, tell me what is it about these poems."

"The duke," she said. "He read Khayyam to me when we were young."

"So, are we Persian?"

"Ah, you with the questions. Look, we're a lotta things. But I never did hold to the idea of countries decided by the whims and wars of men. Now, shared understandings, I believe in. We cover continents of understanding, you and I. And we're better for it. Observe our Swedish ladies, those tender daisies. Which would you rather be?" She pivoted her eye to look me over. "You know," she marveled, "you could be attractive if you didn't carry all your anger here, above your brow, like a storm. A storm for the whole world to see and judge you by."

"Where should I carry it?"

She pointed to her heart. "Like me."

"Like you," I echoed. "Like you with all the secrets."

She chewed on that for a while. Where I expected she'd turn mean, the sun made her mellow, philosophical even.

"No one gets away with life, girl," she said wistfully, her eye closed to the sun. "Trust me, no one. Learn that, and you will save yourself a few surprises. You and you alone get to decide what part of your story you let folks see, 'cause what they see, they'll use to peg you."

All right, then, I decided, if we were going to have this chat, we were going to have it. "The duke is my father," I declared. "There, I've said it. And it didn't kill you or me."

"No," she said, "it didn't kill *you*."

We were quiet then. I had already decided the duke was my father after she went on about him the night she rambled. But knowing it was a different thing. It felt like a punch to the stomach.

"Did you love him?"

"Love? Oh God, is that where this is going?" She took the last bite of the monkey bread and worked it around in her mouth. "Beyond the duke," she said. "Beyond him. Let me tell you: they kill strong-minded women like us. I don't mean they literally kill them. No, what they do is chip at their hearts. If they spot your ambition, they whittle you, dissect you, reduce you. An uncommon woman is to be shunned."

"I won't be shunned," I said. "I don't care what folks say, but I won't be shunned."

"Ha! So, you do think you're exceptional. You once denied it."

I smiled. Having confirmed the bit about the duke, I was content to let that stand. It wasn't untrue.

She was pouring herself more whiskey and I could feel her winding up to say more.

"You think I don't know you," she said. "I know you. I know you because I know me." Her voice shook with emotion. "Let me tell you something, Vera. When your eyes are dark and your skin isn't fair, you will never be in. When you have a sharp tongue. When you fail to compromise, when you are unpleasing, when you are different, when your gaze is piercing, when your eyes see, when you are quiet, when you frown because you are concentrating, when you pull at your nose in public—oh, yes—when your body is made more for work than ease, when you want men till you have them, want friends till they talk, want to be happy till all the happy things bore you, want quiet in the middle of a conversation, when all you hope for is arms around you, until you learn that they come at the price of your soul, when you are melancholy more often than not, when you are fierce in a world of feathers and folly, when you're alone in every room you enter, you do not fit in. You never will. I know you."

She fell back against the pillows and waved a weak hand, dismissing me, now that she was done. She'd hit all her marks. But not every mark.

My head was throbbing. When I was very small, I longed to be near her. When I was some older, I wanted to be like her. Now that I was fifteen—fifteen plus a quake—I wanted only to have what she possessed: power. The power to decide for myself who and what to love.

"I hope . . . I hope I never see the world as grimly as you do," I said. "I'd rather—"

"What, die?" she scoffed. "Come, not you. You're the ultimate survivor." She nodded. "And that, at the end of the end, pleases me."

"You're pleased, but that's as far as you go. You . . . don't love," I said with conviction, though I was just trying it on. "You're afraid to love."

She pulled on the arms of the chaise, struggling to lift herself higher. "You think you know me well enough to talk of my desires? You?"

"I wouldn't . . . say I know you. I don't fully know myself," I admitted.

"There. That's right," she agreed.

"So why don't you tell me. What do you, Rose of The Rose, truly love?"

"There's only one thing worth loving, my girl. Freedom. Always I have loved my freedom."

The Cliffs

I know his body even more so now. All these years, he's in my skin. And to think, when so much else has fallen away. Bobby's body blazes bright, and when little is left, you have the marks to show.

He was too thin. His teeth were too large for his mouth. He smelled of tobacco—it was in his hair, and stained into his fingers. He was careful. I didn't want him to be careful. I wanted him to rush, to get to it. He refused. We had all night—two kids in the moonlight, knocking our bony knees together.

Everyone believes they invented it, the first time. And every time I expect it's true. Every rustle and scoot feeling like the exploration of pioneers. Those nights in the attic, Bobby and I built a new planet out of dust and stars.

And he didn't call me Versus, or Anyway. He called me Vera.

I could give you his body cell by cell, but I won't. I won't give that away.

All the men I've known since, and there have been quite a few, there never was another Bobby—no one so sure, so knowing in that way. That scamp. How did this boy, this scrap of an urchin, with holes in his pockets and raggedy cuffs, his hair cut with a raw blade, his shoes with paper bottoms, how did he know so much about a woman's pleasure? My three husbands never knew as much. Oh, they were kind in their way, and eager to please—that is, when they wished to please.

• • •

We decided the attic was the better place. Throughout that winter of '07, Bobby found me. There was nothing stopping us now from being stupid-silly, or slow and patient, with our love.

And we made that trip to the beach. They'd fixed part of the line and we rode the Ocean Beach trolley to the end. We passed through Golden Gate Park and the Japanese Tea Garden and the Conservatory of Flowers, into the Sunset District, to the Cliff House and the Sutro Baths.

We had a picnic in the sand. Bobby thought to borrow a tablecloth from Tan, and we ate sandwiches and even chocolates. "Where'd you get these?" I asked. While the chocolate was in my mouth, he kissed me.

He'd never seen the Cliff House before. That seven-story white palace built for the city's swells, perched on the rocks with views of the sunset.

"When we're old or rich, let's have tea there," I said.

"Sure, but does it have to be tea?" he asked, laughing. Then his face turned serious and he said, "Do you really think we'll grow old together?"

Well, I don't know what came over me, but I started to cry. "I want to grow young with you, Bobby. Can't we do that first?" Those days had been so very hard.

I don't recall what else we talked about. Nothing of importance. Bobby, he wasn't much of a talker. Then, neither was I. We looked, we touched, we knew, and that was the world—that was more than enough.

The seals were lolling on the rocks, hundreds of them, and we watched their antics as they took their leisure, napping in the sun.

We packed up slowly—reluctantly. The sun was setting beyond the cliffs. A gorgeous yolk of a sunset. We rode the trolley back and walked the rest of the way holding hands. We didn't care who saw us. We were sweethearts.

Pie had been watching from the parlor windows. She ran to meet us as we came up the driveway.

"Rose is gone," she said. "She took everything."

It Isn't Personal

"No one gets away with life," Rose said. I've had many years to think about what she meant. I've decided that Rose was the exception. Rose got away.

Why, she even stripped the bed. She took the heavy silver and her perfumes and the Victrola. She took Mercy and Sophia; Lifang, LowNaa, and Tan. Whatever lived in the safe, she also took. As a final mockery, or perhaps as a sign of having packed in haste, she left the door of the safe open, so we could feast on its emptiness, the shelves bare where the gold and cash had been, the little empty cubbies that used to hold her jewelry. All that remained were some loose papers at the bottom, on which the bars had been stacked.

"Aw, darlin'," Cap said, "you gotta know it isn't personal."

"It sure feels personal."

Cap shrugged. "Johnny Law was coming for her. He was bearing down, and you know Madam Rose wasn't likely to sit to. She needed to disappear and I expect she disappeared good."

"Where do you suppose she'd go, Cap?"

"She wasn't sayin'. She wasn't saying nothin' except get outta my way."

Cap and Valentine took care of me. They put me in a hot bath, washed my hair and feet. I tried to resist but they knew what they were doing, cleaning me. I cried and they washed my tears. Cap said, "That's right, darlin', empty the bowl."

Capability brushed my hair and dried me and put me in soft flannel, and sang me to sleep.

When I woke, it was the middle of the next day. Capability was rocking in the chair, the squeak of the wood a music to me.

"Darlin' child," she said, "I learned a long ways ago, no one can take from you what you don't offer. You didn't offer, then she didn't take it. *Capisci?*"

I thought about that awhile. "Cap?"

"Yeah, sugar?"

"Why didn't you go with them?"

"Let's put it this way"—she sighed—"I've been the caboose on that train for a long, long time."

"Cap?"

"Go on, now," she urged. "Sleep as long as you can stand it. I'll be here, holding the place."

"The place?"

"That's right. This very place."

I hadn't stopped for a single day. Not for the quake, or the fire—certainly not during the days that followed. Oh, I'd slept, I'd eaten, but I hadn't stopped. I hadn't let myself feel it all. But when I did, I fell down a hole that went to the center of the earth.

The next time I woke, Cap said, "You hungry? There's a tray."

On the floor by the cot. The tray had a pot of tea, a plate of hash, and an apple cut in thin slices and fanned.

"Who did this?"

"Who do you think?" Cap chuckled. "Tan, of course. He's fussing awful that you won't eat."

"Tan's back?"

"Why, sure. He took them to the station, said his good-byes, then drove his sorry self back."

I ate everything on that tray, then fell asleep—for another couple of days. Valentine said Bobby demanded to see me, but they told him I had a fever and that he'd best stay away. That bought me time. They put the flowers he'd picked in a vase on the dresser.

I dreamed I was living on Francisco Street. The piano was where it was supposed to be, in the parlor. I heard the bells of the milk wagon and the butcher's call. Mrs. Valdrone, the laundress, was there, hauling her cart to the rocks at Cow Hollow. Foghorns in the distance. Someone was chasing me.

Then the dream turned, and I was being beaten while Pie and Morie looked on. They were judges, dressed in robes. When I woke, I asked Cap, "Has Pie come up to see me?"

"Well, honey," she said, choosing her words carefully. "Pie is very busy with those orphans."

"Cap?"

"Mmm?"

"That's a lot of bull."

"Yes," she said at last, "indeed, it is."

"Cap?"

"Mmm?"

"Do you ever really know someone?"

"Oh, sure. Most folks you know right off. Problem is, then you go deciding to love them, and you forget." She rocked some more, then added, "You, I knew right off. When she brought you back instead of giving you away that first time. You were just a wee bit, sweet to the marrow. Oh, I knew you right off."

"Cap, keep going. Don't stop."

"Lordy, I thought you were gonna sleep."

"What did I do wrong? I must have done something to make her send me away to Morie."

"Not a damn thing," Cap said. "By then you were walking, of course. And, oh my, talking. Asking the questions. This little bitty girl, running down the halls, with the johns due any minute, and you asking why, why, why."

"She gave me away because I asked—?"

"She can't be running a whorehouse with a toddler underfoot."

Valentine swore that Rose had put a spell on me. I don't disagree. The earthquake, the fire, whoa, none of that spiked such a tremor in me.

I had to concentrate. I had to concentrate very hard to see my way. And until I could, I took my meals, everything, in the attic, where it was quiet and small and I could look at the sky through the ox-eye window; I could look at the underside of the sewing machine.

Bobby visited me. He stood at the door and whispered, "Anyway?"

But I'd misplaced my laughter. And my desire.

His kisses felt suffocating; his arms, his heavy legs on mine made me panic, as if I were being crushed.

Of course, being so young, we didn't have the language. I didn't know what to tell him. I'd lost my way, that was the simplest, kindest way to put it. I wasn't sorry she was gone, I didn't miss her, but she took something from me—at the very least my hope—and without it I couldn't put my lips against the scruff of Bobby's chin and feel anything but scratched.

For a time, you see, I left my body on the earth and floated above. My body was just too angry and sad. When I returned to it, I felt I had to catch up quickly, urgently—to be smart in all the ways I had been foolish. I pored over the books in her library, I read the newspapers—morning and evening editions. I was desperate to learn the ways of the world, to know how to be.

Bobby said, "Come back, Vera. Wherever you've gone, come back to me."

I replied, "Bobby, what do you think about the new scheme for the trolleys? What do you think of Roosevelt's plan to limit the number of Japanese people entering the country? It's wrong, isn't it? Do you think Taft will be a good president?" I had a hundred concerns like that.

Bobby said he didn't think much of Taft or any man who allowed himself to get so fat.

"Is that all you have to say about it?"

"Don't worry," he assured me. "I won't get fat."

I didn't bother to hide my disappointment. "Bobby, don't you want to know what is happening in the world? Don't you want to learn—?"

"Tell you what," he said, "if there's food or the scratch we need inside one of those books you're reading, I'll eat it. Meantime, I'm gonna fix the wheel on Tan's pushcart, so he can get to the grocer."

That's when I saw just how far and high Bobby would go, and it would never be with his mind, only his hands.

I said to myself, Vera, you are being ridiculous; you will regret this; he is a good man—all that. I dared myself to look at him. And when I couldn't quite see him and me together, I did an awful thing—truly the most awful. I gave Bobby Del Monte the Invisible.

Tan and I made quite the pair. He was suffering too. He'd begged Lifang to stay; he impressed upon her the possibility of starting over in the new Chinatown. But she'd yearned to get away from the ash and those tong boys, who were already claiming, even expanding, their turf. She yearned to get away from Tan. LowNaa agreed to go as Lifang's chaperone, promising he'd be back, but Tan knew that was unlikely.

To make certain that her father wouldn't follow, Lifang spat at his feet and promised that she despised him.

Lifang's parting gift to me was a dirty pot with a soiled rag she left outside my door—her final insult. I seethed over that pot. Honestly, it took me years to realize that it wasn't an insult. Lifang just needed me to be her witness, that's all. That pot was her declaration of all she was leaving behind. And like any person, she needed someone to know that she intended to become someone new.

March arrived wet and cold. I decided it was time to leave the sewing room. I got dressed and started taking my meals downstairs.

In my absence, Tan, Capability, and Valentine had begun having their meals at the worktable in the kitchen. I joined them. They never asked about Bobby, though once Cap reached across the supper table and cupped my sad chin in her hand. "Shh, now, that's why they call it falling, darlin'. You're falling in reverse."

After I gave him the Invisible, Bobby returned to his former habit of eating with the orphans at the Ladies' Protection. Pie took her meals in her room.

That left Tan, Capability, Valentine, and me free to discuss over supper our shared obsession: money. Where to get it; how little we had. We sold the booze, and with it the art and what remained of Rose's silver.

That's when Valentine and Capability put a toe in. They were seeing their regular clients outside the house, but only here or there. Cap had a trilling soprano, popular at the time, and, of course, whenever Valentine opened her mouth, out boomed a velvet bass.

"We could try it, one or two Sundays," Valentine said. "What harm could it do, charging for a few friendly songs?"

"We'd need someone in the middle," Cap said. "An alto."

Lily worked in the deli shop nearby. A large-breasted gal with thick legs and a gorgeous voice, Lily wasn't opposed to singing, or flirting, or much of anything.

Soon word got around and men started coming for the Sunday sherry recitals, where Cap, Valentine, and Lily performed a couple of sets, and maybe for a little extra they'd sit on a lap, that kind of thing.

Pie was furious. The first chance she had she pulled me into her room. "You promised," she sniped. "You promised me, hearts-cross."

"What did I promise you, Pie? What have I ever promised you I didn't follow through? If you don't want men in the house, and your God-of-the-book isn't providing, then give me another plan. How are we going to live?" I didn't speak kindly, my feelings were still hurt that she hadn't bothered to check on me when I was ill.

"I don't know," she hemmed. "You're the planner. I know if you thought about it, you'd noodle a way—"

"Noodle. What exactly would I noodle, eh, Piper?" That was the first time in forever I used her real name. When I first came to live with them, I called my new sister Pie, and to me that was what she'd always been.

"We counted on you. Morie and I did," she said.

We. Something stirred in me when she said that, an old something, born of the boar-bristle brush and how Pie never once lifted a hand to stop Morie.

So, I asked, "When I was sick, why didn't you come see me? I was so blue, and you didn't come."

"Oh." She stumbled. "You know I don't care to go upstairs where they . . . sleep. And I knew . . . well, I was sure Capability was taking good care of you. She told me so. I did ask, V, and Capability told me you needed rest. I know it was a terrible shock and I thought: That's right, Vera needs to rest. And I had my work at the orphanage—oh, V, don't be sore at me."

"How come you cook for the orphans, but you won't help cook for your family, here?"

Leveling those calm blue eyes at me, she lifted her chin. "I'd cook for my family," she said.

• • •

All that winter, I'd missed running into Sugarman. He'd taken Pearl and their boys to Europe while the city got back on its feet. Pearl's nerves were shot, Sugarman explained to me, in his usual mix of Yiddish, English, and soul-speak. For six months Sugarman and his family visited relatives in Hungary; they met with his colleagues in Vienna. He was present when his former classmate Sigmund Freud met Carl Jung for the first time.

Upon Sugarman's return, as I was just getting on my feet, I ran into him while I was out walking Rogue. The first few times we met by accident, but soon we were arranging our walks. We fell into an easy rhythm. Some nights we'd get so deep in conversation, we'd do five, six, ten laps around the perimeter of the square.

Concerning my predicament, Sugarman, ever the philosopher, put forth his theory that the greater the love, the larger the betrayal. He meant Rose, but I was fixated on Pie.

I'd been stewing on her words.

I found her in her room, getting ready for bed. She was seated at her vanity—the one Rose made sure every bedroom in the house had. In Pie's room, the vanity's trifold beveled mirror had suffered a few nicks in the quake. I took a seat on one of the twin beds and looked on as Pie performed her evening toilette. Morie had taught her what to do with her hair when she was a little girl. She likewise tried to teach me, but I never had much patience for the dabs and doodads.

First, Pie divided her hair into three parts, one on each side, then the back. Her blond hair fell to her waist, with a shy curl at the ends. Using a hairbrush that Rose had given her, Pie gave each section a hundred strokes. First the left side, then the right, then a reach to the back—always the same order, the same ritual Morie had followed and I suppose Morie's mother before her. Pie's lips moved as she counted strokes, and as she relaxed, she forgot about me. Her eyes fluttered closed. If ever I wondered what wouldn't change after the world collapsed, it was this: Pie brushing her hair three hundred strokes.

"Pie?"

"Yah?"

"I've been thinking . . . on what you said. About turning the house into, you know?"

She paused mid-stroke. "Oh, I knew you'd agree with me, once you gave it a good think. There has to be another way."

"Yeah, maybe so."

Relieved, she started in where she'd left off. "Sixty-seven. Sixty-eight." She smiled at me in the mirror. "I bet you've noodled something brilliant. What is it?"

"Well, it concerns you."

"Me?"

"Mmm. Actually, it's not a new idea, you and Morie thought of it a while ago."

"We did?"

"We've got to get you married, Pie. I've gone through the figures and I can give you a month. That's all we've got: one month to find him, woo him, marry him."

She turned slowly. "Are you suggesting that I—"

My heart was pounding with false euphoria, with an old anger I'm not proud of, but there it was. "'Course," I added, "he has to have money."

"Get out!" she cried.

"Thirty days," I said. "That, or we start the business. Oh, and should that happen, I expect we'll need this room."

Pie spent every one of those thirty days away from the house. She left early each morning and returned late from working with Eugenie and the orphans. Every day Bobby took her there and back in the buggy. No one asked him to do so; he just did it. I expect he thought it would please me.

It happened right under my nose. I was so busy avoiding him, I didn't see. I suppose I didn't want to see.

One morning in April, as Bobby was picking the frogs in Monster's hooves and otherwise getting the horse and buggy ready to ferry Pie to the refuge, I returned from walking Rogue. Pie was just coming out of the house; she was wearing a new hat.

"Did you buy her that?" I accused Bobby with my hands on my hips, as if I were an aggrieved wife.

His face turned ugly. "Where would I get the scratch to buy a silly hat?"

But Pie, you see, had remembered her assignment. The one I gave her.

"Bobby," she called sweetly. "Here, I made sandwiches for your lunch." She handed him a basket lined with a fresh linen towel. Then she waited till he helped her into the buggy.

Next thing I heard, Pie had shifted from working at the refuge with Eugenie to spending time with Bobby and the orphans at the Ladies' Protection. She befriended some of the other do-gooder women there, women with fancy hats and deep purses, from the city's finest families. It was Pie's idea that they should form a committee to raise funds to rebuild the orphanage; the women insisted that Pie lead the effort.

Was I convinced that since Bobby loved me so much, he'd never turn to Pie? Did I think I had all the months in the world to change my mind? All I can say is that for a while it was a relief to be alone, with no one demanding more of me. By the time I got my feeling back, weeks had passed.

One night, I waited till the house was asleep. Wearing only my nightgown, I brushed my hair so it was long feathers, the way Bobby liked it. I shut Rogue in our attic room and crept downstairs and out the kitchen door.

There was no moon and I nearly broke my neck tripping over a shovel that was lying on the ground. I was already flustered, and the creak-groan of the heavy garage door rolling on its casters unnerved me more.

"Bobby?"

"Hey!"

"Bobby, please, just let me get this out: I love you. I do. I didn't for a while, I mean, I sort of forgot. But I do—"

"Don't," he said sternly, rushing toward me, the heat of him, naked. "Don't."

I couldn't see his face in the dark, and his tone had a bite. I supposed it was because he was hurt or mad, of course he was. I hung my arms around his neck, and searched for his mouth with my lips.

Then I heard rustling. No, it was more that I felt-heard another animal in that small space.

"Who's that?" I whispered.

"V, it's me," Pie declared. That was all she said.

The next afternoon, when Cap, not knowing, told me that Bobby had taken Pie on a buggy ride to the ocean, I wanted to beg, Why, Bobby, why? But I knew.

Loose Papers

Tomorrow, April 18, they'll come for me. They'll bring me a corsage, wrap me in blankets, and strap me to my chair. They'll take me down the road to Lotta's Fountain. There at the crux of Market Street, they'll take my picture for the paper: the oldest living survivor of the '06 quake.

That's tomorrow. Today, I'm just enjoying the peace.

"Vera, want to tidy a bit before the hoopla?" the nurse asked me this morning when she came to roll me this way and that in my bed.

My hands are spotted lobster claws, my nose and ears are the only parts still growing; if I make it to a hundred and six I can be an elephant for Halloween.

So I asked, "Gloria, just how much tidying do you think is possible for a body this far gone?"

Gloria chuckled. She thinks I'm a funny old bird.

I have lived beyond a century. A hundred years of bombs and push. A century where man's genius made him a devotee of machines. A hundred years of world wars punctuated by the true miracles of penicillin and the silicon wafer and the Beatles. The first half of the century was hard on my body; the second half has been hard on my mind.

Even so, tomorrow they'll park me beside Lotta's cast-iron fountain, two relics of survival, and blast the horns and speak of the great shaker, as if it is a thing of the past. They'll ask, How did you manage to survive the catastrophe?

And I'll be a smart-ass and say, Which one? The last one, or the next one coming?

They won't ask about the fire, that part has faded. It's all quake now, and notions of a once-raucous city of hookers and gin joints on the Barbary Coast, of con men with gold-lined pockets and girls in low-cut dresses doing the cancan. They won't ask about Mayor Schmitz, long dead, also forgotten.

We were more alive after the quake than we had any right to be.

Tan, Valentine, Capability, and I passed the one-year anniversary of the quake, April 18, 1907, in the gold house, where we shared our midday dinner and concerns. We were at the kitchen table one day when the post arrived, with a letter from the assessor's office, which didn't exist anymore, just a couple of desks in the temporary City Hall. The letter was regarding taxes. Taxes due. It turned out Rose hadn't paid the taxes on the house in years.

"Look, your name is on the envelope," Valentine said. "That's gotta be a mistake."

Tan, ever the scrapper, solved the riddle. He gathered those loose papers that had been waiting at the bottom of the safe the whole time and brought them to me. We fanned them across the dining room table. Glory be, they were deeds. Deeds and transfers and escrow documents. Carefully executed, signed in Rose's hand.

Rose, it turned out, didn't just invest in gold. She had her lawyers buy land in the ultimate fire sale, for a fraction of its worth. Barren lots, but one day worth millions. There was even a map on which Rose had charted the path of the aboveground trolleys, knowing that wherever those trolleys stopped, there would be plenty of customers wanting stores and restaurants. My inheritance was the three lots downtown that had been The Rose. Why, she'd even signed over the house, with a sizable mortgage, to me.

Some gifts are curses too. Where would we ever get the money to build, let alone pay the mortgage and taxes that were due?

At night, Tan, Capability, Valentine, and I stared at the papers as if they would magically show us a way forward.

Rose knew I'd be reluctant to sell the land—any fool could see this was my chance. She'd planted the seed to start a parlor house. Cap and Valentine needed an occupation. Tan—even Bobby and Pie—needed to eat. I had so many hearts to care for. And my own, which I could not see.

By then the debris downtown had been plowed and there were speculators with designs on making a killing. With the property records destroyed along with City Hall, there was a free-for-all. Anyone who could show proof of ownership had better get to it.

I went, as I would many times throughout the years, to seek the advice of Sugarman. When he saw me coming not at my usual evening hour but midday, he strapped on his boots and we walked downtown to eyeball my barren plots while turning over my latest problem.

"Vera, my friend," Sugarman said, "what is it you truly want?"

"I don't know," I admitted, but I thought of Rose's answer, freedom, and how for me that was not the first thing.

"Ah," he said, "I think you do know. You merely lack the words. Let's keep walking till you find them. Meantime, what is it you think you need?"

"A lawyer, Dr. Sugarman," I said, "though I also need money. But first I need a good lawyer."

Sugarman introduced me to a young lawyer named Bill Hutchinson. Tall, well-spoken, Harvard-trained. He'd arrived in San Francisco the week before the quake. When the world around him fell to pieces, he decided he'd be part of making it new again. Hutchinson taught me what I needed to know about leases and shares—and what it would cost to keep everything. I left him feeling more certain that I would never find the money.

Bobby took me to those meetings with the lawyer; he waited outside at the curb with Monster. Bobby saw in Hutchinson, who was nothing to me, a young, educated man in a fine suit. Bill Hutchinson was six foot six, patrician, and though I wasn't thinking about him, Bobby was.

"You gonna marry him?" Bobby asked, with such sorrow in his eyes.

"No, Bobby, I'm never getting married," I said. "But you are."

As we worked to rebuild our lives, the days were full. I didn't look back much on my life before the quake; I didn't think about Francisco Street. We'd heard that our block had been cleared and the lots were being sold for next to nothing. On another walk, Sugarman went with me to Francisco Street to claim my dirt.

Pie and I had forgotten about the Haj, but he hadn't forgotten us. He followed Sugarman and me home. The next morning, he returned and rang the bell.

I had just run upstairs to fetch my ledger. Tan answered the door. By the time I came down, the Haj had cracked Tan's knee with his cane and pushed his way into the foyer. Valentine threw a running punch at the Haj, knocking him off his feet. The Haj reached for his knife as Valentine clobbered him in the head with the marble bust of Venus. Cap had a grip on Rogue's collar, but the dog was barking wildly, gnashing his teeth.

"Stop, everyone. Stop!" I shouted as I ran down the stairs. They ignored me. Rogue kept barking—the sound was deafening. "Rogue, off. You hear me, off!" I bellowed. He paused, and shifted to a menacing growl.

I focused on the Haj. He was truly a wretched creature, stalk-thin, bleeding from his nose and mouth.

Valentine, wearing a dress, her wig tossed on the floor, had gotten hold of the knife and was threatening the Haj with it, pinning him to the floor with a heavy knee.

The Haj's hair and coat were filthy. He was gaunt in his bloody cheeks. The quake had been hard on everyone, but maybe especially hard if you were a shark.

"Valentine?" I called.

She wouldn't look at me. "Go upstairs, miss. Go on, now." Valentine turned the handle of the knife so the Haj stayed focused on the blade.

"There . . . she is," the Haj muttered. "Hook . . . hooker's daughter."

"What do you want?" I asked.

"What I'm owed . . . is all. Six hundred . . . twenty dollars."

Tan looked to me. His knee was badly hurt, and even so, he shook his head. The Haj might just as well have said six thousand, or six hundred thousand; we had no chance of paying such a debt.

"Go on, Missy V. Go on up," Tan urged.

I thought, That's what I should do, go up, and let them take care of it. There was no question in my mind what taking care of it meant. And this time it would happen in my house.

"You'll take a hundred," I said. "Or I go up."

"Four hundred fifty," said the Haj.

Valentine flicked him with the knife under his chin.

"Talking to the miss," the Haj spat.

"Two hundred or nothing," I countered. "And I'll need a month."

The Haj dared to turn his head and look at me. "Two fifty . . . two weeks."

"All right," I said.

• • •

The habit of doing things to impress Rose didn't quit me all at once. For a while, I acted as if she were watching me, and in my mind, I heard her clucking her tongue whenever I proved weak or foolish.

After that bit with the Haj, I didn't hear Rose anymore.

But I kept thinking of those couple of nights when I fed her morphine and she confessed her soul, and how much of what she'd obsessed about had to do with money. Well, it was money I needed. Rose talked about the mayor's financial dealings with Abe Ruef, and how the river of cash flowed downstream, with Rose being just one branch of the stream, with other branches including the police and the newspapers and the public works folks and the politicians too. It was a whole lot of money to keep track of, to prosecute, and if a certain bundle went missing, who would miss it?

It got me thinking of money tucked away in little rabbit holes—inside safes and pockets and hidden beneath floors.

A Visit to Ruef

Prior to the start of his criminal trial, Abe Ruef was put under house arrest. Since the temporary city jail was unfit for a man of his stature and celebrity, Ruef was confined to Mayor Schmitz's former home, on Fillmore Street.

I walked from the gold house down the steep hill to the mayor's, careful not to trip. Ruef's Packard was parked at the curb, a chock block wedged under its rear wheel to keep it from rolling down the hill. There were only a few thousand automobiles in the whole of the country then. Rose and the mayor each owned two, and if you added the cars that Abe Ruef possessed—the Rolls, the Packard, and a couple of runabout Fords used to collect the payola—between the three of them, they owned nearly a dozen. Such was the cash that flowed through their respective operations, above and below the sheets, a car then never being just a car: no, a car was cash on wheels.

Two cops sat inside a Ford, also parked at the curb, and another pair guarded the front door. One of San Francisco's finest lounged in a chair in the foyer. The officer in the hallway stood as I came in.

"Abe," he shouted, "there's a young lady here."

Ruef had been having a late lunch in the kitchen. He hurried to see who it was, his napkin still tucked into his collar, his eyes showing a range of emotions, all fleeting, from contempt to surprise.

"What's this," he said.

"Sorry to bother you." I spoke quickly, so I wouldn't lose my nerve.

Ruef wiped his chops on Julia Schmitz's linen napkin and, adjusting his bow tie, this small man in a three-piece brown suit and shined boots tossed the napkin to his guard. "Yes," he said. "Bother me how?"

"Eugenie Schmitz asked me to come. She left behind some things in her room. She asked if I would fetch them for her. She can't, well, you understand, she can't come herself."

He took notice of Lars Johnson's valise, the one I'd carried from Francisco Street on the day of the quake.

"Of course," Ruef said, "have at." And he waved me on with all the impatience of a man who still had a city to run.

My foot was on the top stair when Ruef called to me.

"I remember you," he said.

I turned back. "Yes, Mr. Ruef. I remember you too."

"Beer and ham sandwiches," he answered, the gears of his massive brain grinding.

"That's right. And you, you wanted to relocate the Chinese."

"Ah, lost that one, didn't I?" He grimaced. "But it was the right idea."

"Not to the Chinese."

"Ah, true. True enough," he agreed. "I wasn't supposed to be here that day," he mused, his voice soft, almost nostalgic. "They decided they didn't want me. Even Gene. Maybe especially Gene. But I came anyway. You bet I did." He shrugged. "And look at me now, I can't leave."

"I suppose, as prisons go, it's not the worst?" I put it as a question.

He misheard me. "Prison?" he said. "Ha, don't you worry. I'm not going to prison."

• • •

Eugenie's room was as she'd left it: a world of lace—canopies and antimacassars and bows. The wooden cross, the one that always gave me the creeps, with its sad Jesus, still guarded the bed.

First off, I made a loud business of opening and shutting the drawers of Eugenie's wardrobe. They creaked and thudded. When I felt I'd established sufficient racket, I hurried to the foot of the bed. The carpet was as it had been, covering the spot where the floor had been cut. I rolled it aside and found the hidden metal pull, and lifted the boards. I was so nervous, my hands were clumsy and I kept looking over my shoulder at the door.

I knew enough about Schmitz to understand that he was both reckless and lazy. I guessed that he would have decided against last-ditch measures, and even decided there would be no safer place to store the cash than in a house with half a dozen guards. Besides, if found, couldn't it be Ruef who stashed it there?

The metal box was unlocked. I lifted the lid to find the red plush lining, and . . . nothing. The boodle box, as it was later called in the newspaper—a compartment that was never the right shape for storing violins—was empty. I stuck my nose inside the box to be sure.

In my desperation, I pushed on the velvet ends of the box and they gave way just a bit. I pushed harder—the ends had only been tacked in place. Beyond, in the crude space between the floor and ceiling, a second stash was hidden, on either side of the boodle box. I reached as far as my arm would go. The bills had been tied with the same sort of bands that I'd seen used at The Rose. I stuffed the valise till it couldn't hold any more. Finally, I covered the stash with a dozen of Eugenie Schmitz's hand-embroidered handkerchiefs and did up the leather straps.

The cop was waiting for me at the top of the stairs. "You need help, there, miss? Come, let me." Before I could stop him, he took my heavy bag. "Let's get you down the road, eh," he said.

All I could think was: I just needed to get past the cops at the curb, then up two blocks to where Tan was waiting for me.

"What'd you find?" Ruef called, hurrying once more from the kitchen. He went as far as the front door and paused, there, at the rim of his cage.

"What'd you get?" He gestured at the valise.

Damn, I thought, the jig is up.

"Keepsakes," I said. "This and that."

"Ah, you ladies with your treasures." Ruef squinted, accustoming his eyes to the bright sun. With his middle finger, he pushed back the bridge of his wire-rimmed glasses. They were always slipping down his nose.

"That's right," I agreed.

The cop holding the valise glanced at its worn brass clasps and I feared he had an inkling to cast his eye on what was inside. He set the heavy bag on the walk.

"Vera Johnson!" Ruef exclaimed, laughing.

"What's this," the cop said. "Who?"

"Vera goddamn Johnson, Rose's kid," he bellowed, and he knocked his fist on the mayor's door.

"Right," I agreed. "You got me."

How pleased Ruef was with himself! To have so cleverly knit the pieces, to have pulled from his capacious memory bank, where the city pols and hookers and saloonkeepers resided, among the upstanding Jews and goys, and those who owed the monthly or weekly or every-so-often payola, and the supervisors of easy virtue and the ones who balked, and his lawyers, his bankers, and Joey, the ruthless, who ran the cribs at the Standard, to Teddy Roosevelt himself, who, on the morning of their meeting, ordered his coffee sweet with seven spoons of sugar, and this was just a fraction of what Abe Ruef kept in that noggin of his, all this and my name.

"See that." He wagged his finger at the cop, who was still eyeballing my bag, and the other cops in the Ford—reminding them, those sons of bitches, who would sooner see him in jail, that he was the smart guy, the one and only Abe Ruef.

I suppose I looked properly impressed and even embarrassed.

"Give Eugenie my regards," Ruef said, waving me on. "Tell her I hope she's praying for me."

"I expect she's praying for her father," I said as I picked up the bag.

"Have you seen him?" Ruef asked. "Have you seen Gene?"

"Not recently," I said, thinking, Sweet almighty, just ten more steps and I'm free.

But Ruef wasn't done. The cops were eyeing him, and he wasn't done. "I told you to go to college, didn't I, Vera?"

"Yes. Yes, you did."

"And I was right: you should. Don't let them hold you back just 'cause you're a girl."

She was a girl too, my city. How perfect that her official seal is that of a phoenix rising. After she burned that sixth time, she was born again—headstrong and whimsical, careless as ever. Her trembling, her desire as elemental as her bedrock and curves.

Ruef's trial was the sensation of the spring of '07. The men behind the prosecution included Francis Heney, U.S. district attorney; Fremont Older, editor of the *San Francisco Bulletin*; and Claus Spreckels, father of Alma's AB.

During the proceedings, Francis Heney discovered that one of the jurors, a Morris Haas, was a convicted felon. Heney accused Haas of being on Ruef's payroll. Haas answered the accusation by shooting the district attorney in the face—right there in the courtroom. Incredibly, Heney survived.

The next morning, Morris Haas was found dead in his cell. Everyone suspected Ruef of being the mastermind of a perfectly, audaciously planned execution. The newspapers accused William Biggy, the city sheriff, of negligence. After all, Biggy had allowed a murder to take place in the city jail. Biggy was hounded in the press and on the streets. It was suggested that he too must be on Ruef's payroll. The stench of corruption was everywhere, as was the outcry that the new San Francisco was proving to be just as dirty as the old.

When Sheriff Biggy's body was found floating in the bay, it was yet one more seismic shock. It seemed Biggy had fallen off his boat late one night and drowned. An improbable death that had all the markings of Ruef, who was soon sentenced to fourteen years in San Quentin.

Mayor Schmitz's trial was more straightforward.

On June 13, 1907, fourteen months after the quake, Eugene Schmitz was convicted for extorting twenty-seven hundred dollars from Tony Bloney, proprietor of the Poodle Dog. Schmitz was sentenced to the maximum of five years in San Quentin.

A thousand people gathered in the street to hear the verdict. As it was read, a roar went up. Schmitz turned to his lawyers and said, "What? What happened?"

The mayor's lawyers appealed immediately, based on lack of evidence. Where was the twenty-seven hundred dollars? they demanded. When Schmitz's bank accounts were shown to have negligible balances—when the prosecution discovered that the boodle box, hidden in the floor of a bedroom in the mayor's former house, was empty—his conviction was overturned. The grand house up the hill, yes, the cars, the trips to Europe on a mayor's modest salary all pointed to obvious corruption, but without a cash trail, there was no real proof.

I hoped I'd never run into Schmitz. But San Francisco has always been a small town. The folks you wish to avoid inevitably are the ones you see.

"Vera!" Schmitz called, laughing like a man who didn't have the slightest dent in his conscience. "How well you look. Are you still a pagan?" Schmitz was on his way out of church, the granite steps just behind him; he kept glancing over his shoulder to see who was watching him. He had ash on his forehead. Of course, I realized, it was Ash Wednesday.

"It's the music I love," he said, as if I'd asked, Why church? He spoke as he always did with me, one step too familiar. I suppose that's what I was to him, familiar. "Say, I'll send you an invitation to our premiere. You must have heard from your sister: Eugenie and I have written an opera. Isn't that something? It isn't *Carmen*, of course, but it isn't half bad."

"What's it about?" I asked.

"What's that? The opera? Oh, I guess the usual fare: God, fate . . . love, of course."

Thieves, I thought. Schmitz, you ought to write what you know: cathouses and con men and singers and thieves.

Voile

Here in the home, in what they call the common room, there are sheer voile curtains in the windows. I can't see out, just the vague outline of green and cars. And no one can see in, but for a nurse's passing shadow across the halo of the lamp. My memory is like that now. I can see my hand. I can see the sheers. They lead me to the sheers in the parlor windows of the gold house.

All day the nurses come and go. They speak of me, over me. They are kind and unkind, as humans always are, no two exactly alike.

I can't recall the faces of my children, not as they are in recent years, but I can see them small. I can smell their sweetness as babies; each of the three had a unique, delicious scent. Then I was always in a hurry. Then they played Chopin, badly. In the parlor of that grand gold house, they ran up and down the staircases hollering.

Pie and Bobby made their new life, and so I made mine.

Years later, when I did marry Hutchinson, he would ask me some nights to wear a bit of silk. And I would. I'd put on a little flirty something so he could peel it off me. Ah, Hutch and I had some good, good times. He was bawdy, not tender like Bobby, and that's exactly what I needed. To laugh ha-ha-ha. Hutch died too young. Leaving me with three kids under the age of seven. In that gold house.

My three husbands were all good men, though none I was so

crazy in love with as Bobby. Hutch died in a car wreck. Walt had a heart attack. I divorced Joe. Each time, even when I was the one doing the leaving, the sorrow nearly broke me. Each time, my heart was a boodle box with a lock. But there is something in surviving, I can say that, and in knowing one can.

I've always found it to be a compelling mystery when two unlikely souls collide. What did Bobby Del Monte see in that wild-haired girl with the furious scowl? I do not wonder what he saw in Pie.

I never wished to be a squirrel with that money. Money from then on was just a tool—no more, no less. There was enough to share. That didn't make the money clean, but it made what passed from me to mine something more.

I had to be very careful, should the police come calling. Tan was the only person I trusted—Tan, after all. The rest of them believed what they saw: I sold the three parcels of The Rose and bought two cheaper plots—one nearby and the other in Chinatown. Both bordered the trolleys.

I paid the taxes and the mortgage, and I took care of the Haj.

Then, at my urging, Tan approached Look Tin Eli, a Chinese banker who was much in the news those days. Tin Eli had a vision for a new Chinatown that would be a tourist destination. Tan asked him for a loan to build a restaurant on our parcel on Clay Street. Tan's China Empress with its pagoda and a thirty-foot stone dragon guarding the entrance and a menu of spicy, deliciously prepared meats became an instant hit.

In the beginning, Tan and I shared the expenses and profits on the place in Chinatown, as was our custom, but over time, he took over the whole thing. He did more with it than anyone could have done. He stuck, ol' Tan. He stuck with me, and I with him. The birth records in Chinatown burned in the fire, and no one could prove Tan wasn't American-born; he could own property and no one could stop him. He became a very rich man. His one sorrow was Lifang. Like Rose, Lifang left and never looked back.

Cap and Valentine ran the jazz hall on what became known as Terrific Street. They were my partners, but didn't turn tricks. That was my firm rule. No tricks. I'm not opposed to a woman doing what she will with her body, but until the world views men and women as true equals—something I won't live to see—the money exchanged isn't fine with me, not if I'm the second- or thirdhand party benefiting. It isn't fine with me.

We called our new place the Rogue and we offered dancing—the Texas Tommy and the Turkey Trot were big hits—and jazz. Sophie Tucker and Jelly Roll Morton were regulars.

As for Bobby and Pie? Pie didn't get a rich man, but she got Bobby, and a place where she mattered, at the Ladies' Protection. She and Bobby had the grace to elope. Bobby took them south to Carmel, to the mission down there, where they said their vows. They stayed for two weeks and I had to hear them in my mind's eye walking by the sea, laughing. I had to imagine what they were doing in bed at night. I had to *feel* them doing it. When they came back, I had it so bad I had to disappear. I walked downtown and looked over my dirt. I counted my money, took it in stacks to the office of an architect, and to the surveyor, and to the bank and the tax man. Every day I started work early and kept at it long after dark.

In bed I closed my eyes and imagined Bobby brushing Pie's hair and I thought, Oh God, oh God, why?

But I'd missed my chance. When you're young, you think time is like water—you can put your hand in at will and swirl it around. But time isn't like water. Time is like a quake: irrevocable and crushing. At best you can hope to ride it till it stops.

At my lowest ebb, Alma asked AB to spring for an extra ticket to Paris. I went as her chaperone. We rode the train to New York, and from New York we sailed east on a ship, and I saw that the world was grand. I forgot myself. We were gone for three glorious months.

While we were in Paris, I got in touch with the duke. We had dinner. He was very glad to see me. He'd heard that Rose had died. I didn't correct him—she was dead to me too.

We talked of San Francisco, and at one point, I showed him the book I'd brought: Khayyam. I think he was glad at the thought of another daughter, but, you know, the duke was broke.

"I don't need money," I told him. "It would just be nice to have you as—"

"Amis spéciaux," he suggested, placing his hands on mine.

So the duke and I became special friends. We had some very fine times—you can imagine how much he loved Alma. He introduced her to all the impoverished artists in Paris. Cézanne had recently died poor, his work ridiculed. He'd been working in a field and caught pneumonia. Alma wired Spreckels asking for money and, as tribute, bought a few of Cézanne's paintings that had been in his friend Émile Zola's possession.

Oh, Alma was fierce when she loved someone; that made her a very good friend. She swore that when she got Spreckels to marry her, she'd find a way for us to be neighbors, just so we'd have the pleasure of running into each other on the street again.

She did just that. They bought three adjacent mansions around the corner from me on Washington Street and knocked them all down. She had Spreckels build her a mansion out of white stone that resembled a box of sugar—a palace for the sugar king and his new bride. The neighbors couldn't stand Alma, no more than they could on Francisco Street. She didn't care. On the weekends, she threw garage sales in her mansion to benefit poor widows and children. She got Spreckels to build her a museum at Lands End, and there she housed her Cézannes and Rodins. Yes, the Legion of Honor museum was built by a former nudie artists' model. Until her last days, Alma swam naked every morning in her indoor pool.

Around the corner in the gold house, I gave Tan first pick of the bedrooms. He chose a small bedroom on the third floor, with a view of the fireplace in the garden. Cap and Valentine took over the two bigger bedrooms on that floor. We left Rose's room and Pie's empty, but I used Rose's study as my office. When I married Hutch, he said he wasn't going to make love to his wife in an attic, so we stripped everything in Rose's suite, including the closets, the mirrors, the pink marble bathroom. We made it ours, but I kept the attic for when I needed to be alone. I sat in the rocker and studied the sky out the round window and remembered myself. In time, Tan moved into his own place; Valentine decided to live above the Rogue. I asked Capability if she'd stay with me. She did, till the day she died. When Hutch and I had our babies, Cap and Alma became their godmothers.

So, Bobby made his life with Pie. And I should be glad that they delighted each other—a happiness anybody but a blind ass could see.

Bobby would only accept a loan, which I gladly gave without interest so that they could build a house, a modest place, with a stable in back for Monster. Bobby started a repair shop, for cars and bikes and wagons, and eventually he sold cars.

That first year, we had Sunday dinner when I was in town. At my house, or theirs. Bobby stood at the head of the table and carved the meat—thin, the way I like it. He arranged it on the plate just so, to suit Pie. And for a long string of those Sundays, I would look at him and think, I am the meat.

And maybe we'd exchange a glance, to say: We know what we know.

One afternoon, we took a drive. It was a fair day, dry, and we rode with Rose's Model F's canvas top down. Pie and Bobby were in the back seat. Pie was pregnant by then, and the open air put some color in her cheeks. I sat up front, next to Tan.

It was late afternoon, with San Francisco's tawny sun stretched like a long, lazy tongue down Market Street. The Slot, the steel track that the cable cars ran on, was newly forged in the ground. The sun was so bright you had to squint. Ah, that sun: one of the good, great things.

Now, on both sides of Market the buildings were going up fast, the iron and steel ribs of the new skyscrapers lining the street. The new Call Building, the Emporium with its tall arched windows eye level to the street, and a hundred other structures told the story of a city rising for the sixth time.

I suppose I was rising too. The sun felt glorious on my back. You'd have to be dead not to feel a lift of the heart with that golden light warming your shoulders and kissing the top of your hat.

The road was a hive of motorcars and drays and pedestrians all a jumble, with no one having a bit of sense to look left or right. They never did. And Tan? He drove the car the way he'd commanded the buggy, hissing and scowling, and lurching hell-bent.

In the back seat, Pie was telling us the latest gossip: Eugenie Schmitz had decided to take the veil. She had only to deliver the news to her parents.

I was absorbing that bit, picturing Eugenie Schmitz in a nun's wimple, when a Packard approached, going the opposite way. I could see at a distance that it was ferrying a grande dame. I couldn't see clearly for the sun's glare but the impression I got was of a hat pulled low, a defining nose, a crooked mouth. In other words, my heart saw her.

I leaped to my feet.

"V, sit down," cried Pie.

But Bobby, he got it immediately. Reaching over the seat, he grabbed my hips with both hands and held me so I wouldn't topple. I could feel the warmth of his hands, they were beautiful hands, and I thought: Bobby, don't let me fall.

The car passed by.

I looked behind me, into the back seat. Bobby shrugged and tipped his head, as if to say, And if so, Anyway, what would change?

It might have been, it must have been Rose.

There are only two people I've ever truly wanted, and both I shall never have. Mine was a slow education of the heart.

The Buddhists say there is no such thing as good and bad, it's all life. Well, I never trucked much with the Buddhists; they're entirely too calm. And I never met one who didn't hold back on spice in their cooking, if you know what I mean. That said, it is all life. And anyone who claims to be *good* has yet to shake hands with her dark side. Across a hundred years I've met most of my parts, and I've lived a good deal in the shadows. I've reconciled the anger with the hope, the bitter with the bullshit, the yearning with the grief, the fake with the true. I have an unkempt soul. I am extraordinarily ordinary. But I have known love—great love. Oh, yes, I've known it. And that I will take with me into the night. I like best the parts of us that are contradictory and most human.

Those are the places I visit now. When the nurse brings me my meds and food I won't eat; when my family, what's left of it, comes to see the old bag and brings me chocolate and news, I grin and close my eyes. I return to that year when the world ended and I was most alive.

I apologize for nothing.

Maybe I should have been sent to the Ingleside Jail for Women, same as Abe Ruef was kicked up to San Quentin, but I wasn't. And if Mayor Schmitz spent any time wondering who stole the cash from his boodle box, I don't imagine he lingered. No,

Schmitz was spared and so was I. I'll live out my fate as I began: a single girl in this temblor-riven paradise, this city of prostitutes and thieves and dreamers and me.

There's talk these days of another quake coming, nature's apocalypse. Well, I've seen the apocalypse. I've seen the end of the world and I tell you: I've seen marvelous things.

Acknowledgments

I never know where curiosity will lead me. Some thirty years ago, I began collecting books, maps, and articles related to the 1906 San Francisco earthquake and fire. I kept the best of the lot on a shelf (interestingly, above politics and below medical tomes) and let them talk to one another—and to me.

Across the years of researching and writing *Vera,* I used dozens of source books and websites too numerous to mention here. Still, thanks are due to a few works that informed and inspired my thinking: Dan Kurzman's *Disaster! The Great San Francisco Earthquake and Fire of 1906*; Simon Winchester's *A Crack in the Edge of the World*; Philip Fradkin's *The Great Earthquake and Firestorms of 1906*; *San Francisco Stories* by Jack London; *Lost San Francisco* by Dennis Evanosky and Eric J. Kos; *Big Alma: San Francisco's Alma Spreckels* by Bernice Scharlach; *The Lost Sisterhood: Prostitution in America, 1900–1918* by Ruth Rosen; *Denial of Disaster: The Untold Story and Photographs of the San Francisco Earthquake and Fire of 1906* by Gladys Hansen and Emmet Condon; and Rebecca Solnit's *A Paradise Built in Hell.* Thank you Susie Magnin Grenitz for loaning me your only copy of *Call Me Cyril,* by Cyril Magnin and Cynthia Robins.

My gratitude to the San Francisco Museum and Historical Society and my most ardent thanks to its founder, Charles Fracchia, who took a call from a complete stranger, invited her to tea, then offered to review her manuscript. I cannot thank him enough for his kindness and eagle-eye.

The Museum of the City of San Francisco's photography collection and digital archives were invaluable guides, particularly the timelines of the quake and fire and the remarkable eyewitness accounts. I'm grateful for the bounteous archives of FoundSF, the *Examiner*, the *Call*, the *San Francisco Chronicle*, and the *New York Times*. The collections of historical photographs at the San Francisco Public Library and at the National Archives and Records Administration proved tremendous, as did Wikipedia, for all manner of historical fodder from clothing to curses.

Several films helped me understand the spirit of the city before and after, particularly Harry Miles's thirteen-minute film *A Trip Down Market Street Before the Fire*, shot just four days before the 1906 quake. Miles attached a movie camera to the front of a cable car as it made its way down Market Street, thus capturing the happy mayhem of motors and horse and buggies as they crisscrossed the busy Slot. (Mercifully, the film was shipped off to New York for processing or otherwise it would have been lost.) Two necessary companions to the Miles footage were *After A Trip Down Market Street 1906*, which captured the devastation following the quake and fire, and *The Damnedest, Finest Ruins*, narrated by Peter Coyote.

Where I have strayed from fact into fiction, I've done so in service to story—to the follies, desires, and wayward paths of Vera and her compatriots. Any lapses in place, timing, or persons are mine.

I'm grateful to Jennifer Rudolph Walsh for early *Vera* championing and to Dorian Karchmar for seeing *Vera* home. Thanks to the rest of the crackerjack team at WME: Jill Gillett, Caitlin Mahony, Fiona Baird, Alex Kane, and Erica Nori.

Much thanks to everyone at Scribner, especially Kara Watson, Nan Graham, Katie Monaghan, Clare Maurer, Ashley Gilliam, Roz Lippel, Wendy Sheanin, Jaya Miceli, Sabrina Pyun, and Stephanie Evans. Thank you, Nicole Dewey and Sophie Taylor, for walking with me.

ACKNOWLEDGMENTS

My everlasting gratitude to Ann Beattie, Liv Jenks, Lacy Crawford, Jane Lancellotti, Lori Ogden Moore, Bridget Quinn, Tricia Stone, David Leof, and Wendy Willmot, who read drafts, offered advice, and otherwise kept me together, body and soul. Particular thanks to Daniel Wheeler, who turned on a dime and always with joy. Thank you, Katie and Tom Dickson and Julie Benello, for lending me writing spaces at crucial times. Bless you, Bea Rose, for always being at my side.

My love and admiration to the writers, readers, teachers, supporters, and staff of *Narrative*. You are the truest band of believers I know. Your kindness inspires me.

It is my great fortune and joy to have been gifted with three daughters. Girls, you are my daily bread. Lastly, first and always: with you, Tom.

About the Author

Carol Edgarian is the acclaimed author of the *New York Times* bestseller *Three Stages of Amazement* and the international bestseller *Rise the Euphrates,* winner of the ANC Freedom Prize. Her articles and essays have appeared in the *Wall Street Journal,* on NPR, and in *W,* among many other publications. She is cofounder of *Narrative,* a nonprofit digital publisher of fiction, poetry, and art, and of Narrative in the Schools, which provides free libraries and writing resources to teachers and students around the world. Edgarian lives with her family in San Francisco. Join Carol on Instagram @CEdgarian or at www.CarolEdgarian.com.